EMMA

A young woman in a blue merino dress with three flounces came to the door of the house to receive Monsieur Bovary ... Charles was surprised by the whiteness of her fingernails. They were shiny, thin at the tips, almond-shaped and as spotlessly clean as Dieppe ivories. Her hands, however, were not pretty: not pale enough, perhaps, and a little rough at the joints; they were also too long, and without soft curves. Her eyes were her best feature; they were brown, although they seemed black because of her eyelashes, and they looked straight at you with naïve boldness ...

Her neck rose out of her turned down white collar. Her black hair was divided into two sections by a fine part running down the middle of her head; these sections, drawn tightly over her skull, were so smooth that each seemed to be of one piece. They covered all but the tips of her ears and were joined at the back of her head in a large chignon. The hair over her temples was waved slightly, a refinement which the country doctor now noticed for the first time in his life. The tops of her cheeks were pink. She had a shell-rimmed pince-nez which she carried, like a man, tucked in between two buttons of her bodice.

MADAME BOVARY
by **Gustave Flaubert**

Bantam Literature
Ask your bookseller for the books you have missed

MADAME BOVARY
Gustave Flaubert

Translated by Lowell Bair

**Edited and with an Introduction
by Leo Bersani**

BANTAM BOOKS · TORONTO · NEW YORK · LONDON

MADAME BOVARY

A Bantam Classic / June 1959

2nd printing ...... *June 1960*	*7th printing* ... *January 1966*
3rd printing ...... *June 1961*	*8th printing* . *December 1966*
4th printing .... *October 1962*	*9th printing* .... *August 1968*
5th printing ...... *July 1963*	*10th printing* .. *February 1969*
6th printing .. *November 1964*	*11th printing* ...... *July 1969*

12th printing .... *October 1970*

New Bantam edition / March 1972

2nd printing .... *July 1973*	*3rd printing* .... *January 1975*

4th printing .... *October 1976*

COPYRIGHT NOTICES AND ACKNOWLEDGMENTS

"Gustave Flaubert," by *Emile Zola from* Les Romanciers Naturalistes, *1881.*

"Essay on Gustave Flaubert," by *Guy de Maupassant from an essay written for the Quantin edition of Flaubert's work, 1885. Reprinted in the Conrad edition, translated by Helen Weaver.*

"Gustave Flaubert," by *Henry James. From his* Notes on Novelists. *Copyright 1914 by Henry James. Reprinted by permission of Charles Scribner's Sons.*

"Madame Bovary: *The Cathedral and the Hospital,*" by *Harry Levin. From his* Essays in Criticism, *January, 1952, and reprinted with their permission.*

"Realism in Madame Bovary," by *Erich Auerbach. From his* Mimesis: The Representation of Reality in Western Literature, *translated by Willard Trask. Copyright © 1953 by Princeton University Press and reprinted with their permission.*

"Patterns of Imagery: *Her Dreams Too High, Her House Too Narrow,*" by *Victor Brombert. From his* The Novels of Flaubert: A Study of Themes and Techniques. *Copyright © 1966 by Princeton University Press and reprinted with their permission.*

"The Weaknesses of Madame Bovary," by *Martin Turnell. From his* The Novel in France. *Copyright 1950 by Martin Turnell. All Rights Reserved. Reprinted by permission of Hamish Hamilton, Ltd., London and New Directions Publishing Corporation.*

"Class Consciousness in Flaubert," by *Jean-Paul Sartre. From* LES TEMPS MODERNES, *June, 1966. Reprinted by permission of Jean-Paul Sartre.*

"Flaubert's Silences," by *Gérard Genette. From his* Figures. *Copyright © 1966 by Editions du Seuil. Reprinted by permission of Georges Borchardt, Inc. Literary Agency.*

ISBN 0-553-10479-9

Published simultaneously in the United States and Canada

PRINTED IN THE UNITED STATES OF AMERICA

CONTENTS

Introduction

INTRODUCTION

Is *Madame Bovary* a "great novel"? We have of course been brainwashed to think unreflectively of Flaubert's work as a masterpiece of modern art. But Flaubert's revolutionary position in the history of the novel can largely be explained by his subversion of the traditional criteria of greatness in fiction. The other major novelists of the nineteenth century—think, for example, of Balzac and Stendhal, of Jane Austen and James, of Dostoevsky and Tolstoy—have trained us to identify novelistic talent with the ability to create characters of moral or intellectual distinction and psychological complexity. The heroes of fiction have generally been what James called perceptive "vessels of experience"; because of their sensitivity and intelligence, they are able to articulate what we like to think of as the significance, the "profounder meanings" of human life. To someone reading *Madame Bovary* for the first time, it will therefore come as something of a shock to discover that the central character in this highly praised work should be a stupid, vulgar and cruel woman. Emma has, it could be argued, the intellectual and moral qualities of a housewife from a village near Des Moines who dreams of living in New York and who commits adultery in a desperate attempt to give to her life some of the glamorous pathos of a Rock Hudson movie. If *Madame Bovary* is in fact a great novel, it is perhaps in spite of the triviality of its heroine. And Flaubert's radical proposition would seem to be that literary distinction has little to do (perhaps nothing) with the distinction of the experience and of the personalities which literature represents.

I want to suggest that the importance of *Madame Bovary* has, indeed, less to do with the appeal of Madame Bovary herself as a character than with the questions which the novel raises about the nature of the literary imagination. Nothing is more commonplace in twentieth-century art than the work which takes *itself* as its most profound subject, that is, the work in which the creative act seems to have become a reflection on the very processes of artistic creation. *Madame Bovary* is an early, only half-explicit, not yet fashionable attempt to locate the drama of fiction in an investigation of the impulse to invent fictions rather than in any psychologically, morally or socially significant "content." What *is* a literary fiction? What is its relation to "reality"? Does art ever really imitate life? In spite of her silly sentimentality, Flaubert's heroine lives these questions with unprecedented urgency. As a result, she can be a very mediocre but highly original character: as we shall presently see in more detail, she allows Flaubert to make of his novel an inquiry into the very possibility of correspondences between art and reality. Lacking Balzac's and Stendhal's faith in the capacity of literature to mirror or designate life, Flaubert submits language to a relentless, anguished attention designed to expose its supposedly reflecting powers as an illusion. Like Emma, Flaubert is less interested in the *quality* of the life literature represents than in the questions of whether or not literature *can* represent life. And it is this crucial shift of perspective which defines Flaubert's spectacularly subversive role in the history of fiction.

In a sense, however, *Madame Bovary* is Flaubert's least radical work, and it is undoubtedly best to approach the novel by looking first at some of its more conventionally novelistic elements. In *L'Education sentimentale, Un Coeur simple,* and *Bouvard et Pécuchet,* Flaubert will choose as heroes characters whom he apparently defies us to find interesting, while Emma, for all her mediocrity, is Flaubert's richest, most fully realized creation. She intrigues us from the start by her mere physical presence, by a kind of irresistible sensual glamor. Beginning with Charles's visits to Les Bertaux while he is still married to the unappetizing Héloïse, we see Emma, throughout the novel, in a series of physical poses which perhaps stimulate desire by suggesting an artful absorption in the care and pleasures of her own body. Emma's presence is like a promise of sensual variety and refinement to which Charles, Léon, and especially Rodolphe greedily respond. Our first analytical perspective on Mme Bovary comes after her marriage; before that, we watch her, from

Charles's angle of vision, sucking blood from the fingers she has pricked while sewing, taking a few drops of liqueur in the kitchen with Charles (". . . with her chin tilted upward, her lips pushed forward and her throat taut, she laughed because she felt nothing, while the tip of her tongue, darting out from beneath her delicate teeth, licked the bottom of the glass"), and dazzling poor Bovary with the variety of her voice, the mobility of her face:

> And, according to what she was saying, her voice was either clear or shrill; or, suddenly becoming langorous, it would trail off into inflections that ended almost in a murmur, as though she were talking to herself. Sometimes her eyes would open wide in guileless joy, then her eyelids would droop while her face took on an expression of profound boredom and her thoughts seemed to wander aimlessly.

Léon and Rodolphe are also immediately seduced by this spontaneous sensual inventiveness in Emma's poses and movements. Rodolphe's practised eye misses no detail of Emma's rapid, graceful gestures as she tries to revive Justin from his fainting spell during the bloodletting of Rodolphe's servant. And Léon silently takes in another sexually provocative scene when Mme Bovary warms herself in front of the fireplace at the Lion d'Or the evening of her arrival in Yonville:

> Grasping her skirt at the knees with two fingers and pulling it up to her ankles, she held out her foot, in its black high-topped shoe, toward the flames, over the leg of mutton turning on the spit. The fireplace shone on her from head to toe; its harsh glare illuminated the weave of her dress, the pores of her white skin and even her eyelids when she blinked her eyes. She was enveloped in a reddish glow each time the wind blew in through the half-open door.

The variety of these poses, their frequency in the novel, and the amount of detail in Flaubert's descriptions of them make for an astonishingly concrete presence. And the subtle sensual refinement they suggest is undoubtedly, as the nineteenth-century critic Ferdinand Brunetière claimed, Emma's most exceptional trait. Her insatiable hunger for sensations constitutes a rare if limited openness to the world. Her generosity and her imagination are almost entirely of the senses; as we see, for example, in her indifference to Charles's affection and to Hippolyte's suffering, she is cruelly insensitive to the feelings of others. Emma ruins herself on sexual and sentimental excesses, but neither sex nor sentiment appears to satisfy her most profoundly. Indeed she perhaps has a greater talent for something closer to what Freud described as polymorphous perversity. Emma's sensual life is too richly diffuse to be pre-empted by specifically sexual pleasures, and her pathetic sentimentality is in part a weak attempt to sublimate (to understand and to make sublime) the rich, unreflective life of her body. Thus, while La Vaubyessard becomes a source of absurd fantasy as it recedes into the past, Emma's immediate reactions to the luxurious atmosphere of the ball have a penetrating concreteness. Her actual experience of the ball consists in very precise and varied sense impressions, rather than in the vague and monotonous daydreaming which she indulges in as an escape from sensually unstimulating environments. As she enters the dining room, she feels herself "enveloped by a warm atmosphere in which the fragrance of flowers and fine linen mingled with the odor of hot meat and truffles." She shivers from head to toe at the unaccustomed taste of iced champagne, and notices that the powdered sugar looks "whiter and finer than any she had seen before." As she dances that evening, "she smiled gently at some of the violinist's flourishes . . ."; and, with a quiet and deeply contented sensuality, she eats a maraschino ice "from a silver-gilt shell that she was holding in her left hand; the spoon was between her teeth and her eyes were half shut."

This acute sensuality both cheapens Emma's spiritual life and yet provides the only escape from her exhausting daydreams of love. Incapable of imagining occasions for happiness which do not cater luxuriantly to the senses, Emma rejects her ugly provincial world but continues to think of "bliss" as immediate sensual gratification. Her reckless spending is a desperate attempt to make the fabulous decors of literary romance believable by making them visible. She has an extravagant but exceptionally limited imagination: nothing is harder for her to conceive of than the novelistic adventures which she hungrily but rather perplexedly devours. Therefore, the immediate cause of her suicide is, appropriately, her debts, for money is the talisman with which Emma tries to materialize love. It is as if luxury alone could convince her of the concrete reality of literary fantasy. Hopelessly sentimental but, as Flaubert says, impatient of anything which she can't immediately "consume," which doesn't provide an instant "personal profit," she seeks sensual stimulation from an extravagantly rich world unavailable to her senses. Bored with what she knows but unable to find pleasure in what she can only think about, Emma tries to feel what she can only weakly imagine, to induce sensations from fantasies. The exhausted debauchery into which she falls more and more deeply as the novel proceeds is due less to her actual adventures than to this more debilitating adventure of exciting her mind to satisfy her body.

It is in literature that Emma seeks the excitement her environment almost never provides, and *Madame Bovary* is obviously a novel about the dangers of reading novels. Now Flaubert's work is *not* a very serious attack on romantic fiction, and this fact should help us to see both the exact relation of *Madame Bovary* to a period of literary history, and the radical, "non-historical" nature of its critique of literature. Emma can hardly bear the burden of serious reflection about romanticism; *any* cultural or spiritual style can be made to appear absurd if it is "studied" through someone who doesn't understand it. The metaphysical, esthetic and social revolution which we identify with romanticism is as short-changed in *Madame Bovary* as Leibniz's philosophy is in Voltaire's *Candide*. Instead of giving us a certain kind of sensibility in its most distinguished and abstractly typical form, Flaubert depicts the trivial but pervasive ways in which a powerful style of being comes to affect the expectations which the most unremarkable people have of life. Emma's romanticism is that of the fashion magazines, of keepsakes, of the novels which the old woman who washes in the laundry of the convent reads to the girls:

> They were filled with love affairs, lovers, mistresses, persecuted ladies fainting in lonely country houses, postriders killed at every relay, horses ridden to death on every page, dark forests, palpitating hearts, vows, sobs, tears and kisses, skiffs in the moonlight, nightingales in thickets, and gentlemen brave as lions, gentle as lambs, virtuous as no one really is, and always ready to shed floods of tears.

Who is the author of these adventures? Obviously, no one; the great romantic talents have been filtered through a process which leaves only a sediment of anonymous, parodically simplified images. This is the market of originality, a stage in the diffusion of art in which good literature has not disappeared but is consumed for the images it has inspired in women's magazines. As in all popularization, literature is judged by its success; and the simplified forms in which it effectively penetrates ordinary social life finally provide even the standards it has "to live up to."

This popularizing process was of course slower in Madame Bovary's day than it is today, so there was a gap between the diffusion of romantic themes in the literature Emma reads and their treatment (or invention) in the great works of romantic literature. And because of that gap, the mental style of an Emma Bovary is probably a better index of the cultural atmosphere of her period than the romantic art we still admire. For, like most interesting art of the past, those masterpieces are too personal, too idiosyncratic to be spoken of primarily as representative, and we would be more likely to find something like "the spirit of an age" in the pages of the fashion magazines Emma reads than in works where that problematic spirit is obscured by the particularities of individual talent. This distinction is important to remember, for today we are used to the instant popularization of art. In a sense, TV and the press have become our avant-garde; they are, in their hunger for the new, ahead of all experimental art, emptily ready to advertise the still unimaginable. As a result, the time between original art and the public awareness of it has been reversed. Instead of the artist having to wait for recognition, a voracious willingness to recognize everything is necessarily more daring and more advanced than *any* artistic production which, however explosive or "spontaneous," can never be ahead of that which anticipates it.

But Flaubert's novel has, of course, more than an historical interest. Essentially, *Madame Bovary* is about an exasperated and disastrous attempt to equate reality with its representations in art. In the disappointment she feels after her marriage, Emma "tried to find out exactly what was meant by the words 'bliss,' 'passion' and 'rapture,' which had seemed so beautiful to her in books." Emma's tragedy is obviously that she can't connect these literary fantasies with her own experience, and the sympathy which Flaubert clearly feels for her suggests that the trivial content of her fantasies is irrelevant to the profound truth about imagination which she discovers in her suffering. The mediocrity of Emma's thought is less important than the artistic rigor of her refusal to accept *any* equivalence between imagination and reality. Significantly, she is never more exasperated than during her love affairs. The affair with Rodolphe could, one imagines, have gone on indefinitely; it is Emma who ends it with her frantic insistence on transporting it to other, more "suitable" climates. And Léon doesn't really break with her; with docility and terror, he plays the pathetic game of an extravagant, brutal sexuality meant to deaden Emma's constant sense of "the insufficiency of life." Nor does Flaubert suggest that Emma would have felt any less strongly that "instant decay of the things she leaned on" had she found lovers superior to Rodolphe and Léon. Emma comes to understand what was for Flaubert the central fact about literature: its infinitely seductive fictions *resemble nothing*. Flaubert in *Madame Bovary* is certainly mocking literary clichés of romance, but nothing in any of his works suggests that so-called great art can provide more accurate images of reality. The autonomous, arbitrary, futilely rich universe of words and ideas which Emma inhabits produces what might be called a totally abstract sickness, that is, an agony and a death whose insignificant cause is simply the exercise of imagination.

Rodolphe, Flaubert harshly notes, stupidly doubts Emma's love because he has heard the same language of passion from his other mistresses, "as though the fullness of the soul did not sometimes overflow into the emptiest phrases, since no one can ever express the exact measure of his needs, his conceptions or his sorrows, and human speech is like a cracked pot on which we beat out rhythms for bears to dance to when we are striving to make music that will wring tears from the stars." An inadequate vehicle for our feelings, language for Flaubert is no less resistant to adequate descriptions of the world: weeks of tortuous revision might finally produce a more or less satisfactory passage describing the atmosphere of an agricultural fair. An ineffable self, an ineffable reality outside of the self; "between" the two, a language enigmatically indifferent to anything but its own seductive suggestiveness. All human expression and, more particularly, all literature may therefore be (to use the title of one of Samuel Beckett's works) "texts for nothing." That is, the coherence of our language may have nothing to do with its epistemological accuracy; it perhaps *describes* neither the self using it nor the world we like to believe it designates.

Flaubert, as we see in his letters, was both terrified and fascinated by the verbal orgies, "the debaucheries of the imagination" which Emma impatiently waits for life to realize. He rightly recognizes in the fantastic heroine of *Madame Bovary* a fellow realist (she expects art to be an accurate reflection of life)—minus his own sense of the difficulties and dangers of realism. When Emma naively wonders what in life corresponds to the literary notions of "bliss" and "passion," she is repeating, in reverse, the question with which Flaubert made a torment of art. His verbal asceticism is the strategy by which he would avoid Emma's fate; he withholds his linguistic choices as long as possible, resists the temptation to write freely, without stopping, thus hoping to subdue language into an exact conformity with "nature as it is." Flaubert had an almost Platonic view of reality. He speaks in his correspondence as if "subjects" existed somewhere outside of language, and the exhausting labor to which he condemned himself was to find the expressions which would merely convert reality, without changing its nature, into language. But in spite of the killing discipline to which he submitted himself in order to reach this goal, Flaubert naturally could not help but recognize that language provides its own inspirations; it is a creator rather than simply a translator of reality. As Flaubert writes in an extraordinary letter to Louise Colet, nothing is more dangerous than "inspiration," than those "masked balls of the imagination" during which the writer betrays his subject by allowing himself to write freely and profusely. And so, while devoting his life to finding the "right" words and the "right" rhythms, Flaubert came to have a polemical distrust of *all* fictive versions of reality. He tended, it could be said, to define the highest artistic integrity as a *reluctance to produce*. The subject of all his work, in spite of the obvious but superficial distinction between the realistic and the non-realistic novels, is the excesses of imagination. Flaubert both reveled in and deeply mistrusted those excesses. *Madame Bovary, L'Education sentimentale* and *Bouvard et Pécuchet* are the equivalents, in his career, of that familiar stylistic "fall" which, in so many of his sentences, deflates an eloquent fantasy with a prosaic detail. Emma, Frédéric Moreau, and Bouvard and Pécuchet are the scapegoats through whom Flaubert does penance for the extravagances of *La Tentation de Saint Antoine* and *Salammbô;* scrupulously masochistic, Flaubert sadistically punishes those inferior versions of himself for his own intoxicating inventions.

But is the prosaic any more "real" than the extravagantly romantic? Tostes and Yonville in *Madame Bovary,* while they are meant to provide an ironic commentary on Emma's sense of life's possibilities, are treated as negatively, in spite of their "material" existence, as Emma's dreams of romance. What Albert Thibaudet called Flaubert's *vision binoculaire* (the simultaneous perception of opposite poles of a subject which cancel each other out) is less a corrective vision of reality than a repetitively nihilistic one. The most spectacular example of the *vision binoculaire* is the scene of the fair at Yonville: fragments of Rodolphe's seduction of Emma alternate with fragments of Lieuvain's speech to the citizens of Yonville, and we see both scenes, as it were, from above and at the same time. Neither side of the Flaubertism vision is allowed to settle into a definitive version of reality, although both are presented with a kind of maddening literalness and attention to detail. Indeed, the *vision binoculaire* actually exposes the fundamental similarity between the world of Emma and the world of Homais, between the exceptional and the banal.

The conflict between Emma and her community obscures a profound resemblance: she is as cliché-ridden as Homais, incapable, as Flaubert writes, "of believing in anything that did not manifest itself in conventional forms." Flaubert runs the gamut of these *formes convenues* in *Madame Bovary* (from the trite provincial formulas to Emma's dreams of exotic landscapes) and, given the impossible rigor of his demand for exact correspondence between language and reality, we could say that he comes close to condemning *all* expression as cliché. Flaubert is aware of but essentially indifferent to the cheap quality of Emma's fantasies. More *interesting* fantasies would not necessarily be more accurate representations of reality. And perhaps as important as Flaubert's sympathy for Emma is his less explicit, more troubled identification (as Sartre has argued) with Homais. For the druggist's magnificently comical enthusiasm for clichés parodies but may not be essentially different from the artist's less complacent but perhaps no more successful efforts to make language contain reality.

Indeed, the cliché is the lowest and the clearest form of

imaginative extravagance; it condenses both the appeal and the dangers of imagination. Flaubert had the admirable dream of an ideally free language, of a literature in which, as he writes in a letter, "form, as it becomes more skillful, is attenuated, it abandons all liturgy, all rules, all measure. . . ." This "liberation from materiality" would be the democratization of literature; it "can be found in everything, for example, in the way governments have evolved, from oriental despotisms to the socialist states of the future." The enemy of democracy is the rigid "orthodoxy" of dictatorships; the enemy of a free style is the *formes convenues* of the *Dictionnaire des idées reçues,* that compilation of clichés on which Flaubert worked all his life with a savage joy. But Flaubert's horror of cliché is of course equaled only by his fascination with it. For the cliché is, in a sense, the purest art of intelligibility; it tempts us with the possibility of enclosing life within beautifully inalterable formulas, of obscuring the arbitrary nature of imagination with an appearance of necessity. Thus the drifting of imagination among its unaccountable fancies is checked not by the adherence of words to reality, but by the ideal *un*reality of a language which disciplines the mind by making it merely predictable. Obsessed by the distance between words and things, both Emma and Flaubert regularize imagination by mechanically formalizing it. Flaubert's prose, far from being "free," inflicts upon us the external ternary rhythm, the non-connective "and" to introduce a final clause, the adverb at the end of the sentence, and the deadening *c'était* at the beginning of descriptions. The high priest of style is thus the master of the rhythmical tic.

By an irony which should now be clear, the care with which Flaubert sought to make language transparent to reality consecrates the very opaqueness of language which he dreaded. For his realism entails a kind of attention to words which can only make them appear heavy and unmanageable. Tirelessly worked over, they finally settle into combinations which represent a difficult but somewhat unconvincing victory over verbal excesses. Flaubert develops, clings to formal procedures which replace the real as an object of literary imitation. Because the terror of art in the name of life seems to be the death of life in art, the Flaubertian style often strikes us as referring only to its own achievements, as expressing little more than an inflexible model of linguistic coherence.

The extraordinary richness of *Madame Bovary* undoubtedly lies in its availability to the different kinds of critical approaches I have briefly illustrated. On the one hand, Emma is an unforgettable presence; her beauty, her sentimental vulnerability and her suffering elicit a sympathy which we like to think we feel in front of fully realized "human beings" in literature. But perhaps the modernity—and the deeper interest—of *Madame Bovary* can best be explained by a certain indifference on Flaubert's part to those very values which make it easy for us to admire his novel at once. The subject of this successfully "realistic" novel is the impossibility of realistic representation in art. More generally, *Madame Bovary* is a novel of epistemological failure: the instruments of human knowledge are incapable of closing the gap between the mind and reality. *All* language is essentially "stupid." And, in a sense, Flaubert's least interesting, least distinguished characters are the ideal "carriers" of his obsessive theme: no one is better equipped than the intellectually dull and psychologically superficial Bouvard and Pécuchet—those tireless pursuers of "truth"—to expose all forms of knowledge as equally arbitrary, insubstantial and insignificant.

The uneasy feeling of nineteenth-century critics about Flaubert's work is understandable. No one had ever made such a rageful case against "content" in art, or so radically separated the quality of a work from the quality of the life it represents, or sought (so hopelessly?) to compensate for the unreality of imagination by the abstract perfection of pure style. In essays partially reproduced in this volume, Zola, naively confident that literary realism constituted an enormous progress in the history of art's relation to life, recalls his exasperation at Flaubert's insistence on being judged only for his "well-made sentences," and Henry James indirectly suggests the novelistic revolution accomplished by Flaubert in his puzzled displeasure with the thinness of Emma Bovary's character. But the educative value of truly original art reveals itself slowly, and even today we may find something shocking or at least puzzling in Gérard Genette's praise of Flaubert as the first writer to express the essence of literature by an enterprise involving the murder of meaning in language. Indeed, we may be more sympathetic to Sartre's brilliant attempt, part of which is also included here, to study the individual and social situation in which such an enterprise can become a writer's fundamental project. Essentially hostile to the high critical fashion illustrated in Genette's manifesto-like "truths" about literature's "essence," Sartre is less interested in continuing and refining the Flaubertian attitude toward literary language than in making that attitude historically intelligible. Genette, at any rate, sharply summarizes the most profound implications for literature of Flaubert's work: namely, its subversion of both realistic and idealistic esthetic criteria, and its shattering identification of literary authenticity with literary failure.

Failure, and boredom, and silence. Undoubtedly, nothing is more upsetting than this assault on the moral and intellectual distinction of art, not to speak of this indifference to art as entertainment. For the literary agony which Flaubert inaugurates is by no means a devaluation of "seriousness" in literature in the name of "play"; the source of Flaubert's comedy—as well as of comedy in Joyce and in Beckett—is perhaps more an exasperation at language than an enjoyment of it. In the tension between these writers' dream of a new, "purer," more authentically expressive language and their absorption in the resistant forms (and formulas) they detest, the reader becomes the victim of a theoretically interminable attack on a shared system of communication. The nightmare of *Finnegans Wake* is the lifelong effort required to decode it. And in Flaubert and Beckett, writing incorporates the nausea of writing. The artist's extraordinary hatred of his own inventiveness creates the drama of his work: unable to *stop* producing, he nonetheless aspires to the proud sterility of silence by replacing his own talent with the inanities of Flaubert's *Dictionnaire* or the meaningless sounds (such as "plof" and "quaqua") which punctuate the monologues of Beckett's derelicts.

But the compromise of actual literary activity of course produces literary values, that is, a text open to our critical appreciation. There is, consequently, more to be said about *Madame Bovary* (and more to be enjoyed) than I have just suggested; if the novel tends, most deeply, to condemn the very temptation to novelize, it also cannot help but give us more than this extreme negativity. It gives us, for one thing, passages of extraordinary beauty which describe the sensuality I began by discussing. Emma's sensuality provides occasions for the relaxation of Flaubert's satirical treatment of her faith in literature; in her least verbal moments Emma perhaps allows Flaubert to suspend his distrust of literature, to indulge in his natural sympathy for fantasies which he usually condemns. At certain privileged points in the novel— for example, when Rodolphe makes love to Emma in the forest, or when they spend their last evening together in the Bovarys' garden, or when Léon visits Emma after the opera in her hotel room in Rouen—the gap is temporarily closed between fantasy and the senses, between present and past, between the mind and the world. Ironically, Emma's dreams of ecstasy are occasionally realized by their very extinction in an absorbing sensuality, and at such moments Flaubert gives us the poetry of torpor—of an *engourdissement,* or *mollesse*— as an interlude in the comedy of language.

The countries of romance which Emma has yearned to visit are then used as *images* to describe this engulfing, pleasantly heavy sensuality. The only legitimate romantic talk in *Madame Bovary* is when Flaubert "fills in" Emma's silences with the dreams she has momentarily forgotten. Thus we see the world of romance in its only "realistic" form: as a verbal luxury. Emma would like to go, so to speak, where the pleasing images are, but she never finds her language in the world. When, on the other hand, Flaubert comparts her languorous anticipation of physical pleasure to the odorous breezes of a tropical shore, he is sympathetically using the literature of romance not to "test" reality, but to illustrate how poetry is made from the life of the senses. There is no equation between those tropical shores and the world's geography; more important, there is no way of demonstrating the exact equivalence between Flaubert's language and Emma's essentially indescribable sensations. His language merely (but adequately) approximates Emma's physical life by re-creating it verbally. The exotic lands of the literary imagination are the *fables* of our sensations.

They are, that is to say, the metaphors which enrich our experience by their very "inaccuracy," by the gap between their own suggestiveness and the experience they are meant to translate. But metaphor is generally the disaster of Flaubert's style. Proust claimed, with some exaggeration, that he couldn't find a single beautiful metaphor in Flaubert. The startlingly clumsy similes in *Madame Bovary* express Flaubert's impatience with the epistemologically approximative nature of metaphor: things were not to be *like* other things, but each expression was meant to cover and absorb its hypothetically real subject with literal precision. Only rarely—as in the passage describing Emma's sensuality—does Flaubert show that indulgence toward imaginative versions of reality which consists in using them to construct a style—or a life—while recognizing them as fictive. More often, Flaubert invokes the notion of the real in order to condemn the fictive or the imaginary. And this dream of an uncompromising realism made of his art an art of retrenchment, of calculated verbal denials for the sake of a more than verbal expressiveness.

But the fictions of language may in fact *be* reality, or at least the only reality we can know. And what we like to think of as living in harmony with reality may be simply a knack for multiplying fictions, for accommodating new versions of experience to older ones so that we may impose a personal if always tentative unity on the inexplicable richness of our imagination. That unity is our personal style, which, as Maupassant rightly suggests, is not at all what Flaubert meant in his ascetic devotion to an idea of style which necessarily crippled his own inventiveness. What we miss in Flaubert is some trust in those fictions which tempted but frightened him; for, as his work and his career movingly illustrate, the alternative to that trust is a panic at the mind's inventions and the impressive but perhaps unnecessary torture of trying to be "realistic."

Leo Bersani

To

MARIE-ANTOINE-JULES SENARD *
Member of the Paris Bar,
Ex-President of the National Assembly, and
Former Minister of the Interior

Dear and illustrious friend,
Allow me to inscribe your name at the head of this
book and above its dedication, for it is to you, more
than anyone else, that I owe its publication. In passing through your magnificent plea in court, my work
has acquired, in my eyes, a kind of unexpected authority. I therefore ask you to accept here the tribute
of my gratitude, which, however great it may be,
will never reach the height of your eloquence or
your devotion.

Gustave Flaubert

Paris, April 12, 1857

---

* The lawyer who successfully defended Flaubert when the publication of *Madame Bovary* as a magazine serial caused him to be
tried for "committing an outrage against public and religious
morality."—L.B.

Part One

We were in study hall when the headmaster walked in, followed by a new boy not wearing a school uniform, and by a janitor carrying a large desk. Those who were sleeping awoke, and we all stood up as though interrupting our work.

The headmaster motioned us to sit down, then turned to the teacher and said softly, "Monsieur Roger, I'm placing this pupil in your care. He'll begin in the eighth grade, but if his work and conduct are good enough, he'll be promoted to where he ought to be at his age."

The newcomer hung back in the corner behind the door, so that we could hardly see him. He was a country boy of about fifteen, taller than any of us. He wore his hair cut straight across the forehead, like a cantor in a village church, and he had a gentle, bewildered look. Although his shoulders were not broad, his green jacket with black buttons was apparently too tight under the arms, and the slits of its cuffs revealed red wrists accustomed to being bare. His legs, sheathed in blue stockings, protruded from his yellowish trousers, which were pulled up tight by a pair of suspenders. He wore heavy, unpolished, hobnailed shoes.

We began to recite our lessons. He concentrated all his attention on them, as though listening to a sermon, not daring even to cross his legs or lean on his elbow, and when the bell rang at two o'clock the teacher had to tell him to line up with the rest of us.

When we entered a classroom we always tossed our caps on the floor, to free our hands; as soon as we crossed the threshold we would throw them under the bench so hard that they struck the wall and raised a cloud of dust; this was "the way it should be done."

But the new boy either failed to notice this maneuver or was too shy to perform it himself, for he was still holding his cap on his lap at the end of the prayer. It was a headgear of composite nature, combining elements of the busby, the lancer cap, the round hat, the otter-skin cap and the cotton nightcap—one of those wretched things whose mute ugliness has great depths of expression, like an idiot's face. Egg-shaped and stiffened by whalebone, it began with three rounded bands, followed by alternating diamond-shaped patches of velvet and rabbit fur separated by a red stripe, and finally there was a kind of bag terminating in a cardboard-lined polygon covered with complicated braid. A network of gold wire was attached to the top of this polygon by a long, extremely thin cord, forming a kind of tassel. The cap was new; its visor was shiny.

"Stand up," said the teacher.

He stood up; his cap fell. The whole class began to laugh.

He bent down and picked it up. A boy beside him knocked it down again with his elbow; he picked it up once again.

"Will you please put your helmet away?" said the teacher, a witty man.

A loud burst of laughter from the other pupils threw the poor boy into such a state of confusion that he did not know whether to hold his cap in his hand, leave it on the floor or put it on his head. He sat down again and put it back on his lap.

"Stand up," said the teacher, "and tell me your name."

The new boy mumbled something unintelligible.

"Say it again!"

The same mumbled syllables came from his lips again, drowned out by the jeers of the class.

"Louder!" cried the teacher. "Louder!"

With desperate determination the new boy opened his enormous mouth and, as though calling someone, shouted this word at the top of his lungs: *"Charbovari!"*

This instantly touched off an uproar which rose in a crescendo of shrill exclamations, shrieks, barks, stamping of feet and repeated shouts of *"Charbovari! Charbovari!"* Then it subsided into isolated notes, but it was a long time before it died down completely; it kept coming back to life in fits and starts along a row of desks where a stifled laugh would occasionally explode like a half-spent firecracker.

A shower of penalties gradually restored order in the classroom, however, and the teacher, having managed to understand Charles Bovary's name after making him repeat it, spell it out and read it to him, immediately ordered the poor devil to sit on the dunce's seat at the foot of the rostrum. He began to walk over to it, then stopped short.

"What are you looking for?" asked the teacher.

"My ca—" the new boy said timidly, glancing around uneasily.

"The whole class will copy five hundred lines!" Like Neptune's *"Quos ego"* in the *Aeneid*, this furious exclamation checked the outbreak of a new storm. "Keep quiet!" continued the teacher indignantly, mopping his forehead with a handkerchief he had taken from his toque. "As for you," he said to the new boy, "you will write out *'Ridiculus sum'* twenty times in all tenses." He added, in a gentler tone, "Don't worry, you'll find your cap: it hasn't been stolen."

Everything became calm again. Heads bent over notebooks, and for the next two hours the new boy's conduct was exemplary, despite the spitballs, shot from the nib of a pen, that occasionally splattered against his face. He merely wiped himself with his hand each time this happened, then continued to sit motionless, with his eyes lowered.

That evening, in study hall, he took sleeveguards from his desk, put his things in order and carefully ruled his paper. We saw him working conscientiously, looking up all the words in the dictionary and taking great pains with everything he did. It was no doubt because of this display of effort that he was not placed in a lower grade, for, while he had a passable knowledge of grammatical rules, his style was without elegance. He had begun to study Latin with his village priest, since his parents, to save money, had postponed sending him off to school as long as possible.

His father, Monsieur Charles-Denis-Bartholomé Bovary, had once been an assistant surgeon in the army. Forced to leave the service in 1812 for corrupt practices with regard to conscription, he had taken advantage of his masculine charms to pick up a dowry of sixty thousand francs being offered to him in the person of a hosier's daughter who had fallen in love with his appearance. He was a handsome, boastful man who liked to rattle his spurs; his side whiskers

joined his mustache, his fingers were always adorned with
rings and he wore bright-colored clothes. He had the look of
a pimp and the affable exuberance of a traveling salesman.
He lived on his wife's money for the first two or three years
of their marriage, eating well, getting up late, smoking big
porcelain pipes, staying out every night to see a show and
spending a great deal of time in cafés. His father-in-law died
and left very little; indignant at this, he "went into the textile
business" and lost some money, then he moved to the country,
where he intended to "build up a going concern." But since
he knew little more about farming than he did about calico,
since he rode his horses instead of sending them off to work
in the fields, drank his bottled cider instead of selling it,
ate the finest poultry in his barnyard and greased his hunting
shoes with the fat of his pigs, he soon realized that he
would do well to give up all thought of business endeavor.

So for two hundred francs a year he rented a residence
that was half farm and half gentleman's estate, on the border
between Picardy and the Caux region of Normandy. Melancholy, consumed with regrets, cursing heaven, envious of
everyone, he withdrew into seclusion at the age of forty-
five, disgusted with mankind, he said, and resolved to live
in peace.

His wife had been mad about him in the beginning; she
had loved him with a boundless servility that made him
even more indifferent to her. She had been vivacious, expansive and brimming over with affection in her youth, but
as she grew older she became peevish, nagging and nervous,
like sour wine turning to vinegar. She had suffered so much
at first without complaining, watching him run after every
village strumpet in sight and having him come home to her
every night, satiated and stinking of alcohol, after carousing
in a score of ill-famed establishments! Then her pride rebelled; she withdrew into herself, swallowing her rage with a
mute stoicism which she maintained until her death. She
was always busy with domestic and financial matters. She
was constantly going to see lawyers or the judge, remembering
when notes were due and obtaining renewals; and at home
she spent all her time ironing, sewing, washing, supervising
the workmen and settling the itemized bills they presented
to her, while Monsieur, totally unconcerned with everything
and continually sinking into a sullen drowsiness from which
he roused himself only to make disagreeable remarks to her,
sat smoking beside the fire and spitting into the ashes.

When she had a child it had to be placed in the care of a wet-nurse. The boy was pampered like a prince when he came back to live with them. His mother fed him on jam and candied fruit; his father let him run barefoot and even carried his philosophical pretensions to the point of saying that he might as well go naked, like a young animal. In opposition to his wife's maternal tendencies, he had a certain virile ideal of childhood, and he tried to form his son in accordance with it. He wanted him to be raised harshly, Spartan-style, in order to give him a sturdy constitution. He sent him to bed without a fire, taught him to take hearty swigs of rum and to jeer at religious processions. But, placid by nature, the child showed little response to his father's efforts. His mother kept him tied to her apron-strings; she cut out cardboard figures for him, told him stories and talked to him in endless monologues full of melancholy gaiety and wheedling chatter. In the isolation of her life she transferred all her shattered, abandoned ambitions to her child. She dreamed of high positions, she saw him already grown up, handsome and witty, making a successful career for himself in the Department of Civil Engineering or the magistracy. She taught him to read and even to sing two or three sentimental songs, using an old piano she had. But Monsieur Bovary, who cared little for culture, maintained that such things were "a waste of time." Would they ever have enough money to put him through the government schools, buy him a government position or set him up in business? Besides, "a man could always get ahead in life if he had enough nerve." Madame Bovary bit her lips and the boy continued to run wild in the village.

He tagged after the farmhands and drove the crows away by throwing clods of earth at them. He ate the blackberries growing along the ditches, kept watch over the turkeys with a long stick, pitched hay during harvest time, wandered through the woods, played hopscotch under the church porch on rainy days and, on important holidays, begged the sexton to let him toll the bells, so that he could hang his whole body on the thick rope and feel it lift him into the air when the bells were ringing in full peal.

Thus he grew like an oak. He acquired strong hands and a healthy complexion.

When he was twelve his mother succeeded in arranging for him to begin his education. The village priest agreed to give him lessons. But they were so short and irregular that they accomplished very little. The priest gave them in the sacristy, at odd moments, between a christening and a funeral, hurriedly, without even sitting down; or else he sent for his pupil after the Angelus, on evenings when he did not have to go out. They would go up to his bedroom and set to work while the gnats and moths flew around the candle. It was warm there; the boy would fall asleep and the old man, his hands folded over his stomach, would soon doze off and begin snoring with his mouth open. At other times, when the priest was on his way back to the village after giving the Eucharist to some sick person in the vicinity, he would catch sight of Charles frolicking in the fields, call him over, lecture him for several minutes and take advantage of the opportunity to make him conjugate a verb beneath a tree. They would be interrupted by rain, or some acquaintance passing by. He was always satisfied with his pupil, however, and even said that the "young man" had a good memory.

Charles's mother was determined that he should not stop there. Ashamed, or rather weary, his father gave in without further resistance. They waited another year, until the boy had made his First Communion.

Six more months went by; then, the following year, Charles was finally sent to the lycée in Rouen. His father took him there himself toward the end of October, during the Saint-Romain fair.

It would now be hard for any of us to remember very much about him. He was a boy of moderate temperament; he played during recess, worked in study hall, listened in class, slept well in the dormitory and ate heartily in the dining hall. His temporary guardian was a wholesale hardware dealer on the Rue Ganterie who called for him once a month, on a Sunday, after his shop was closed, and sent him off to take a walk along the waterfront to look at the boats, then brought him back to school at seven o'clock, before supper. Every Thursday evening he wrote a long letter to his mother, using red ink and three sealing wafers; then he would go over his history notebooks or read an old volume of *Anacharsis* that lay around in the study hall. During class outings he talked with the servant, a countryman like himself.

By working hard he always managed to keep himself somewhere near the middle of the class; once he even earned an honorable mention in natural history. But when he had finished the tenth grade his parents took him out of the lycée and put him in medical school, confident that he would be able to get his baccalaureate degree by his own efforts.

His mother rented a room for him in the house of a dyer with whom she was acquainted. It was on the fifth floor, overlooking the brook known as the Eau-de-Robec. She made arrangements for his board, got him a table and two chairs and sent home for an old cherrywood bed. She also bought a small cast-iron stove and a supply of firewood so that her poor boy could keep himself warm. Then she left at the end of the week, after urging him countless times to behave himself now that he was going to be on his own.

He was staggered by the list of courses he read on the bulletin board: anatomy, pathology, physiology, pharmacy, chemistry, botany, clinical practice and therapeutics, not to mention hygiene and materia medica; to him these were all words of unknown etymology, and they were like so many doors leading into sanctuaries full of solemn shadows.

The lectures were equally baffling; he listened attentively but understood nothing. He worked hard just the same. He took notes, went to all his classes and never missed a single visit to the hospital. He performed his daily tasks like a mill horse walking blindfolded in a circle, ignorant of what he is grinding.

To save him money, his mother sent him a veal roast by the stagecoach each week. He had some of it for lunch every day when he came in from the hospital, kicking the mud off his shoes as he ate. Then he would hurry off again, walking all over town to go to lectures, the amphitheater or another hospital, and finally walking home at the end of the day. In the evening, after the meager dinner his landlord served him, he climbed back up to his room and went to work again, his damp clothes steaming as he sat in front of the red-hot stove.

On clear summer evenings, at the hour when the warm streets are deserted and servant girls are playing battledore and shuttlecock in front of the houses, he would open his window and look out, leaning on his elbows. The brook, which makes this part of Rouen a kind of sordid little Venice, flowed past below him, yellow, violet or blue between its bridges and railings. Workmen, squatting on the bank, were washing their arms in the water. Draped over poles projecting from attics, skeins of cotton were drying in the open air. Opposite him, beyond the rooftops, the vast, pure sky stretched out, and the setting sun cast a reddish glow. How pleasant it must be out there, how cool in the beech grove! He opened his nostrils wide, trying to breathe in the good odors of the country, but they were too far away to reach him.

He became thinner and taller, and his face took on a kind of pained expression which made it almost interesting.

His natural irresponsibility eventually led him to break all his good resolutions. One day he missed a visit to the hospital, the next day a lecture; he liked this first taste of idleness and gradually abandoned his courses altogether.

He began going to taverns and developed a passion for dominoes. To spend every evening shut up in a dirty public room, clicking black-dotted pieces of sheep bone on a marble tabletop, seemed to him a precious exercise of his freedom, and it increased his self-esteem. It was like an initiation into the world, an admission into a realm of forbidden pleasures; and he felt an almost sensual delight each time he took hold of the doorknob to enter the tavern. Many things formerly pent up inside him now burst into the open; he learned verses by heart and sang them at parties, became an enthusiastic admirer of Béranger, learned how to make punch and finally came to know the pleasures of love.

Thanks to this preparatory work, he failed miserably when he took his examination to qualify as an *officier de santé.** And his parents were expecting him to come home that very night to celebrate his success!

He set out on foot and stopped at the outskirts of his village. He sent for his mother and told her everything. She excused him, blaming his failure on the unfairness of the examiners, and reassured him a little by promising to smooth things over.

Monsieur Bovary did not learn the truth until five years later; it was an old story by then and he accepted it, especially since he could not admit the possibility that his own offspring might be stupid.

Charles set to work again and ceaselessly crammed for his examination, memorizing the answers to all the questions in advance. He passed with a fairly good grade. What a proud day for his mother! She gave a large dinner party.

Where should he go to prctice his new profession? To Tostes. The town had only one elderly doctor. Madame Bovary had been awaiting his death for a long time, and the

---

* A man authorized to practice medicine without an M.D. degree.—L.B.

old man had not yet given up the ghost when Charles moved in across the road as his successor.

But it was not enough to have raised a son, sent him to medical school and discovered Tostes for him to practice in: he needed a wife. She found him one: a Dieppe bailiff's widow, forty-five years old, with a yearly income of twelve hundred francs.

Although she was ugly and thin as a rail, with pimples blossoming on her face like buds in springtime, Madame Dubuc had no shortage of suitors to choose from. Madame Bovary had to oust them all to achieve her purpose; her skill was particularly evident in the way she foiled the schemes of a butcher who had the backing of the clergy.

Charles had envisaged marriage as the beginning of a more pleasant life, feeling that he would be freer and able to dispose of his time and money as he saw fit. But it was his wife who ruled: in front of other people he had to say this and not say that, he had to eat fish every Friday, dress the way she wanted him to and follow her orders in dunning patients who had not paid their bills. She opened his letters, spied on him and listened through the thin wall when women came to his office.

She had to have her hot chocolate every morning, and endless other attentions. She was constantly complaining about her nerves, her chest, her dizzy spells or her fits of depression. The sound of footsteps was painful to her; when people stayed away from her she found her solitude unbearable; when they came to see her it was no doubt because they wanted to watch her die. When Charles came home at night her long, thin arms would emerge from beneath the covers and twine around his neck; after making him sit down on the edge of the bed, she would begin to tell him of her woes: he was neglecting her, he was in love with another woman! She should have listened when people warned her she'd be unhappy! And then she would end by asking him for some kind of tonic to make her feel better, and a little more love.

II

One night, toward eleven o'clock, they were awakened by the hoofbeats of a horse which stopped in front of their house. The maid opened the attic window and parleyed for some time with a man who remained in the street below. He had been sent to bring the doctor; he had a letter. Nastasie came down the stairs, shivering, unlocked the door and pushed back the bolts one after the other. The man left his horse, followed the maid and walked directly into the bedroom behind her. He reached into his gray-tasseled wool cap, drew out a letter wrapped in a piece of cloth and respectfully handed it to Charles, who raised himself on one elbow to read it while Nastasie, standing beside the bed, held the light for him. Out of modesty, Madame continued to lie facing the wall, with her back to the visitor.

The letter, sealed with a small blue wax seal, begged Monsieur Bovary to come immediately to a farm known as Les Bertaux to set a broken leg. It is at least fifteen miles from Tostes to Les Bertaux, going by way of Longueville and Saint-Victor. It was a dark night. Madame Bovary was afraid her husband might have an accident, so it was decided that the farmhand would start back ahead of him. Charles would leave three hours later, at moonrise. A boy would be sent out to meet him, to show him the way to the farm and open the gates for him.

Carefully wrapped in his overcoat, Charles set out for Les Bertaux at about four o'clock in the morning. He was still drowsy from the warmth of his sleep, and his horse's peaceful trot lulled him like the rocking of a cradle. Each time the animal stopped of its own accord before one of those holes surrounded by thorns that are dug along the borders of cultivated fields, Charles would awake with a start, immediately remember the broken leg and try to recall all the fractures he had studied. The rain had stopped; day was breaking and there were birds perched motionless on the bare branches of the apple trees, ruffling up their little feathers in the cold morning wind. The flat countryside stretched out as far as the eye could see, and the clumps of trees around the farmhouses formed widely separated dark purple stains on that vast gray surface which merged at the horizon into the dull hue of the sky. From time to time Charles would open his eyes, but then his mind would grow weary, sleep would again overwhelm him and he would sink back into a drowsiness in which recent sensations were confused with more distant memories; he saw a double image of himself as both a sudent and a married man, lying in bed as he had been a short time before, and walking through a surgical ward as he had done in the past. The warm smell of poultices was mingled with the fresh smell of the dew; he heard the clatter of curtain rings sliding along the metal rods of hospital beds, and the sound of his wife's breathing as she slept. . . .

As he was nearing Vassonville he saw a young boy sitting on the grass beside a ditch.

"Are you the doctor?" asked the child.

When he heard Charles's answer, he took his wooden shoes in his hands and began to run in front of him.

On the way, the *officier de santé* gathered from his guide's remarks that Monsieur Rouault must be an extremely well-to-do farmer. He had broken his leg the night before as he was returning from a Twelfth Night celebration at a neighbor's house. His wife had been dead for two years. He had with him only his daughter, who helped him run the household.

The ruts in the road became deeper; they were approaching Les Bertaux. The boy darted through a hole in the hedge, disappeared, then reappeared in a farmyard, opening the gate. Charles's horse began to slip on the wet grass and he had to bend down to avoid overhanging branches. Watchdogs were barking in the kennel, tugging at their chains. When he went through the gate of Les Bertaux, his horse took fright and shied violently.

It was a prosperous-looking farm. Through the open upper halves of the stable doors, big work horses could be seen placidly eating from new hayracks. Alongside the farm buildings lay a wide, steaming manure pile; among the chickens and turkeys pecking at its surface were five or six peacocks, a favorite luxury in the barnyards of the Caux region. The sheepfold was long and the barn was high, with walls as smooth as your hand. In the shed were two large carts and four plows, complete with whips, horse collars and all the other trappings, including blue wool pads that were slowly becoming soiled by the fine dust falling from the lofts. The barnyard, with its symmetrically planted trees, sloped upward, and from near the pond came the merry sound of a flock of geese.

A young woman in a blue merino dress with three flounces came to the door of the house to receive Monsieur Bovary. She led him into the kitchen, where a big fire was blazing. Around it the farmhands' breakfast was bubbling in small pots of various sizes. Damp clothes were drying inside the fireplace. The fire shovel, the tongs and the nozzle of the bellows, all of colossal proportions, shone like burnished steel, and along the walls hung an abundant array of kitchen utensils reflecting the flickering firelight and the first rays of dawn coming in through the windows.

Charles went up to the second floor to see the patient. He found him in bed, sweating under the blankets; he had thrown off his cotton nightcap. He was a fat little man of fifty, with pale skin and blue eyes, bald in front and wearing earrings. On a chair beside him was a big decanter of brandy from which he had been pouring himself a drink now and then to pluck up his spirits; but as soon as he saw the doctor he calmed down: instead of cursing as he had been doing for the past twelve hours, he began to groan weakly.

The fracture was a simple one, without complications of any kind. Charles could not have wished for anything easier. Recalling his teachers' bedside manner with accident cases, he cheered up the patient with all sorts of jovial remarks, surgical caresses that are like the oil used to lubricate a scalpel. A bundle of laths was brought in from the cart shed to be used as splints. Charles chose one of them, cut it into pieces and smoothed it down with a piece of broken glass while the maidservant tore sheets to make bandages and Mademoiselle Emma tried to sew some pads. It took her a long time to find her sewing box and her father complained impatiently; she made no reply, but as she sewed she kept pricking her fingers and raising them to her lips to suck them.

Charles was surprised by the whiteness of her fingernails. They were shiny, thin at the tips, almond-shaped and as spotlessly clean as Dieppe ivories. Her hands, however, were not pretty: not pale enough, perhaps, and a little rough at the joints; they were also too long, and without soft curves. Her eyes were her best feature; they were brown, although they seemed black because of her eyelashes, and they looked straight at you with naïve boldness.

When the splints were bound, Monsieur Rouault himself invited the doctor to "have a bite to eat" before leaving.

Charles went down to the parlor on the first floor. At the foot of a big canopied bed covered with calico whose design represented people in Turkish costumes, a small table had been set for two, with silver mugs beside the plates. A smell of orrisroot and damp sheets came from the tall oaken cupboard facing the window. In the corners, sacks of grain were standing in rows, the overflow from the adjoining granary, to which three stone steps led. To decorate the room, there was a black pencil drawing of a head of Minerva hanging from a nail in the middle of the wall, whose green paint was flaking off beneath the saltpeter rot; it was set in a gilded frame and bore this inscription at the bottom, in Gothic letters: "To my dear Papa."

They spoke about the patient first, then about the bitterly cold weather and the wolves that roamed the fields at night. Mademoiselle Rouault did not enjoy living in the country, especially now that she was burdened with nearly the full responsibility of running the farm. Since the room was chilly, she shivered as she ate; this called attention to her full lips, which she was in the habit of biting when she was not speaking.

Her neck rose out of her turned-down white collar. Her black hair was divided into two sections by a fine part running down the middle of her head; these sections, drawn tightly over her skull, were so smooth that each seemed to be of one piece. They covered all but the tips of her ears and were joined at the back of her head in a large chignon. The hair over her temples was waved slightly, a refinement which the country doctor now noticed for the first time in his life. The tops of her cheeks were pink. She had a shell-rimmed pince-nez which she carried, like a man, tucked in between two buttons of her bodice.

When Charles came back downstairs after going up to say good-by to Monsieur Rouault, he found her standing with her forehead pressed against the windowpane, looking out at the garden, where the beanpoles had been toppled by the wind. She turned around.

"Are you looking for something?" she asked.

"Yes, my riding crop," he answered.

She began to look around on the bed, behind the doors, under the chairs; it had fallen on the floor, between the sacks of grain and the wall. She saw it and bent down over the sacks. He gallantly hurried over to her, and as they both reached down at the same time he felt his chest graze her back, which was curved beneath him. She straightened up, blushing deeply, and looked at him over her shoulder as she handed him his riding crop.

Instead of coming back to Les Bertaux three days later, as he had promised, he returned the very next day, and from then on he came twice a week regularly, not counting the un-expected calls he made from time to time, as if by chance.

Everything went well; the bone knit according to the rules, and when, forty-six days later, Monsieur Rouault was seen trying to walk around his house unaided, Monsieur Bovary began to acquire a reputation as a man of great ability. Monsieur Rouault said he could not have been healed better by the greatest doctors of Yvetot, or even Rouen.

As for Charles, he never wondered why he enjoyed going to Les Bertaux. If he had thought about it, he would no doubt have attributed his zeal to the seriousness of the case, or perhaps to the sizable fee he hoped to collect. But was this really why his visits to the farm were such charming interludes in an otherwise drab existence? On those days he would get up early and set off at a gallop, urging on his horse; and before entering the house he would wipe his feet on the grass and put on his black gloves. He was always happy when he rode into the farmyard; he liked the feel of the gate as he pushed it open with his shoulder, the rooster crowing on the wall, the boys who came out to meet him. He liked the barn and the stables; he liked Monsieur Rouault, who gripped his hand vigorously and called him his savior; he liked the sound of Mademoiselle Emma's little shoes on the scrubbed flagstones of the kitchen floor. Her high heels made her a little taller, and when she walked in front of him her wooden soles made a sharp little tapping sound each time they rose against the leather uppers.

She always accompanied him to the foot of the front steps. If his horse had not yet been brought around, she would wait there with him. Since they had already said good-by to each other, they would remain silent; the breeze would swirl all around her, ruffling the stray wisps of hair on the back of her neck or making her apron strings twist and flutter like streamers on her hip. Once during a thaw, the bark of the trees in the barnyard was oozing and the snow on the roofs of the farm buildings was melting; she stood in the doorway, then went back inside for her parasol, brought it out and opened it. The sun shone through the iridescent silk, illuminating the white skin of her face with shifting patches of light. She smiled beneath it at the soft warmth of the day, and drops of water could be heard falling one by one on the taut moiré.

When Charles first began his visits to Les Bertaux, his wife never failed to ask about the patient's progress, and she had even chosen a fine new page for Monsieur Rouault in the double-entry ledger she kept. But when she found out he had a daughter, she began to make inquiries; she learned that Mademoiselle Rouault had gone to boarding school in a Ursuline convent, where she had received what was known as a "fine education"; she had therefore been taught dancing, geography, drawing, needlework and piano. This opened her eyes! "So that's why he looks so happy when he goes to see her!" she said to herself. "That's why he puts on his new vest, even when there's a chance he may ruin it in the rain! Oh, that woman! That woman!"

And she hated her instinctively. At first she gave vent to her anger by making insinuations, but Charles did not understand them. Then she began to make parenthetical remarks which he pretended not to notice, for fear of stirring up a storm. Finally she hurled point-blank accusations at him which he did not know how to answer. Why did he keep going back to Les Bertaux when Monsieur Rouault was well again and hadn't even paid his bill yet? Why? Because of a certain person who lived there! Someone who had a glib tongue, who knew how to add spice to a story and make witty remarks. That was what he liked: he had to have city girls! And she went on:

"Rouault's daughter, a city girl! What a joke! Their grandfather was a shepherd, and they have a cousin who almost went to prison for stabbing a man during a quarrel. And yet she gives herself airs, and wears silk dresses to church on Sunday, like a countess! Why, if it hadn't been for his rapeseed crop last year, her father, poor old man, would have had a hard time paying his debts!"

Out of weariness, Charles stopped going to Les Bertaux. After many sobs and kisses, in a great explosion of love, she had made him put his hand on a prayer book and swear that he would never go back there again. He kept his word, but the boldness of his desire protested against the servility of his conduct, and, with a kind of naïve hypocrisy, he felt that being forbidden to see her gave him a right to love her. And then the widow he had married was skinny; she had long teeth; all year round she wore a little black shawl, with one corner of it hanging down between her shoulder blades; her bony figure was always encased in scabbard-like dresses that were too short; they revealed her ankles, and the ribbons of her wide shoes crisscrossing over her gray stockings.

Charles's mother came to see them from time to time. After a few days her daughter-in-law always seemed to impart some of her own sharpness to her, and, like two knives, they would begin scarifying Charles with their observations and critical comments. He shouldn't eat so much! Why was he always ready to offer a drink to anyone who came to see him? How stubborn he was not to wear flannels!

Early in spring it happened that a notary of Ingouville, custodian of the widow Dubuc's funds, sailed away one fine day, taking all his clients' money with him. Héloïse still owned her house on the Rue Saint-François, it is true, along with a six-thousand-franc share in a ship; and yet, of all that wealth which had been vaunted so highly, nothing except a few pieces of furniture and some clothes had ever appeared in the household. The state of her fortune now had to be cleared up. It turned out that her house in Dieppe was mortgaged up to the rafters; God alone knew how much money she had entrusted to the notary, and her share in the boat was actually worth no more than three thousand francs. So the good lady had been lying! The elder Monsieur Bovary was so outraged that he smashed a chair against the floor and accused his wife of having ruined their son's life by yoking him with a broken-down nag whose harness was worth even less than her carcass. They came to Tostes. The matter was thoroughly discussed. There were scenes. Héloïse, in tears, threw herself in her husband's arms and begged him to defend her against his parents. Charles tried to vindicate her. His parents flew into a rage and left.

But the blow had been struck. A week later, as she was hanging out washing in the yard, she suddenly began to spit blood, and the next day, just at the moment when Charles turned away from her to draw the window curtain, she said "Oh, my God!" sighed deeply and collapsed. She was dead! Who would have believed it?

When everything was over at the cemetery, Charles went

back home. He found no one downstairs; he went up to the
bedroom on the second floor and saw her dress hanging in
the alcove. He leaned against the writing desk and stayed
there till nightfall, lost in sorrowful thoughts. After all, she
had loved him.

III

One morning Monsieur Rouault brought Charles his payment for setting his broken leg: seventy-five francs in two-
franc coins, plus a turkey. He had learned of his loss, and he
consoled him as best he could.

"I know how it is," he said, patting him on the shoulder.
"I've gone through the same thing myself. After I lost my
poor wife I used to go out into the fields to be alone. I'd lie
down under a tree and cry, then I'd talk to God and say
all kinds of silly things to him. I wished I could be like the
moles I saw hanging from the branches, with maggots crawling
in their bellies—dead, in other words. And when I thought
that right then, at that very moment, other men were holding
their sweet little wives in their arms, I'd start pounding on
the ground with my stick. I was almost out of my mind. I
couldn't eat, and even the thought of going to a café made
me feel sick—you can't imagine how it was! Well, gradually,
with one day coming after another, with a spring after a
winter and a fall on top of a summer, I got over it, little by
little, bit by bit. It went away, vanished; or rather it sank
out of sight, because there's always something left, something
like a weight that you carry around inside you, here, in your
chest! But sooner or later it will happen to all of us, so you
mustn't let yourself waste away; there's no sense in wanting
to die just because somebody else is dead! You must pull
yourself together, Monsieur Bovary; you'll get over it! Come
to see us. My daughter thinks about you every once in a
while, you know, and she says you're forgetting her. It's
almost spring now; we'll go out and shoot a rabbit in the
warren, that will cheer you up a little."

Charles followed his advice. He came back to Les Bertaux.
He found everything unchanged since his last visit, five
months before. The pear trees were already blossoming, and

Monsieur Rouault, back on his feet now, bustled to and fro, which made the farm seem livelier.

Thinking it his duty to show the doctor the greatest possible consideration because of his bereavement, he urged him not to take off his hat, talked to him in a low voice as though he were ill, and even pretended to be angry that nothing especially light had been prepared for him, such as little dishes of custard or stewed pears. He told funny stories. Charles surprised himself by laughing, but he was sobered when the memory of his wife came back to him. Then coffee was served and he stopped thinking about her.

He thought of her less and less as he became accustomed to living alone. The new delights of independence soon made his solitude more bearable. He could now change the hours of his meals, come and go without giving any explanations, lie down and spread his arms and legs from one side of the bed to the other when he was tired. He pampered and coddled himself, and accepted all the consolations that were offered to him. Furthermore, his wife's death had been quite useful to him in his profession, because for a month people had kept repeating, "Poor young man! What a tragedy!" His name had become well known, his patients had become more numerous. And now he could go to Les Bertaux whenever he pleased. He was filled with hope that had no specific goal, with vague happiness; he found his face more attractive as he brushed his side whiskers in front of his mirror.

He arrived one day at about three o'clock. Everyone was out in the fields. He went into the kitchen, but at first he did not see Emma; the shutters were closed. The sun was shining in between the slats, casting long, thin rays of light which stretched across the stone floor, broke sharply over the corners of the furniture and shimmered on the ceiling. On the table, flies were crawling up the sides of dirty glasses and buzzing as they drowned in the cider remaining at the bottom. The light coming down through the chimney turned the soot on the fireback to velvet and gave a bluish tinge to the cold ashes. Emma was sitting between the window and the fireplace, sewing; she was not wearing a shawl, and he could see little beads of sweat on her bare shoulders.

As is customary in the country, she offered him something to drink. He refused, she insisted, and finally she laughingly invited him to have a glass of liqueur with her. She went to get a bottle of curaçao from the cupboard, took down two small glasses, filled one of them to the brim and poured a few drops into the other. After they had touched their glasses together, she raised hers to her lips. Since it was nearly empty, she leaned back to drink from it; with her chin tilted upward, her lips pushed forward and her throat taut, she laughed because she felt nothing, while the tip of her tongue, darting out from between her delicate teeth, licked the bottom of the glass.

She sat down again and resumed her work, which consisted of darning a white stocking; she sewed with her head bowed and did not speak. Neither did Charles. A draft coming in under the door was blowing little clouds of dust across the floor; he watched them swirling and heard only the pounding inside his head, along with the cackling of a hen laying an egg in the barnyard outside. From time to time Emma cooled her cheeks with the palms of her hands, then cooled her hands again by placing them on the iron knobs of the big andirons.

She complained of having been troubled by dizzy spells since the beginning of the season and asked if bathing in the sea would help her. She began to talk about her convent school, Charles about his lycée; words came more easily to them. They went upstairs to her room. She showed him her old music exercise books, the little books she had won as prizes, and the wreaths of oak leaves lying abandoned at the bottom of a closet. She talked to him about her mother and the cemetery, and even showed him the flower bed in the garden from which, on the first Friday of every month, she picked flowers to place on her grave. But their gardener had no understanding of such things: none of their servants was worth his keep! She wished she could live in town, at least during the winter, although the days were so long in summer that the country was perhaps even more boring then than ever. . . . And, according to what she was saying, her voice was either clear or shrill; or, suddenly becoming languorous, it would trail off into inflections that ended almost in a murmur, as though she were talking to herself. Sometimes her eyes would open wide in guileless joy, then her eyelids would droop while her face took on an expression of profound boredom and her thoughts seemed to wander aimlessly.

On his way home that evening, Charles went over her remarks one by one, trying to recall them exactly and fathom their full implications in order to picture what her life had been like before he met her. But he was never able to imagine her any differently from the way she had been the first time he saw her, or as she had been when he left her. Then he wondered what would become of her, whether she would marry, and whom. Alas, Monsieur Rouault was quite rich . . . and she was so beautiful! But her face appeared constantly before his eyes, and something like the monotonous humming of a top kept buzzing in his ears: "But what if *you* got married? What if *you* got married?" He couldn't sleep that night. His throat was tight, he was thirsty; he got up to drink from his water jug and opened the window. The sky was covered with stars; a warm wind was blowing and dogs were barking in the distance. He turned his face in the direction of Les Bertaux.

Thinking that, after all, it would do no harm to try, Charles promised himself he would ask the question at the next opportunity; but each time an opportunity presented itself the fear of not finding the right words sealed his lips.

Monsieur Rouault would not have been at all unhappy to have someone take his daughter off his hands, for she was of little use to him on the farm. In his heart he forgave her, feeling that she was too intelligent for farming, which he regarded as an accursed occupation because it had never made anyone a millionaire. Far from making a fortune at it, the old man lost money every year; he did very well for himself in the market place, where he enjoyed using all the tricks of the trade, but no one was ever less suited to the work of raising crops and managing a farm. He never lifted a finger if he could avoid it, and he spared no expense where his personal comfort was concerned: he insisted on good food, a good fire and a good bed. He liked hard cider, legs of mutton cooked rare and coffee with rum or brandy in it. He took his meals alone in the kitchen; he sat facing the fire and ate from a little table that was brought in to him already set, as in the theater.

So when he noticed that Charles's cheeks turned red in his daughter's presence, which meant that one of these days he would ask for her hand, he pondered the whole matter in advance. He found Charles rather thin and frail, not the kind of son-in-law he would have preferred, but he was said to be level-headed, thrifty and very well educated, and he probably wouldn't haggle too much over the dowry. Furthermore, since Monsieur Rouault was soon going to be forced to sell forty-five acres of his land, since he owed a great deal to the mason and the harness-maker, and since the cider press needed a new shaft, he said to himself, "If he asks me for her, I won't say no."

Toward the end of September, Charles spent three days at Les Bertaux. The last day went past like the others, with the big moment being put off from one hour to the next. Monsieur Rouault was accompanying him a short distance before seeing him off; they were walking along a sunken road; they were about to part. The time had come. Charles told himself he must make his declaration before they came to the corner of the hedge; finally, when they had passed it, he murmured, "Monsieur Rouault, there's something I'd like to say to you."

They stopped. Charles fell silent.

"Go on, tell me what's on your mind—as if I didn't know already!" said Monsieur Rouault, laughing gently.

"Monsieur Rouault—Monsieur Rouault—" stammered Charles.

"As far as I'm concerned, I'd like like nothing better," continued the farmer. "I'm sure my daughter agrees with me, but I'll have to ask her just the same. I'll leave you here and go back to the house. Listen to me now: if she says yes, you'd better not come in, because of all the people around; and besides, it would upset her too much. But I don't want to keep you in suspense, so I'll open one of the shutters all the way against the wall; you'll be able to see it if you look back over the hedge."

And he walked away.

Charles tied his horse to a tree, ran back to the path and waited. Half an hour went by, then he counted nineteen minutes by his watch. Suddenly he heard a sound from the house: the shutter had slammed against the wall; the catch was still quivering.

He returned to the farm at nine the next morning. Emma blushed when he came in, but she forced herself to laugh a little in order not to seem flustered. Monsieur Rouault embraced his future son-in-law. They postponed all discussion of financial arrangements: there was still plenty of time, since the wedding could not decently take place until the end of Charles's mourning, toward spring of the following year.

The winter was spent in waiting. Mademoiselle Rouault busied herself with her trousseau. Part of it was ordered in Rouen, and she made herself a number of nightgowns and nightcaps patterned after some fashion drawings she had

borrowed. During Charles's visits to the farm they talked
about preparations for the wedding, wondering which room
the dinner should be served in, dreaming of all the different
courses that would be required and trying to decide what the
entrées ought to be.

Emma would have preferred to be married at midnight,
by torchlight, but this idea seemed senseless to her father.
So there was a traditional wedding with forty-three guests who
remained at table for sixteen hours, began the celebration
all over again the next day and kept it up more or less for
several days afterward.

IV

The guests arrived early in a variety of vehicles: carryalls,
two-wheeled charabancs, old gigs without tops, vans with
leather curtains; and the young men from the nearby villages
came in carts, standing beside each other in rows and gripping
the rails to keep from falling as they bumped along behind
the trotting horses. They came from twenty-five miles around,
from Goderville, Normanville and Cany. All the relatives of
both families had been invited; quarrels between friends had
been patched up; letters had been written to acquaintances
who had long since dropped out of sight.

Now and then the crack of a whip would be heard behind
the hedge; soon afterward the gate would open and a carryall
would roll in. It would go on at a gallop as far as the front
steps, then stop short and begin discharging its passengers,
who would climb out on all sides, rubbing their knees and
stretching their arms. The ladies wore bonnets and city-style
dresses, with gold watch chains, tippets whose ends were
crossed and tucked into their belts, or small colored scarves
pinned at the back and leaving the neck bare. The boys,
dressed exactly like their papas, looked uncomfortable in
their new clothes (many of them, in fact, were wearing boots
for the first time in their lives), and beside them there was
often some tall, red-faced girl of fourteen or fifteen, probably
their cousin or older sister, standing speechless and bewildered
in her white First Communion dress lengthened for the occasion, her hair sticky with rose pomade, terribly worried

about soiling her gloves. Since there were not enough stable-men to unharness all the vehicles, the men rolled up their sleeves and did it themselves. According to their social status, they wore tail coats, frock coats, long jackets or short jackets. The tail coats were fine garments, each one held in high esteem by an entire family and taken out of the closet only on great occasions; the frock coats had full skirts that billowed in the wind, cylindrical collars and pockets as wide as bags; the long jackets, made of coarse woolen cloth, were in most cases worn with a cap whose visor was trimmed with brass; the short jackets had two buttons in back, set close together like a pair of eyes, and stubby tails which looked as though they had been cut from a single block by a carpenter's ax. A few guests (these, of course, would sit at the foot of the table) wore dress smocks; that is, smocks with collars turned down over the shoulders, pleated backs and stitched belts worn very low.

And the shirts bulged out like breastplates! Every man was freshly shorn, ears stuck out sharply from every head, every face was closely shaven. Some of the men, having gotten up before dawn, had not been able to see clearly when they shaved; as a result, they had diagonal gashes under their noses, or patches of skin as wide as a three-franc coin sliced from their jaws. These cuts had been inflamed by the wind during the journey, so that the big, beaming white faces were mottled with red spots.

Since the town hall was only a little more than a mile from the farm, the entire party went there on foot and re-turned the same way after the church ceremony. At first the procession was like a single brightly colored scarf undulating across the countryside along the narrow path that wound through the green grain, but it soon began to stretch out thin and break up into separate groups which lingered along the way to talk. The fiddler walked in front with his violin, which was adorned with ribbons hanging from its scroll; then came the bride and groom with their relatives behind them; the other guests followed in a disorderly band, and the children dallied behind, amusing themselves by pulling the bellflowers from among the oat stalks, or frolicking with each other, out of sight of their parents. Emma's dress, too long, trailed on the ground a little; she would stop now and then to pull it up and daintily pick off the coarse blades of grass and thistle spikes with her gloved fingers while Charles stood by empty-handed, waiting for her to finish. Monsieur Rouault, wearing

a new silk hat and a black tail coat whose sleeves hung down
to his fingertips, had given his arm to the elder Madame
Bovary. As for the elder Monsieur Bovary, who, basically
despising all those people, had come wearing merely a long
single-breasted coat of military cut, he was busy addressing
barroom gallantries to a blond young peasant girl who nodded
and blushed, not knowing what to answer. The other members
of the wedding party were discussing business matters or
playing tricks behind each other's backs, working themselves
up in advance for the merriment that was to come. And, if
they listened, they could hear the fiddler, who continued to
scrape his instrument as he walked across the fields. Whenever he noticed that the others were lagging far behind him,
he would stop to catch his breath, carefully rub his bow
with rosin to make the strings squeak better, then set off again,
bobbing the neck of his violin up and down to keep time. His
music frightened away all the birds within a wide radius.

The table had been set up in the cart shed. On it were
four sirloin roasts, six chicken fricassees, a veal casserole,
three legs of mutton and, in the center, a beautiful roast
suckling pig flanked by four large sausages made of chitter-
lings and sorrel. At the corners stood decanters of brandy.
The cider was foaming up around the corks and every glass
had been filled to the brim with wine. Big dishes of yellow
custard, on whose smooth surface the newlyweds' initials had
been inscribed in arabesques of sugar-coated almonds, quivered
whenever the table was given the slightest knock. The pies
and nougat had been ordered from a confectioner in Yvetot.
Since he had just opened up shop in the district he had done
his best to make a good impression, and when it was time
for dessert he personally carried in a wedding cake which
brought forth a chorus of exclamations. Its base was a square
of blue cardboard representing a temple with porticos and
colonnades, adorned on all sides with stucco statuettes standing in niches studded with gilded paper stars. The second tier
consisted of a fortified castle tower made of spongecake,
surrounded by smaller fortifications of angelica, almonds,
raisins and sections of orange. And finally, on the top layer,
which was a green meadow with rocks, jelly lakes and hazel-
nut-shell boats, a little cupid was swinging in a chocolate
swing whose two uprights were tipped with real rosebuds.

The eating went on till nightfall. When some of the guests
became tired of sitting down, they would take a stroll through

the barnyards or go into a barn and play a game of cork-penny, then they would return to the table. Toward the end, a few people fell asleep and snored. But everything came to life again when the coffee was served: there were songs and feats of strength; the men carried heavy weights, put their heads under their arms while holding their thumbs on the table, tried to raise carts on their shoulders, told spicy stories, kissed the ladies. Later in the evening, when it was time to leave, the horses, stuffed to the nostrils with oats, were placed between the shafts only with great difficulty; they kicked, reared and broke their harnesses while their masters cursed or laughed; and all night long, in the moonlight on the country roads, there were runaway carryalls bouncing along ditches at a wild gallop, leaping over piles of stones and sideswiping embankments, with women leaning out, trying to catch hold of the reins.

Those who stayed behind at Les Bertaux spent the night drinking in the kitchen. The children went to sleep under the benches.

The bride had begged her father to see to it that she was spared the usual practical jokes. However, one of their cousins, a fishmonger (who had brought a pair of soles as a wedding gift), was about to squirt water from his mouth through the keyhole when Monsieur Rouault came along just in time to stop him, explaining that the dignity of his son-in-law's position forbade such unseemly pranks. The cousin gave in to him with extreme reluctance. He inwardly accused Rouault of snobbishness and went off to a corner to join four or five other guests who had, by chance, been given inferior cuts of meat at table several times in succession and therefore felt that they too had been badly treated; they all whispered malicious remarks about their host and, in veiled language, expressed hopes for his ruin.

The elder Madame Bovary had not opened her mouth all day. She had not been consulted about her daughter-in-law's wedding dress or the arrangements for the celebration; she retired early. Instead of going with her, her husband sent to Saint-Victor for cigars and stayed up till dawn, smoking and drinking hot toddies made with kirsch, a mixture that was new to the other guests; it made him feel that they held him in even greater esteem.

Charles was not jocular by nature, and his conversation during the festivities had not been sparkling. He made feeble

replies to the witticisms, puns, equivocal remarks, compliments and broad jokes which everyone felt duty-bound to
toss at him all through the meal.

The next day, however, he seemed a different man. It was
he who acted as though he had lost his virginity during the
night, while the bride's behavior revealed nothing whatever.
Even the shrewdest observers were puzzled, and they carefully scrutinized her whenever she came near. But Charles
hid nothing. He called her "my wife," used the intimate form
of address when he spoke to her, kept asking everyone where
she was and looking for her everywhere, and often took her
out into the yard, where he could be seen in the distance,
through the trees, walking with his arm around her waist,
leaning over her and rumpling with his head the tucker she
was wearing over her bodice.

The bride and groom left two days after the wedding:
because of his patients, Charles could stay no longer. Monsieur
Rouault had them taken back in his carryall and went with
them as far as Vassonville. There he gave his daughter one
last kiss, got out and began walking back toward Les Bertaux.
He turned around after taking a hundred steps or so, and
as he watched the carryall moving away from him, its wheels
spinning in the dust, he heaved a deep sigh. He recalled his
own wedding, his own youth, his wife's first pregnancy; he,
too, had been happy the day he took her from her father's
house to his own. She had ridden behind him on his horse
as it trotted through the snow, for it had been close to
Christmas and the fields were white; she had held onto him
with one arm while her basket hung from the other; she was
wearing the traditional headdress of the Caux region, and
the long lace streamers fluttered in the wind, occasionally
blowing across his mouth. Each time he looked around he
saw her rosy little face pressed up against his shoulder,
smiling silently at him from beneath the gold plaque of her
bonnet. From time to time she would warm her fingers by
putting them inside his coat. It was all so long ago! Their
son would now be thirty if he were still alive! He looked back
again and saw nothing on the road. He felt desolate and dreary,
like an empty, deserted house, and as tender memories and
gloomy thoughts mingled in his mind, which was still beclouded
by the vapors of the feast, he had a momentary impulse to
head toward the church. Since he was afraid the sight of it
might make him even sadder, however, he went straight
home.

Monsieur and Madame Charles Bovary reached Tostes at about six o'clock. The neighbors came to their windows to see their doctor's new wife.

The old servant appeared, presented her respects, apologized for not having dinner ready and suggested that Madame look over her new house in the meantime.

V

The brick front of the house was flush with the street, or rather the road. Behind the door hung a coat with a short cape, a bridle and a black leather cap, and on the floor in one corner lay a pair of gaiters still caked with mud. To the right was the "parlor," which was actually a living room and dining room combined. The canary-yellow wallpaper, embellished at the top by a border of pale flowers, rippled everywhere over its loose cloth backing; white calico curtains edged with red braid overlapped each other down the length of the windows, and on the narrow mantelpiece a clock adorned with a bust of Hippocrates stood majestically between two silver-plated candlesticks with oval glass shades. Across the hall was Charles's office. It was a small room, no more than six paces wide, with a table, three simple chairs and an office armchair. The six shelves of the fir bookcase were filled almost entirely by a set of the *Dictionary of the Medical Sciences* whose pages were uncut, but whose bindings had suffered in the process of being bought and sold by a long succession of different owners. The smell of cooking sauces came through the wall during consultations, and from the kitchen one could hear the patients coughing and giving detailed descriptions of their symptoms. Next came a big dilapidated room which opened directly onto the courtyard, where the stable was, and contained an oven. Now being used as a woodshed, wine bin and storeroom, it was filled with old, rusty iron, empty barrels, broken agricultural implements and a number of other dusty objects whose uses were impossible to guess.

The garden, longer than it was wide, ran along between two clay walls covered with espaliered apricot trees until it came to the thorn hedge that marked it off from the fields.

In the middle was a slate sundial on a masonry pedestal. Four beds of scrawny wild rose bushes were symmetrically laid out around the useful square plot of ground devoted to more serious vegetation. At the far end, beneath the spruces, a plaster priest was reading his breviary.

Emma went up to the bedrooms. The first one was not furnished, but the second one, the conjugal chamber, had a mahogany bed standing in an alcove hung with red draperies. A box made of sea shells decorated the dresser, and on the writing desk near the window there was a bouquet of orange blossoms standing in a decanter and tied with white satin ribbons. It was a bride's bouquet, the *other* bride's bouquet! She looked at it. Charles noticed, picked it up and went off to put it in the attic. Sitting in an armchair while her belongings were being piled up around her, Emma thought of her own bridal bouquet, which was packed in a cardboard box, and wondered what would be done with it if she were to die.

She spent the first two days planning changes in the house. She took the glass shades off the candlesticks, had the walls repapered, the stairs repainted and benches made for the garden, to be placed around the sundial; she even made inquiries as to how to go about constructing a fish pond with a fountain. And her husband, knowing she liked to go for drives, bought a secondhand two-wheeled buggy which, after being fitted out with new lanterns and quilted leather mudguards, looked almost like a tilbury.

He was happy, without a care in the world. A meal alone with her, an evening stroll along the highway, the movement of her hand as she smoothed her hair, the sight of her straw hat hanging from a window hasp, and many other things which he had never dreamed would give him pleasure—such were the components of his unceasing happiness. Each morning, lying in bed with his head beside hers on the pillow, he watched the sunlight shining through the golden down on her cheeks, half covered by the scalloped flaps of her nightcap. Seen from so close, her eyes seemed larger than usual, especially when she opened and shut them several times on awakening; black when seen in shadow, dark blue in bright light, they seemed to have different layers of color which became lighter and more transparent as they approached the glossy surface. His eyes became lost in those depths and he saw himself in miniature down to his shoulders, with a silk scarf around his head and his nightshirt open. After he had gotten up, she would go to the window to watch him leave;

she would lean on her elbows between two pots of geraniums, her dressing gown hanging loosely around her. Outside in the street, Charles would put his foot on the curbstone to buckle his spurs and she would go on talking to him from above, occasionally biting off a piece of a flower or a leaf and blowing it down to him; it would flutter and seem to hover momentarily, making little half-circles in the air like a bird, and finally, before reaching the ground, it would catch in the tangled mane of the old white mare standing motionless in front of the door. Charles would throw her a kiss after climbing into the saddle; she would reply with a wave of her hand; he would set off. And then, on the endless dusty ribbon of the highway, on sunken roads lined with overhanging branches, on paths running through grainfields whose stalks came up to his knees, with the sun on his shoulders and the morning air in his nostrils, his heart full of the night's bliss, his mind at peace and his flesh content, he would ride along ruminating his happiness, like those who, after dinner, still savor the taste of the truffles they are digesting.

Up till now, had there ever been anything really good in his life? Was it the time he had spent in the lycée, where he had been shut in by those high walls, lonely among richer or more intelligent schoolmates who laughed at his accent and made fun of his clothes, and whose mothers brought them cookies in their muffs when they came to the visiting room? Or was it the time he had later spent studying medicine, when he had never had enough money to go dancing with some little working girl who would have become his mistress? Then he had lived fourteen months with the widow, whose feet, in bed, had been as cold as icicles. But now he possessed, for life, this pretty wife whom he adored. For him the universe did not go beyond the silken confines of her petticoat; and he would reproach himself for not loving her enough, and yearn to be with her again; he would ride back at top speed and run upstairs, his heart pounding. Emma would be in her room, combing her hair; he would tiptoe up to her and kiss her from behind; she would cry out in surprise.

He could not keep from constantly touching her comb, her rings, her shawl; sometimes he gave her big, full-lipped kisses on the cheek, or a string of little kisses all the way up her bare arm, from her fingertips to her shoulder; and she would push him away, half smiling and half annoyed, like a mother with a clutching child.

Before her marriage she had believed herself to be in love;

but since the happiness which should have resulted from this love had not come to her, she felt that she must have been mistaken. And she tried to find out exactly what was meant in life by the words "bliss," "passion" and "rapture," which had seemed so beautiful to her in books.

VI

She had read *Paul and Virginia* and dreamed of the bamboo cabin, the Negro Domingo and the dog Fidèle, and especially of the sweet friendship of a devoted little brother who would climb trees higher than a steeple to pick red fruit for her, or run barefoot across the sand, bringing her a bird's nest.

When she was thirteen her father took her to town to place her in the convent school. They stopped at an inn in the Saint-Gervais quarter where they ate their supper from plates on which scenes from the life of Mademoiselle de la Vallière were painted. The explanatory captions, interrupted here and there by knife scratches, all glorified piety, the sensibilities of the heart and the pomp of the court.

At first, far from being bored in the convent, she enjoyed the company of the nuns, who, to amuse her, would take her into the chapel by way of a long corridor leading from the dining hall. She played very little during the recreation periods and understood her catechism well: it was always she who answered the curate's most difficult questions. Living constantly in the warm atmosphere of the classrooms and among those pale women who wore rosaries with copper crosses attached to them, she gradually succumbed to the mystic languor which she breathed in with the perfumes of the altar, the coolness of the water in the holy-water fonts, the radiance of the candles. Instead of following the Mass, she looked at the blue-bordered religious pictures in her book; she loved the sick sheep, the Sacred Heart pierced by sharp arrows, and poor Jesus stumbling and falling beneath his cross. She tried to fast for a whole day, to mortify herself. She tried to think of some vow she could fulfill.

When she went to confession she invented little sins so that she could stay longer, kneeling in the shadows, her hands clasped and her face in front of the grille, with the priest whispering above her. Metaphorical expressions such as "betrothed," "spouse," "heavenly lover" and "eternal wedlock," which constantly recur in sermons, stirred previously unknown depths of sweet emotion in her soul.

Every evening before prayers a passage from some religious work was read aloud in the study hall. On weekdays it was from a summary of Biblical history, or Abbé Frayssinous' lectures; on Sundays, as a special treat, there was a reading from Chateaubriand's *The Genius of Christianity*. How intently she listened, the first few times, to the sonorous lamentations of that romantic melancholy expressing itself again and again in all the echoes of this world and the next! If her childhood had been spent in a shopkeeper's apartment in the business district of a city, she might now have opened herself to the lyric appeal of nature, which usually reaches us only through the medium of literature. But she knew the country too well; she was thoroughly acquainted with bleating sheep, dairy produce and plows. Accustomed to peaceful sights, she was drawn to scenes of contrast and unrest. She liked the sea only because of its storms, and verdure only when it was scattered among ruins. She had to be able to extract some kind of personal benefit from things, and she rejected as useless anything which did not contribute to the immediate gratification of her heart, for her temperament was more sentimental than artistic and she sought emotion, not landscapes.

There was an old spinster who came to the convent for a week each month to mend the linen. As a member of an ancient noble family ruined by the Revolution, she enjoyed the patronage of the archdiocese; she ate at the nuns' table in the dining hall and always stayed to have a little chat before going back upstairs to her work. The schoolgirls often slipped out of study hall to pay her a visit. She knew a number of eighteenth-century love songs, and she sang them in a low voice as she plied her needle. She told stories, reported the latest news, ran errands in town for the girls and secretly let the older ones read the novels she always had in her apron pocket (the good lady herself devoured long chapters from them during the intervals in her work). They were filled with love affairs, lovers, mistresses, persecuted ladies fainting in lonely country houses, postriders killed at every relay, horses ridden to death on every page, dark forests, palpitating hearts, vows, sobs, tears and kisses, skiffs in the moonlight, nightingales in thickets, and gentlemen brave as lions, gentle as lambs, virtuous as no one really is, and always ready to shed floods of tears. For six months, at the age of fifteen, Emma soiled her hands with this dust from old lending libraries. Later, with Sir Walter Scott, she developed a passion for things historical and dreamed of wooden chests, palace guards and wandering minstrels. She wished she could have lived in some old manor house, like those chatelaines in low-waisted gowns who spent their days with their elbows on the stone sill of a Gothic window surmounted by a trefoil, chin in hand, watching a white-plumed rider on a black horse galloping toward them from far across the countryside. In those days she worshiped Mary Queen of Scots and venerated other illustrious or ill-starred women. For her, Joan of Arc, Héloïse, Agnès Sorel, La Belle Ferronnière and Clémence Isaure stood out like comets against the dark vastness of history; also visible to her, though unrelated and less clearly distinguishable among the shadows, were Saint Louis and his oak, the dying Bayard, some of Louis XI's atrocities, a few details of the Massacre of Saint Bartholomew, the plume of Henri IV's helmet, and always the memory of the painted plates glorifying Louis XIV.

The sentimental songs she sang in music class were concerned with nothing but little angels with golden wings, madonnas, lagoons and gondoliers; they were placid compositions whose silly words and inept music gave her glimpses of the alluring phantasmagoria of genuine emotion. Some of her schoolmates brought to the convent the keepsake albums they had received as New Year's gifts. They had to be kept hidden, which was no easy matter; they were read at night, in the dormitory. Handling their beautiful satin bindings with great care, Emma would stare, dazzled, at the unfamiliar names of the authors, most of them counts or viscounts, whose signatures were placed beneath their contributions.

She quivered as she blew back the tissue paper from the engravings; it would curl up, then gently fall and spread over the page again. Behind the balustrade of a balcony, a young man in a short cloak was embracing a girl in a white dress with an alms-purse hanging from her belt; or there were anonymous portraits of English ladies with blond curls, their wide, light-colored eyes looking out from beneath their round straw hats, Some were shown lolling in carriages gliding through parks, with a greyhound running ahead of the trotting horses driven by two little postilions in white knee breeches. Others were dreaming on sofas with an opened letter beside them, looking out at the moon through a window that was half open and half draped with a black curtain. Innocent maidens with tears on their cheeks were kissing turtledoves through the bars of a Gothic cage; or, smiling, with their heads tilted over one shoulder, they were pulling the petals from a daisy with their tapering fingers which curved upward like the tips of medieval slippers. And there were sultans with long pipes swooning under arbors in the arms of dancing girls; there were Giaours, Turkish sabers and fezzes; and above all there were wan landscapes of fantastic countries: palm trees and pines were often combined in one picture, with tigers on the right, a lion on the left, Tartar minarets on the horizon, Roman ruins in the foreground, and a few kneeling camels—all framed by a clean, tidy virgin forest, with a big perpendicular sunbeam shimmering on the surface of the water and floating white swans etched on a steel-gray background at distant intervals.

And the shaded lamp fixed to the wall above Emma's head illuminated all these pictures of the world as they passed before her one after the other in the silence of the dormitory, broken only by the faraway sound of some belated cab rolling along the boulevards.

When her mother died, she wept profusely for several days. She had a funeral picture made with the dead woman's hair and sent her father a letter, filled with gloomy reflections on life, in which she asked to be buried in the same tomb when she died. He thought she must be ill and came to see her. Emma was inwardly pleased to feel that she had so quickly attained that rare ideal of a pale, languid existence, beyond the reach of mediocre spirits. She drifted along winding Lamartinian paths, listened to the music of harps floating over lakes, to all the songs of dying swans, to the fall of every leaf, to the sound of pure virgins ascending to heaven, and to the voice of the Eternal discoursing in the valleys. She became bored with this, refused to admit it to herself, continued first from force of habit, then out of vanity, until she was finally surprised to discover that she felt quite tranquil again and that she had no more sadness in her heart than wrinkles in her forehead.

The good nuns, who had felt so confident about her vocation, noticed with great surprise that Mademoiselle Rouault now seemed to be slipping away from them. They had showered her so lavishly with prayers, retreats, novenas and sermons, preached to her so much about the respect due to the saints and the martyrs, and given her so much good advice about bodily modesty and the salvation of her soul, that she reacted like a horse being pulled by the bridle: she stopped short and the bit fell from her teeth. Even in the midst of her raptures she had always maintained a propensity for the concrete; she had loved the church for its flowers, music for the sentimental words of the songs, and literature for its power to stir up the passions. She rebelled against the mysteries of faith and became increasingly irritated by discipline, which was antipathetic to her nature. When her father took her out of school, no one was sorry to see her go. The Mother Superior, in fact, felt that she had recently become rather disrespectful toward the community.

For a short time after her return, Emma enjoyed giving orders to the servants, then she became disgusted with the country and began to miss the convent. By the time of Charles's first visit to Les Bertaux she regarded herself as extremely disillusioned, a woman with nothing more to learn and no more emotions to experience.

Her anxiety over her new position in life, or perhaps the stimulation of this man's presence, had been enough to make her believe that she at last possessed that marvelous passion which, until then, had been like a great rosy-plumaged bird soaring in the splendors of poetic skies. And now she could not bring herself to believe that the calm in which she was living was the happiness she had dreamed of.

VII

It sometimes occurred to her that these were nevertheless the best days of her life: the honeymoon days, as they were commonly called. To taste their sweetness, she and her husband would probably have had to go off to those countries with romantic names where newlyweds can savor their bliss in such delicious languor! They would have slowly climbed the steep slopes in a post chaise with blue silk curtains, listening to the postilion's song echoing among the mountains, along with the tinkling of goat bells and the muffled roar of waterfalls. At sunset they would have breathed in the fragrance of lemon trees on the shore of a bay; and at night, alone on the terrace

of a villa with their fingers intertwined, they would have
looked up at the stars and made plans for the future. It
seemed to her that certain parts of the earth must produce
happiness like a plant indigenous to that soil and unable to
flourish anywhere else. If only she could lean over the balcony
of a Swiss chalet, or enclose her melancholy in a Scottish
cottage, with a husband wearing a long black velvet cloak,
a sugar-loaf hat and fancy cuffs!

She might have liked to confide all these things to someone,
but how can one describe an elusive malaise which continually
changes form like a cloud and whirls like the wind? She
could not find the words she needed, and she had neither
the opportunity nor the courage to speak.

And yet it seemed to her that if Charles had made the
slightest effort, if he had been at all perceptive, if his glance
had only once penetrated her thoughts, an abundance of feeling would suddenly have been released from her heart, like
ripe fruit falling from a tree at the touch of a hand. As their
daily life became more and more intimate, she was separated
from him by a growing feeling of inner detachment.

Charles's conversation was as flat as a sidewalk, and it was
traversed by a steady stream of the most commonplace ideas,
all wearing their usual garb and appealing to neither the emotions, the sense of humor nor the imagination. When he had
lived in Rouen, he said, he had never had any desire to go
to the theater to see the Parisian companies that performed
there. He did not know how to swim, fence or shoot a pistol,
and one day he was unable to tell her the meaning of a riding
term she had come across in a novel.

But shouldn't a man know everything, excel in all sorts of
activities, initiate you into the turbulence of passion, the
refinements and mysteries of life? *This* man taught nothing,
knew nothing, wanted nothing. He believed her to be happy;
and she resented his steadfast calm, his serene dullness, the
very happiness she gave him.

She drew occasionally, and Charles loved to stand beside her
and watch her as she leaned over her sketch, squinting her
eyes to see it better, or rolling little balls of soft bread between
her thumb and finger. As for the piano, the faster her fingers
moved the more he marveled. She played boldly, sweeping
up and down the keyboard without faltering. Thus shaken by
her vigorous touch, the old instrument, whose strings jangled,
could be heard at the other end of the village if the window

was open, and the bailiff's clerk, bareheaded and holding a sheet of paper in his hand, would often stop to listen as he walked past the house in his cloth shoes.

Emma also knew how to run her household. She wrote to all of Charles's patients, reminding them of how much they owed, yet phrasing her letters so well that they did not sound like bills. Whenever one of the neighbors came to dinner on Sunday, she always managed to present some attractive dish; she knew how to arrange greengage plums in pyramids on vine leaves, she served jelly turned out of the jar onto a plate, and she even spoke of buying finger bowls for dessert. All this greatly enhanced the esteem in which Charles was held.

And he finally began to esteem himself more highly for having such a wife. He proudly showed his visitors two of her little pencil sketches which he had placed in very wide frames and hung on the papered wall of the parlor with long green cords. People returning from Mass saw him on his doorstep wearing a beautiful pair of carpet slippers.

He usually came home late, at ten o'clock, sometimes at midnight. He would ask for something to eat, and since the maid was in bed, Emma herself would serve him. He would take off his coat to be more comfortable while he ate and tell her about everyone he had met, every village he had gone to and every prescription he had written. Exuding self-satisfaction, he would eat what remained of the stew, pare his cheese, munch an apple and empty the decanter of wine; then he would get ready for bed, lie down on his back and begin to snore.

Since he had long been accustomed to wearing a cotton nightcap, his foulard always slipped off his head during the night, so that by the time he awoke in the morning his hair was hanging over his face, white with down from his pillow, whose strings had come untied while he slept. He always wore heavy boots which had two deep creases running diagonally from the instep to the ankle, while the rest of the upper rose in a straight line, as taut as if it had been stretched over a boot tree. He said they were "good enough for the country."

His mother approved of his thriftiness in this regard. As in the past, she came to see him whenever she had had a violent scene with her husband. She seemed to be prejudiced against her daughter-in-law, however. She felt that she was inclined to "live beyond her means"; the amount of firewood, sugar and candles consumed in the house was "enough to keep a palace going," and they burned enough charcoal to cook for twenty-five people! She rearranged the linen in the closets and taught Emma to keep an eye on the butcher when he brought the meat. Emma listened to these lectures and the elder Madame Bovary dispensed them liberally; the words "mother" and "daughter" were exchanged all day long, accompanied by a little twitch of the lip, and both women uttered sugary words in a voice quavering with anger.

In Madame Dubuc's day, the old lady had felt that she was still the favorite, but now Charles's love for Emma seemed to her a withdrawal of his affection, an invasion of what rightly belonged to her; and she observed her son's happiness in sad silence, like a ruined man looking in through a window at the people sitting in the dining room of what was once his house. On the pretext of reviving old memories, she reminded him of all her sufferings and sacrifices; then, comparing them with Emma's carelessness and neglect, she concluded that he was wrong to adore her so exclusively.

Charles did not know what to answer; he respected his mother and idolized his wife; he considered his mother's judgment infallible, and yet everything about Emma was irreproachable to him. After the elder Madame Bovary had gone, he would timidly try to repeat, using her own words, one or two of the mildest criticisms he had heard her express; Emma would quickly prove to him that he was wrong and send him back to his patients.

Meanwhile, following theories in which she believed, she made determined efforts to experience love. In the garden, by moonlight, she would recite to him all the passionate verses she knew by heart and sing him mournful adagios accompanied by sighs; but afterward she found herself as calm as before, and Charles did not seem to be any more amorous or stirred up.

Unable to produce the slightest spark of love in her heart by such means, and as incapable of understanding what she did not feel as she was of believing in anything that did not manifest itself in conventional forms, she easily convinced herself that there was no longer anything extraordinary about Charles's love for her. His raptures had settled into a regular schedule; he embraced her only at certain hours. It was one habit among many, like a dessert known in advance, after a monotonous dinner.

A gamekeeper whom Monsieur had cured of pneumonia gave Madame a little Italian greyhound bitch. She took her with her whenever she went out for a walk, which she did now and then in order to be alone for a while without having to look at the everlasting garden and the dusty road.

She would walk to the beech grove at Banneville, near the abandoned pavilion which stands at the corner of the wall facing the fields. The bottom of the ditch there is overgrown with grass and rushes with sharp-edged leaves.

She would begin by looking around to see if anything had changed since her last visit. She always found everything in the same place: the foxgloves and gillyflowers, the clumps of nettles around the stones and the patches of lichen along the three windows, whose shutters, always closed, were rotting away from their rusty iron bars. Her thoughts were usually vague at first, wandering at random, like her greyhound, which would begin to run in circles in the fields, barking at yellow butterflies, chasing shrewmice and chewing on the poppies at the edge of a wheatfield. Then her mind would gradually focus; sitting on the grass and poking at it with the tip of her parasol, she would ask herself over and over, "Oh, why did I ever get married?"

She wondered if there might not have been some way, through a different set of circumstances, of meeting another man; and she tried to imagine those events which had not happened, that different life, that husband whom she did not know. Not all men were like Charles. Her husband might have been handsome, witty, distinguished and attractive. Her former schoolmates had no doubt married men like that. What were they doing now? In cities, with their animated streets, buzzing theaters and glittering ballrooms, they were leading lives which allowed them to give free rein to their emotions and develop their senses. But *her* life was as cold as an attic facing the north, and boredom, like a silent spider, was weaving its web in the shadows, in every corner of her heart. She recalled the Prize Days at school when she had mounted the platform to receive her little wreaths. She had been charming, with her braids, her white dress and her open prunella slippers. When she went back to her seat, the gentlemen had leaned over to pay her compliments. The courtyard had been full of carriages, with people looking out the windows to tell her good-by; the music teacher had bowed to her as he walked past with his violin case. How far away it all was, how far away!

She would call Djali, take her between her knees, stroke her long, delicate head and say to her, "Come on, give your mistress a kiss; there's no trouble or sorrow in *your* life!" As the slender Djali yawned slowly, Emma would look at her melancholy face and grow wistful; then, comparing her to herself, she would speak to her aloud as though consoling someone in distress.

Sometimes the wind would begin to blow in strong gusts which came from the sea and swept across the plateau of the Caux region, filling the whole countryside with cool salt air. The rushes would hiss, flattened against the ground, and the quivering beech leaves would rustle loudly while the tops of the trees swayed and murmured. Emma would pull her shawl tight around her shoulders and stand up.

Green light, filtered through the leaves, shone down on the thin layer of moss that crunched softly beneath her feet as she walked along the avenue. The sun was setting; the sky showed red through the branches, and the straight line of identical tree trunks looked like a row of brown columns against a golden background. Suddenly afraid, she would call Djali and hurry back to Tostes along the highway; when she came home she would sink into an armchair and say nothing all evening.

But toward the end of September an extraordinary thing happened to her: she was invited to La Vaubyessard, home of the Marquis d'Andervilliers.

Having been a cabinet minister under the Restoration, the marquis now wished to return to political life, and for a long time he had been making preparations to assure his election to the Chamber of Deputies. In winter he distributed firewood generously, and in the Departmental Council he always made impassioned pleas for the construction of better roads in his district. During the hot weather he had had an abscess in his mouth which Charles had relieved, as though by magic, with a well-timed stroke of his lancet. His steward, sent to Tostes to pay the bill for the operation, reported that evening that he had seen some magnificent cherries in the doctor's little garden. Since the cherry trees at La Vaubyessard were not doing well, the marquis asked Bovary for a few grafts and made a point of going to thank him personally. When he saw Emma he noticed that she had a shapely figure and that she did not bow to him like a peasant, so at the château it was decided that the young couple could be invited without going beyond the limits of gracious condescension or causing anyone any embarrassment.

One Wednesday, at three in the afternoon, Monsieur and

Madame Bovary set out for La Vaubyessard in their buggy
with a big trunk tied to the back, a hatbox in front and another
box between Charles's legs.

They arrived at nightfall, just as the lanterns in the park
were being lit to enable the carriages to find their way.

VIII

The château, a modern Italian-style building with two
projecting wings and three front entrances, was spread out
at the far end of an immense lawn on which several cows
were grazing among widely spaced clumps of tall trees.
Clusters of shrubbery—rhododendrons, syringas and snowballs
—lined the curving graveled drive with irregular tufts of
verdure. There was a stream flowing under a bridge; through
the haze, farm buildings with thatched roofs could be seen
scattered over a meadow flanked by two gently sloping wooded
hills; at the rear, among dense groups of trees, were two
parallel lines of coach houses and stables, remains of the old
château which had been torn down.

Charles's buggy drew up in front of the middle door;
servants appeared; the marquis stepped forward, gave the
doctor's wife his arm and led her into the entrance hall.

It had a marble floor and a very high ceiling; footsteps and
voices echoed in it as in a church. At the far end rose a straight
staircase, and to the left a gallery facing the garden led to
the billiard room, from which the clicking of ivory balls could
be heard as one approached the door. Passing through it on
her way to the drawing room, Emma saw a group of dignified-
looking men around the table; their chins were resting on their
high cravats, they all wore decorations and they smiled silently
as they wielded their cues. On the dark paneling of the walls
hung large gilded frames with names inscribed at the bottom
in black letters. She read: *"Jean-Antoine d'Andervilliers
d'Yerbonville, Comte de la Vaubyessard and Baron de la
Fresnaye, killed in the Battle of Coutras on October 20, 1587."*
And beneath another picture: *"Jean-Antoine-Henry-Guy
d'Andervilliers de la Vaubyessard, Admiral of the Fleet and
Knight of the Order of St. Michael, wounded in the Battle
of La Hogue on May 29, 1692, died at La Vaubyessard on*

January 23, 1693." The other inscriptions were scarcely visible, for the lamps were shaded to make them shine down on the green felt of the billiard table, leaving part of the room in shadow. The pictures along the walls were darkened, except for thin streaks of light reflected from the cracks in the varnish, and details painted in lighter colors than the rest stood out here and there in each of those big black squares framed in gold: a pale forehead, a pair of eyes looking down at you, a wig hanging over the powder-flecked shoulder of a red coat, or a garter buckle at the top of a plump calf.

The marquis opened the door of the drawing room; one of the ladies (the marquise herself) rose, came forward to greet Emma, invited her to sit down beside her on a settee and began a friendly conversation with her, as though she had known her for a long time. She was a woman of forty or so, with pretty shoulders, an aquiline nose and a drawling voice; she was wearing a simple lace shawl over her auburn hair, with one of the corners hanging down behind. A blond young woman was sitting near her in a high-backed chair, and around the fireplace gentlemen with little flowers in their buttonholes were chatting with the ladies.

Dinner was served at seven. The men, more numerous than the ladies, sat down at a table in the entrance hall, while the ladies took their places in the dining room with the marquis and the marquise.

On entering the dining room, Emma felt herself enveloped by a warm atmosphere in which the fragrance of flowers and fine linen mingled with the odor of hot meat and truffles. Blazing candelabra cast long gleams on the silver dish-covers; the facets of the cut glass, covered with a dull film of moisture, gave off pale reflections; there was a row of bouquets from one end of the table to the other, and on each of the wide-bordered plates was a napkin folded into the shape of a bishop's miter, with an oval roll lying in the center. The red claws of the lobsters protruded from the platters; choice fruit was piled up on moss in openwork baskets; the quail still had their feathers; steam rose from various parts of the table. The maître d'hôtel, solemn as a judge and wearing knee breeches, silk stockings, a white cravat and a ruffled shirt front, held platters of carved meat between the guests and placed the chosen pieces on their plates with a flick of his spoon.

Madame Bovary noticed that several ladies had not put their gloves in their wine glasses.

At the head of the table, alone among the ladies, an old man sat hunched over his filled plate, wearing his napkin around his neck like a child and letting drops of gravy fall from his mouth as he ate. He had bloodshot eyes and wore his hair in a little pigtail tied with a black ribbon. He was the marquis' father-in-law, the old Duc de Laverdière; he had been the Comte d'Artois' favorite in the days of the Marquis de Conflans' hunting parties at Le Vaudreuil, and he was said to have been Marie-Antoinette's lover, between Monsieur de Coigny and Monsieur de Lauzun. He had led a life of wild debauch, filled with duels, wagers and abducted women, squandered all his money and horrified his whole family. He would occasionally stammer something and point to various dishes; a servant standing behind his chair would lean down close to his ear and loudly call out their names to him. Emma's eyes kept turning back to this pendulous-lipped old man as though he were an extraordinary and awe-inspiring sight. He had lived at court and gone to bed with queens!

Iced champagne was served. Emma shivered from head to toe when she felt the cold wine in her mouth. She had never seen pomegranates or eaten pineapple. Even the granulated sugar seemed to her whiter and finer than any she had seen before.

Then the ladies went up to their rooms to get ready for the ball.

Emma groomed and dressed herself with the meticulous care of an actress about to make her debut. She arranged her hair in accordance with the hairdresser's recommendations and slipped into her barège gown, which had been laid out on the bed. Charles's trousers were too tight at the waist.

"These shoestraps will bother me when I'm dancing," he said.

"When you're *dancing?*" exclaimed Emma.

"Yes."

"Have you lost your mind? They'd all laugh at you! Stay in your place. Besides," she added, "doctors shouldn't dance anyway."

Charles made no reply. He paced up and down, waiting for her to finish dressing.

He looked at her from behind in the mirror, between two candles. Her eyes seemed darker than ever. There were bluish glints in her lustrous hair, drawn smooth and tight against both sides of her head, with a gentle outward curve over each ear. Attached to her chignon, a rose quivered on its flexible stem, with artificial dewdrops on the ends of its leaves. Her pale saffron gown was adorned with three bouquets of pompon roses mingled with foliage.

Charles walked over and kissed her on the shoulder.

"Stop!" she said. "You're mussing me up!"

They heard a violin begin to play, then a horn. As she walked down the stairs she had to restrain herself from running.

The quadrilles had begun. More people were coming in, jostling one another. She sat down on a padded bench near the door.

When the first quadrille ended, the dance floor was taken over by men who stood talking to one another in groups, and liveried servants carrying large trays. Along the line of seated women, painted fans were fluttering, smiles were half hidden by bouquets, and scent bottles with gold stoppers turned in hands whose white gloves showed the form of the nails and gripped the wrist tightly. Lace trimmings quivered on dresses, diamond brooches sparkled on bosoms and medallion bracelets jingled on bare arms. The hair on each head was smooth in front and twisted at the back, with a wreath, bunch or sprig of forget-me-nots, jasmine, pomegranate blossoms, wheat or cornflowers. Sour-faced mothers, sitting tranquilly in their places, wore red turban-style headdresses.

Emma's heart pounded a little when her partner led her by the fingertips to the line of dancers and she waited for the opening notes of the violin. But her nervousness soon vanished and she glided forward, swaying her head and body to the rhythm of the orchestra. She smiled gently at some of the violinist's flourishes during the solos he occasionally performed while the other instruments were silent; for a time the clinking of gold coins on the gambling tables in the next room would be clearly audible, then the cornet would blare and everything would begin again: the dancers' feet would resume their rhythmic tramping, skirts would billow and brush against each other, hands would join and part, eyes would be lowered in front of you, then return and stare into yours a moment later.

Scattered among the dancers or talking in doorways, there were about a dozen men, ranging in age from twenty-five to forty, who were distinguished from the rest of the crowd by what almost amounted to a family resemblance, despite their differences of age, dress or feature.

Their coats fitted them better and seemed to be made of

finer cloth; their hair, brought forward over the temples in curls, seemed to glisten with more delicate pomades. They had the complexion of wealth, that white complexion which goes so well with the pallor of porcelain, the sheen of satin, the luster of fine furniture, and is kept in perfect condition by a moderate diet of exquisite foods. Their necks turned freely above low cravats; their long side whiskers descended to their turned-down collars; they wiped their lips with scented handkerchiefs bearing large embroidered monograms. Those who were beginning to age seemed youthful, while those who were young had a certain look of maturity. Their faces wore that placid expression which comes from the daily gratification of the passions; and beneath their polished manners one could sense the special brutality that comes from half-easy triumphs which test one's strength and flatter one's vanity— the handling of thoroughbred horses, the pursuit of loose women.

A few feet away from Emma, a gentleman in a blue coat was talking about Italy with a pale young woman wearing pearls. They extolled the massive pillars of St. Peter's, Tivoli, Vesuvius, Castellamare and the Cascine, the roses in Genoa, the Colosseum by moonlight. With her other ear, Emma was listening to a conversation full of words she did not understand. A circle had formed around a young man who had "beaten Miss Arabelle and Romulus" the week before and won two thousand louis by jumping a ditch in England. One man complained that his racers were getting fat, another that the name of his horse had been mutilated by misprints.

The air in the ballroom was stuffy and the lamps were growing dim. There was a flow of people into the billiard room. A servant climbed up on a chair and broke two window-panes; at the sound of the shattering fragments, Madame Bovary turned her head and saw peasants looking in from the garden, their faces pressed against the glass. Thoughts of Les Bertaux came into her mind. She saw the farm, the muddy pond, her father in his smock beneath the apple trees, and she saw herself as she had once been, skimming the cream with her finger from the jars of milk in the dairy. But, in the dazzling splendor that now surrounded her, the memory of her past life, hitherto so vivid, began to fade away completely, and she almost doubted that she had ever lived it. She was there in the ballroom; everything beyond it was shrouded in darkness. She was eating a maraschino ice from a silver-gilt shell that she was holding in her left hand; the spoon was between her teeth and her eyes were half shut.

A lady near her dropped her fan just as one of the dancers was passing by. "Would you be good enough to pick up my fan for me, monsieur?" the lady said to him. "It's fallen behind the sofa."

The gentleman bowed, and as he put out his arm Emma saw the young lady drop into his hat a white object folded into a triangle. He recovered the fan and respectfully handed it to the lady; she thanked him with a nod and began to sniff her bouquet.

After supper—which included a wide assortment of Spanish and Rhine wines, bisque and almond-milk soup, Trafalgar pudding and all sorts of cold meats surrounded by aspic that quivered on the platters—the carriages began to leave one after the other. Drawing back one corner of a muslin curtain, Emma saw their gleaming lanterns slipping away in the darkness. The padded benches grew bare; some of the gamblers still remained; the musicians were cooling their fingertips by putting them on their tongues; Charles was leaning against a door, half asleep.

At three o'clock in the morning the cotillion began, marking the end of the ball. Emma did not know how to waltz. Everyone else was waltzing, even Mademoiselle d'Andervilliers and the marquise. Only the hosts and their house guests now remained, a dozen or so people in all.

One of the waltzers, a man who was familiarly called "Viscount," and whose low-cut vest seemed molded over his chest, came up to Madame Bovary for the second time to invite her to dance, assuring her he would guide her and that she would do quite well.

They began slowly, then quickened their pace. They whirled and everything whirled around them—lamps, furniture, walls and floor—like a disk on a spindle. As they passed near a door, the hem of Emma's gown caught on her partner's trousers; their legs interlocked; he looked down at her, she looked up at him; a kind of torpor came over her and she stopped moving. They began to dance again; drawing her along more swiftly, the viscount led her to a remote corner at the end of the gallery, where, out of breath, she almost fell, and for a moment she rested her head on his chest. Then, still whirling, but more slowly, he led her back to her seat; she leaned against the wall and put her hands over her eyes.

When she opened them, a lady was sitting on a low stool in the middle of the room with three waltzers kneeling in front of her. She chose the viscount and the violin began to play again.

Everyone watched them. They glided back and forth, she with her body rigid and her head lowered, he always in the same posture, back arched, elbow extended, chin forward. Now he was dancing with someone who knew how to waltz! They went on for a long time, after everyone else was exhausted.

After chatting for a few minutes more and bidding one another good night, or rather good morning, the hosts and house guests went off to bed.

Charles dragged himself up the stairs, gripping the handrail and complaining that his legs were "about to fall off." He had spent five solid hours standing beside the tables watching people play whist, unable to make any sense of the game. He therefore heaved a great sigh of relief when he took off his shoes.

Emma put a shawl around her shoulders, opened the window and leaned out.

It was a dark night. A few drops of rain were falling. She breathed in the moist air, which cooled her eyelids. The music of the ball was still throbbing in her ears and she forced herself to stay awake in order to prolong the illusion of that luxurious life which she would soon have to abandon.

Day began to break. She looked at the windows of the château for a long time, trying to guess which bedrooms were occupied by the people she had seen that night. She longed to know all about their lives, to enter into them and become part of them.

But she was shivering with cold. She undressed, slipped into bed and pressed up against Charles, who was sleeping soundly.

There were many people at breakfast. The meal lasted ten minutes; no liqueurs were served, which surprised the doctor. Then Mademoiselle d'Andervilliers gathered up the remains of the rolls in a basket to feed the swans in the pond, and everyone went off to take a stroll through the greenhouse, where odd bristly plants were piled up in pyramids beneath suspended vases from which long, intertwined green tendrils hung down like snakes crawling out of an overcrowded nest. From the orangery, which was at the far end of the greenhouse, a covered passage led to the outbuildings of the château. To entertain the young woman, the marquis took her to see the stables. Above the basket-shaped racks there were porcelain plaques bearing the names of the horses in black letters. They all stirred restlessly in their stalls when the visitors passed by, clicking their tongues. The floor of the harness room was as highly polished as the parquet of a drawing room. In the middle stood two revolving posts on which the carriage harnesses were hung, while the bits, whips, stirrups and curbs were lined up along the wall.

Meanwhile Charles had gone to ask a servant to harness his horse to his buggy. It was brought to the front door; after all their bundles had been crammed into it, the Bovarys politely thanked the marquis and the marquise and started back to Tostes.

Emma watched the turning wheels in silence. Charles, perched on the edge of the seat, held his arms far apart as he drove, and the little horse trotted along at a leisurely pace between the shafts, which were too wide for him. The slack reins became wet with lather as they slapped against his rump, and the box tied to the back of the buggy bumped loudly at regular intervals.

When they reached the rising ground near Thibourville they suddenly saw a group of riders coming toward them. As they went past, puffing on their cigars and laughing, Emma thought she recognized the viscount; she turned around, but she saw only heads outlined against the sky, bobbing up and down to the uneven rhythm of a trot or a gallop.

Half a mile further on, the breeching broke and Charles had to stop and repair it with a piece of rope.

As he was checking the harness before setting off again, he saw something lying on the ground between the horse's hooves. He picked it up: it was a cigar case embroidered all over with green silk and bearing a coat of arms in the center, like a carriage door.

"It even has two cigars in it," he said. "I'll save them for tonight, after dinner."

"What? Do you smoke?"

"Once in a while, whenever I get a chance."

He put his find in his pocket and flicked the horse with his whip.

When they reached home, dinner was nowhere near ready. Madame flew into a rage. Nastasie talked back to her.

"Get out!" cried Emma. "I won't stand for that kind of insolence! Pack up your things and leave."

For dinner there was onion soup and veal with sorrel. Charles, sitting opposite Emma, rubbed his hands together in satisfaction and said cheerfully, "It's good to be home again!"

They could hear Nastasie weeping. He was rather fond of the poor girl: she had kept him company during many an idle evening while he was a widower. She had been his first patient and acquaintance in the village.

"Are you really going to let her go?" he finally asked.

"Yes," she replied. "What's to stop me?"

They warmed themselves in the kitchen while their bedroom was being made ready for them. Charles began to smoke. He pursed his lips, spat every few moments and recoiled after every puff.

"You're going to make yourself sick," she said scornfully.

He put down his cigar and rushed to the pump to drink a glass of cold water. Emma quickly snatched up the cigar case and threw it into the back of the closet.

The next day seemed endless to her. She went out into her little garden and walked up and down the same paths over and over again, stopping in front of the flower beds, the apricot trees along the wall, the plaster priest, staring in amazement at all those familiar things from the past. How long ago the ball seemed already! Why was there such a great distance between this evening and the morning of the day before yesterday? Her trip to La Vaubyessard had made a gap in her life, like those great crevasses which a storm will sometimes hollow out on a mountainside in a single night. But she managed to resign herself; she opened her drawer and reverently put away the clothes she had worn to the ball, including even her satin slippers, whose soles were yellow from the slippery wax of the dance floor. Her heart was like them: contact with wealth had left something on it which would not wear away.

Remembering the ball became an occupation for her. Every Wednesday morning she said to herself when she awoke, "Ah! A week ago . . . two weeks ago . . . three weeks ago, I was there!" And, little by little, the faces became confused in her memory; she forgot the melody of the quadrilles; she could no longer picture the liveries and the rooms so clearly; some of the details vanished, but her longing remained.

IX

Often, when Charles was out, she would go to the closet and take the green silk cigar case from the pile of linen in which she had left it.

She would look at it, open it and sniff its lining, which was impregnated with an odor of verbena and tobacco. Whose was it? . . . The viscount's. A present from his mistress, perhaps. It had been embroidered on a charming little rosewood frame, kept hidden from everyone else, which had occupied many long hours, and over which the curls of some pensive young lady had swayed gently as she worked. A breath of love had passed through the mesh of the canvas; each stroke of the needle had fixed a hope or a memory there, and all those intertwined silken threads were the continuation of a single silent passion. And then the viscount had taken it with him one morning. What had they talked about while it lay on broad mantelpieces, between vases of flowers and Pompadour clocks? She was in Tostes. He was now in Paris. Paris! What was Paris like? What a titanic name! She repeated it to herself softly, for the pleasure of hearing it; it resounded in her ears like the great bell of a cathedral; it blazed forth before her eyes everywhere, even on the labels of her pomade jars.

At night she would awaken when the fishmongers passed beneath her windows in their carts, singing *La Marjolaine*; listening to the clatter of the iron-rimmed wheels, which abruptly changed to a dull rumble when the carts reached the dirt road at the end of the village, she would say to herself, "They'll be there tomorrow!"

And she followed them in her imagination, up and down the hills, through the villages, along the highway by the light of the stars. Then, after covering an indeterminate distance, she always came to a vague public square where her dream quickly faded away.

She bought herself a map of Paris; following the streets with her fingertip, she traveled all over the capital. She walked along the boulevards, stopping at every corner, between the lines of the streets, in front of the white squares representing houses. Finally her eyes would grow tired and she would close them; then, in the darkness, she could see gas streetlamps flickering in the wind and carriage steps being noisily lowered in front of theaters.

She subscribed to *La Corbeille,* a women's magazine, and to *Le Sylphe des Salons.* She devoured, without skipping a word, every article about first nights in the theater, horse races and soirées; she was interested in the debut of every new singer, the opening of every new shop. She knew the latest fashions, the addresses of the best tailors, the days when one went to the Bois or the opera. She studied the descriptions of furniture in the works of Eugène Sue; she read Balzac and George Sand, seeking imaginary gratifications of her desires. She would even bring a book with her at meals and turn the pages while Charles ate and talked to her. The memory of the viscount kept coming back to her as she read. She frequently found similarities between him and the fictitious characters in her books. But the circle at whose center he stood gradually widened, and the aureole around his face spread far beyond it, illuminating other dreams.

Paris, vaster than the ocean, glittered before Emma's eyes in a rosy light. The teeming life of the tumultuous city was divided into parts, however, separated into distinct scenes. She distinguished only two or three which overshadowed the others and represented all mankind for her. The world of the ambassadors moved across gleaming parquets, in drawing rooms paneled with mirrors, around oval tables covered with gold-fringed velvet. It was a world of trailing gowns, profound mysteries, and anguish concealed beneath smiles. Then came the circle of the duchesses: here everyone was pale and got up at four in the afternoon; the women—poor darlings!—wore English lace on the hems of their petticoats; and the men, each one with unknown abilities masked by a frivolous exterior, amused themselves by riding their horses to death, spent their summers in Baden-Baden and finally, when they were about forty, married heiresses. The motley crowd of writers and actresses gathered after midnight in the candlelit private rooms of restaurants for riotous supper parties. They squandered their money like princes and were full of idealistic ambitions and fantastic frenzies. They lived above other people, in a sublime region of their own, somewhere between heaven and earth, amid the storms. As for the rest of the world, it was lost to her; it had no specific location and scarcely seemed to exist at all. And the closer things were to her, the farther her mind turned away from them. Everything immediately surrounding her—the boring countryside, the idiotic bourgeois people, the mediocrity of everyday life— seemed to her an exception in the world, something she had fallen into by accident, while beyond all this the realm of bliss and passion stretched forth as far as the eye could see. In her longing she confused the pleasures of luxury with the joys of the heart, elegant customs with refined feelings. Did not love, like Indian plants, require prepared soil and special temperatures? Sighs in the moonlight, long embraces, tears flowing onto yielding hands, all the fevers of the flesh and the languors of love—these things were inseparable from the balcony of a great castle in which life moved at a leisurely pace, from a boudoir with silk curtains, a thick carpet, filled flower stands and a bed mounted on a platform, from the sparkle of precious stones or the aiguillettes of liveried servants.

The boy who worked in the post house came to rub down the mare every morning; he walked through the hall in his heavy wooden shoes; his smock had holes in it and he wore no stockings. This was the groom in knee breeches she had to content herself with! He left as soon as his work was done and did not come back until the next day, for when Charles came home he personally put his horse in the stable, took off the saddle and put on the halter, while the maid brought a bundle of straw and tossed it into the manger as best she could.

To replace Nastasie (who finally left Tostes, shedding torrents of tears), Emma had hired a fourteen-year-old orphan girl with a sweet face. She forbade her to wear cotton nightcaps and taught her to address her superiors in the third person, bring a glass of water on a tray, knock on doors before entering, iron and starch clothes and help her dress; in short, she tried to make her into a lady's maid. The girl obeyed without a murmur, for fear of being discharged; and since Madame always left the key in the sideboard, Félicité took a small supply of sugar every night and ate it when she was all alone in her bed, after she had said her prayers.

Sometimes she would walk across the road and talk with the postilions while Madame was upstairs in her room.

Emma wore a low-cut dressing gown with a shawl collar and a pleated dicky with three gold buttons. Her belt was a cord with large tassels, and her little garnet-red slippers had tufts of wide ribbons at the instep. She had bought herself a blotter, a writing case, a pen and some envelopes, although she had no one to write to; she would dust off her whatnot, look at herself in the mirror, pick up a book, then begin to daydream between the lines and let it fall to her lap. She longed to travel, or to go back and live in the convent. She wanted both to die and to live in Paris.

Charles rode all over the countryside, through snow and rain. He ate omelets at farmhouse tables, thrust his hand between damp bedclothes, had his face splattered by spurts of warm blood during bleedings, listened to death rattles, examined the contents of basins and drew back a great deal of dirty underwear; but every night he came home to a blazing fire, a table already set for him, comfortable furniture and a charming wife, attractively dressed and so delicately fragrant that he could not tell where the scent came from and wondered if her skin might not be perfuming the clothes it touched.

She delighted him with all sorts of little refinements: a new way of making paper shields for the candlesticks, a flounce she had changed on her dress, or a fancy name given to some simple dish which the maid had prepared badly, but which he enjoyed to the last bite. In Rouen she saw ladies with charms attached to their watch chains; she bought herself some charms. She decided she had to have a pair of large blue glass vases for her mantelpiece; a short time later she needed an ivory sewing box with a silver-gilt thimble. The less Charles understood these elegant whims, the more they captivated him. They added something to the pleasure of his senses and the charm of his home. They were like a layer of golden dust sprinkled over the narrow path of his life.

His health was excellent; he looked hearty and good-natured. His reputation was completely established. The country people liked him because he was unpretentious. He fondled their children and never went to a tavern; furthermore, his morals inspired confidence. He was particularly successful in treating catarrhs and chest ailments. Afraid of killing his patients, he usually prescribed only sedatives, occasionally an emetic, foot-bath or leeches. It was not that he shrank from surgery, however: he bled people abundantly, like horses, and no one had a more powerful grip when it came to pulling teeth.

Finally, "to keep himself up to date," he subscribed to *La*

Ruche Médicale, a new professional journal whose prospectus had been sent to him. He began to read it after dinner, but the warmth of the room, combined with his digestion, always made him fall asleep within five minutes; and there he sat, with his chin in his hands and his hair falling down to the base of the lamp, like a mane. Emma would look at him and shrug her shoulders. Why didn't she at least have for a husband one of those taciturn, dedicated men who pore over books at night and eventually, by the time they are sixty and the age of rheumatism has begun, acquire a row of decorations to wear on their ill-fitting black coats? She would have liked the name of Bovary, which was her name too, to be famous, displayed in all the bookshops, constantly mentioned in the newspapers, known all over France. But Charles had no ambition! A doctor from Yvetot with whom he had recently consulted had made some rather humiliating remarks to him, right in front of the patient and the assembled relatives. When Charles told her about it that evening, she burst into violent anger against this colleague. Charles was touched by this. He kissed her on the forehead with tears in his eyes. But shame was the cause of her rage, and she had to restrain herself from beating him with her fists. She went out into the hall, opened a window and breathed in the fresh air to calm herself.

"What a pitiful specimen!" she said to herself softly, biting her lip in despair.

She was increasingly annoyed with him in general. As he grew older his manners became cruder than ever: he whittled the corks of empty wine bottles at the end of the meal, he ran his tongue over his teeth after eating, he made a gulping sound each time he swallowed a spoonful of soup; and as he became fatter his eyes, already small, seemed to be pushed up toward his temples by the puffiness of his cheeks.

Emma sometimes tucked the red edge of his sweater into his vest, straightened his tie, or threw away a pair of faded gloves he was about to put on; this was not for his sake, as he believed, but for her own: she did it out of vanity and nervous irritation. And sometimes she talked to him about things she had read: a passage in a novel, a new play, or an anecdote of "high society" life recounted in a gossip column; for Charles was at least a person, an ear that was always open, an unfailing source of approval. After all, she even confided in her greyhound! She would have talked to the logs in the fireplace if necessary, or the pendulum of the clock.

Meanwhile, in the depths of her soul, she was waiting for something to happen. Like a sailor in distress, she kept scanning the solitude of her life with anxious eyes, straining to sight some far-off white sail in the mists of the horizon. She did not know how it would come to her, what wind would bring it to her, to what shores it would carry her, whether it would be a launch or a towering three-decker, laden with sorrow or filled to the gunwales with bliss. But every morning when she awoke she expected it to arrive that day; she listened to every sound, periodically leapt to her feet with a start and was surprised when she saw it had not come; then, at sundown, sadder than ever, she longed for the next day.

Spring came again. She had difficulty in breathing during the first warm days, when the pear trees were blossoming.

Early in July she began to count on her fingers how many more weeks were left till October, thinking that the Marquis d'Andervilliers might give another ball at La Vaubyessard. But the whole month of September went by without a single letter or visitor.

After the chagrin of this disappointment, her heart was once more left empty, and the series of identical days began all over again.

So they were going to continue like this, one after the other, always the same, innumerable, bringing nothing! In other people's lives, dull as they might be, there was at least a chance that something might happen. One event sometimes had infinite ramifications and could change the whole setting of a person's life. But God had willed that nothing should ever happen to her. The future was a long, dark corridor with only a locked door at the end.

She abandoned her music. Why should she play? Who would hear her? Since she could never sit on a concert stage in a short-sleeved velvet gown, running her light, graceful fingers over the ivory keys of an Erard piano and feeling the ecstatic murmur of the audience flow around her like a warm breeze, there was no point in going through the boredom of practicing. She left her sketchbooks and embroidery in the closet. What was the use? Sewing irritated her.

"I've read everything," she said to herself.

And she spent her time holding the fire tongs in the flames until they were red-hot, or watching the rain fall.

How sad she was on Sundays when the church bell rang for vespers! She listened to each dull stroke with a kind of dazed attention. A cat walking slowly across the roofs would arch its back in the pale sunlight. The wind blew trails of dust along the highway. Sometimes a dog would howl in the distance. And the regular, monotonous tolling would continue to float from the belfry, dying away over the surrounding countryside.

People came out of the church: women in polished wooden shoes, peasant men in new smocks, little children skipping bareheaded in front of them; they were all going home. And until nightfall five or six men, always the same ones, played cork-penny before the main entrance of the inn.

The winter was cold that year. The windowpanes were covered with frost every morning, and sometimes the whitish light that shone through them, as though through ground glass, did not vary all day long. The lamps usually had to be lit by four o'clock in the afternoon.

On sunny days she went out into the garden. The dew had left silvery lace on the cabbages, with long shiny threads stretching from one to the other. She never heard any birds; everything seemed to be asleep: the espaliered fruit trees were covered with straw, and the vine was like a long sick snake under the coping of the wall, where she could see many-legged wood lice crawling when she came near. Among the spruces near the hedge, the priest wearing a three-cornered hat and reading his breviary had lost his right foot, and the plaster, flaking off in the frost, had left white scabs on his face.

Then she would go back upstairs, close her door and stir up the glowing coals; and as the heat of the fire filled her with torpor she would feel boredom descend on her again, heavier than ever. She would have liked to go downstairs and chat with the maid, but her pride held her back.

Every day at the same hour the schoolmaster, in his black silk skullcap, opened the shutters of his house, and the village policeman passed by with his saber buckled around his smock. Morning and evening, the post horses crossed the road in groups of three to drink from the pond. Now and then the little bell on the door of a tavern would tinkle, and when there was a wind she could hear the copper basins that served as the barber's sign creaking on their two iron rods. His shop was decorated with an old-fashioned drawing pasted against one of the windowpanes, and a wax bust of a woman with yellow hair. The barber, too, bewailed his frustrated ambitions, his bleak future; dreaming of a shop in some big city, such as Rouen, for example, on the waterfront, near the theater, he would gloomily pace back and forth between the town hall and the church all day, waiting for customers. When Madame Bovary looked up she always saw him there, like a sentry on duty, in his smooth woolen jacket and his fez pulled down over one ear.

A man's face would sometimes appear outside the parlor windows in the afternoon, a sun-tanned face with black side whiskers and a broad, slow, white-toothed smile. A waltz would soon be heard, and dancers the size of a finger would begin to move in a miniature drawing room on top of the hurdy-gurdy. There were women in pink turbans, Tyroleans in cutaways, monkeys in black tail coats and gentlemen in knee breeches; they all whirled among armchairs, sofas and console tables, and were reflected in pieces of mirror glass joined at the corners by strips of gold paper. The man would keep turning his crank, looking to the right, to the left, and toward the windows. From time to time he would shoot a jet of brown saliva against the curbstone and raise his knee to lift the instrument, whose hard strap made his shoulder hurt; and the music, sometimes plaintive and slow, sometimes joyous and quick, came wheezing out of the box through a pink taffeta curtain under a complicated copper grille. It consisted of melodies that were heard in other places, that were played in theaters, sung in drawing rooms, danced to at night beneath lighted chandeliers—echoes of the world which were now reaching Emma's ears. Endless sarabands ran through her head and, like dancing girls on a flowered carpet, her thoughts skipped with the notes, moving from dream to dream, from sorrow to sorrow. When the man had collected his alms in his cap, he would pull down an old blue wool cover, put his hurdy-gurdy on his back and plod off down the road. Emma always watched him leave.

But it was especially at mealtimes that she felt she could bear her life no longer, in that little room on the ground floor with its smoking stove, squeaking door, sweating walls and damp stone floor. All the bitterness of life seemed to be served up to her on her plate, and as the steam rose from the boiled meat, waves of nausea rose from the depths of her soul. Charles was a slow eater; she would nibble a few hazelnuts, or lean on her elbow and idly make lines in the oilcloth with her knife.

She now neglected her household duties entirely, and the

elder Madame Bovary was amazed by this change when she came to spend part of Lent in Tostes. Emma, once so well-groomed and refined, now went for days at a time without putting on a dress, wore gray cotton stockings and used cheap tallow candles. She repeatedly said they had to keep their expenses down, since they weren't rich, and added that she was very contended, very happy, that she liked Tostes very much. These surprising remarks, along with others of the same kind, shut up her mother-in-law before she could open her mouth. However, Emma showed no more inclination than ever to follow her advice. Once, in fact, when Madame Bovary ventured to state that employers ought to make sure their servants led proper religious lives, Emma replied with such an angry look and such an icy smile that from then on the good woman was careful not to cross her again.

Emma was steadily growing more capricious and hard to please. She would order special dishes for herself and then not touch them; one day she would drink nothing but milk, the next day she would down cups of tea by the dozen. Often she stubbornly refused to leave the house, then she would feel stifled, open the windows and put on a light dress. After she had thoroughly browbeaten the maid she would give her presents or tell her she could go visit the neighbors, just as she would occasionally give all the silver coins in her purse to the poor, even though she usually tended to be rather hardhearted and insenitive to the distress of others, like most people born of country parents, whose souls always keep something of the callousness of their fathers' hands.

Toward the end of February Monsieur Rouault brought his son-in-law a magnificent turkey in memory of his recovery, and he stayed at Tostes for three days. Emma kept him company, since most of Charles's time was taken up with his patients. He smoked in her bedroom, spat on the andirons, talked about crops, calves, cows, poultry and the town council; as a result, when he left she shut the door behind him with a feeling of relief which even she found surprising. She no longer hid her contempt for anything or anyone. She sometimes expressed peculiar opinions, condemning what other people approved and approving perverse or immoral things, which made her husband open his eyes wide in astonishment.

Would this misery last forever? Was there no escape from it? And yet she was certainly just as good as all those other women whose lives were happy! She had seen duchesses at

La Vaubyessard who had dumpier figures and cruder manners than she, and she cursed God's injustice; she leaned her head against the wall and wept; she envied those who led tumultuous lives, spent whole nights at masked balls, pursued dissolute pleasures and all the wild raptures, unknown to her, which they must bring with them.

She grew pale and had palpitations of the heart. Charles gave her valerian and camphor baths. Everything he tried seemed to make her more overwrought than ever.

There were days when she chattered feverishly for hours on end; and this overexcitement would be abruptly followed by a period of torpor during which she neither spoke nor moved. She would then revive herself by pouring a bottle of eau de Cologne over her arms.

Since she continually complained about Tostes, Charles decided that something about the town or its location must be causing her illness; seizing on this idea, he began to think seriously of going somewhere else to live.

From then on she drank vinegar to lose weight, developed a little dry cough and lost her appetite completely.

It was hard for Charles to leave Tostes after living there for four years, and "just when he was starting to get established." But, since he had no choice . . . He took her to Rouen to see one of his old teachers. She had a nervous malady and required a change of air.

After casting about here and there, Charles learned that in the district of Neufchâtel there was a good-sized market town named Yonville-l'Abbaye whose doctor, a Polish refugee, had decamped only the week before. He wrote to the local pharmacist to find out the exact size of the town's population, how far away the nearest doctor was, how much his predecessor had earned per year, etc. Having received satisfactory answers, he decided to move by spring if Emma's health did not improve.

One day as she was tidying up a drawer in preparation for her departure, she pricked her fingers on something. It was a piece of wire on her bridal bouquet. The orange-blossom buds were yellowed with dust and the silver-edged satin ribbons were frayed. She threw it into the fire. It blazed up like dry straw, then it was consumed more slowly, lying on the ashes like a glowing red bush. She watched it burn. The little cardboard berries burst open, the brass wire twisted, the braid melted; and the shriveled paper petals hovered along the back of the fireplace like black butterflies, then finally flew up the chimney.

When they left Tostes in March, Madame Bovary was pregnant.

Part Two

Yonville-l'Abbaye (so named because of an ancient Capuchin abbey which has vanished without even leaving any ruins) is a market town twenty miles from Rouen, between the roads to Abbeville and Beauvais in the valley of Rieule, a small river which flows into the Andelle after turning the wheels of three mills near its mouth, where there are a few trout which boys like to fish for on Sundays.

The road to the town branches off the highway at La Boissière and runs level until it reaches the hill at Les Leux, which overlooks the valley. The river flowing through this valley divides it into two dissimilar regions: everything to the left is pasture, everything to the right is cultivated farmland. The pastures stretch forth alongside a chain of low hills until they join the grasslands of the Bray country, while the gently rising plain broadens as it extends eastward, spreading its golden grainfields as far as the eye can see. The stream running along the edge of the grass forms a white line which separates the color of the meadow from that of the plowed land, thus making the countryside look like an enormous outspread cloak which has a green velvet collar edged with silver braid.

On the horizon beyond the town are the oaks of the Argueil forest and the steep slopes of the Saint-Jean hill, which is streaked from top to bottom with long irregular red lines, marks left by rain water flowing down its sides; their rusty color, standing out sharply against the gray background of the hill, is due to the high iron content of the many springs in the surrounding countryside.

This is where Normandy, Picardy and the Ile-de-France come together, a bastard region whose speech is as flat as its landscape is characterless. It is here that the worst Neuf-châtel cheeses in the whole district are made; and farming is costly because it takes a great deal of manure to fertilize the crumbly, sandy, stony soil.

Until 1853 there was no decent road leading to Yonville, but at about that time the Abbeville and Amiens highways were connected by a local road which is sometimes used by carters going from Rouen to Flanders. Despite this "new channel for trade," however, Yonville-l'Abbaye has stood still. Instead of improving their crops, the farmers obstinately stick to their pastures, no matter how worn-out they may be; and the lazy town has naturally continued to grow in the direction of the river, moving away from the plain. Seen from a distance, stretched out along the bank, it reminds one of a cowherd taking a siesta beside a stream.

At the foot of the slope, starting at the bridge, a straight street lined with young aspen trees leads to the first houses of the town. They are enclosed by hedges and their yards are full of straggling outbuildings: cider presses, cart sheds and brandy distilleries are scattered among thick trees with ladders or poles propped up against them, or scythes hooked over their branches. Like fur hats pulled down over eyes, the thatched roofs cover the top third or so of the low windows, whose thick, bulging panes each have a bull's-eye in the middle, like the bottom of a bottle. Sometimes one sees emaciated pear trees pressed up against the plastered walls of the houses, with their black diagonal timbers. Each doorway has a little swinging gate to keep out the young chickens which gather on the threshold to peck crumbs of brown bread soaked in cider.

Gradually the yards become narrower, the houses move closer together, the hedges disappear; a fern broom dangles beneath a window, a blacksmith's forge appears, and a cart-maker's shop with two or three new carts outside, partially blocking the road. Then, through an iron fence, one can see a white house whose round lawn is decorated by a cupid holding his fingers to his lips; two cast-iron urns stand on either side of the small terrace at the top of the front steps; there are gleaming metal plaques on the door: this is the notary's house, the finest in town.

The church is on the other side of the street, twenty yards further on, at the entrance to the public square. The little cemetery surrounding it is so full of graves that the old tombstones, lying flat on the ground, form a continuous pavement on which the grass has traced out green rectangles. The church was rebuilt during the latter part of the reign of Charles X. The arched wooden ceiling is beginning to rot at the top, and its blue surface is marred here and there by black cavities. Above the door, where most churches have an organ, is a gallery for the men, reached by a spiral staircase which echoes beneath their wooden soles.

The daylight coming in through the plain glass windows falls obliquely on the pews projecting from the wall. There are straw mats tacked on some of them with these words in big letters below: "Monsieur So-and-So's Pew." Further on, where the nave narrows, is the confessional. Beside it stands a statue of the Virgin; she is dressed in a satin gown and a tulle veil sprinkled with silver stars, and her cheeks are painted bright red like an idol from the Sandwich Islands. Finally, the view is terminated by a copied painting—"The Holy Family, Presented by the Minister of the Interior"—hanging above the main altar between four candlesticks.

The market shed, a tile roof supported by a score of pillars, takes up about half of the public square of Yonville. The town hall, "built from the plans of a Paris architect," is a kind of Greek temple standing at one corner of the square, beside the pharmacist's house. Its ground floor has three Ionic columns. On the second floor there is a gallery with a semi-circular arched roof, and the culminating tympanum is filled by a Gallic cock, one of its claws resting on the Constitution while the other holds the scales of justice.

But the most eye-catching sight of all is across the street from the Lion d'Or inn: Monsieur Homais' pharmacy! At night, when his lamp is lit, the colored glass jars which embellish his front window cast their red and green glow on the ground; looking through them, as though through Bengal lights, one can see the shadow of the pharmacist leaning over his desk. The front of his shop is covered from top to bottom with signs written in running script, round hand or block letters: *"Vichy, Seltzer and Barège Waters, Depurative Syrups, Raspail's Medicine, Arabian Racahout, Darcet Lozenges,*

Regnault Paste, Bandages, Baths, Dietetic Chocolates," etc. And his name is written on a sign which runs across the entire width of the shop: *"Homais, Pharmacist."* At the rear of the shop, behind the big scales fastened to the counter, the word *"Laboratory"* is spread out above a glazed door in the middle of which *"Homais"* appears again, in gold letters on a black background.

After this there is nothing else to see in Yonville. The street (the only one in town), long as a rifle shot and lined with a few shops, abruptly changes into a road at the first bend. Leaving it on the right and following the base of the Saint-Jean hill, one soon arrives at the cemetery.

It was enlarged during the cholera epidemic; one of its walls was torn down and six acres of adjoining land were purchased. But this whole new section is almost uninhabited: the graves continue, as always, to crowd into the area near the gate. The caretaker, who is also the gravedigger and the church sexton (thus making a double profit from the corpses of the parish), has taken advantage of the empty land to plant potatoes. His little field shrinks from year to year, however, and each time there is an epidemic he does not know whether to rejoice at the deaths or lament the new graves.

"You're feeding on the dead, Lestiboudois!" the priest said to him one day.

These somber words made him think, and for a time he gave up his potatoes; but now he continues to cultivate them, calmly maintaining that they grow naturally.

And nothing else has changed in Yonville since the events we are about to relate. The tin tricolor still turns atop the church steeple; the two calico streamers outside the dry-goods shop still wave in the wind; the pharmacist's foetuses continue to rot in their turbid alcohol, looking like lumps of white amadou; and, above the main entrance of the inn, passers-by can still see the old golden lion, faded by the rains, with his curly, poodle-style mane.

On the evening when the Bovarys were due to arrive in Yonville, Madame Lefrançois, the widow who ran the inn, was so busy that there were big drops of sweat on her face as she worked among her pots and pans. Tomorrow was a market-day. She had to prepare everything in advance: cut the meat, clean the chickens, make the soup and grind the coffee. Besides all this she had to cook dinner for her regular boarders, the new doctor, his wife and their maid. Shouts of laughter came from the billiard room; in the small dining room three millers were calling for brandy; the wood fire was blazing, the embers were crackling, and on the long kitchen table, among the quarters of raw mutton, stood piles of plates which trembled as the spinach was chopped on a block. From the barnyard came the squawking of chickens which the maid was trying to catch in order to cut off their heads.

A slightly pockmarked man, wearing green leather slippers and a velvet fez with a gold tassel, was warming himself with his back to the fire. His face expressed nothing but self-satisfaction, and he seemed to take life as calmly as the goldfinch in the wicker cage hanging above his head. This was the pharmacist.

"Artémise!" shouted the mistress of the inn. "Chop some kindling, fill the decanters, bring some brandy! Hurry! If I only knew what dessert to make for those people you're all waiting for! Good heavens, now the moving-men are starting to make a racket in the billiard room again! And they've left their van in front of the door—the Hirondelle will probably crash into it if it stays there! Call Polyte and tell him to put it in the shed. . . . Just think of it, Monsieur Homais: since this morning they've played at least fifteen games and drunk eight jugs of cider! . . . Oh! They're going to tear the cloth on my table!" she said, looking into the billiard room with her skimming ladle in her hand.

"That wouldn't be much of a loss," remarked Monsieur Homais. "You could buy another table."

"Another billiard table?" exclaimed the widow.

"That's right. This one's falling apart. I've said it before and I'll say it again: it's foolish of you to keep it, Madame Lefrançois, very foolish! And nowadays players want narrow pockets and heavy cues. They don't play the way they used to, everything's different now! We've got to keep up with the times! Take Tellier, for example . . ."

The hostess turned red with anger. The pharmacist went on:

"Say what you like, his billiard table is nicer than yours. Now suppose someone gets the idea of holding a patriotic tournament to raise funds for Poland, or the victims of the Lyons flood—"

"We're not worried about a nobody like him!" interrupted the hostess, shrugging her burly shoulders. "People will always come to the Lion d'Or, Monsieur Homais, you know that! We're on solid ground. But the Café Français is another story. Just wait: one of these days you'll see it closed, with a great big notice stuck on the shutters. . . . Get a new billiard table?" she went on, as though talking to herself. "Why should I do that when this one's so useful to fold my washing on? And in the hunting season I've has as many as six people sleeping on it! . . . But what's keeping that slowpoke Hivert?"

"Are you going to wait for him to get here before you serve dinner to your gentlemen?" asked the pharmacist.

"Wait for him? And what about Monsieur Binet? You'll see him walk in here on the stroke of six—there's nobody like him in the whole world when it comes to being on time. He always has to sit at the same place in the little room. He'd rather die than eat anywhere else! And he's so finicky, especially about his cider! He's not like Monsieur Léon! Monsieur Léon sometimes comes in at seven, or even seven-thirty, and he doesn't even look at what's on his plate. What a nice young man! I've never once heard him raise his voice."

"Yes, there's a big difference between someone who's had a good upbringing and an old soldier who's been turned into a tax collector."

The clock struck six. Binet entered.

His blue frock coat hung straight down all around his skinny body, and beneath the upturned visor of his leather cap, whose earflaps were tied together at the top, could be seen a bald forehead, permanently compressed by the helmet which had pressed down on it for years. He was wearing a black vest, a haircloth collar, gray trousers and—as he did in all seasons—a pair of well-shined boots with two parallel bulges over his big toes. His jaw was outlined by a fringe of impeccably neat blond whiskers which framed, like the border of a flower bed, his long, gloomy face, with its small eyes and hooked nose. He played all card games well, was a good hunter and wrote a fine hand. He had his own lathe and amused himself by turning out napkin rings which he piled up all over his house with the jealousy of an artist and the egotism of a bourgeois.

He walked toward the dining room, but first the three millers had to be cleared out. During the whole time his place was being set, he stood silently beside the stove; then he closed the door and took off his cap as usual.

"He'll never wear out his tongue with polite conversation!" said the pharmacist as soon as he was alone with the hostess.

"He never talks any more than that," she replied. "One

night last week two cloth salesmen came in, both of them just as funny as they could be; they told me stories that made me laugh till I cried, but he just sat there like a clod and never opened his mouth!"

"Yes," said the pharmacist, "he has no imagination, no wit, none of the things that make a polished gentleman."

"And yet they say he's a pretty smart man," objected the hostess.

"Smart!" retorted Monsieur Homais. "Him, smart? Well, maybe he does all right in his work," he added in a calmer tone. Then, after a pause, "Ah! If an important businessman, a lawyer, a doctor or a pharmacist gets so absorbed in his work that he becomes eccentric or even surly, I can understand it; there are examples of it in history. But at least it's because he's thinking about something! Take me, for instance: I can't tell you how many times I've looked all over my desk for my pen when I needed to write out a label, and then finally found out I've put it behind my ear!"

Meanwhile Madame Lefrançois had gone over to the door to see if the Hirondelle was coming. She started when a man dressed in black suddenly walked into the kitchen. His florid face and athletic build were distinguishable in the fading twilight.

"What can I offer you, father?" she asked, taking down one of the brass candlesticks lined up along the mantelpiece with their candles already in them. "Would you like a drink? A little black-currant brandy? A glass of wine?"

The priest politely refused. He had come to pick up his umbrella, which he had left in the Ernemont convent the other day, and after asking Madame Lefrançois to have it brought to him that evening he left for the church, where the Angelus was ringing.

When the sound of his footsteps in the square had died away, the pharmacist passed extremely adverse judgment on his conduct. His refusal to accept a drink struck him as the most odious kind of hypocrisy; all priests were secret guzzlers, and they were all trying to bring back the days of the tithe.

The hostess countered with a defense of her priest. "And besides," she concluded, "he could take on any four men like you and break them all in half. Last year when he helped our men bring in the straw he sometimes carried six bundles at a time—that's how strong he is!"

"Good for him!" cried the pharmacist. "Go on, send your

daughters to confess to fine, husky men like that! If I were the government I'd have all priests bled once a month. That's right, Madame Lefrançois, once a month! A nice big phlebotomy for the sake of public order and morality!"

"Keep quiet, Monsieur Homais, you're an irreligious man!"

"Not at all! I have my own religion, and I'm a lot more religious than all those priests with their ludicrous ceremonies and their hypocrisy! No, I'm not an irreligious man: I worship God! I believe in a Supreme Being, a Creator—it doesn't matter what you call him—who put us on this earth to fulfill our duties as citizens and parents. But I don't have to go into a church and kiss silver plates and give away my hard-earned money to fatten a lot of rascals who eat better than we do! You can honor God just as well in a forest, in a field, or by simply looking up at the celestial vault, like the ancients. My God is the God of Socrates, of Franklin, of Voltaire, of Béranger! I stand for the religious credo set forth in Rousseau's *Emile*, and for the immortal principles of '89! That's why I can't accept the idea of a God who goes walking in his garden with his cane in his hand, lodges his friends in the bellies of whales, dies with a groan and comes back to life three days later. Such things are absurd in themselves, and besides that they're completely opposed to all the laws of physics. This proves, incidentally, that priests have always wallowed in abject ignorance and done their best to drag everyone else down to their level."

He looked around for an audience, so carried away by his own eloquence that for a moment he thought he was making a speech before the town council. But the mistress of the inn was no longer listening to him: she was straining her ears to catch a distant rumble. It gradually separated into the rattle of a carriage and the pounding of loose horseshoes on the road, and finally the Hirondelle drew up in front of the door.

It was a big yellow box mounted on two enormous wheels which came all the way up to the luggage rack on top, blocking the passengers' view and throwing dirt on their shoulders. The little panes of its narrow windows quivered in their frames when the carriage was closed, and they had mud stains scattered over their thick coating of dust, which even heavy rainstorms never washed off completely. It was drawn by three horses, the first one alone and the other two abreast, and when it went downhill its bottom bumped against the road.

A number of local citizens arrived in the square; they all talked at once, asking for news, explanations and packages. Hivert did not know whom to answer first. It was he who ran errands in Rouen for the people of Yonville. He went to various shops, brought back rolls of leather for the shoe-maker, scrap iron for the blacksmith, a keg of herrings for Madame Lefrançois, his employer, bonnets from the milliner, wigs from the hairdresser; and all along the road on the way back he distributed packages, standing up on his seat and throwing them over fences with loud shouts as the horses went on unguided.

He had been delayed by an accident: Madame Bovary's greyhound had run off across the fields and vanished. They had spent a good fifteen minutes whistling for it. Hivert had even gone back more than a mile, thinking he had seen it every minute or so, but finally he had to resume his journey. Emma had wept and lost her temper, blaming Charles for her misfortune. Monsieur Lheureux, the dry-goods dealer, who was also in the stagecoach, tried to comfort her with a num-ber of stories about lost dogs recognizing their masters many years later. He had heard of one, he said, which had come back to Paris from Constantinople. Another one had traveled a hundred and twenty-five miles in a straight line, swim-ming across four rivers on the way; and his own father once had a poodle which, after twelve years of absence, had jumped on his back one night in the street as he was going out to dinner.

II

Emma got out first, then Félicité, Monsieur Lheureux and a wet-nurse. Charles had to be awakened in his corner, where he had fallen sound asleep as soon as it was dark.

Homais introduced himself, paid his compliments to Madame and his respects to Monsieur. He said he was de-lighted to have been of service to them and added jovially that he had taken the liberty of inviting himself to join them for dinner, his wife being out of town.

When she was in the kitchen, Madame Bovary walked

over to the fireplace. Grasping her skirt at the knees with two fingers and pulling it up to her ankles, she held out her foot, in its black high-topped shoe, toward the flames, over the leg of mutton turning on the spit. The firelight shone on her from head to toe; its harsh glare illuminated the weave of her dress, the pores of her white skin and even her eyelids when she blinked her eyes. She was enveloped in a reddish glow each time the wind blew in through the half-open door.

A fair-haired young man was silently watching her from the other side of the fireplace.

Since he was terribly bored in Yonville, where he was a clerk in the office of Monsieur Guillaumin the notary, Monsieur Léon Dupuis, the second of the Lion d'Or's regular diners, often had his dinner late in the hope that some traveler would come to the inn with whom he could spend the evening talking. On days when he finished his work early, he had no choice but to arrive on time, not knowing what else to do, and sit through a conversation with Binet from one end of the meal to the other. He was therefore overjoyed to accept the hostess's suggestion that he dine with the newcomers, and they all went into the large dining room, for, in honor of the occasion, it was here that she had had their four places set.

Homais asked permission to keep his fez on, for fear of catching a head cold. Then he turned to Emma, who was sitting beside him, and said, "I imagine you're rather tired, madame. It's a terribly rough ride in our Hirondelle!"

"Yes, it is," replied Emma, "but I always like to travel. I enjoy a change of scene."

"It's so dull to spend your life rooted to one spot!" sighed the law clerk.

"If you were like me," said Charles, "always having to be on horseback . . ."

"But I don't think there's anything more pleasant than riding," said Léon, addressing Madame Bovary, "when you can do it," he added.

"Anyway," said the pharmacist, "the practice of medicine isn't very arduous in this region, because the condition of our roads makes it possible to use a gig and, in general, the people here pay well; the farmers are prosperous. As far as illness is concerned, besides the usual cases of enteritis, bronchitis, liver trouble, and so on, we have an occasional intermittent fever at harvest time, but on the whole we have very few serious illnesses, nothing special to point out, except for a considerable amount of scrofula, which is no doubt due to the deplorable hygienic conditions in which our peasants live. Ah, you'll find many prejudices to fight against, Monsieur Bovary! Every day your scientific efforts will be blocked by people who stubbornly cling to the past, because may of them still resort to novenas, relics or the priest instead of naturally calling on the doctor or the pharmacist. Actually, however, the climate isn't bad; we even have a number of people in their nineties. The thermomenter—I've made some observations myself—goes down to four degrees in winter, and in the hottest weather it goes up to twenty-five or thirty degrees Centigrade at the most, which gives us a maximum of twenty-four degrees Réamur, or fifty-four degrees Fahrenheit, the English scale—no more! You see, we're sheltered from the north winds by the Argueil forest on one side and from the west winds by the Saint-Jean hill on the other. However, this warmth, which, because of the water vapor given off by the river and the presence in the pastures of a considerable number of animals, which, as you know, exhale a great deal of ammonia, in other words, nitrogen, hydrogen and oxygen (no, just nitrogen and hydrogen), and which, sucking up the humus from the soil, mingling all those different emanations, binding them into one bundle, so to speak, and combining of itself with the electricity in the atmosphere when there is any, could eventually engender unhealthy miasmas, as in the tropical countries . . . as I was saying, this warmth happens to be moderated from the direction from which it comes, or rather the direction from which it would come, namely, the south, by the southwest winds, which, having been cooled in passing over the Seine, sometimes burst upon us all at once, like icy winds from Russia!"

"Are there at least a few nice places to go for walks in the vicinity?" continued Madame Bovary, speaking to the young man.

"Oh, very few!" he replied. "There's one place called the Pasture, on top of the hill, at the edge of the forest. Sometimes I go there on Sunday with a book and watch the sunset."

"I don't think there's anything more beautiful than a sunset," she said, "but I like them especially on the seashore."

"Oh, I love the sea!" said Monsieur Léon.

"Doesn't it seem to you," asked Madame Bovary, "that the mind moves more freely in the presence of that boundless expanse, that the sight of it elevates the soul and gives rise to thoughts of the infinite and the ideal?"

"The same is true of mountain scenery," said Léon. "I have a cousin who traveled in Switzerland last year, and he told me it's impossible to imagine how poetic the lakes are, how charming the waterfalls are, or how overwhelming the glaciers are. You can see pines of incredible size standing on the banks of swift streams, chalets built on the very edge of a cliff, and you can look down and see whole valleys a thousand feet below you, when there's an opening in the clouds. Scenes like that must be thrilling to see, they must be conducive to prayer, to ecstasy! I'm not at all surprised by that famous musician who used to play the piano in front of some imposing landscape, to stimulate his imagination."

"Are you a musician?" she asked.

"No, but I love music," he answered.

"Don't listen to him, Madame Bovary," interrupted Homais, leaning across his plate. "He's just being modest. How can you say that, my friend? Why, just the other day, in your room, you were singing *The Guardian Angel* beautifully. I heard you from my laboratory: you put real feeling into it, like an actor."

Léon lived in the pharmacist's house, in a small room on the third floor, overlooking the square. He blushed at this compliment from his landlord, who had already turned back to the doctor and was giving him a list of all the leading citizens of Yonville. He told anecdotes about them and gave assorted bits of information. No one knew exactly how rich the notary was, and then there was the Tuvache family, who caused a great deal of trouble.

Emma went on: "And what kind of music do you prefer?"

"Oh, German music, the kind that makes you dream."

"Do you know Italian opera?"

"Not yet; but I'll hear some of it next year when I go to live in Paris, to finish my law studies."

"As I was just telling your husband, talking about that poor Yanoda who ran away," said the pharmacist, "thanks to his extravagance you're going to enjoy one of the most comfortable houses in Yonville. The most convenient thing about it for a doctor is that it has a door opening on the lane, which means that people can come and go without being seen. And it has everything necessary to make a pleasant household: a wash-house, a kitchen with a pantry, a living room, a fruit storeroom, and so on. There was a man who didn't count his pennies! He built an arbor at the far end of the garden, near the river, just so he could drink beer in it during the summer, and if Madame likes gardening she can—"

"My wife isn't very interested in gardening," said Charles. "I keep advising her to get some exercise, but she'd rather stay in her room and read."

"I'm the same way," said Léon. "What could be better than to sit beside the fire at night with a hook and a glowing lamp while the wind beats against the windows . . ."

"You're quite right," she said, staring at him with her big dark eyes wide open.

"Your mind is free then," he went on. "The hours pass, and, without leaving your chair, you wander through countries that are clearly visible to you. Your imagination is caught up in the story and you see all the details, experience all the adventures; it seizes the characters and you have the feeling that *you* are living in their costumes."

"Oh, yes, it's true!" she said.

"Have you ever had the experience of finding in a book some vague idea that's already occurred to you, some obscure image that comes back to you from the depths of your mind, or a perfect expression of your most subtle feelings?"

"Yes, that's happened to me," she replied.

"That's why I especially like to read poetry," he said. "It affects me more strongly than prose, it's much more likely to bring tears to my eyes."

"But it's tiring in the long run," said Emma. "I've come to love a different kind of book much more: stories that keep you in suspense all the way through, and frighten you. I hate commonplace heroes and lukewarm emotions, the kind you find in real life."

"Yes," observed the clerk, "it seems to me that books which don't touch the heart are far removed from the true goal of art. In the midst of all the disenchantments of life, it's so comforting to be able to turn your thoughts to noble characters, pure sentiments and scenes of happiness. Cut off from the world as I am, it's my only distraction; Yonville has so little to offer!"

"It must be like Tostes," said Emma. "That's why I always had a subscription to a lending library."

"If Madame will do me the honor of accepting," said the pharmacist, who had overheard her last words, "I'll be glad

to offer her the use of a library composed of the best authors: Voltaire, Rousseau, Delille, Sir Walter Scott, the
Écho des Feuilletons, and so on. Furthermore, I receive a
number of periodicals, including the *Fanal de Rouen* every
day; I have the good fortune to be its local correspondent
for Buchy, Forges, Neufchâtel and the surrounding area."

They had been at table for two and a half hours, for
Artémise, the maid, casually dragged her cloth slippers over
the floor, brought in plates one by one, forgot everything,
paid no attention to what was said to her and constantly
left the door of the billiard room ajar, so that its latch kept
banging against the wall.

Without realizing what he was doing, Léon had put his
foot on one of the rungs of Madame Bovary's chair as he
talked. She was wearing a little blue silk scarf which held her
pleated batiste collar as stiff as a ruff; according to the movements of her head, the lower part of her face either sank
into the folds or gently emerged from them. Sitting side by
side while Charles and the pharmacist chatted, they entered
into one of those vague conversations in which every topic
leads back to a fixed center of mutual attraction. The Paris
theater, the titles of novels, new quadrilles, the world which
neither of them knew, Tostes where she had lived, Yonville
where they both were now—they examined everything, talked
about everything until the end of dinner.

When coffee was served, Félicité went off to prepare the
bedroom in the new house, and soon they all got up from
table. Madame Lefrançoise was asleep beside the smoldering
fire, and the stableboy, lantern in hand, was waiting to take
Monsieur and Madame Bovary to their new home. There
were wisps of straw in his red hair, and his left leg was
lame. He took the priest's umbrella in his other hand and
they left.

The town was asleep. The pillars of the market shed cast
long shadows. The ground was gray, as though it were a
summer night.

But since the doctor's house was only fifty yards from
the inn, they had to bid each other good night almost as
soon as they were outside, and they went their separate ways.

The moment she stepped into the entrance hall, Emma felt
the cold of the plaster descend on her shoulders like a damp
cloth. The walls were new, and the wooden steps creaked.
In the bedroom, on the second floor, a whitish light was coming in through the curtainless windows. They could glimpse

the tops of trees and, beyond them, the grasslands half smoth-ered in the mist that was rising along the river in the moon-light. In the middle of the room was a jumble of dresser drawers, bottles, iron rods, gilded wooden ones, mattresses on chairs and basins on the floor—the two men who had carried in the furniture had left everything there in disorder.

This was the fourth time she had gone to bed in a strange place. The first was the day she entered the convent, the second was the day she arrived in Tostes, the third at La Vaubyessard, and now the fourth; and each one had marked the beginning of a new phase of her life. She did not believe that things could be the same in different places; and since her life so far had been bad, the remainder of it would surely be better.

III

When she got up the next morning she saw the clerk out-side in the square. She was in her dressing gown. He looked up and bowed to her. She nodded quickly and closed the window.

Léon waited all day for six o'clock to come; but when he walked into the inn he found only Monsieur Binet, in his usual place at table.

The dinner of the previous evening had been a notable event for him; never before had he spoken for two whole hours with a "lady." Why had he been able to tell her so many things that he would not have been able to express so well before? He was usually shy and maintained a reserve that was composed of both modesty and dissimulation. In Yonville he was regarded as having "refined manners." He listened to the reasoning of older people and did not seem to be ex-cited about politics—a remarkable thing in a young man. And then he was talented: he painted in water colors, could read the treble clef, and often devoted himself to literature after dinner, when he was not playing cards. Monsieur Homais respected him for his learning, Madame Homais liked him for his obligingness: he often stayed in the garden for a while with the Homais children, impudent brats who were always dirty and had sluggish temperaments, like their mother. Besides the maid, they were looked after part of the time by Justin, the pharmacist's apprentice, a distant cousin of his whom they had taken into their house out of charity, and who also worked in it as a servant.

The apothecary proved to be the best of neighbors. He gave Madame Bovary information about the tradesmen, had his cider dealer make a special trip to her house, tasted the cider himself and made sure the cask was properly placed in the cellar; he also told her how to go about supplying herself with butter at low cost and made an arrangement for her with Lestiboudois, the sexton, who, in addition to his ecclesiastical and mortuary functions, took care of the principal gardens in Yonville by the hour or by the year, according to the owners' preference.

His need to concern himself with others was not the only thing that prompted the pharmacist to such obsequious cordiality: it was also part of a plan.

He had violated the law of the 19th of Ventôse, Year XI, Article I, which forbids anyone not holding a diploma to practice medicine, and as a result of anonymous denunciations he had been summoned to the private office of the Public Prosecutor in Rouen. The magistrate had received him standing, wearing his official robe, with ermine on his shoulders and a toque on his head. It was in the morning, before the opening of the day's court session. The pharmacist could hear the tramp of heavy-booted gendarmes in the hall, and the sound of strong locks being shut in the distance. His ears rang so loudly that he thought he was about to have a stroke; he had visions of deep dungeons, his family in tears, his pharmacy sold, all his glass jars scattered; and later he had to go to a café and drink a glass of rum and Seltzer water to steady his nerves.

The memory of this warning gradually faded away, and he continued as before to give innocuous consultations in the back room of his shop. But the mayor was against him and some of his colleagues were jealous of him: he had to watch his step. His friendly attentions to Monsieur Bovary would earn his gratitude and keep him quiet if he should notice anything. So every morning Homais brought him "the paper," and often left the pharmacy for a few moments in the afternoon to go and talk to him.

Charles was sad: he had no patients. He sat for long hours without speaking, took naps in his office or watched his wife sew. He did odd jobs around the house to distract himself, even trying to paint the attic with some paint which the workmen had left behind. But money worries filled his mind. He had spent so much on repairs at Tostes, dresses for Madame, and the expenses of moving, that the entire dowry, over nine thousand francs, had melted away in two years. And how many things had been broken or lost on the way from Tostes to Yonville! The plaster priest, for example, had been thrown from the cart by a particularly violent jolt and shattered into a thousand pieces on the pavement of Quincampoix.

He had a more cheerful concern: his wife's pregnancy. As her term drew near he cherished her more than ever. Another bond of the flesh was being formed between them, and he was continuously aware of a more complex union. When he saw her indolent walk and the way her body swayed gently above her uncorseted hips; when, sitting opposite her, he contemplated her at leisure and saw her take on a tired pose in her chair—at such moments his happiness knew no bounds. He would stand up, kiss her, stroke her face, call her "little mother," try to make her dance with him; and half laughing, half weeping, he would shower her with all the lighthearted, affectionate remarks he could think of. The idea of having begotten a child delighted him. Now he had everything he could wish for. He knew human life from one end to the other, and he looked forward with confidence to what it would offer him in the future.

At first Emma felt only great astonishment, then she was eager to be delivered, so that she could know what it was like to be a mother. But since she could not spend as much money as she would have liked, since she could not buy embroidered baby bonnets and a boat-shaped cradle with pink silk curtains, she abandoned all her plans for the layette in a fit of bitterness and ordered everything at once from a seamstress in the village without choosing or discussing anything. Thus she did not amuse herself with those preparations which whet the appetite of maternal love, and this may have weakened her affection from the very beginning.

However, since Charles talked about the baby at every meal, she soon began to think about it more seriously.

She wanted a son. He would be strong and dark, and his name would be Georges. This idea of giving birth to a male was like a hope of compensation for all her past frustrations. A man, at least, is free; he can explore the whole range of the passions, go wherever he likes, overcome obstacles, savor the most exotic pleasures. But a woman is constantly thwarted. Inert and pliable, she is restricted by her physical weakness and her legal subjection. Her will, like the veil tied to her hat with a cord, quivers with every wind; there is always some desire urging her forward, always some convention holding her back.

The baby was born at six o'clock on a Sunday morning, at sunrise.

"It's a girl!" said Charles.

She turned her head away and fainted.

Almost immediately Madame Homais rushed in and kissed her; so did Madame Lefrançois of the Lion d'Or. Being a man of discretion, the pharmacist confined himself for the moment to congratulating her briefly through the half-open door. He asked to see the child and declared it to be well formed.

During her convalescence she spent a great deal of time trying to find a name for her daughter. First she went over all those with Italian endings, such as Clara, Louisa, Amanda, Atala; she was rather fond of Galsuinde, still fonder of Yseult or Léocadie. Charles wanted to name the girl for her mother, but Emma refused. They went over every saint's name from one end of the calendar to the other and asked outsiders for suggestions.

"I was talking to Monsieur Léon the other day," said the pharmacist, "and he told me he's surprised you haven't chosen Madeleine: it's a very fashionable name these days."

But the elder Madame Bovary protested loudly against naming the child after a sinner. As for Monsieur Homais, he had a predilection for names which recalled great men, illustrious deeds or noble ideas, and he had christened his four children accordingly. Thus Napoléon represented glory, Franklin liberty; Irma was perhaps a concession to romanticism, but Athalie was a tribute to the most immortal masterpiece of the French theater, for his philosophical convictions did not prevent him from admiring great works of art: the thinker in him did not stifle the man of feeling. He was capable of seeing differences, of discriminating between imagination and fanaticism. In the tragedy of *Athalie*, for example, he condemned the ideas but admired the style, cursed the conception but praised all the details, was exasperated by the characters but enthusiastic about their speeches. He was carried away when he read the famous passages, but he was distressed when he reflected that the

priests were turning them to their own advantage; these contradictory feelings were so confusing to him that he would
have liked to place a wreath on Racine's brow with his
own hands and argue with him at the same time.

Finally Emma remembered that at La Vaubyessard she had
heard the marquise call a young woman Berthe; she immediately decided on this name. Since Monsieur Rouault was
unable to come, Monsieur Homais was asked to be the god-
father. All his presents were products from his pharmacy,
namely, six boxes of jujubes, a whole jar of racahout and
three packages of marshmallow paste, plus six sticks of sugar
candy which he had found in a cupboard. On the evening of
the ceremony there was a large dinner. The priest was there,
and the conversation became rather heated. When the liqueurs
were served, Monsieur Homais burst out with *Le Dieu des
Bonnes Gens,* Monsieur Léon sang a barcarolle, and the
elder Madame Bovary, who was the godmother, sang a
sentimental song from the time of the Empire. Finally
Charles's father demanded that the child be brought downstairs and proceeded to baptize her by pouring a glass of
champagne over her head. Father Bournisien complained indignantly about this mockery of the first secrament and the
elder Madame Bovary, who was the godmother, sang a
Guerre des Dieux. The priest stood up to leave, the ladies
begged him to stay, Homais intervened, and they finally
managed to make him sit down again, after which he calmly
picked up his saucer and his half-finished demitasse.

Charles's father stayed in Yonville for a month, dazzling
the inhabitants with a magnificent silver-braided policeman's
hat which he wore each morning when he smoked his pipe
in the square. Being accustomed to drinking a great deal of
brandy, he often sent the maid to the Lion d'Or to buy him
a bottle, which was charged to his son's account; and to
perfume his foulards he used up his daughter-in-law's entire
supply of eau de Cologne.

Emma did not find his company at all unpleasant. He had
seen the world: he spoke of Berlin, Vienna and Strasbourg,
and of his years as an army officer, of the mistresses he had
had, of the great banquets he had attended. Then his manner would become engaging, and sometimes, on the stairs or
in the garden, he would even put his arms around her waist
and exclaim, "You'd better look out, Charles!"

The elder Madame Bovary became alarmed for her son's
happiness and, fearing that her husband might eventually

have an immoral influence on the young woman, she did her best to hasten their departure. Perhaps she had more serious worries: Monsieur Bovary was a man to whom nothing was sacred.

One day Emma suddenly felt a need to see her little girl, who had been put out to nurse with the cabinet-maker's wife, and without looking at the almanac to see whether the six weeks of the Virgin had elapsed, she went to Rollet's house, which was on the edge of the village at the foot of the hill, between the highway and the meadows.

It was noon; the houses all had their shutters closed, and the slate roofs, gleaming under the harsh light of the blue sky, seemed to be giving off sparks beneath their ridges. A sultry wind was blowing. Emma felt weak as she walked; the pebbles on the footpath hurt her feet; she considered going back home or stopping in somewhere to sit down.

Just then Monsieur Léon stepped out of a nearby door with a sheaf of papers under his arm. He came over to greet her and stood in the shade of the gray awning in front of Lheureux's shop.

Madame Bovary said she was on her way to see her child, but that she was beginning to feel tired.

"If . . ." Léon began, not daring to go any further.

"Do you have an appointment somewhere?" she asked.

And when she heard his reply she asked him to accompany her. This was known all over Yonville by evening, and Madame Tuvache, the mayor's wife, said in front of her maid that Madame Bovary was "compromising herself."

To reach the wet-nurse's house they had to turn left at the end of the street, as though going to the cemetery, and follow a narrow privet-lined path that ran between cottages and yards. The privet hedges were in bloom, and so were the veronicas, wild roses and nettles, and the thin brambles growing out from the bushes. Through the holes in the hedges they could look into farmyards and see a pig on a manure pile, or cows wearing breast harnesses rubbing their horns against tree trunks. They walked along slowly, side by side, she leaning on his arm and he shortening his steps to match hers, while in front of them a swarm of flies buzzed in the warm air.

They recognized the house by the old walnut tree that shaded it. It was low, with a brown tile roof, and from its

attic window hung a string of onions. A thorn hedge reinforced with brushwood enclosed a plot of land in which grew
lettuce, a few lavender plants and sweet peas climbing on
poles. A stream of dirty water was trickling over the grass,
and all around were a number of nondescript rags, knitted
stockings, a short red calico wrapper and a large, thick sheet
spread out on the hedge. At the sound of the gate the wet-
nurse appeared, carrying with one arm a child that was
sucking her breast. With her other hand she was pulling
a poor sickly little boy whose face was covered with scrofula
sores. He was the son of a Rouen knit-goods dealer; too busy
with their shop to take care of him, his parents had boarded
him out in the country.

"Come in," she said. "Your little girl's inside, sleeping."

The ground-floor bedroom, the only one in the house, had
a wide uncurtained bed standing against the wall at the far
end, while the kneading trough occupied the side of the
room with the window, one of whose panes had been mended
with a patch of blue paper. In the corner beside the door, beneath the washing slab, stood a row of heavy shoes with
gleaming hobnails, and a bottle of oil with a feather in its
mouth; a Mathieu Laensberg almanac lay on the dusty mantelpiece among gun flints, candle ends and pieces of tinder.
The clutter in the room was completed by a picture of Fame
blowing her trumpet; it had no doubt been cut out of some
perfume advertisement and was now fastened to the wall
with six shoe nails.

Emma's child was sleeping in a wicker cradle on the floor.
She picked her up in her blanket and began to sing to her,
rocking her in her arms.

Léon walked around the room; it seemed strange to him
to see that beautiful lady in a nankeen dress standing in the
midst of such squalor. Madame Bovary blushed; he turned
away, fearing there might have been a certain impertinence
in his eyes. Then she put the baby back in its cradle: it had
just thrown up on her collar. The wet-nurse quickly wiped
it off, assuring her it wouldn't show.

"That's not all she does!" she said. "She keeps me busy
washing her all the time! I'd appreciate it if you'd tell
Camus the grocer to let me have a little soap whenever I
need it. It'll be easier for you, because that way I won't
have to bother you about it."

"All right, all right," said Emma. "Good-by, Madame
Rollet."

And she walked out, wiping her feet on the doorsill.

The wet-nurse accompanied her to the end of the yard, telling her how hard it was for her to get up during the night.

"Sometimes I'm so worn out I fall asleep in my chair, so you ought to at least let me have a pound of ground coffee. That would be enough to last me for a month. I'd drink it in the morning, with milk."

After undergoing her thanks, Madame Bovary walked away. She had gone a little way along the path when the sound of wooden soles made her turn around: it was the wet-nurse again.

"What now?"

The peasant woman drew her aside behind an elm and began to talk to her about her husband, who, with his trade and six francs a year which the captain . . .

"Come to the point," said Emma.

"Well, I'm afraid he'd be pretty upset if he saw me drinking coffee all by myself," said the wet-nurse, sighing between each word. "You know how men are . . ."

"You'll have enough coffee for both of you! I'll give it to you, I've told you that already! Stop bothering me!"

"But you see, madame, he has terrible cramps in his chest, because of his wounds. He says cider makes him even weaker . . ."

"Hurry, come to the point!"

Madame Rollet curtsied and went on: "So, if I'm not asking too much"—she curtsied again—"if you'd just let me have"—she gave her a supplicating look—"a little jug of brandy," she said at last. "I'll rub your little girl's feet with it; they're as tender as your tongue."

When she was rid of the wet-nurse, Emma took Monsieur Léon's arm again. She walked swiftly for a time, then she slowed down, and as she looked back and forth her eyes fell on the young man's shoulder. His smooth, neatly combed brown hair came down to the black velvet collar of his frock coat. She noticed his fingernails, which were quite a bit longer than those of most people in Yonville. Taking care of them was one of his major occupations: he kept a special penknife in his desk for the purpose.

They walked back to Yonville along the river. Its level sank in summer, widening its banks and revealing the bottoms of the walls of the gardens, each of which had a few steps leading down to the water. It ran silently, swift and cold-looking; long

thin grass swayed with the current, like disheveled green hair
growing in its limpid depths. Here and there an insect with
delicate legs was crawling or sitting on a water-lily leaf
or the tip of a reed. Sunbeams pierced the little blue bub-
bles which kept forming and bursting on the ripples; branch-
less old willows mirrored their gray bark in the water; the
meadows around them seemed empty. It was dinnertime on
the farms. As the young woman and her companion walked
along they heard nothing but the rhythm of their footsteps
on the dirt path, the words they were saying to each other
and the sound of her dress rustling all around her.

The garden walls, with their copings of pieces of broken
bottles, were as warm as the glass of a greenhouse. Wallflowers had taken root between the bricks, and the edge of
Madame Bovary's open parasol crumbled some of their blossoms into yellow dust as she passed; or an overhanging
branch of honeysuckle or clematis would catch on the fringe
and brush against the silk for a moment.

They were talking about a company of Spanish dancers
scheduled to appear soon at the theater in Rouen.

"Are you going to see them?" she asked.

"If I can," he replied.

Was this all they had to say to each other? Yet their eyes
were full of more serious talk, and as they forced themselves
to find commonplace phrases they both felt the same kind
of languor stealing over them; it was like a deep, continuous
murmur of the soul, dominating that of their voices. Astonished by this new sweetness, they had no thought of
describing the sensation to each other or trying to discover
its cause. Future joys, like tropical shores, project their native
softness in a perfumed breeze that blows into the vastness
stretching out before them and makes us sink into a kind of
drowsy intoxication in which we care nothing for whatever
may lie over the horizon.

In one spot the ground had been made boggy by the
trampling of cattle; they had to walk on big green stones
spaced out in the mud. She often stopped for a moment to see
where to put her foot down, and teetering on the unsteady
stone with her elbows raised, her body bent forward and her
eyes glancing around hesitantly, she would laugh, afraid she
might fall into a puddle.

When they reached her garden, Madame Bovary opened the
little gate, ran up the steps and disappeared.

Léon went back to his office. His employer was out; he

looked at the dossiers and sharpened a quill pen, then he took his hat and left.

He went to the Pasture, on top of the Argueil hill at the edge of the forest; he lay down on the ground beneath the firs and looked up at the sky through his fingers.

"I'm so bored!" he said to himself. "So bored!"

He felt he ought to be pitied for having to live in that village with Homais as his friend and Monsieur Guillaumin as his employer. The latter's mind was completely taken up with his business; he wore gold-framed glasses, red side whiskers and a white cravat; he knew nothing of refined feelings, although he still affected the stiff English manner that had strongly impressed the clerk at first. As for Madame Homais, she was the best wife in Normandy: she was as gentle as a lamb and she cherished her children, her parents and her whole family; she wept over other people's misfortunes, let everything in her house go and hated corsets. But she was so slow-moving, so boring to listen to, so common-looking and so limited in conversation that, although she was thirty and he twenty, although they slept in adjoining rooms and she spoke to him every day, it had never occurred to him that anyone could regard her as a woman, or that she might have other attributes of her sex besides the dress she wore.

And then who else was there? Binet, a few shopkeepers, two or three tavern-keepers, the priest, and finally Monsieur Tuvache, the mayor, and his two sons: a prosperous, surly, dull-witted family who farmed their own land and ate Gargantuan meals which they invited no one to share; they were devout churchgoers and their company was completely unbearable.

Against the background of all these faces, Emma's stood out in isolation, yet farther away than any of the others, for he felt that he was separated from her by some sort of shadowy abyss.

At first he had gone to her house several times with the pharmacist. Charles had not seemed too eager to receive him, and Léon felt paralyzed between his fear of being indiscreet and his desire for an intimacy that he considered all but impossible.

IV

As soon as the cold weather set in, Emma left her bedroom and moved into the parlor, a long, low-ceilinged room in which a thick cluster of coral stood on the mantelpiece, leaning against the mirror. Sitting in her armchair beside the window, she watched the people of the village go by on the sidewalk.

Twice a day Léon went from his office to the Lion d'Or. Emma could hear him coming from a distance; she would lean forward to listen, and the young man would slip past the curtain, always dressed in the same way, without turning his head. But at twilight, when she had put her unfinished embroidery on her lap and was sitting with her chin in her left hand, she often started at the appearance of that gliding shadow. She would then stand up and order the maid to set the table.

Monsieur Homais would come in during dinner. Fez in hand, he would walk in quietly in order not to disturb anyone, and he always repeated the same greeting: "Good evening, everybody!" Then when he had sat down between them at table, he would ask the doctor for news of his patients, and Charles would ask him about the possibilities with regard to fees in each case. Next they would discuss what was "in the paper." By this time of day Homais knew it almost by heart, and he would give a full report, down to the editorials and the details of every individual catastrophe that had occurred in France and abroad. When this subject had been pumped dry, he soon began to make comments on the food they were eating. Sometimes, half rising in his chair, he would graciously point out to Madame the tenderest piece, or turn to the maid and give her advice on the preparation of stews and the hygienic use of seasoning; he spoke brilliantly about aromas, osmazomes, juices and gelatines. And there were more recipes in his head than jars in his pharmacy: he excelled in making all sorts of jams, vinegars and liqueurs. He knew about all the latest fuel-saving stoves and the arts of preparing cheeses and treating sick wines.

At eight o'clock Justin would come in to notify him it was

time to close the pharmacy. Monsieur Homais would give him a mocking look, especially if Félicité happened to be present, for he had noticed that his apprentice had a great fondness for the doctor's house. "The young blade is starting to get ideas," he would say. "I could swear he's in love with your maid!"

But the boy had a more serious failing, for which the pharmacist often rebuked him: he was always listening to other people's conversations. On Sundays, for example, there was no way of getting him out of the parlor when Madame Homais summoned him there to take the children, who were falling asleep in the armchairs, pulling down the loose calico slip covers with their backs.

Not many people came to these soirées in the pharmacist's house, for his malicious gossip and his political opinions had alienated one respectable person after another. The clerk never failed to come. As soon as he heard the bell he would hurry to the door to greet Madame Bovary, take her shawl and put away under the desk in the pharmacy the thick cloth overshoes she wore when it was snowing.

First they would play a few games of *trente-et-un*, then Monsieur Homais would play *écarté* with Emma while Léon stood behind her and advised her. Leaning his hands on the back of her chair, he would look at the teeth of her comb biting into her chignon. The right side of her dress rose each time she threw down a card; from her upswept hair a zone of dark color ran down her back, gradually growing lighter until it was lost in the shadows. Then her dress would fall down on each side of her chair, billowing and full of folds, and spread out on the floor. Sometimes Léon would feel the sole of his shoe press down on it, and he would quickly draw back, as though he had stepped on someone.

When the card games were over, the apothecary and the doctor played dominoes, and Emma would move to another chair, lean her elbows on the table and look through a copy of *L'Illustration* or the fashion magazine she had brought with her. Léon would sit down beside her; they would look at the pictures together and wait for each other to finish before turning a page. She often asked him to read a poem to her; he would declaim it in a languid voice which he carefully lowered to a sigh when he came to the love passages. But the noise of the dominoes irritated him. Monsieur Homais was an expert player and he usually beat Charles soundly. When the score had reached three hundred they would both stretch out in front of the fireplace and quickly fall asleep. By now the fire had died down and the teapot was empty; Léon continued to read and Emma listened to him, absent-mindedly turning the lampshade decorated with paintings of pierrots in carriages and tightrope dancers with their balancing poles. Léon would stop and make a gesture calling her attention to his sleeping audience; then they would talk to each other in low voices, and their conversation seemed sweeter to them because no one else could hear it.

Thus a bond was established between them, a continual exchange of books and songs; Monsieur Bovary, little inclined to jealousy, took it as a matter of course.

For his birthday he received a magnificent phrenological head, marked all over with figures down to the thorax and painted blue. It was a present from the clerk. He was obliging to Charles in many other ways, too, even going so far as to run errands for him in Rouen. When a book written by a novelist made cactuses the latest fad, Léon bought some for Madame and brought them back in the Hirondelle, holding them on his lap and pricking his fingers on their spines.

She had a shelf with a railing along it installed in her window to hold her flowerpots. The clerk also had his little hanging garden; they could look out of their respective windows and see each other tending their plants.

Among the windows of the village there was one that was even more often occupied than theirs: all day long on Sunday, and every afternoon when the weather was good, Monsieur Binet's lean profile could be seen through his attic window as he leaned over his lathe, whose steady drone was audible as far away as the Lion d'Or.

One night when Léon came back to his room he found a velvet and wool bedspread with foliage designs on a pale background. He called in Madame Homais, Monsieur Homais, the children and the cook, and he later spoke about it to his employer. Everyone wanted to see it: why should the doctor's wife be so generous to the clerk? It seemed suspicious, and everyone concluded that she must be his mistress.

He strengthened this opinion by constantly talking about her charm and intelligence. One day Binet said to him peevishly, "What's it to me? She's no friend of mine!"

He racked his brains trying to decide how to "declare himself" to her; and, continually torn between fear of displeasing her and shame at his own faint-heartedness, he shed tears of despair and desire. Finally he began to make firm decisions: he wrote letters and tore them up, set himself time limits and then extended them. He often set out with the intention of daring all, but his resolution quickly abandoned him in Emma's presence, and if Charles came in to invite him to get into his buggy with him and go off to see a patient living somewhere nearby, he would always accept immediately, bow to Madame and leave. After all, wasn't her husband part of her, in a way?

As for Emma, she never made any effort to determine whether or not she was in love with him. Love, she felt, ought to come all at once, with great thunderclaps and flashes of lightning; it was like a storm bursting upon life from the sky, uprooting it, overwhelming the will and sweeping the heart into the abyss. It did not occur to her that rain forms puddles on a flat roof when the drainpipes are clogged, and she would have continued to feel secure if she had not suddenly discovered a crack in the wall.

V

It was on a snowy Sunday afternoon in February.

Monsieur and Madame Bovary, Homais and Monsieur Léon had all gone to see a new spinning mill that was being built in the valley, a mile or so from Yonville. The apothecary had brought Napoléon and Athalie along, to give them some exercise, and Justin accompanied them, carrying several umbrellas on his shoulder.

Nothing, however, could have been less interesting than this point of interest. A long rectangular building pierced with many little windows stood in the middle of a large expanse of bare land dotted with piles of sand and gravel and a few already rusty gearwheels. It was still unfinished, and the sky could be seen through the timbers of its roof. Attached to the ridge beam was a bouquet of straw and wheat tied with tricolored ribbons that flapped in the wind.

Homais was speaking. He explained to them how important the establishment was going to be, estimated the strength of the floors and the thickness of the walls, and expressed great regret that he had no metric ruler, such as Monsieur Binet owned for his own use.

He had given Emma his arm; she leaned on his shoulder a little and looked up at the faraway disk of the sun flooding the mist with its dazzling pallor. Then she turned her head: Charles was there. His cap was pulled down to his eyebrows, and his thick lips were quivering, which added a certain stupidity to his face; even his back, his placid back, was irritating to look at: it was as though she could see all his dullness spread across his coat.

As she was looking at him, drawing a kind of perverse pleasure from her irritation, Léon took a step forward. The cold that had made his face turn pale seemed to give it a sweeter languor; his skin was visible between his cravat and the rather loose collar of his shirt; the tip of an ear showed from beneath his hair, and his big blue eyes, raised toward the clouds, seemed to Emma more limpid and beautiful than a mountain lake mirroring the sky.

"Stupid brat!" the apothecary suddenly cried out.

And he ran over to his son, who had just rushed into a pile of lime to paint his shoes white. Napoléon howled in reply to his father's angry lecture while Justin scraped his shoes with a piece of plaster. But a knife was needed: Charles offered his.

"Ah!" she said to herself. "He carries a knife in his pocket, like a peasant!"

Frost was beginning to form, and they went back to Yonville.

That night Madame Bovary did not visit her neighbors. When Charles was gone and she felt herself alone, the comparison came into her mind again, almost as vivid as an immediate sensation, and with the greater perspective given to things by memory. Watching the brightly burning fire from her bed, she could still see Léon as he had been that afternoon, bending his slender cane as he leaned on it with one hand, while with the other he held Athalie, who was calmly sucking a piece of ice. She found him charming; she could not take her mind off him; she recalled how he had looked on other days, things he had said, the sound of his voice, everything about him; and she said over and over again, advancing her lips as though for a kiss, "Yes, charming! Charming!" Then she asked herself, "Isn't he in love with someone? Who could it be? . . . Why, it's me!"

All the evidence immediately became clear to her and her heart leapt. The flames in the fireplace cast a joyful, flickering light on the ceiling; she rolled over on her back and stretched out her arms.

Then began the eternal lament: "Oh, if only fate had willed it! Why couldn't things have been different? What would have been wrong with it?"

When Charles came in at midnight she pretended to wake up. He made some noise as he undressed and she complained of a headache; then she casually asked him what had happened during the evening.

"Monsieur Léon went up to his room early," he said.

She could not help smiling, and she soon went to sleep, her soul filled with a new kind of bliss.

The following afternoon, jut as it was getting dark, she received a visit from Monsieur Lheureux, the dry-goods merchant. He was a clever man, this shopkeeper.

A Gascon by birth and a Norman by adoption, he combined his southern volubility with the wily caution of the Caux region. His soft, fat, beardless face seemed to have been tinted with a light decoction of licorice, and his white hair accentuated the audacious brightness of his little black eyes. No one knew what he had been before coming to Yonville: a peddler, said some; a banker in Routot, said others. One thing was certain: he could work out calculations in his head that were complicated enough to frighten Binet himself. Polite to the point of obsequiousness, he always stood in a half-bent position, like someone bowing or extending an invitation.

After leaving his hat with its mourning band at the door, he placed a green cardboard box on the table and began by complaining to Madame, with profuse compliments, that until now he had not been fortunate enough to gain her confidence. A poor shop like his was not likely to attract a lady of such elegance (he stressed this word). However, she had only to give him her orders and he would undertake to supply her with anything she might want, whether it be ribbons, lace, lingerie, stockings, knit goods or fine cloth, for he went to the city four times a month regularly. He was in contact with all the biggest firms. She could mention his name at the Trois Frères, the Barbe d'Or or the Grand Sauvage: all those gentlemen knew him like the backs of their hands! But today he merely wanted to show Madame a few articles he happened to have acquired by taking advantage of a rare opportunity. And he took out half a dozen embroidered collars from the box.

Madame Bovary examined them.

"I don't need anything," she said.

Monsieur Lheureux delicately exhibited three Algerian scarves, several packets of English needles, a pair of straw slippers, and finally four cocoanut-shell eggcups which had been carved in openwork designs by convicts. Then, with both hands on the table, neck outstretched, body bent forward from the waist and mouth open, he followed Emma's eyes as she hesitantly looked over his merchandise. Now and then, as though to remove a speck of dust, he flicked the unfolded silk scarves with his fingernail; they quivered and rustled, and their gold sequins sparkled like little stars in the greenish twilight.

"How much are they?"

"Practically nothing," he replied, "practically nothing. But there's no hurry: you can pay whenever you like—we're not Jews!"

She pondered for a few moments and finally declined again.

"All right," he said impassively, "we'll get together some other time. I've always managed to get along well with ladies —except for my wife!"

Emma smiled.

"I just wanted to let you know," he went on good-naturedly, after his little jest, "that I'm not worried about the money . . . I could even lend you a little, in fact, if you should need it."

She made a gesture of surprise.

"Oh," he said quickly, in a low voice, "I wouldn't have to go far to find it for you, believe me!"

He then began to ask about Monsieur Tellier, the owner of the Café Français, whom Monsieur Bovary was treating: "What's the matter with Tellier, anyway? He coughs so hard he shakes his whole house, and I'm afraid he'll be needing a pine overcoat instead of a flannel nightshirt before long! He used to go on so many sprees when he was young! He and his friends never knew when to stop, madame! He's burnt out his insides with brandy! Just the same, though, it's hard to see someone go when you've known him for so long."

And as he closed up his box again he went on talking about the doctor's patients.

"It's probably the weather," he said, looking out the window with a scowl, "that's causing all this sickness. I don't feel so well myself; one of these days I'll have to come and see your husband about a pain I've got in my back. . . . Well, good-by, Madame Bovary; and don't forget: I'm at your service."

He closed the door softly behind him.

Emma had her dinner brought up to her room on a tray. She ate it slowly beside the fire; everything tasted good to her.

"I was so sensible!" she said to herself, thinking of the scarves.

She heard footsteps on the stairs: it was Léon. She stood up, went over to the dish towels that were piled on the dresser, waiting to be hemmed, and picked up the one on top. She looked very busy when he came in.

Their conversation languished; she kept lapsing into silence, and he seemed extremely ill at ease. He sat on a low chair near the fireplace and toyed with her ivory needle-case; she continued to sew, occasionally gathering the cloth with her fingertip. She said nothing and neither did he; he was as captivated by her silence as he would have been by her words.

"Poor boy!" she thought.

"What is there about me that she dislikes?" he wondered.

Finally he told her he would soon make a trip to Rouen to take care of a business matter for his employer.

"Your music subscription has expired: shall I renew it for you?"

"No," she replied.

"Why not?"

"Because . . ."

And, pursing her lips, she slowly drew out a long stretch of gray thread.

Her sewing irritated him. It seemed to be hurting the tips of her fingers. A gallant remark came into his mind, but he was afraid to say it.

"You're giving it up?"

"What?" she asked quickly. "My music? Oh, yes! I have my house to run, my husband to take care of, a thousand other things to do: all kinds of duties that come first!"

She looked at the clock. Charles was late. She pretended to be worried and said two or three times, "He's such a good man!"

The clerk was fond of Monsieur Bovary, but her tender

feelings for him came as an unpleasant surprise; nevertheless he also said a few kind words about Charles and added that he had heard everyone else praise him, especially the pharmacist.

"He's a fine man," said Emma.

"He certainly is," said the clerk.

And he began to talk about Madame Homais, whose slovenly appearance usually made him laugh.

"What does that matter?" Emma interrupted. "A good wife and mother doesn't worry about how she looks."

She then became silent again.

She was the same during the days that followed; her talk, her manner—everything about her had changed. She took her household duties very seriously, went to church regularly and treated her maid more strictly.

She took Berthe back from the wet-nurse. Félicité brought her in whenever there were visitors, and Madame Bovary undressed her to show off her arms and legs. She claimed to adore children; her daughter, she said, was her consolation, her joy and her passion, and she accompanied her caresses with lyrical outpourings that would have reminded anyone except Yonvillians of Paquette in *The Hunchback of Notre Dame.*

When Charles came home he found his slippers warming in front of the fireplace. His vests always had linings now, there were never any buttons missing from his shirts, and it was a pleasure to see his nightcaps stacked up neatly in the closet. She no longer showed any aversion when he asked her to take a walk in the garden with him; she agreed to everything he proposed, although she never anticipated any of the wishes to which she submitted without a murmur. And when Léon saw him after dinner—sitting beside the fire with his hands folded over his stomach, his feet on the andirons, his cheeks flushed from his digestion, his eyes moist with happiness, the baby crawling on the carpet, and that slender woman leaning over the back of his armchair to kiss him on the forehead—he said to himself, "What madness! How can I ever come near her?"

She seemed so virtuous and inaccessible to him that all his hopes, even the vaguest, abandoned him.

But in thus placing her beyond his reach he endowed her with extraordinary qualities. For him, she was now divested of those bodily attributes from which he could obtain nothing, and in his heart she rose higher and higher, soaring away from him in a glorious apotheosis. It was one of those pure feelings which do not interfere with everyday life and are cultivated because they are rare; the pain of losing them would be greater than the happiness of possessing them.

Emma lost weight, her face became pale and gaunt. With her smooth black hair, her big eyes, her straight nose, her birdlike walk and the silence that had now become almost constant with her, did she not seem to be passing through life without touching it, bearing on her brow the mysterious mark of a sublime destiny? She was so sad and serene, so sweet and yet so withdrawn, that Léon felt himself gripped by a kind of icy enchantment in her presence, just as one shivers in a church when the fragrance of flowers is mingled with the coldness of marble. Others also fell under this spell. "She's a remarkable woman!" the pharmacist would sometimes say. "She wouldn't be out of place in a district capital!"

The housewives all admired her for her thriftiness, Charles's patients for her courtesy, the poor for her generosity.

Yet she was full of covetous desires, anger and hatred. The smooth folds of her dress concealed a tumultuous heart, and her modest lips told nothing of her torment. She was in love with Léon, and she sought solitude because it allowed her to revel in thoughts of him at leisure. His actual presence disturbed the voluptuous pleasure of her reveries. Her heart palpitated at the sound of his footsteps, but her agitation always began to subside as soon as he appeared, and she was left with nothing but deep astonishment which eventually turned to sadness.

Léon did not know, when he left her house in despair, that she immediately went to the window and watched him walk away. She worried over everything he did, scrutinized his face, and made up an elaborate story to give herself a pretext for visiting his room. She regarded the pharmacist's wife as extremely fortunate because she slept under the same roof with him, and her thoughts constantly returned to that house, like the pigeons from the Lion d'Or which alighted on it to wet their pink feet and white wings in the rain-gutters. But the more clearly aware of her love she became, the more she tried to repress it in order to conceal and diminish it. She wished Léon would guess it, and she imagined chance occurrences and catastrophes that would have facilitated its consummation. She was no doubt held back by indolence or fear, and also by shame. She felt that she had kept him at too great a distance, that it was now too late, that all was lost. Furthermore, the pride and pleasure she felt when she said to herself "I'm virtuous," or watched herself in the mirror as she struck various poses of resignation, consoled her a little for the sacrifice she thought she was making.

Her carnal desires, her longing for money and the melancholy of her unfulfilled passion merged into one vast anguish, and instead of trying to distract herself from it she concentrated her attention on it, stirring up her pain and always looking for a chance to suffer. She complained bitterly about a badly served dish or a door left ajar, she lamented the velvet she did not own, the happiness that eluded her, her too lofty dreams, her too narrow house.

She was exasperated by Charles's apparent unawareness of her ordeal. His conviction that he was making her happy seemed to her an idiotic insult, and his placid confidence about it struck her as ingratitude. For whom was she being virtuous? Was he not the obstacle to any kind of happiness, the cause of all her misery, the sharp-pointed tongue in the buckle of the strap that wound around her, binding her on all sides?

She therefore made him the sole object of the complex hatred engendered by her frustrations, and all her efforts to lessen it served only to increase it, for their failure gave her one more reason to despair and made her feel still more alienated from him. She sometimes rebelled against her own meekness. The drabness of her daily life made her dream of luxury, her husband's conjugal affection drove her to adulterous desires. She wished he would beat her so that she could feel more justified in hating him and taking vengeance on him. She was sometimes amazed by the horrible conjectures that came into her mind; and yet she had to go on smiling, hearing herself told over and over that she was lucky, pretending to be happy, letting everyone believe it!

Sometimes, however, this hypocrisy became so repugnant to her that she was tempted to run away with Léon to some faraway place where she could begin a different life; but then she always felt as though some dark, mysterious abyss were opening up before her.

"Anyway, he doesn't love me any more," she would think. What was to become of her? What help could she look forward to, what consolation, what relief?

And for a time she would be despondent and almost lifeless,

gasping and sobbing softly with tears running down her cheeks.

"Why don't you tell Monsieur?" the maid asked whenever she came into the room during one of these crises.

"It's just my nerves," Emma would reply. "Don't mention it to him, it would only upset him."

"Oh, yes," Félicité said once, "you're just like the daughter of old Guérin, the fisherman at Le Pollet. I met her in Dieppe, before I came here. She was so sad! When you saw her standing in her doorway she made you think of a funeral pall hanging in front of the house. They say it was some kind of fog in her head that was bothering her. The doctors couldn't do anything for her, and neither could the priest. When it got too bad she used to go down to the beach all by herself, and sometimes the customs officer would find her lying face down on the pebbles, crying. Then after she got married it went away, or so they say."

"In my case," said Emma, "it didn't *begin* till after I was married."

VI

One evening when the window was open and she had just been sitting in it watching Lestiboudois, the sexton, trimming the boxwood, she suddenly heard the Angelus ringing.

It was the beginning of April, when the primroses begin to bloom, when warm breezes blow over spaded flower beds, and gardens, like women, seem to be primping for summer's festivities. Through the slats of the arbor and all around beyond, she could see the river flowing through the meadows, tracing sinuous, wandering curves on their grassy surface. The evening mist was seeping in among the leafless poplars, blurring their outlines with a purple tint that was paler and more transparent than a curtain of filmy gauze caught on their branches. Cattle were walking in the distance, but neither their lowing nor the sound of their hooves could be heard; and the bell continued to ring, filling the air with its peaceful lament.

As Emma listened to its steady tolling, her mind began to stray among old memories of her childhood and the convent school. She recalled the big altar candlesticks towering above the vases full of flowers and the tabernacle with its little columns. She wished she could again be part of the long line of white veils dotted with black here and there by the stiff cowls of the nuns bowing on their *prie-dieus*. On Sundays during Mass, when she raised her head she would always see the sweet face of the Virgin through the rising, swirling, bluish clouds of incense. She was filled with tender emotion when she thought of it; she felt limp and abandoned, like a wisp of bird down being whirled along in a storm; and unconsciously she began to walk toward the church, ready for any kind of devotion, as long as it would humble her heart and blot out the rest of the world.

In the square she met Lestiboudois on his way back from the church, for in order not to shorten his workday he preferred to interrupt his gardening and then return to it—as a result, he rang the Angelus whenever it suited him. Anyway, by ringing early he notified the boys that it was time for catechism class.

Some of them were already there, playing marbles on the stone slabs in the cemetery. Others, sitting astride the walls, were swinging their legs and mowing with their wooden shoes the tall nettles that grew between the end of the cemetery and the nearest graves. This was the only green spot: all the rest was covered with stones on which there was always a layer of fine dust, despite the sexton's broom.

Boys shod only in their cloth undershoes were running around on the flat stones as though they formed a floor made especially for them, and their shouts could be heard above the tolling of the bell, now growing softer as the oscillations of the thick rope, which hung down from the high bell tower, its lower end dragging on the ground, became shorter and shorter. Swallows twittered as they swiftly sliced through the air overhead, then hurried back to their yellow nests under the eave tiles. At the far end of the church a lamp was burning; it consisted merely of a wick in a hanging glass, and from a distance its light seemed to be only a whitish spot dancing on the surface of the oil. A long sunbeam cut across the nave, making the side aisles and corners look even darker.

"Where's the priest?" Madame Bovary asked a boy who was amusing himself by shaking the turnstile in its loose socket.

"He'll be here before long," he answered.

Just then the door of the presbytery creaked open and Father Bournisien appeared; the boys fled helter-skelter into the church.

"The brats!" he muttered. "They're always the same!" He picked up a tattered catechism which he had just bumped with his toe. "No respect for anything!

When he saw Madame Bovary he said, "Excuse me, I didn't recognize you at first." He stuffed the catechism into his pocket and stood still, swinging the heavy key to the sacristy between two fingers.

The glow of the setting sun struck him full in the face and gave a lighter tinge to his woolen cassock, which was shiny at the elbows and frayed at the hem. Grease spots and snuff stains followed the row of little buttons on his broad chest; they became more numerous below his neckband, on which abundant folds of ruddy skin rested. This skin was sprinkled with yellow splotches only partially visible among his stiff, graying whiskers. He had just finished his dinner and he was breathing heavily.

"How are you?" he went on.

"Not well at all," replied Emma. "I'm suffering."

"So am I," said the priest. "These first hot days make you feel terribly faint, don't they? But there's nothing to be done about it. After all, we're born to suffer, as Saint Paul says. . . . But what does your husband think about your condition?"

"Oh, him!" she said with a scornful gesture.

"What!" exclaimed the priest, taken aback. "Hasn't he prescribed anything for you?"

"It's not earthly remedies I need!" said Emma.

But the priest kept glancing into the church, where the kneeling boys were shoving each other with their shoulders and falling down like lead soldiers.

"I'd like to know . . ." she went on.

"Just you wait, Riboudet!" he shouted angrily. "I'll box your ears, you good-for-nothing rascal!"

Then he turned back to Emma and explained, "That's the son of Boudet the carpenter; his parents are well off and they let him do as he pleases. He'd learn fast if he wanted to, though, because he's a bright boy. Sometimes, just for fun, I call him Riboudet, like that hill you go over on the way to Maromme, and sometimes I say '*mon Riboudet*.' Ha! Ha! It sounds like the name of the hill: Mont-Riboudet! The other day I told my little joke to the bishop and he laughed . . . he was kind enough to laugh. . . . And how's Monsieur Bovary these days?"

She seemed not to have heard. He went on: "Still as busy as ever, I suppose. I'm sure he and I are the two busiest people in the parish. The only difference," he added with a heavy laugh, "is that he takes care of bodies and I take care of souls!"

She looked at him beseechingly and said, "Yes . . . you relieve all kinds of suffering."

"Oh, don't talk to me about that, Madame Bovary! Why, just this morning I had to go to Bas-Diauville for a sick cow—they thought someone had cast a spell on her. For some reason, all their cows . . . Excuse me a minute. Longuemarre! Boudet! What's wrong with you, anyway? Stop it!"

And he ran into the church.

Some of the boys were crowding around the high lectern, climbing on the cantor's stool and opening the missal; others were stealthily approaching the confessional, about to venture inside it. The priest suddenly burst upon them and dealt out slaps all around. Seizing them by the coat collar, he lifted them into the air and then set them down on their knees on the stone floor of the choir, pushing hard, as though he wanted to plant them there.

"Yes," he said when he came back to Emma, unfolding his big calico handkerchief as he held one corner of it between his teeth, "farmers certainly have their troubles!"

"They're not the only ones," she replied.

"Of course not! Workmen in the cities, for example."

"I didn't mean them . . ."

"Oh, I've been to a few cities, and while I was there I knew poor mothers, virtuous women, almost saints, believe me, who didn't have enough bread to eat."

"I was thinking of women who have enough bread, father," said Emma, the corners of her mouth twisting as she spoke, "but who don't have—"

"Any firewood for winter?" asked the priest.

"What does that matter?"

"What do you mean, what does that matter? It seems to me that if you're warm, well fed . . . because, after all . . ."

"Oh, dear God!" sighed Emma.

"Are you feeling ill?" he asked, stepping forward with a worried look on his face. "Have you eaten something that didn't agree with you? You'd better go home, Madame Bovary, and drink a cup of tea; that will make you feel better. Or a glass of water with a little brown sugar in it."

"Why?"

She looked like someone awakening from a dream.

"You were rubbing your forehead with your hand. I thought you were feeling faint." Then, changing his mind, he said, "Let's see now, weren't you asking me something? What was it? I can't remember."

"I? Oh, nothing . . . nothing . . ." said Emma.

And her eyes, which had been glancing around her, slowly settled on the old man in the cassock. They looked at each other, face to face, without speaking.

"Well, Madame Bovary," he said at length, "I'm sorry, but my duty comes first, you know: I have to go deal with my boys. It'll be time for their First Communion before long, and I'm afraid it may come too soon for some of them! That's why I'll keep them for an extra hour every Wednesday after Ascension. Poor children! It's never too early to direct their feet in the paths of the Lord, as He Himself told us to do through the mouth of His divine Son. . . . I hope you'll be feeling better, madame. Remember me to your husband."

And he walked into the church, genuflecting in the doorway.

Emma saw him disappear between two rows of pews, walking heavily, his head slightly tilted to one side, his half-open hand held palm outward.

She turned around stiffly, like a statue on a pivot, and headed back toward her house. But behind her she could still hear the booming voice of the priest and the lighter voices of the children:

"Are you a Christian?"

"Yes, I am a Christian."

"What is a Christian?"

"A person who, having been baptized . . . baptized . . . baptized . . ."

She climbed the stairs, clutching the rail, and when she was in her room she sank limply into an armchair.

The whitish light coming in through the windowpanes wavered as it slowly died away. The furniture, standing in its usual place, seemed somehow more motionless, and lost in the shadows as in an ocean of darkness. There was no fire in the fireplace, the clock was still ticking, and Emma felt vaguely amazed that all those things should be so calm when there was such turmoil inside her. Then she saw little

Berthe between the window and the sewing table, tottering in her knitted shoes as she tried to approach her mother and take hold of her apron strings.

"Leave me alone!" said Emma, pushing her away.

The little girl soon came back, closer still; leaning her arms on her mother's knees, she looked up at her with her big blue eyes while a stream of clear saliva flowed from her lip to the silk apron.

"Leave me alone!" Emma repeated angrily.

The look on her face frightened the child and she began to shriek.

"I told you to leave me alone!" said Emma, shoving her away with her elbow.

Berthe fell at the foot of the dresser, cutting her cheek on one of its brass ornaments. She began to bleed; Madame Bovary rushed over to pick her up, broke the bell cord and called the maid at the top of her lungs. She was about to begin reproaching herself bitterly when Charles appeared. It was dinnertime and he had just come home.

"Look at this, darling," said Emma in a steady voice. "The baby fell down and hurt herself while she was playing."

Charles reassured her: it was nothing serious. He went off to get some adhesive plaster.

Madame Bovary did not come down to the parlor: she insisted on staying with her child. As she watched her sleeping, the last of her anxiety gradually wore off, and she felt that she had been stupid and oversensitive to let such a small matter upset her. Berthe had stopped sobbing. The cotton blanket was now rising and falling almost imperceptibly with her breathing. Big tears had gathered at the corners of her half-closed eyelids; her pupils, pale and deep-set, could be seen through her lashes; the skin of her cheek was drawn taut diagonally by the adhesive stuck to it.

"It's amazing how ugly that child is!" thought Emma.

At eleven o'clock, when Charles returned from the pharmacy, where he had gone after dinner to take back the diachylon that was left over, he found his wife standing beside the cradle.

"It's nothing at all, believe me!" he said, kissing her on the forehead. "Don't worry about it, darling: you'll make yourself ill!"

He had stayed with the apothecary a long time. Although he did not seem terribly upset, Monsieur Homais had made great efforts to cheer him up, to "raise his morale." Then they had talked of the various dangers threatening children, and of the carelessness of servants. Madame Homais certainly knew something about *that*, for she still bore on her chest the scars left by a panful of burning coals which a cook had dropped inside her smock when she was a little girl. That was why she and her husband took all sorts of precautions. Their knives were never sharpened, their floors were never waxed. There were iron grilles on the windows and strong bars across the fireplaces. Despite their independence, the Homais children could not make a move without someone behind them to watch them; their father stuffed them with cough syrups at the slightest sign of a cold, and they were all mercilessly made to wear padded caps until they were over four years old. This, it is true, was one of Madame Homais' manias; her husband was secretly worried about it, fearing that such pressure might have a bad effect on the intellectual organs, and he sometimes went so far as to say, "Are you trying to make them into Caribs or Botocudos?"

Charles, meanwhile, had tried several times to break off the conversation. "There's something I want to talk to you about," he had whispered in the clerk's ear.

Finally Léon had begun to walk down the stairs ahead of him. "Does he suspect something?" he wondered. His heart pounded and his mind was flooded with conjectures.

After closing the door behind him, Charles asked him to find out in Rouen how much a good daguerreotype would cost. He had thoughtfully decided to surprise his wife with a sentimental gift: a portrait of himself in his black tail coat. But first he wanted to "know what to expect." It shouldn't be too much trouble for Monsieur Léon to make a few inquiries, since he went into Rouen nearly every week.

What was the purpose of these trips? Monsieur Homais suspected that he was "sowing a few wild oats," carrying on some sort of amorous intrigue. But he was mistaken: Léon was not involved in a love affair. He was more melancholy than ever, as Madame Lefrançois saw clearly from the amount of food he now left on his plate. To find out what was behind it, she questioned the tax collector: Binet replied gruffly that he "wasn't being paid by the police."

His table companion did seem extremely odd to him, however, for Léon often leaned back in his chair, stretched out his arms and complained vaguely about life.

"That's because you don't have enough recreation," said the tax collector.

"What would you suggest?"

"If I were you, I'd get a lathe."

"But I wouldn't know how to use it," answered the clerk.

"That's true," said Binet, stroking his chin with an air of mingled disdain and satisfaction.

Léon was tired of loving without having anything to show for it; and then he was beginning to feel that dejection which comes from a routine life when there is no interest to guide it or hope to sustain it. He was so bored with Yonville that the sight of certain people and certain houses irritated him almost to the breaking point; and the pharmacist, good-natured though he might be, was becoming completely unbearable to him. And yet the prospect of a new situation frightened him as much as it delighted him.

This apprehension soon turned to impatience, and Paris beckoned to him from afar with the fanfare of its masked balls and the laughter of its wanton girls. Since he was supposed to finish his law studies there, why couldn't he leave right away? What was to stop him? He began to make inner preparations, mapping out his new life in advance. He furnished an apartment for himself, in his imagination. He would lead an artist's life! He would take guitar lessons! He would wear a dressing gown, a Basque beret, blue velvet slippers! And already he admired his mantelpiece with two crossed fencing foils above it, surmounted by a skull and the guitar.

The difficulty lay in getting his mother's consent, although no request could have been more reasonable. Even his employer urged him to work for a while in another office where he could broaden his experience. Adopting a middle course, therefore, he looked for a position as second clerk in some office in Rouen, found nothing and finally wrote his mother a long, detailed letter in which he set forth his reasons for wanting to go to live in Paris immediately. She consented.

He did not hurry. Every day for a month, Hivert carried trunks, suitcases and packages for him from Yonville to Rouen, from Rouen to Yonville, and when Léon had restocked his wardrobe, had his three armchairs reupholstered, bought himself a supply of foulards—in short, when he had made more preparations than would have been necessary for a trip around the world—he still kept putting off his departure from one week to the next, until at last he received a second letter from his mother urging him to leave, since he wanted to take his examination before the beginning of summer vacation.

When the time came for farewell embraces, Madame Homais wept and Justin sobbed; Homais, being a strong man, concealed his emotion and insisted on carrying his friend's overcoat to the house of the notary, who was to take Léon to Rouen in his gig.

Léon just had time to say good-by to Monsieur Bovary. When he reached the top of the stairs he was so breathless that he had to stop for a moment. Madame Bovary stood up quickly when he walked in.

"Here I am again," said Léon.

"I was sure you'd come!"

She bit her lip, and blood rushed under her skin, turning it pink from the roots of her hair to the edge of her collar. She remained standing, leaning her shoulder against the wooden paneling of the wall.

"Monsieur isn't here?" he asked.

"He's out."

She repeated: "He's out."

There was a silence. They looked at each other, and their thoughts, united in a single surge of anguish, clung together like two palpitating bosoms.

"I'd like to kiss Berthe good-by," said Léon.

Emma went down a few steps and called Félicité.

He quickly glanced around at the walls, the shelves, the fireplace, as though to take in everything and carry it away with him.

She came back, and the maid brought in Berthe, who was swinging a pinwheel upside down on a string.

Léon kissed her several times on the neck. "Good-by, little girl! Good-by, little darling, good-by!" And he handed her back to her mother.

"Take her away," said Emma.

They were left alone.

With her back to him, she stood pressing her face against a windowpane; Léon was holding his cap in his hand and softly tapping his thigh with it.

"It's going to rain," said Emma.

"I have a coat," he answered.

"Ah!"

She turned toward him a little, her face lowered. The light gleamed on her forehead as on a marble statue, down to her arched eyebrows, and it was impossible to tell what she was looking at on the horizon, or what she was thinking deep inside herself.

"Well, good-by!" she sighed. She looked up abruptly. "Yes, good-by. . . . Go now!"

They moved toward each other. He held out his hand; she hesitated.

"All right, we'll shake hands, English style," she said with a forced laugh, abandoning her hand to his.

He felt it between his fingers, and the very essence of his being seemed to flow down into that moist palm.

Then he opened his hand; their eyes met once again and he left.

When he was under the market shed he stopped and hid behind a pillar to take one last look at the white house with its four green jalousies. He thought he saw a shadow behind the bedroom window, but the curtain, released from its hook as though of its own accord, slowly began to move its long oblique folds, then suddenly spread out and remained as straight and motionless as a plaster wall. Léon ran away.

He saw his employer's gig on the road in the distance, with a man wearing an apron beside it, holding the horse. Homais and Monsieur Guillaumin were chatting together. They were waiting for him.

"Embrace me," said the apothecary with tears in his eyes. "Here's your overcoat, my dear friend, put it on if you get chilly. Take care of yourself! Don't wear yourself out!"

"Come on, Léon, climb in," said the notary.

Homais leaned over the mudguard and, in a voice broken by sobs, uttered these sad words: "Have a good trip!"

"Good-by," said Monsieur Guillaumin. "We're off!"

They left, and Homais went home.

Madame Bovary had opened the window facing the garden and was now looking out at the clouds.

They were gathering in the west, in the direction of Rouen, swiftly rolling in black spirals with enormous sunbeams emerging from them in back, like the golden arrows of a hanging trophy, while the rest of the sky was empty and as white as porcelain. But a gust of wind bent the poplars and suddenly rain was pattering on the green leaves. Then the sun came out again, chickens cackled, sparrows fluttered their wings in the wet bushes and little streams of water flowing from puddles in the gravel carried away the pink flowers of an acacia.

"Oh, he must be far away by now!" she thought.

Monsieur Homais paid his usual visit at six-thirty, during dinner.

"Well, we've sent our young man off to the big city, haven't we?" he said as he sat down.

"I suppose so," replied the doctor. Then, turning in his chair, he asked, "What's new at your house?"

"Nothing much—just that my wife was a little upset this afternoon. You know how women are: the slightest little thing gets them all stirred up, especially my wife! There's no use complaining about it, though, because their nervous system is much more delicate than ours."

"Poor Léon!" said Charles. "How will he get along in Paris? . . . Do you think he'll get used to living there?"

Madame Bovary sighed.

"Don't worry about him!" said the pharmacist, clicking his tongue. "Fancy meals in restaurants, masked balls, champagne—he'll have plenty of things like that to keep him busy, believe me!"

"I don't think he'll let himself be corrupted," objected Bovary.

"Neither do I," Monsieur Homais said quickly, "although he *will* have to go along with the others if he doesn't want them to think he's a Jesuit. You can't imagine what kind of a life those bohemians lead in the Latin Quarter, with their actresses! And students are highly regarded in Paris. If they have any social graces at all, they're admitted into the very best circles, and there are even some ladies in the Faubourg Saint-Germain that fall in love with them, which gives them a chance to make a very good marriage."

"But," said the doctor, "I'm afraid that in Paris he may—"

"You're right," interrupted the apothecary. "That's the other side of the coin! You've got to keep your hand on your watch pocket every minute there! Let's say you happen to be in a park; a man comes up to you: he's well dressed, he may even be wearing a decoration, he looks as though he might be a diplomat. He says something to you and you get into a conversation with him. He's very friendly; he offers you a pinch of snuff or picks up your hat for you. Then he gets even friendlier: he takes you to a café, invites you to his country house, gets you a little drunk and introduces you to all sorts of people—and nine times out of ten it's to steal your money or get you mixed up in some kind of underhanded business."

"That's true," said Charles, "but I was mainly thinking about diseases—typhoid fever, for example; it often attacks students from the provinces."

Emma started.

"That's because of the change of diet," said the pharmacist. "It upsets the whole system. And then there's the Paris water! Sooner or later your blood gets overheated by the things they serve in restaurants, all those spicy foods. I'd rather have a good stew any day, no matter what some people say. I've always liked home cooking better than anything else: it's more wholesome. That's why I took my meals in a boarding house when I was studying pharmacy in Rouen; I ate with the teachers."

And he went on expounding his general opinions and personal preferences until Justin came in to tell him someone wanted him to prepare some eggnog.

"Never a moment's peace!" he cried out. "Always slaving away! I can't leave the shop for a minute. I have to keep sweating blood, like a plow horse! What drudgery!"

When he was at the door he asked, "By the way, have you heard the news?"

"What news?"

"It's quite probable," said Homais, raising his eyebrows and taking on a deeply serious expression, "that the agricultural fair of the department of the Seine-Inférieure will be held at Yonville-l'Abbaye this year. At least that's the rumor. There was something about it in this morning's paper. It will be extremely important for our district if it happens! But we'll talk about it later. I can find my way, thank you: Justin has the lantern."

VII

The next day was a gloomy one for Emma. Everything seemed shrouded in a kind of vague, floating black atmosphere, and sorrow sank into her soul, moaning softly like the winter wind in an abandoned castle. She was oppressed by the brooding melancholy that arises from the thought of things that will not return, by the lassitude that follows every irrevocable action, by the pain resulting from the interruption of any established habit or the abrupt cessation of a prolonged vibration.

She now felt the same dull depression, the same numb despair that she had felt after her return from La Vaubyessard, while the music of the quadrilles was still whirling in her head. Léon now seemed taller, handsomer, more charming, less distinct; although he was separated from her, he had not left her: he was still there, and everything in the house seemed to retain his shadow. She could not take her eyes from the carpet he had walked on, the empty chairs he had sat in. The river was still flowing, still rippling gently against the slippery bank. They had walked along it many times, listening to that same murmur of the water over the moss-covered stones. How beautiful the sunshine had been! And those wonderful afternoons they had spent alone together in the shade at the end of the garden! He had read aloud to her, bareheaded, sitting on a wooden stool, while the cool wind from the meadows fluttered the pages of the book and the nasturtiums in the arbor. . . . And now he was gone, her only pleasure in life, her only possible hope of happiness! Why hadn't she seized that happiness when it offered itself to her? And when she saw it slipping away from her, why hadn't she clutched it with both hands, begged it on her knees to stay? She cursed herself for not having surrendered to her love for Léon; she thirsted for his lips. She suddenly longed to run after him, to throw herself in his arms and say to him, "Here I am: I'm yours!" But she was discouraged in advance by the difficulties of such an action, and her desire, augmented by regret, became all the more intense.

From then on, this memory of Léon stood at the center of her boredom, crackling and glowing there like a traveler's campfire abandoned in the snow of a Russian steppe. She hurried toward it, pressed up against it, carefully stirred the dying embers, looked all around her for anything that might make the flames burn more brightly. Distant memories and present realities, genuine feelings and flights of imagination, her gradually withering sensual desires, her plans for happiness that rattled like dead branches in the wind, her sterile virtue, her blighted hopes, the litter of her domestic life—she seized on everything and used it as fuel with which to warm her grief.

Nevertheless the flames died down, whether because the supply of fuel became exhausted or because it was piled on too thickly. Little by little, love was extinguished by absence, regret was smothered by routine; and the fiery glow that reddened her pale sky grew dimmer and gradually faded away. In the growing torpor of her mind she even mistook her aversion to her husband for a yearning that was drawing her toward her lover, the hot breath of hatred for a rekindling of love. But the stormy wind continued to blow until her passion had burnt itself to ashes, and since no help came and no sun appeared, total darkness and horrible, piercing cold closed in all around her.

Then the bad days of Tostes began all over again. She considered herself much more unhappy now, for she had experienced grief and knew it would never end.

A woman who had imposed such great sacrifices on herself certainly had a right to indulge in a few whims. She bought herself a Gothic *prie-dieu;* she spent fourteen francs in one month on lemons with which to bleach her fingernails; she sent for a blue cashmere dress from Rouen; she bought the finest scarf in Lheureux's shop. She tied it around her waist over her dressing gown and, in this costume, she closed the shutters and lay on the sofa with a book in her hand.

She often rearranged her hair: she wore it Chinese style, in soft curls and in braids; she parted it on one side and turned it under, like a man's.

She decided to learn Italian; she bought dictionaries, a grammar and a supply of white paper. She tried reading serious books: history and philosophy. Sometimes at night Charles would wake up with a start, thinking someone had come to call him to a patient's bedside. "I'm coming," he would stammer, and it would be only the sound of the match that Emma was striking to light her lamp. But her books were like the pieces of embroidery which she put away in the cupboard almost as soon as they were begun: she would read a little in each one, give it up and go on to another one.

She had spells during which it would have been easy to push her to extremes. One day she maintained that she felt like drinking half a glass of brandy; when Charles expressed disbelief and foolishly dared her, she drained the glass to the bottom.

Despite her "flightiness" (as the ladies of Yonville described it), Emma did not seem happy; at the corners of her mouth there was usually that stiff contraction which marks the faces of old maids and men who have seen their ambitions destroyed. She was pale all over, white as a sheet; the skin of her nose was pinched around the nostrils and her eyes stared vaguely. When she discovered three gray hairs at her temples she began to talk about growing old.

She often had dizzy spells. One day she even spat blood, and when Charles made a great fuss over her, showing his anxiety, she said to him, "Oh, what's the difference?"

Charles shut himself in his consulting room, put his elbows on his desk and wept, sitting in his office armchair beneath the phrenological head.

Then he wrote his mother a letter asking her to come, and they had long discussions about Emma.

What should they decide? What was to be done, since she refused all treatment?

"Do you know what your wife needs?" said the elder Madame Bovary. "She needs hard work, with her hands! If she had to work for a living, like so many other people, she wouldn't have those vapors; they come from the silly ideas she fills her head with, and the idle life she leads."

"But she's busy a good part of the time already," said Charles.

"Oh, busy! Busy doing what? Reading novels and other bad books that are against religion and make fun of priests with quotations from Voltaire! It can lead to all kinds of things, my son—a person who isn't religious always comes to a bad end."

It was therefore decided to keep Emma from reading novels. It would probably not be an easy thing to do. The good lady agreed to take care of it herself: she would go to see the owner of the lending library when she passed through Rouen and tell him Emma was canceling her subscription. And wouldn't they have a right to go to the police if he refused to stop spreading his poison?

Emma and her mother-in-law bade each other a curt farewell. During the three weeks they had been together, they had not exchanged four words apart from routine greetings and inquiries at mealtime and bedtime.

The elder Madame Bovary left on a Wednesday, the regular market-day in Yonville.

From early morning a line of uptilted carts with their shafts in the air stretched along the square in front of the houses between the church and the inn. On the other side there were canvas booths in which cotton goods, woolen blankets and stockings were sold, along with horse halters and bundles of blue ribbon whose ends fluttered in the wind. Heavy hardware was spread out on the ground between pyramids of eggs and baskets of cheese from which sticky straw protruded; beside the agricultural machines, hens were clucking in flat cages and sticking their heads between the bars. The crowd, gathering in one spot and refusing to move, sometimes threatened to break the front window of the pharmacy. The shop was always full on Wednesdays; people pushed their way into it, less to buy medicine than to consult Monsieur Homais, for he had a brilliant reputation in the surrounding villages. The country folk were all fascinated by his robust self-assurance. They regarded him as a greater doctor than all the doctors.

Emma was leaning out her window, as she often did (in the provinces windows replace theaters and promenades), amusing herself by watching the herd of yokels, when she caught sight of a gentleman in a green velvet frock coat. His hands were covered with yellow gloves, even though he was wearing heavy gaiters, and he was coming toward the doctor's house, followed by a peasant who looked down at the ground as he walked along with a thoughtful expression on his face.

"May I see Monsieur?" he asked Justin, who was chatting in the doorway with Félicité. Taking him for a servant of the house, he added, "Tell him Monsieur Rodolphe Boulanger de la Huchette is here."

It was not out of pride in his estate that he added "de la Huchette" to his name, but simply to indicate more clearly who he was. La Huchette was an estate near Yonville; he had recently bought the château and two farms which he managed personally, though not too seriously. He was a bachelor and was rumored to have "an income of at least fifteen thousand francs a year!"

Charles came into the parlor. Monsieur Boulanger introduced his man, who wanted to be bled because he "felt prickly all over."

"It'll clean me out inside," he objected to all arguments.

So Bovary told the maid to bring in a bandage and a basin, which he asked Justin to hold. Then he said to the peasant, who was already pale, "Don't be afraid."

"I'm all right," he replied. "Go ahead."

And he held out his thick arm with an air of bravado. At the prick of the lancet the blood spurted out and splattered against the mirror.

"Hold the basin closer!" cried Charles.

"Look at the way it comes out!" exclaimed the peasant. "Like a little fountain! My blood is really red! That's a good sign, isn't it?"

"Sometimes they don't feel anything at first," said the *officier de santé,* "then they pass out all at once, especially husky people like this man."

At these words the peasant dropped the lancet case he had been toying with. His shoulders jerked, striking the back of his chair and making it creak. His hat fell to the floor.

"I was expecting that," said Bovary, pressing his finger to the vein.

The basin began to shake in Justin's hands; his knees wobbled and he turned pale.

"Emma! Emma!" cried Charles.

She ran down the stairs.

"Get some vinegar!" he said. "Good God! Two at once!"

And in his excitement he had trouble applying the compress.

"It's nothing," said Monsieur Boulanger as he held Justin in his arms. He set him down on the table, leaning his back against the wall.

Madame Bovary began to take off the boy's tie. There was a knot in the laces of his shirt; she moved her light fingers around his neck for a few moments, then she poured some vinegar on her batiste handkerchief, patted his temples with it and blew on them gently.

The peasant revived, but Justin was still unconscious; his pupils had sunk into the whites of his eyes like blue flowers in milk.

"We'd better hide this from him," said Charles.

Madame Bovary took the basin and put it under the table. As she bent down, her dress—a long-waisted, full-skirted yellow summer dress with four flounces—flared out around her on the floor; and as she put out her hands to steady herself, the billowing cloth settled in various places, following the curves of her body. Then she brought in a pitcher of water. She was dissolving some lumps of sugar when the pharmacist arrived. The maid had gone off to get him during the commotion. When he saw his apprentice with his eyes open he began to breathe more easily; then he walked around him and looked him up and down.

"Idiot!" he said. "Stupid little idiot! After all, a bloodletting's a horrible thing to see, isn't it? And to think that he's usually a brave boy who's not afraid of anything! Why, I've seen him climb after nuts like a squirrel, all the way to the top of the tallest trees! Go on, say something, brag about your courage! You'll make a fine pharmacist some day! You may be called into court to give important testimony before the judges, and if you can't keep your self-control, talk intelligently and act like a man, you'll make an utter fool of yourself!"

Justin made no reply. The apothecary went on: "Who asked you to come here, anyway? You're always bothering Monsieur and Madame Bovary! And besides, I need you on Wednesdays more than any other day. There are at least twenty people in the shop right now. I left everything because I was worried about you. Go on, hurry back! Wait for me there, and keep an eye on the jars."

After Justin had straightened his clothes and left, they talked a little about fainting. It had never happened to Madame Bovary.

"That's very unusual for a lady!" said Monsieur Boulanger. "But some men are delicate that way, too. I once saw a second in a duel faint before a shot had been fired, just from the sound of the pistols being loaded."

"The sight of other people's blood doesn't bother me at all," said the apothecary, "but the very idea of my own blood flowing would be enough to make me feel faint if I thought about it too much."

Meanwhile Monsieur Boulanger sent his man away, telling him to stop worrying, now that his whim had been granted. "And his whim has given me the privilege of making your acquaintance," he added, looking at Emma.

Then he put three francs on the corner of the table, bowed casually and left.

He was soon on the other side of the river (he had to cross it to go back to La Huchette), and Emma saw him walking across the meadow beneath the poplars, slowing his pace from time to time, like someone lost in thought.

"She's very nice, that wife of the doctor's!" he was saying to himself. "Beautiful teeth, black eyes, dainty feet, and graceful as a Parisian! How the devil did she get here? How did such a clumsy oaf ever get a wife like her?"

Monsieur Rodolphe Boulanger was thirty-four. He had a brutal temperament and a shrewd intelligence; futhermore, he had had a great many mistresses and was a good judge of women. He had judged this one to be pretty, so he was now thinking about her, and her husband.

"He seems very stupid. She must be tired of him by now. His fingernails are dirty and he hasn't shaved in three days. While he trots off to see his patients, she stays home and darns his socks. And she's bored! She wishes she could live in town and dance the polka every night. Poor woman! She's gasping for love like a carp gasping for water on a kitchen table. A few sweet words and she'd adore me, I'm sure of it! She'd be affectionate, charming. . . . Yes, but how could I get rid of her later?"

The thought of all the bothersome complications involved in such an amorous intrigue reminded him, by contrast, of his mistress, an actress he kept in Rouen. But even her image gave him a feeling of satiation, and he said to himself, "Ah, Madame Bovary is prettier, and much fresher! Virginie is starting to get fat, no doubt about it. She annoys me with her fits of gaiety. And what a mania she has for shrimps!"

The countryside was deserted; he heard nothing around him but the regular swishing of the grass against his shoes and the chirping of the crickets hidden in the distant oatfields. He thought of Emma in the parlor, dressed as he had seen her, and he undressed her.

"Oh, I'll get her!" he exclaimed as he smashed a clod of earth in front of him with his stick.

And he immediately began to consider the strategic aspects of the undertaking. "Where could we meet?" he wondered. "How could we arrange it? We'd always have that brat of hers to contend with, and the maid, the neighbors, her husband—all kinds of things to worry about. . . . No, the whole thing would take too much time."

Then he reconsidered: "But she's got eyes that bore right into you. And that pale complexion! I love pale women!"

By the time he reached the top of the Argueil hill he had made up his mind.

"All I have to do is keep my eyes open for opportunities. I'll stop by to see them every once in a while and send them game and poultry; I'll even ask her husband to bleed me, if I have to. We'll get to be friends, I'll invite them to my house. . . . Aha! The fair will open before long—she'll be there and I'll see her! I'll use the direct approach—it works better than anything else."

VIII

The day of the fair finally came! Early that morning all the inhabitants of the town were standing in their doorways discussing the preparations: the pediment of the town hall had been hung with ivy, a tent had been set up for the banquet in one of the meadows, and in the middle of the square was an old cannon that would signal the arrival of the prefect and the announcement of the names of the prize winners. The Buchy national guard (there was none in Yonville) had come to join forces with the fire brigade, of which Binet was the captain. He was wearing an even higher collar than usual that day, and his chest, squeezed into his tunic, was so stiff and motionless that all the living force of his body seemed to have gone down into his legs, which abruptly rose and fell in cadence, without bending. Since there was a certain rivalry between the tax collector and the colonel, each showed off his talents by drilling his men separately. The spectators saw the red epaulettes and the black breastplates march past alternately. It never seemed to end, it was always beginning again! Never before had there been such a display of pomp! Several of the local citizens had washed their houses the day before; tricolor flags were hanging from half-open windows; all the taverns were full; and in the perfect weather the starched bonnets looked whiter than snow, the gold crosses glittered in the bright sunlight and the multicolored scarves relieved the somber monotony of the frock coats and blue smocks. As the farm women dismounted from their horses they pulled out the big pins that held their dresses tucked up around them to avoid mudstains; their husbands were worried about their hats: to protect them they had covered them with pocket hand-kerchiefs, holding one corner in their teeth.

The crowd was gathering in the main street from both

ends of the village. People were pouring out of alleys, lanes and houses, and knockers could be heard falling against doors as housewives wearing cotton gloves came out to watch the festivities. Especially admired were two long triangular frames covered with lamps that flanked the platform on which the dignitaries were to sit; and against the four columns of the town hall stood four poles, each bearing a greenish banner with an inscription in gold letters. One said "Commerce," another "Agriculture," the third "Industry" and the fourth "Fine Arts."

But the jubilation that shone in all faces seemed to cast a pall of gloom over Madame Lefrançois, the innkeeper. Standing on her kitchen steps, she muttered to herself, "It's so stupid, that canvas shack of theirs! Do they think the prefect is going to enjoy eating in a tent, like a circus acrobat? They claim it's all for the good of the village! In that case, why did they have to bring in a third-rate cook from Neufchâtel? And who's it for? A bunch of cowherds! Good-for-nothing clodhoppers!"

The apothecary walked by. He was wearing a black tail coat, nankeen trousers, beaver shoes and, contrary to his habits, a hat—a low-crowned one.

"Good morning, madame," he said. "Excuse me, I'm in a hurry."

When the fat widow asked him where he was going he replied, "It probably seems odd to you, since I'm usually cooped up in my laboratory like the old man's rat in his cheese."

"What cheese?" asked the innkeeper.

"O, nothing, nothing!" answered Homais. "I just wanted to say, Madame Lefrançois, that I usually stay in my house like a recluse. But today, in view of the circumstances, I must . . ."

"Oh, you're going *there?*" she asked with a disdainful look.

"Oh course I am," replied the apothecary, surprised. "After all, I'm on the advisory committee."

Madame Lefrançois studied him for a few moments and finally said, smiling, "That's different! But what have you got to do with farming? Do you know anything about it?"

"Certainly I know something about it! I'm a pharmacist, which means I'm also a chemist. And the subject of chemistry, Madame Lefrançois, is the reciprocal and molecular action of all natural bodies, so it follows that agriculture lies within its domain! Take the composition of manure, for example, or the fermentation of liquids, the analysis of gases, the influence of noxious vapors—what are such things, I ask you, if not chemistry, pure and simple?"

The innkeeper made no reply. Homais went on: "Do you think a man must personally till the soil and fatten chickens before he can become an agronomist? No. But he must know the composition of the substances involved, he must know about mineral deposits, atmospheric phenomena, the qualities of different kinds of soil, minerals and water, the density and capillarity of various natural bodies—and all sorts of other things besides! He must have a thorough knowledge of all the principles of hygiene so that he can direct and criticize the construction of farm buildings, the feeding of livestock, the diet of farmhands! And then he must know botany, Madame Lefrançois; be must he able to distinguish all the different plants. Do you know what I mean 'Vhich ones are beneficial and which are harmful, which ones are unproductive and which are nutritive, whether they ought to be weeded out here and planted there, whether some ought to be destroyed and others propagated. In short, he must keep abreast of all the latest developments in science by reading pamphlets and other publications; he must always be on his toes to point out possibilities of improvement. . . ."

Madame Lefrançois had never taken her eyes off the door of the Café Français during the whole time he was speaking. He continued: "Would to God that our farmers were all chemists, or at least that they'd listen more closely to the counsels of science! I recently wrote a long article, a treatise of over seventy-two pages, entitled 'Cider: Its Manufacture and Effects, Followed by a Number of New Observations on the Subject.' I sent it to the Agronomical Society of Rouen and it brought me the honor of becoming one of its members—Agricultural Section, Pomology Division. Now if my article had been made available to the public—"

The apothecary broke off at this point, for it had become obvious to him that Madame Lefrançois' mind was not on what he was saying.

"Just look at them!" she said. "I can't understand it! Why should anyone want to go to a filthy place like that?"

She shrugged her shoulders so vigorously that her sweater was pulled tight over her bosom, then she pointed with both hands to her rival's tavern, from which the sound of singing could be heard.

"Well, he won't be there much longer," she added. "In less than a week he'll be through."

Homais drew back in amazement. She came down three steps and whispered in his ear: "What! Didn't you know? The place is going to be seized and put up for auction this week. It's Lheureux's doing. Tellier finally signed so many notes that he signed himself right out of business."

"What a frightful catastrophe!" cried the apothecary, who always had an appropriate expression ready for any situation imaginable.

Madame Lefrançois proceeded to tell him the story, which she had heard from Théodore, Monsieur Guillaumin's servant. Although she detested Tellier, she condemned Lheureux: he was a whining, groveling hypocrite.

"Look, there he is now, under the market shed," she said. "He's bowing to Madame Bovary. She's wearing a green hat. . . . And she's holding Monsieur Boulanger's arm."

"Madame Bovary!" said Homais. "I'll hurry over and pay my respects to her. She might like to have a seat in the enclosure, under the porch."

And, without listening to Madame Lefrançois as she tried to retain him to give him further details, he strode away with a swift, springy step, smiling and nodding right and left and filling a great deal of space with his long black coattails, which floated in the wind behind him.

Rodolphe had spotted him and quickened his pace, but Madame Bovary was now out of breath, so he slowed down, smiled at her and said bluntly, "I wanted to avoid that fat man—you know, the apothecary."

She nudged him with her elbow.

"What does that mean?" he wondered.

And he watched her out of the corner of his eye as they walked along.

Her profile was so calm that it revealed nothing to him. Her features stood out sharply in the bright sunlight, framed by the oval of her bonnet, whose pale ribbons looked like reed leaves. Her eyes, with their long curving lashes, stared straight ahead; although they were wide open, they appeared to be slightly narrowed, because of the blood pulsing gently beneath the delicate skin of her cheekbones. The light shone through the pink flesh between her nostrils. Her head was tilted to one side, and between her lips he could see the pearly tips of her white teeth.

"Is she laughing at me?" he thought.

But Emma's nudge had been only a warning, for Monsieur Lheureux was walking with them. He spoke to them occasionally, as though trying to begin a conversation.

"What a beautiful day! Everybody's out! The wind is from the east."

Madame Bovary and Rodolphe seldom replied to him, but at their slightest movement he would draw close to them, touch his hat and say, "Beg your pardon?"

When they were in front of the blacksmith's house, instead of following the road as far as the gate, Rodolphe abruptly turned and began to walk along a path, drawing Madame Bovary with him.

"Good-by, Monsieur Lheureux!" he called out. "We'll be seeing you."

"You certainly got rid of him!" she said, laughing.

"Why should we let anyone intrude on our privacy?" he said. "Since I'm lucky enough to be with you today . . ."

Emma blushed. He did not finish his sentence; instead, he began to talk about the good weather and how pleasant it was to walk on the grass, in which a few daisies were growing.

"Look at the pretty daisies," he said. "There are enough of them to tell every girl in the village whether her sweetheart really loves her or not. . . . Should I pick some? What do you think?"

"Are *you* in love?" she asked, coughing a little.

"Ah! Who knows?" replied Rodolphe.

The meadow was beginning to fill up, and housewives were bumping into everyone with their big umbrellas, their baskets and their children. People often had to turn aside to avoid long lines of peasant girls, farm servants wearing blue stockings, flat shoes and silver rings and smelling of milk when they passed nearby. They held each other by the hand as they walked along, forming chains that stretched the entire length of the meadow, from the row of aspens to the banquet tent. It was now time for the judging to begin, and the farmers were filing into a kind of hippodrome marked off by a long rope draped over a series of stakes.

Inside it stood the animals, their noses turned toward the rope, their uneven rumps forming a ragged line. Pigs were lethargically rooting in the ground; calves were lowing; sheep were bleating; cows with their legs folded under them were lying on the grass, slowly chewing their cud and blinking their heavy eyelids at the gnats buzzing around them. Bare-armed teamsters gripped the halters of stallions that kept rearing and neighing loudly in the direction of the mares. The latter remained calm, their manes drooping from their outstretched necks, while their colts rested in their shadows or came up to suckle them from time to time. Now and then, above the long, undulating line of all those closely packed bodies, one could see a white mane rising in the wind like a wave, a pair of sharp horns abruptly thrust upward, or a man's head bobbing as he ran. A hundred yards off to one side, outside the enclosure, there was a big black muzzled bull with an iron ring through his nose, motionless as a bronze statue. A ragged boy was holding him by a rope.

Meanwhile a group of gentlemen were ponderously walking between the two rows, examining each animal and then conferring in low voices. One of them (he seemed to be the most important) occasionally wrote down a few words in a notebook as he walked along. He was the chairman of the board of judges, Monsieur Derozerays de la Panville. When he recognized Rodolphe he quickly stepped forward and said to him with a cordial smile, "Why, Monsieur Boulanger! Have you deserted us?"

Rodolphe assured him he would come in a little while. But when the chairman was gone he said, "No, I won't go: I prefer your company to his."

Although he kept making fun of her, Rodolphe showed the gendarme his blue card so that they could walk around more freely, and sometimes he even stopped in front of some fine specimen. Madame Bovary never showed much interest, however; he noticed this and began to joke about the Yonville ladies and their clothes, then he apologized for the slovenliness of his own. He was dressed with that incongruous mixture of casualness and refinement which the common people regard as evidence of an eccentric life, tumultuous passions, artistic aspirations, and always a certain contempt for social convention, which either fascinates or exasperates them. Thus his batiste shirt with pleated cuffs puffed out from the opening of his gray twill vest each time the wind blew on it, and the bottoms of his broad-striped trousers revealed nankeen ankle-boots vamped with patent leather so shiny that the grass was reflected in it. He trampled horse dung with these boots, his hand in his coat pocket and his straw hat tilted over one ear.

"Besides," he added, "when you live in the country . . ."

"All your efforts are wasted," said Emma.

"Exactly!" replied Rodolphe. "Just think: not one of these good people around us is even capable of appreciating the cut of a coat!"

Then they talked about provincial mediocrity, the lives it smothered and the illusions it destroyed.

"So," said Rodolphe, "I keep sinking deeper and deeper into melancholy. . . ."

"You?" she exclaimed in surprise. "I thought you were very lighthearted!"

"Yes, I give that impression, because I've learned to wear a mask of mockery when I'm with other people. And yet how often the sight of a cemetery in the moonlight has made me wonder whether it wouldn't be better for me to join those who are sleeping there!"

"Oh! And what about your friends? You're forgetting about them."

"My friends? What friends? What makes you think I have any? Who cares about me?"

And he accompanied these last words with a little hiss.

But they had to move apart to make way for a man who came up behind them carrying an enormous pile of chairs. He was so overloaded that they could see only the tips of his wooden shoes and part of his outstretched arms. It was Lestiboudois, the gravedigger: he was renting chairs to the crowd. Full of imagination where his own interests were concerned, he had hit upon this way of making a profit from the fair, and his plan was successful, for he was now being called from all directions at once. The villagers were hot; they almost fought over those straw-bottomed chairs which smelled of incense, and they leaned with a certain veneration against the high backs stained with candlewax.

Madame Bovary took Rodolphe's arm; he went on talking, as though to himself.

"Yes, so many things have passed me by! Always alone! Oh, if only I'd had a goal in life! If only I'd met someone who could give me affection, someone who . . . Oh, I'd have poured out all the energy at my command, I'd have surmounted everything, broken down every obstacle!"

"Still, though," said Emma, "it seems to me you're scarcely to be pitied."

"Really?"

"Yes, because, after all, you're free . . ." She hesitated. ". . . rich . . ."

"Don't make fun of me," he said.

She swore she wasn't making fun of him. Just then there was a loud cannon shot and everyone began to hurry helter-skelter toward the village.

It was a false alarm. The prefect had not arrived, and the judges were in a quandary, not knowing whether to begin the ceremony or go on waiting.

Finally at the far end of the square appeared a big hired landau drawn by two bony horses that were being vigorously whipped by a coachman wearing a white hat. Binet scarcely had time to shout "Fall in!" and the colonel followed suit. Their men ran to their stacked rifles. There was a moment of frantic confusion. Some of them even forgot to button their collars. But the prefect's team seemed to sense the difficulty: the two nags, swaying at the end of their chain, drew up at a slow trot in front of the peristyle of the town hall just as the national guard and the fire brigade were lining up to the beating of a drum.

"Mark time!" cried Binet.

"Halt!" cried the colonel. "Column left, march!"

After a present-arms during which the metal bands of the rifles rattled like a copper cauldron rolling down a flight of stairs, the men all lowered their weapons.

Then the spectators saw a man in a short silver-embroidered coat step out of the carriage. He had a bald forehead, a tuft of hair on the back of his head, a pale complexion and an extremely benign expression. He squinted his large, heavy-lidded eyes to peer at the crowd, raised his pointed nose and curved his sunken lips into a smile. He recognized the mayor by his sash and announced to him that the prefect had been unable to come. He was a prefectorial councilor, he said; then he added a few words of apology. Tuvache replied with profuse courtesy, the councilor confessed his embarrassment and they stood there, face to face with their foreheads almost touching, surrounded by the judges, the municipal council, the notables, the national guard and the crowd. The councilor reiterated his greetings, holding his little three-cornered hat to his chest, while Tuvache, bent like a bow, returned his smiles, stammered, tried to find the proper words, protested his devotion to the monarchy and his appreciation of the honor that was being bestowed on Yonville.

Hippolyte, the stableboy of the inn, came up to take the

coachman's horses by the bridle; then, limping on his club-foot, led them under the porch of the Lion d'Or, where a crowd of peasants gathered to look at the carriage. The drum sounded, the howitzer thundered and the gentlemen filed up on the platform to sit down in the red velvet arm-chairs lent by Madame Tuvache.

These men all looked alike. Their flabby, fair-skinned, slightly sun-tanned faces were the color of sweet cider, and their bushy side whiskers protruded over high, stiff collars held in place by white cravats tied with wide bows. Every vest was of velvet, with a shawl collar; an oval cornelian seal hung from every watch at the end of a long ribbon; and every man sat with his hands on his thighs, carefully keeping apart the legs of his trousers, whose hard-finished cloth shone more brightly than the leather of his heavy shoes.

The ladies of the official group sat behind, under the porch among the columns, while the rest of the crowd was opposite them, either sitting on chairs or standing. Lestiboudois had transferred all the chairs that had been in the meadow and was now running back and forth, bringing new ones from the church; his rental business had caused such great congestion that it was difficult to reach the little staircase leading up to the platform.

"I think," said Monsieur Lheureux, addressing the pharmacist, who was passing by on his way to take his seat, "that they should have put up two Venetian flagpoles, with a string of flags made of some rich, subdued material; it would have been a pretty sight."

"Yes, of course," replied Homais. "But what can you expect? The mayor took everything into his own hands. Poor Tuvache doesn't have much taste; in fact, he's completely lacking in what's known as the esthetic sense."

Meanwhile Rodolphe had taken Madame Bovary up to the second floor of the town hall, into the "meeting room"; since it was empty he had told her they could sit comfortably there and have a good view of the ceremony. He took three of the stools that stood around the oval table, beneath the bust of the monarch, and placed them in front of a window. He and Emma sat down beside each other.

There was a flurry of agitation on the platform, long whispered conversations and consultations. Finally the councilor stood up. By now it was known that he was Monsieur Lieuvain, and his name was repeated from one person to another through the whole crowd. After checking over a few

sheets of paper, holding them close to his eyes to see them
more clearly, he began:

"Gentlemen: I should like, with your permission, before
speaking to you about the object of our meeting today—
and I am sure you will all share my feeling on the matter—
I should like, with your permission, to pay tribute to the
national administration, to the government, to the monarch,
gentlemen, to our sovereign, that beloved king who is not
indifferent to any aspect of public or private welfare and who,
with so wise and firm a hand, guides the chariot of the
State through the constant perils of a stormy sea, maintaining
public respect for peace as well as for war, and for industry,
commerce, agriculture and the fine arts."

"I ought to move back a little," said Rodolphe.

"Why?" asked Emma.

But just then the councilor's voice rose to an extraordinary
pitch. He was declaiming:

"Gone forever, gentlemen, are the days when civil strife
caused blood to flow in our public squares, when the landowner, the businessman, even the worker, closed their eyes
in peaceful slumber at night, trembling for fear they might
be abruptly awakened by the sound of inflammatory tocsins,
when the most subversive doctrines were audaciously under-
mining the foundations . . ."

"Because someone down there might see me," said Rodolphe. "Then I'd have to spend the next two weeks apologizing, and with my bad reputation . . ."

"Oh!" exclaimed Emma. "You're slandering yourself."

"No, no, I have an abominable reputation, really."

"But, gentlemen," continued the councilor, "if I thrust these
dark scenes from my memory and cast my eyes on the present
situation of our glorious fatherland, what do I see? Commerce and the arts are flourishing everywhere; everywhere
new channels of communication, like so many new arteries
in the body of the State, are establishing new contacts within
it; our great manufacturing centers have resumed their
activities; a strengthened religion appeals to every heart; our
ports are full of ships, confidence is being reborn, and France
breathes freely at last!"

"Futhermore," added Rodolphe, "from the point of view
of society I may well deserve it."

"What do you mean?" she asked.

"What! Don't you know there are some souls that are
constantly tormented? They need dreams and action, one

after the other, the purest passions, the most frenzied pleasures, and it leads them to throw themselves into all sorts
of fantasies and follies."

She looked at him as one looks at a traveler who has been
in fabulous lands and said, "We poor women can't even
enjoy that kind of distraction!"

"It's a poor distraction, because there's no happiness in
it."

"But do we ever find happiness?" she asked.

"Yes, sooner or later it comes our way," he answered.

"And that is exactly what you have realized," the councilor
was saying. "You, farmers and country workmen; you,
peaceful pioneers in a great work of civilization; you, men of
progress and morality—you have realized that political storms
are truly even more to be dreaded than the disorders of the
elements!"

"Sooner or later it comes our way," repeated Rodolphe.
"One day, just as we're about to give up hope, it suddenly
appears. Then new horizons open up, and it's as though a
voice had called out, 'Here it is!' You feel a need to tell
a certain person everything about your life, to give him
everything, sacrifice everything to him! You don't have to
explain anything to each other, you guess each other's
thoughts. You've already seen each other in your dreams."
(He was looking at her.) "At last the treasure you sought so
long is there in front of you, gleaming and sparkling. Yet
you still have doubts, you're afraid to believe in it, you're
dazzled, as though you'd suddenly come from darkness into
light."

As he spoke these last words, Rodolphe emphasized them
with pantomime: he passed his hand over his face like a man
who has suddenly been dazed; then he let it fall on Emma's.
She withdrew hers. The councilor was still reading:

"Who could doubt this, gentlemen? Only someone so blind,
so deeply sunk in the prejudices—I am not afraid to use
the word—in the prejudices of another age that he still
misunderstands the spirit of our farming population. Where
can one find more patriotism than in rural areas, more devotion
to the common welfare—in short, more intelligence? And I
am not speaking, gentlemen, of that superficial intelligence
which is nothing but the useless ornament of idle minds; no,
I am speaking of that profound and moderate intelligence
which applies itself above all to the pursuit of useful ends,
thus contributing to the good of all, to public improvement

and the support of the State. Such intelligence is the fruit of respect for law and performance of duty."

"Again!" said Rodolphe. "Duty, always duty! I'm sick of the word! There's always a bunch of old fogeys in flannel vests, pious prigs with footwarmers and rosaries, constantly yelling 'Duty! Duty!' in our ears. Well, here's what duty really means: our duty is to feel what's great and cherish what's beautiful—not to accept the conventions of society and the ignominy it forces on us!"

"Still, though . . ." objected Madame Bovary.

"No! Why preach against the passions? Aren't they the only beautiful thing in this world, the source of heroism, enthusiasm, poetry, music, the arts, everything?"

"Just the same," said Emma, "we have to pay some attention to the opinions of society and follow its moral standards."

"Ah, but there are two moralities!" he replied. "There's the petty, conventional, human morality that's constantly changing; it brays loudly and bustles around on the ground, like that crowd of imbeciles you see down there. But the other morality, the eternal one, is all around us and above us, like the landscape that surrounds us and the blue sky that gives us light."

Monsieur Lieuvain had just wiped his mouth with his pocket handkerchief. He went on:

"Surely it would be pointless, gentlemen, for me to demonstrate to you the usefulness of agriculture. Who is it that provides for our needs? Who is it that maintains our food supply? Is it not the farmer? The farmer, gentlemen, sowing with laborious hand the fertile furrows of our countryside, brings forth the wheat, which, having been ground and reduced to powder by means of ingenious machinery, comes out under the name of flour, and from there it is transported to our cities and speedily delivered to the bakers, who make it into a food for the poor as well as the rich. And is it not the farmer who fattens his abundant flocks in the pastures to provide us with our clothing? For how would we be clothed, how would we be fed, without the farmer? In fact, gentlemen, is there any need to seek so far afield for examples? Who has not reflected on the enormous benefits we derive from that modest fowl, the pride of our barnyards, which gives us soft pillows for our beds, succulent flesh for our tables, and eggs? But I should never finish if I were to enumerate one after the other all the various products which the well-tilled soil lavishes on her children like a generous mother. Here we have the vine, there we have the cider apple, elsewhere we have rapeseed, further on we have cheese; and flax, gentlemen, let us not overlook flax, whose production has considerably increased in recent years, and to which I should particularly like to call your attention."

There was no need for him to call their attention, for every mouth in the crowd was open, as though to drink in his words. Tuvache, sitting beside him, was listening to him wide-eyed; Monsieur Derozerays gently lowered his eyelids from time to time; and further on, the pharmacist, sitting with his son Napoléon between his legs, was holding his cupped hand to his ear in order not to miss a single syllable. The other members of the board of judges were slowly nodding their chins against their vests to express their approval. The fire brigade, at the foot of the platform, were leaning on their bayonets, and Binet stood motionless with his elbows turned outward and his saber pointed upward. He could hear, perhaps, but he was no doubt unable to see anything, for the visor of his helmet came down over his nose. His lieutenant, Monsieur Tuvache's younger son, was wearing a still more voluminous helmet which kept wobbling and revealed the edge of the calico scarf he had wrapped around his head. He smiled beneath it with childish sweetness, and his pale little face, dripping with sweat, wore an expression of pleasure, exhaustion and drowsiness.

The square was packed with people as far as the houses. Spectators were leaning out of every window and standing on every doorstep. Justin, in front of the pharmacy window, seemed transfixed as he contemplated what lay before his eyes. Despite the silence, Monsieur Lieuvain's voice was lost in the air. Only scraps of sentences interrupted by the scraping of chairs could be heard; then suddenly, from behind the audience, an ox would let out a long bellow, or sheep would bleat to one another on the street corners, for the cowherds and shepherds had driven their animals in close, and occasionally a cow would low as she stretched out her tongue for some bit of foliage hanging from her muzzle.

Rodolphe had moved nearer to Emma and was now saying softly and rapidly, "Aren't you disgusted by the way society conspires against us? Is there a single feeling they don't condemn? The noblest instincts and the purest affinities are persecuted and slandered, and if two poor hearts manage to find each other, everything is organized to keep them apart. They'll try anyway, though: they'll beat their wings and call out to each other. And you can be sure of this: sooner or later, in six months or ten years, they'll come together and bring their love to fruition, because fate requires it and they were born for each other."

He was leaning forward with his elbows on his knees; raising his face to Emma's, he looked at her intently from close up. In his eyes she could see little streaks of gold radiating from his black pupils, and she could even smell the fragrance of the pomade that made his hair glisten. She suddenly felt languid; she recalled the viscount who had waltzed with her at La Vaubyessard and whose beard had given off the same odor of vanilla and lemon as Rodolphe's hair; and unconsciously she half closed her eyes so that she could smell it better. But as she did so she leaned back in her chair and saw in the distance, on the furthest horizon, the old stage-coach, the Hirondelle, slowly coming down the Les Leux hill, trailing a long plume of dust behind it. It was in that yellow carriage that Léon had so often come back to her, and it was along that road that he had left her forever! For a moment she thought she saw him at his window on the other side of the square, then everything became confused and clouds passed before her eyes; it seemed to her that she was again whirling in the waltz, beneath the blazing chandeliers, in the viscount's arms . . . and yet she could still smell Rodolphe's hair beside her. The sweetness of the sensation permeated her past desires, and, like grains of sand in a gust of wind, they swirled in the cloud of subtle fragrance that was spreading through her soul. She opened her nostrils wide several times to breathe in the freshness of the ivy twined around the capitals of the columns outside. She took off her gloves and wiped her hands, then she fanned her face with her handkerchief, while above the pounding in her temples she heard the murmur of the crowd and the voice of the councilor intoning his speech.

He was saying:

"Continue! Persevere! Listen to neither the suggestions of routine nor the hasty advice of rash empiricism! Apply yourselves above all to the improvement of the soil, to good fertilizers, to the development of good breeds of horses, cattle, sheep and pigs. May this fair be for you a peaceful arena in which the victor, as he leaves, will shake hands with the vanquished and fraternize with him, hoping that he will do better in the future! And you, venerable servants, humble domestic workers, whose arduous labors had not been taken into consideration by any government up till now, step forward to receive the reward of your silent virtues, and rest assured that henceforth the State has its eyes on you, that it encourages you, that it protects you, that it will honor your just demands and lighten, insofar as it lies within its power, the burden of your painful sacrifices!"

Monsieur Lieuvain now sat down. Monsieur Derozerays stood up and began another speech. His was perhaps not as flowery as the councilor's, but it had the advantage of a more positive style: it combined more specialized knowledge with loftier considerations. Less time was devoted to praising the government and more to discussing religion and agriculture. He brought out the connection between them and showed how they had always worked together in the development of civilization. Rodolphe was talking to Madame Bovary about dreams, presentiments and magnetism. Going back to the infancy of society, the orator depicted the savage times when men lived on acorns in the depths of the forest. Then they had stopped wearing animal skins, put on cloth, dug furrows in the ground and planted vines. Had this really been beneficial to mankind? Did not the discovery involve more disadvantages than advantages? Monsieur Derozerays pondered this question. From magnetism, Rodolphe had gradually come to the subject of affinities, and while the chairman was citing Cincinnatus at his plow, Diocletian planting cabbages and the Chinese emperors beginning the new year by sowing seeds, the young man was explaining to the young woman that the cause of such irresistible attractions lay in some previous existence.

"Take us, for example," he said. "Why have we met? What circumstances brought it about? It must have been because our particular inclinations made us move toward each other across the distance separating us, like two rivers flowing together."

And he took her hand; she did not withdraw it.

"First prize for general excellence of crops," said the chairman.

"When I came to your house this morning, for instance . . ."

"To Monsieur Bizet of Quincampoix."

". . . did I know I'd come here with you?"

"Seventy francs!"

"I tried to make myself leave a hundred times, yet I followed you, I stayed with you . . ."

"Manures!"

". . . just as I'd stay with you tonight, tomorrow, every day, all my life!"

"To Monsieur Caron of Argueil, a gold medal!"

"I've never been so completely captivated by anyone before."

"To Monsieur Bain of Givry-Saint-Martin!"

"I'll take the memory of me with you . . ."

"For a merino ram . . ."

". . . but you'll forget me, I'll have passed through your life like a shadow."

"To Monsieur Belot of Notre-Dame . . ."

"No, it's not true, is it? I *will* have a place in your thoughts, in your life, won't I?"

"For pigs, Monsieur Lehérissé and Monsieur Cullembourg are tied for first place: sixty francs!"

Rodolphe pressed her hand and felt that it was warm and trembling like a captive turtledove struggling to fly away; but, either because she was trying to free it or because she was responding to his pressure, she moved her fingers.

"Oh, thank you!" he cried out. "You're not repulsing me! You're so kind! You realize that I'm yours! Let me see you, let me look at you!"

A puff of wind came through the windows and ruffled the cloth on the table; and down in the square the big bonnets of the peasant women rose like fluttering white butterfly wings.

"For the use of oil cake," continued the chairman. He was hurrying now: "Liquid manure . . . Flax . . . Drainage, long-term leases . . . Domestic service."

Rodolphe had stopped talking. They were looking at each other. A supreme desire made their dry lips quiver; and languidly, without effort, their fingers intertwined.

"Catherine-Nicaise-Elisabeth Leroux, of Sassetot-la-Guerrière, for fifty-four years of service on the same farm, a silver medal—worth twenty-five francs!"

"Where is Catherine Leroux?" asked the councilor.

She did not appear, but voices could be heard whispering:

"Go on!"

"No."

"To the left!"

"Don't be afraid!"

"Oh, she's so stupid!"

"Is she coming or not?" cried Tuvache.

"Yes . . . Here she is!"

"Then tell her to come up here!"

Everyone watched a frightened-looking little old woman climb onto the platform. She seemed to have shriveled up inside her shabby clothes; she was wearing heavy wooden-soled shoes and a long blue apron. Her face, framed by a close-fitting hood without a border, was more wrinkled than a withered apple, and from the sleeves of her red blouse hung two long, knotty hands. They had been so thoroughly encrusted, roughened and hardened by barn dust, washing potash and wool grease that they looked dirty even though she had rinsed them in clear water, and from long years of service they hung half open, as though humbly bearing witness to all the hardships she had endured. Her face was ennobled by a certain monastic rigidity. Her pale eyes were not softened by the slightest hint of sadness or compassion. She had lived so long with animals that she had taken on their mute placidity. This was the first time she had ever been in the midst of such a large crowd and, inwardly ter-rified by the flags, the drums, the gentlemen in black coats and the councilor's decoration, she stood still, not knowing whether to go forward or turn and flee, not understanding why the crowd was urging her on or why the judges were smiling at her. Thus stood half a century of servitude before the beaming bourgeois.

"Step forward, venerable Catherine-Nicaise-Elisabeth Le-roux!" said the councilor, who had taken the list of prize winners from the hands of the chairman. Looking back and forth between the sheet of paper and the old woman, he repeated in a fatherly tone, "Step forward, step forward."

"Are you deaf!" cried Tuvache, leaping up from his chair. And he shouted in her ear: "Fifty-four years of service! A silver medal! Twenty-five francs! It's for you."

She took the medal and stared at it, then a blissful smile spread over her face, and as she walked away she could be heard mumbling, "I'll give it to our priest, so he'll say Masses for me."

"What fanaticism!" exclaimed the pharmacist, leaning toward the notary.

The ceremony was over; the crowd dispersed and, now

that the speeches had all been read, everyone resumed his
rank and everything returned to normal: the masters shouted
crossly at their servants, the servants beat the animals, and
the animals returned to their barns in indolent triumph with
green wreaths between their horns.

Meanwhile the national guard had gone up to the second
floor of the town hall with soft rolls impaled on their
bayonets; and their drummer was carrying a basketful of bottles. Madame Bovary took Rodolphe's arm and he escorted
her home; after they had parted in front of her door, he
went for a stroll in the meadow until it was time for the
banquet to begin.

The feast was long, noisy and badly served; the guests
were so tightly packed that they could scarcely move their
elbows, and the narrow planks that served as benches threatened to break beneath their weight. They ate abundantly,
each making sure he got full value for his contribution. Sweat
streamed down every forehead, and over the table, between
the hanging lamps, hung a whitish vapor, like a river mist
on an autumn morning. Rodolphe, sitting with his back against
the cotton tent, was thinking so hard about Emma that he
heard nothing. Behind him, on the grass, servants were
piling up dirty dishes; the people around him spoke to him
but he did not answer; someone kept refilling his glass and
there was silence in his mind, despite the growing clamor.
He was thinking about the things she had said, and about the
shape of her lips; her face shone in the plaque of each shako
as in a magic mirror; the folds of her dress hung down along
the walls, and days of love-making stretched forth endlessly
into the future.

He saw her again that evening, during the fireworks display,
but she was with her husband, Madame Homais and the
pharmacist. The latter was terribly worried about the danger
of stray rockets, and he often left the others to go and make
a few suggestions to Binet.

The fireworks had been sent to Monsieur Tuvache and in
an excess of caution he had stored them in his cellar. As a
result, the damp powder could scarcely be ignited, and the
main attraction, which was to represent a dragon biting its
own tail, was a total failure. Now and then a poor little
Roman candle would go off and a roar of admiration would
rise from the gaping crowd, mingled with the shrieks of
women who were being tickled in the dark. Emma nestled

silently against Charles's shoulder, raising her head to follow the blazing trail of the rockets across the black sky. Rodolphe looked at her in the light of the glass lamps.

They went out one by one. The stars began to shine more brightly. A few raindrops fell. She tied her scarf over her bare head.

Just then the councilor's carriage drove away from the inn. The coachman, who was drunk, suddenly dozed off, and in the distance the mass of his body could be seen above the hood, between the two lanterns, swaying back and forth with the pitching of the thorough braces.

"Drunkenness ought to be dealt with more severely!" said the apothecary. "I'd like to see a bulletin board put up on the door of the town hall for the special purpose of posting a list of the names of everyone who's been intoxicated by alcohol during the week. It would be useful from a statistical point of view, too, because it would constitute a public record that could . . . Excuse me."

And again he hurried over to the captain.

The latter was on his way home. He would soon be with his lathe again.

"It might be a good idea," Homais said to him, "to send one of your men, or go yourself . . ."

"Leave me alone," replied the tax collector. "Everything's all right!"

"Don't worry," said the apothecary when he came back to his friends, "Monsieur Binet has just assured me that all precautions have been taken. No sparks have fallen. The pumps are full. Let's all go home to bed."

"I could certainly use some sleep," said Madame Homais, who had been yawning considerably. "Just the same, though, we did have a very beautiful day for our celebration."

"Oh, yes, very beautiful!" said Rodolphe softly, with a tender look in his eyes.

They bade each other good night, turned and went their separate ways.

Two days later there was a long article on the fair in the *Fanal de Rouen*. Homais, full of enthusiasm, had written it the following day:

"Why these festoons, these flowers, these garlands? What was the destination of this crowd rushing along like the waves of an angry sea, beneath the torrential rays of the tropical sun pouring its heat upon our furrowed fields?"

Then he spoke about the condition of the peasants. The

government was doing a great deal for them, to be sure, but not enough! "Let not your spirits falter!" he exhorted its officials. "Countless reforms are necessary: let us carry them out!" Then, turning to the arrival of the councilor, he did not forget "the warlike air of our militia," or "our most vivacious village maidens," or the bald-headed old men, "veritable patriarchs, some of whom, survivors of our immortal phalanxes, felt their hearts beat strongly once again to the virile sound of the drums." He placed his own name high on the list of judges, and even reminded his readers in a footnote that Monsieur Homais, the pharmacist, had sent an article on cider to the Agronomical Society. When he came to the distribution of the prizes he depicted the joy of the winners in lyrical phrases: "Father embraced son, brother embraced brother, husband embraced wife. More than one man proudly displayed his humble medal, and, on returning home to his worthy helpmeet, no doubt hung it on the modest wall of his cottage, weeping tears of joy.

"At six o'clock the leading figures in the celebration gathered at a banquet held in Monsieur Liégeard's pasture. The greatest cordiality reigned throughout. Toasts were proposed by the following: Monsieur Lieuvain: 'To the king'; Monsieur Tuvache: 'To the prefect'; Monsieur Derozerays: 'To agriculture'; Monsieur Homais: 'To those twin sisters, industry and the fine arts'; Monsieur Leplichey: 'To progress.' Later in the evening a brilliant fireworks display suddenly illuminated the heavens. It was a veritable kaleidoscope, a true stage-setting for an opera, and for a few brief moments it was as though our little locality had been transported into the midst of a dream of the Arabian Nights.

"Let us mention that this family reunion was not marred by a single regrettable incident."

And he added:

"Only the absence of the clergy was noted. The sacristies no doubt have a different conception of progress. As you wish, gentlemen of Loyola!"

Six weeks went by. Rodolphe did not come back. One evening he finally appeared.

The day after the fair he had said to himself, "I mustn't go back right away. That would be a mistake." And at the end of the week he had gone off on a hunting trip.

When he returned he thought it was too late, then he reasoned thus: "But if she fell in love with me right from the start, by now her impatience to see me again must have made her love me even more. So let's go back into action!"

And he knew he was right when he saw Emma turn pale as he walked into the parlor.

She was alone. It was growing dark. The little muslin curtains over the windowpanes deepened the twilight, and a sunbeam reflected from the gilded barometer was blazing in the mirror through the open spaces of the coral.

Rodolphe remained standing; Emma scarcely replied to his first formal remarks.

"Things have been pretty hectic for me," he said. "I was ill."

"Seriously ill?" she cried.

"No, not really," he said, sitting down beside her on a stool. "It was just that I didn't want to come back."

"Why not?"

"Can't you guess?"

He looked at her again, but this time there was such violent emotion in his eyes that she blushed and lowered her head.

"Emma . . ."

"Monsieur!" she said, drawing back a little.

"Ah, you see: I was right not to want to come back!" he said in a melancholy tone. "I spoke your name without meaning to, because my heart's filled with it, and you forbade me to say it! Madame Bovary! Everyone calls you that! And it's not even your name—it's someone else's . . . someone else's!" He buried his face in his hands. "Yes, I think about you all the time! The thought of you drives me mad. . . . Oh, forgive me! I'll leave . . . Good-by . . . I'll go away, so far away that you'll never hear of me again! . . . And yet . . . today . . . I don't know what force it was that drove me to you. We can't struggle against fate! We can't resist the smile of an angel! When something beautiful, charming and adorable comes our way, we give in to its power!"

It was the first time Emma had ever heard such things said to her, and her pride, like someone relaxing in a steam bath, stretched languidly and thoroughly in the warmth of his words.

"I didn't come here, I didn't see you," he went on, "but I often looked at the things around you. At night, every night, I got up and came to look at your house, at its roof shining in the moonlight, the trees in the garden swaying outside your window, and a little lamp, just a glimmer, shining through the windowpanes in the dark. Oh, you didn't know a poor, unhappy man was standing there, so near to you and yet so far!"

She turned to him with a sob and said, "Oh, you're so good!"

"No, I love you, that's all! You don't doubt it, do you? Tell me you know it! A word, just one word!"

And Rodolphe was sliding almost imperceptibly from the stool to the floor when he heard the sound of wooden soles in the kitchen and noticed that the parlor door was open.

"I'd be so grateful to you," he said, sitting back down on the stool, "if you'd satisfy a whim of mine!"

His whim was to be shown through the house: he wanted to know what it was like. Madame Bovary saw no reason to refuse, and they were both standing up when Charles came in.

"Good evening, doctor," said Rodolphe.

Flattered by this unexpected title, the *officier de santé* replied with profuse and obsequious courtesy, and Rodolphe took advantage of the respite to recover some of his composure.

"Madame was talking to me about her health . . ." he began.

Charles interrupted him: he was terribly worried, because his wife was again having difficulty in breathing. Rodolphe asked whether horseback riding might not do her good.

"Yes, of course!" exclaimed Charles. "That would be excellent, perfect!" He turned to Emma and said, "It's a wonderful idea—you ought to do it!"

She objected that she did not have a horse; Monsieur

Rodolphe offered her one. She declined and he did not insist; then, to give a reason for his visit, he said that his carter, the man who had been bled, was still having dizzy spells.

"I'll stop by to see him," said Bovary.

"No, no, I'll send him to you; we'll come here: that will be more convenient for you."

"All right. Thank you."

As soon as he was alone with Emma, Charles asked her, "Why didn't you accept Monsieur Boulanger's offer? It was very nice of him."

She took on a sulky expression, made all sorts of excuses and finally said it "might not look right."

"Oh, what do I care about that?" cried Charles, turning sharply. "Health comes first! You're wrong!"

"But how do you expect me to go riding when I have no riding habit?"

"You'll have to order one," he replied.

The riding habit decided her.

When it was ready, Charles wrote to Monsieur Boulanger that his wife was at his disposal and that he was counting on his kindness.

The next day at noon Rodolphe arrived in front of Charles's door with two riding horses. One of them had pink pompons on its ears and a doeskin lady's saddle on its back.

Rodolphe had put on a pair of long soft boots, telling himself she had probably never seen anything like them; and Emma was indeed charmed by his appearance when he came upstairs in his long velvet coat and white tricot riding breeches. She was ready and waiting for him.

Justin slipped out of the pharmacy to see her, and the apothecary also bestirred himself. He gave Monsieur Boulanger a number of warnings: "An accident can happen so quickly! Be careful! Your horses may be high-spirited!"

She heard a sound above her head: it was Félicité drumming on the windowpanes to amuse little Berthe. The child blew down a kiss and her mother replied with a movement of her riding crop.

"Have a good ride!" cried Monsieur Homais. "Remember: caution above all! Caution!"

And he waved his newspaper as they rode away.

As soon as it felt bare earth beneath its hooves, Emma's horse broke into a gallop. Rodolphe galloped along beside her. Now and then they exchanged a few words. With her head slightly lowered, her hand raised and her right arm outstretched, she abandoned herself to the rhythmic rocking of the saddle.

At the foot of the hill Rodolphe gave his horse its head and they both shot forward at once; they stopped abruptly at the top, and Emma's big blue veil fell back in place.

It was early in October. There was a mist over the country-side. Long wisps of vapor lay on the horizon, clinging to the contours of the hills, while others were rising, disintegrating until they vanished entirely. Sometimes, when the clouds parted, a ray of sunlight would fall on the faraway rooftops of Yonville, with its gardens along the river, its courtyards, its walls and the steeple of its church. Emma squinted, trying to pick out her house, and never before had the wretched village she lived in seemed so small to her. From that height the whole valley looked like an enormous pale lake evaporating in the air: clumps of trees stood out here and there like black rocks, and the lines of tall poplars jutting up through the mist were like sandbars shifting in the wind.

To one side, over the grass between the firs, the daylight was dim in the warm air. The reddish, snuff-colored earth deadened the sound of the horses' shod hooves, and they kicked fallen fir cones before them as they walked.

Rodolphe and Emma followed the edge of the wood. She turned away occasionally to avoid his eyes, and then she would see only orderly rows of fir trunks whose endless succession made her feel a little dizzy. The horses were breathing loudly. The leather of the saddles was creaking.

The sun came out just as they entered the forest.

"God is watching over us!" said Rodolphe.

"You think so?" she asked.

"Let's go on!"

He clicked his tongue. Both horses began to trot.

Tall ferns growing along the path kept catching in Emma's stirrup. Rodolphe leaned down and pulled them out as he rode. Sometimes he came near her to push aside low branches and she felt his knee brush against her leg. The sky had become blue. The leaves were no longer rustling. There were wide spaces full of heather in bloom, and patches of violet gave way here and there to tangled clumps of trees with gray, reddish-brown or golden foliage. They often heard a faint fluttering of wings under the bushes, or the hoarse, soft cries of crows flying away through the oaks.

They dismounted. He tied the horses. She walked ahead of him on the moss between the ruts.

Her long dress hampered her, even though she held it up in back. As he walked along behind her, Rodolphe kept his eyes on the delicate white stockings which showed between her black skirt and her black shoes like part of her naked flesh.

She stopped and said, "I'm tired."

"Keep going a little longer. Don't give up yet!"

A hundred yards further on she stopped again; and through the veil that hung down obliquely from her masculine-looking hat to her hips, he could see her face bathed in a bluish transparence, as though she were floating beneath azure water.

"Where are we going?"

He did not answer. She was breathing heavily. He glanced around, biting his mustache.

They came to a broader clearing in which some saplings had been felled. They sat down on a log and Rodolphe began to tell her of his love.

He did not frighten her at first with compliments. He was calm, serious and melancholy.

Emma listened to him with her head bowed, pushing chips of wood on the ground with the toe of her shoe.

But when he asked, "Our destinies are united now, aren't they?" she answered, "No, they're not! You know that! It's impossible!"

She stood up to leave. He gripped her wrist. She stopped. After looking at him for several moments with moist, amorous eyes, she said rapidly, "Please, let's not talk about it any more! Where are the horses? Let's go back."

He made a gesture of anger and displeasure. She repeated: "Where are the horses? Where are the horses?"

Then, smiling a strange smile, his eyes fixed on her, his teeth clenched, he moved toward her with outstretched arms.

She drew back, trembling, and stammered, "Oh! You're frightening me! You're hurting me! Let's leave!"

"If you insist," he said, and his expression changed. He immediately became as respectful, tender and timid as before. She took his arm and they turned back.

"What's the matter?" he asked. "Why did you act that way? I don't understand it. You must be mistaken about me. You're in my heart like a Madonna on a pedestal, in a lofty, secure, immaculate place. But I can't live without you! I need your eyes, your voice, your thoughts. Be my friend, my sister, my angel!"

He put his arm around her waist. She halfheartedly tried to free herself. He held her as they walked.

Then they heard the horses munching leaves.

"Oh, not yet!" said Rodolphe. "Let's not go back! Stay!"

He drew her further on, around a little pond whose rippling surface was green with duckweed. Wilted water lilies lay motionless among the reeds. At the sound of their footsteps in the grass, frogs hopped away to hide.

"I'm wrong, wrong!" she said. "I'm mad to listen to you!"

"Why? Emma! Emma!"

"Oh, Rodolphe," said the young woman slowly, leaning on his shoulder.

The broadcloth of her dress clung to the velvet of his coat. She tilted back her head and her white throat swelled in a sigh. She suddenly felt weak and a long tremor ran through her body; weeping and hiding her face, she abandoned herself.

Evening shadows were falling; the sun's rays, streaming horizontally through the branches, dazzled her eyes. Here and there, all around her, among the leaves and on the ground, were shimmering patches of light, as though hummingbirds had scattered their feathers in flight. Silence lay over everything; the trees seemed to be giving off something soft and sweet; she felt her heart beating again, and the blood flowing through her flesh like a river of milk. Then she heard a long, lingering, indistinct cry coming from one of the hills far beyond the forest; she listened to it in silence as it mingled like a strain of music with the last vibrations of her overwrought nerves. Rodolphe, a cigar between his teeth, was mending a broken bridle with a penknife.

They went back to Yonville by the same route. They saw the tracks left by their horses in the mud, side by side, and the same bushes, the same stones in the grass. Nothing around them had changed; and yet, for her, something more momentous had happened than if the mountains had been shoved aside. Rodolphe leaned over occasionally to take her hand and kiss it.

She was charming on horseback! She sat erect and slender, with one bent knee on her horse's mane, her face slightly colored by the open air and the reddish twilight.

On entering Yonville she made her horse prance on the pavement.

People looked at her from their windows.

At dinner that night her husband found that she was looking well, but when he asked about her ride she did not seem to hear him; she sat leaning her elbow on the table beside her plate, between the two lighted candles.

"Emma!" he said.

"What?"

"Well, I went to see Monsieur Alexandre this afternoon; he has a mare several years old, but still in fine shape, except that she's a little knee-sprung. I'm sure he'd sell her for three hundred francs or so. . . . I thought you'd like to have her, so I reserved her. . . . I bought her. . . . Did I do right? Tell me."

She nodded. Then, a quarter of an hour later, she asked, "Are you going out tonight?"

"Yes. Why?"

"Oh, nothing . . . nothing, dear."

As soon as she was rid of Charles she went upstairs and shut herself in her room.

At first she felt dazed; she saw the trees, the paths, the ditches and Rodolphe; and again she felt his arms tighten around her while the leaves quivered and the reeds rustled.

But when she saw herself in the mirror she was amazed by the way her face looked. Never before had her eyes been so big, so dark, so deep. She was transfigured by something subtle spread over her whole body.

She repeated to herself, "I have a lover! I have a lover!" and the thought gave her a delicious thrill, as though she were beginning a second puberty. At last she was going to possess the joys of love, that fever of happiness she had despaired of ever knowing. She was entering a marvelous realm in which everything would be passion, ecstasy and rapture; she was surrounded by vast expanses of bluish space, summits of intense feeling sparkled before her eyes, and everyday life appeared far below in the shadows between these peaks.

She remembered the heroines of novels she had read, and the lyrical legion of those adulterous women began to sing in her memory with sisterly voices that enchanted her. It was as though she herself were becoming part of that imaginary world, as though she were making the long dream of her youth come true by placing herself in the category of those amorous women she had envied so much. Furthermore, she had a satisfying feeling of vengeance. How she had suffered! But now she was triumphing, and love, so long repressed, was gushing forth abundantly with joyous effervescence. She savored it without remorse, anxiety or distress.

She spent the next day in a kind of bliss that was new to her. She and Rodolphe exchanged vows. She told him of her sorrows. He interrupted her with kisses; looking at him with half-closed eyes, she asked him to call her by her first name again and tell her once more that he loved her. They were in the forest, as they had been the day before, in a hut used by a maker of wooden shoes. It had thatched walls and its ceiling was so low that they could not stand upright. They were sitting side by side on a bed of dried leaves.

From that day on they wrote to each other regularly every evening. Emma would take her letter to the end of the gardén, near the river, and slip it into a crack in the terrace wall. Rodolphe would come to pick it up and leave one for her in its place; she always complained that his was too short.

One morning when Charles had left the house before dawn she suddenly felt that she had to see Rodolphe immediately. She could quickly go to La Huchette, stay an hour and be back before anyone else was awake. This idea made her pant with desire; she was soon walking swiftly across the meadow without looking back.

Day was beginning to break. From a distance she recognized her lover's house, with its two swallow-tailed weathervanes silhouetted in black against the pale light of dawn.

Beyond the farmyard was a building that was no doubt the château. She entered it as though the walls had opened of their own accord at her approach. A wide, straight staircase led up to a hall. She turned the latch of a door: at the far end of a bedroom she saw a man asleep. It was Rodolphe. She uttered a cry.

"It's you!" he said. "It's you! How did you manage to come here? . . . Oh, your dress is wet!"

"I love you," she replied, putting her arms around his neck.

Since this first daring venture had been successful, from then on whenever Charles left early in the morning she quickly got dressed and furtively walked down the steps leading to the river.

When the cow plank had been raised she had to follow the walls that ran along the water's edge. The bank was slippery and she would clutch tufts of withered wallflowers to keep from falling. Then she would set out across the plowed fields, stumbling, sinking into the soft ground and occasionally getting her light shoes stuck in it. Her scarf, tied around her head, fluttered in the wind as she crossed the pastures; afraid of the oxen, she would begin to run, and she always arrived breathless, with her cheeks pink and her whole body giving off a fragrance of sap, verdure and fresh air. Rodolphe would still be asleep at that hour. She was like a spring morning entering his bedroom.

Soft, dull, golden light filtered in through the curtains in front of the windows. Emma would grope her way across the room, straining her eyes to see, with dewdrops still clinging to her hair like a topaz aureole around her face. Rodolphe would laugh, draw her to him and press her to his heart.

Afterward she would examine the room, opening drawers, combing her hair with his comb and looking at herself in his shaving mirror. Often she even put between her teeth the stem of a big pipe which lay on the night table among the lemons and lumps of sugar spread out beside a pitcher of water.

It would take them a good quarter of an hour to say good-by. Emma always wept; she wished she never had to leave him. Something stronger than herself kept driving her to him, until one day when she had arrived unexpectedly he frowned as though he were displeased about something.

"What's the matter?" she asked. "Are you ill? Tell me!"

At length he told her gravely that her visits were becoming reckless and that she was compromising herself.

X

Little by little, she came to share Rodolphe's fears. Love had intoxicated her at first, and she had thought of nothing beyond it. But now that it had become an essential part of her life she was afraid she might lose part of it, or even that something might arise to interfere with it. Each time she returned from his house she glanced around uneasily, looking intently at every figure moving on the horizon, at every dormer window in the village from which she might be seen. She listened for the sounds of footsteps, voices and plows, and whenever she heard something she would stop in her tracks, paler and more trembling than the leaves of the poplars swaying above her head.

One morning as she was coming back she suddenly thought she saw a long rifle being aimed at her. It was protruding at an angle from the edge of a small barrel half hidden in the grass beside a ditch. She nearly fainted from terror, but she walked forward nevertheless, and a man emerged from the barrel like a jack-in-the-box. He was wearing gaiters buckled up to his knees, his cap was pulled down to his eyes, his lips were quivering with cold and his nose was red. It was Captain Binet, lying in wait for wild ducks.

"You should have said something before you got so close!" he cried. "When you see a gun you must always give warning."

In saying this, the tax collector was trying to cover up the fright she had just given him, for the prefect had issued a decree prohibiting duck-hunting except from boats, so that Monsieur Binet, despite his respect for law, was now in the act of violating it. Every few minutes he had thought he heard the game warden coming. But his fear had added spice to his pleasure and, all alone in the barrel, he had been feeling highly satisfied with his good luck and his devilishness.

The sight of Emma seemed to relieve him of a heavy burden, and he immediately tried to open a conversation.

"It's chilly out here! The cold bites right into you!"

She made no reply. He went on:

"You're up bright and early, aren't you?"

"Yes," she stammered, "I've been to the wet-nurse's house to see my baby."

"Oh, I see, I see! As for me, I've been right here ever since dawn, but it's so hard to see anything in weather like this that if a bird doesn't practically perch on the barrel of your gun—"

"Good-by, Monsieur Binet," she interrupted, turning on her heel.

"Good-by, madame," he answered curtly.

And he went back into his barrel.

Emma regretted having taken leave of him so brusquely. He was no doubt going to make some unfavorable conjectures. Her story about the wet-nurse was the worst explanation she could have given, for everyone in Yonville knew that little Berthe had been back with her parents for the past year. Furthermore, no one lived around there, and the path led only to La Huchette. Binet had therefore guessed where she was coming from, and he would not keep it to himself:

he would gossip she was sure of it! She racked her brain till evening, going over every scheme of lies imaginable, and during all that time the imbecile with his game bag never left her mind.

Seeing that she looked worried, Charles insisted on taking her to see the pharmacist after dinner, to distract her; and the first person she saw in the pharmacy was, again, the tax collector! He was standing at the counter in the glow of the red jar, and he was saying, "Let me have half an ounce of vitriol, please."

"Justin," shouted the apothecary, "bring in the sulphuric acid!"

Then he said to Emma, who was about to go up to Madame Homais' room, "No, don't bother to go up: she'll be down soon. You can warm yourself in front of the stove while you're waiting . . . Excuse me . . . Hello, Doctor." (For the pharmacist took great pleasure in pronouncing the word "doctor," as though by addressing it to someone else he made some of its glory rub off on himself.) "Be careful not to knock over the mortars, Justin! No, go get some chairs from the little room—you know very well we never move the armchairs in the parlor!"

And Homais was rushing out from behind the counter to put his armchair back in its right place when Binet asked him for half an ounce of sugar acid.

"Sugar acid?" asked the pharmacist disdainfully. "I don't know what that is, I never heard of it. Perhaps it's oxalic acid you want. It *is* oxalic, isn't it?"

Binet explained that he needed acid to make some metal polish with, because he wanted to clean the rust off some of his hunting equipment. Emma started. The pharmacist said, "Yes, the weather is unpropitious, because of the humidity."

"Still, though," said the tax collector slyly, "there are some people who don't mind it."

She was choking.

"And I also want . . ."

"Won't he ever leave?" she thought.

". . . half an ounce of rosin and turpentine, four ounces of unbleached wax, and an ounce and a half of boneblack, please, to clean the patent leather parts of my outfit."

The apothecary was beginning to cut the wax when Madame Homais appeared with Irma in her arms, Napoléon at her side and Athalie behind her. She seated herself on the velvet-covered bench by the window and the boy sat down on a stool while his elder sister hovered around the jujube box, near her dear papa. The latter was pouring various liquids into funnels, corking bottles, pasting on labels and wrapping packages. Everyone around him remained silent; they heard only the weights clinking in the scales from time to time, and the pharmacist giving his apprentice a few words of advice in a low voice.

"How's your little girl these days?" Madame Homais suddenly asked.

"Quiet!" cried her husband, who was writing figures on his scratch-pad.

"Why didn't you bring her?" she went on in an undertone.

"Sh!" said Emma, pointing to the apothecary.

But Binet, completely absorbed in checking the bill, had probably heard nothing. Finally he left. Emma heaved a deep sigh of relief.

"You're breathing so heavily!" said Madame Homais.

"It's the heat," replied Emma.

The next day she and Rodolphe discussed how they ought to arrange their meetings. She suggested bribing her maid with a present, but they decided it would be better to find a safe house in Yonville. He promised to look for one.

During the entire winter he came to the garden three or four times a week. Emma had taken the key to the gate, which Charles believed to be lost.

To announce his arrival, Rodolphe always threw a handful of gravel against the shutters. She would stand up with a start, but sometimes she had to wait, for Charles loved to chat beside the fire, and he went on endlessly.

She would be consumed with impatience; if he had obeyed the look in her eyes, he would have jumped out a window. Finally she would begin to get ready for bed, then she would pick up a book and calmly read it as though she were interested in it. But Charles, lying in bed, would call to her:

"Come on, Emma, it's time."

"All right, I'm coming."

But, since the candlelight hurt his eyes, he would turn toward the wall and fall asleep. She would then slip out, holding her breath, smiling, palpitating, half undressed.

Rodolphe wore a large cape; he would wrap it around her, put his arm around her waist and silently lead her to the far end of the garden.

They would go to the arbor, to the same rotting wooden

bench on which Léon had once looked at her so amorously on summer evenings. She almost never thought about him now.

The stars shone through the leafless branches of the jasmine. They heard the river flowing behind them, and occasionally the crackle of the dry reeds on the bank. Massive shadows loomed up here and there in the darkness, and sometimes they would all shudder at once, rise up and lean forward, like enormous black waves about to break over them. The cold of the night made them cling more tightly to each other; the sighs that came from their lips seemed more profound; their eyes, scarcely distinguishable in the darkness, looked larger; and, in the midst of the silence, there were soft-spoken words that fell on their hearts with a crystalline ring, echoing and re-echoing inside.

On rainy nights they took shelter in the consulting room, between the shed and the stable. Emma would light a kitchen candle she had hidden behind the books. Rodolphe would settle down as though he were at home. He was amused by the bookcase, the desk and everything else in the room, and he could not help making a great many jokes about Charles. This bothered Emma: she would have liked him to be more serious, and even more dramatic when the circumstances called for it, as he had been on the night when she heard the sound of approaching footsteps in the lane.

"Someone's coming!" she said.

He blew out the candle.

"Do you have your pistols?"

"What for?"

"Why . . . to defend yourself!" said Emma.

"Against your husband? Poor man . . ."

And he finished his sentence with a gesture that meant, "I could crush him with a flick of my finger."

She was amazed at his bravery, although she sensed beneath it a kind of tactlessness and unconcerned vulgarity that shocked her.

Rodolphe gave a great deal of thought to this pistol incident. If she had spoken seriously, he felt, it was a ridiculous thing for her to say; it was even ignoble, in fact, because he had no reason to hate poor Charles. He was by no means "devoured by jealousy." Emma had made him a solemn vow in this connection, and he did not find that in very good taste either.

Furthermore, she was becoming terribly sentimental. They had had to exchange miniatures and cut off locks of their hair, and she was now asking him for a ring, a real wedding ring, as a symbol of their eternal union. She often spoke to him about the "bells of evening" or the "voices of nature"; then she would tell him about her mother and ask about his. Rodolphe's mother had been dead for twenty years, but Emma kept consoling him in the affected language she would have used in speaking to a bereaved child; and sometimes she would even look at the moon and say to him, "I'm sure they're both up there together, and I know they approve of our love."

But she was so pretty! He had possessed so few women with such guileless charm! This love without licentiousness was something new to him; it made him alter his usual easygoing habits, and it aroused both his pride and his sensuality. While his bourgeois common sense was disdainful of her exalted raptures, in his heart he found them delightful, since it was he who inspired them. Eventually, sure of her love, he stopped making any special effort to please her, and little by little his manner changed.

He no longer spoke to her in words so sweet they made her weep, and there were no more of those fiery caresses that threw her into a frenzy. Their great love, in which she lived totally immersed, seemed to be subsiding around her, like the water of a river sinking into its bed, and she could see the mud at the bottom. Refusing to believe it, she redoubled her tenderness; and Rodolphe hid his indifference less and less.

She did not know whether she regretted having given in to him or whether, instead, she wished she could love him more. Her humiliating awareness of her own weakness was turning into resentment, which was tempered by her voluptuous pleasures. It was not an attachment, it was a kind of continuous seduction. She was under his domination. She was almost afraid of him.

In appearance, however, everything was calmer than ever, for Rodolphe had succeeded in conducting their adulterous affair as he pleased; and at the end of six months, when spring came, they were like a married couple placidly keeping a domestic flame alive.

This was the time of year when Monsieur Rouault always sent his turkey, to commemorate the healing of his broken leg. A letter came with the present, as usual. Emma cut the string with which it was tied to the basket and read the following:

> My dear children,
> I hope this letter finds you in good health and that this turkey will be as good as the others. It seems a little tenderer to me, if you don't mind my saying so, and meatier. But next time I'll send you a rooster for a change, unless you'd rather have another turkey, and please send me back the basket, along with the two others. I had an accident with my cart shed, a strong wind blew the roof off into the trees one night. Crops haven't been too good either. I don't know when I'll come to see you. It's so hard for me to leave the place now that I'm all alone, Emma dear!

Here there was a space between the lines, as though the old man had put down his pen to think a while.

> As for me, I'm all right, except for a cold I caught at the Yvetot fair. I went there to hire a new shepherd. I got rid of the one I had because he was too fussy about what he ate. Those bandits give you so much trouble! This one was disrespectful, too.
> I heard from a peddler who had a tooth pulled when he passed through your town last winter that Bovary was working as hard as ever. It doesn't surprise me, and he showed me the tooth. We had a cup of coffee together. I asked him if he saw you, Emma, and he said no, but he saw two horses in the stable, so I suppose business is good. I'm glad of it, my dear children, and may God give you every kind of happiness you can think of.
> It grieves me that I haven't seen my darling granddaughter Berthe Bovary yet. I've planted a plum tree for her in the garden under your window, and I won't let anyone touch it except to make some stewed plums for her later. I'll keep them in the cupboard for her till she comes.
> Good-by, my dear children. Here's a kiss for my daughter, and one for my son-in-law too, and one on each cheek for my little granddaughter.
> > With best wishes,
> > Your loving father, Théodore Rouault.

Emma sat for several minutes with the sheets of coarse paper in her hand. Misspelled words were piled one on top of the other in the letter, and she followed the gentle thoughts that cackled through them like a hen half hidden in a thorn hedge. The ink had been dried with ashes from the fireplace, for a little gray dust fell from the letter onto her dress, and she could almost see her father leaning toward the hearth to pick up the tongs. How long it had been since she had sat beside him on the bench inside the vast fireplace, burning the end of a stick in the tall flames of the crackling gorse! She remembered summer afternoons full of sunshine. The colts whinnied whenever anyone came near them, and they galloped and galloped. . . . There had been a beehive beneath her window, and sometimes the bees, buzzing around in the sunlight, would strike against the panes like bouncing golden balls. What happiness there had been in those days! What freedom! What hope! What an abundance of illusions! She had none left now. Each new venture had cost her some of them, each of her successive conditions: as virgin, wife and mistress; she had lost them all along the course of her life, like a traveler who leaves some of his wealth at every inn along the road.

But what was making her so unhappy? Where was the extraordinary catastrophe that had wrecked her life? She raised her head and looked around, as though trying to find the cause of her suffering.

An April sunbeam was sparkling on the china in the whatnot; the fire was burning; she felt the softness of the rug beneath her slippers; it was a clear day, the air was warm and she could hear her child's shouts of laughter.

The little girl was rolling on the lawn, in the cut grass that had piled up to dry. She was lying face downward on one of the piles while the maid held her by the skirt. Lestiboudois was raking nearby, and each time he came near her she leaned forward and waved her arms.

"Bring her to me!" said her mother; and she rushed up to her to kiss her. "How I love you, darling! How I love you!"

Then, noticing that the tips of Berthe's ears were a little dirty, she quickly rang for some warm water and washed her, changed her underwear, stockings and shoes, asked countless questions about her health, as though she had just come back from a trip, and finally, kissing her again and weeping a little, she gave her back to the maid, who was dumbfounded by this lavish display of affection.

That night Rodolphe found her more serious than usual. "It'll pass," he thought. "It's just a whim."

He failed to appear for three consecutive meetings. When he finally came back she treated him coldly and almost disdainfully.

"You're wasting your time, my girl. . . ." And he pretended not to notice her melancholy sighs or the handkerchief she kept taking out.

It was then that Emma repented!

She even wondered why she detested Charles, and whether it might not be better if she could love him. But there was so little about him to which she could attach this revival of feeling that she was baffled whenever she thought seriously of carrying out her sacrifice. Then one day the apothecary gave her an opportunity.

XI

He had recently read an article praising a new method of curing clubfoot, and since he was all for progress he conceived the patriotic idea that, "to keep up with the times," Yonville ought to be the scene of operations for "talipes, commonly known as clubfoot."

"After all, what's there to lose?" he said to Emma. "And look at what's to be gained!" He enumerated on his fingers the advantages of the attempt: "Almost certain success, cure and improved appearance for the patient, swift fame for the surgeon. Why shouldn't your husband, for example, relieve poor Hippolyte, at the Lion d'Or? He'd be sure to talk about his cure to every traveler at the inn, and then" (Homais lowered his voice and looked around) "what's to stop me from sending a little article about it to the newspaper? And an article gets around! People talk about it and it builds up like a snowball rolling down a hill! After that, who knows? Who knows?"

Emma was convinced: Charles had a good chance of succeeding; she had no reason to doubt his skill, and what a satisfaction it would be for her to have persuaded him to take a step that would enhance his reputation and add to his fortune! She was eager to have something more solid than love to lean on.

Urged on by the apothecary and Emma, Charles agreed to go through with it. He sent to Rouen for Dr. Duval's book and buried himself in it every night, holding his head between his hands.

While Charles was studying talipes equinus, talipes varus and talipes valgus, in other words, *strephocatopodia, strephendopodia* and *strephexopodia* (or, to put it more clearly, deviations of the foot downward, inward or outward), along with *strephypopodia* and *strephanopodia* (downward or upward torsion), Monsieur Homais was using every possible argument to talk the stableboy into consenting to the operation:

"You'll feel nothing more than a slight pain at the very most; it's just a prick, like a little bloodletting, less painful than the removal of some kinds of corns."

Hippolyte thought it over, stupidly rolling his eyes.

"Look, it means nothing to me," the pharmacist went on, "I'm only trying to convince you for your own sake, out of pure humanity! I'd like to see you get rid of that hideous limp, my friend, and that swaying of the lumbar region—it must hinder you considerably in your work, no matter what you claim."

Homais then described how much more vigorous and active he would feel, and even gave him to understand that he would be more successful with women, which made the stableboy smile foolishly. After that, Homais appealed to his pride:

"Are you a man or not? What would have happened if you'd been called to the colors, to go out and defend our country against her enemies? . . . Ah, Hippolyte!"

And Homais walked away, declaring that he was totally unable to understand how anyone could so stubbornly refuse the benefits of science.

Poor Hippolyte eventually gave in, for there was a veritable conspiracy against him. Binet, who never meddled in other people's affairs, Madame Lefrançois, Artémise, the neighbors, even the mayor, Monsieur Tuvache—everyone urged him, preached to him, shamed him; but what finally decided him was the fact that it would cost him nothing. Bovary even agreed to furnish the apparatus for the operation. This generosity had been Emma's idea, and he had accepted it, inwardly telling himself that his wife was an angel.

Following the pharmacist's advice he managed, after two failures, to have the cabinetmaker and the locksmith construct a kind of box weighing about eight pounds, using generous quantities of iron, wood, tin, leather, screws and nuts.

Meanwhile, in order to know which of Hippolyte's tendons to cut, he had to determine which kind of clubfoot he had.

The foot formed almost a straight line with the leg, although it also turned inward, so that it was an equinus mingled with a little varus, or perhaps a slight varus with a strong admixture of equinus. But with his equinus—which actually was as wide as a horse's hoof, with rough skin, hard tendons and huge toes whose black nails were like the nails of a horseshoe— the taliped galloped like a deer from morning to night. He was constantly seen in the square, hopping around the carts, thrusting his crippled leg forward. In fact, this leg seemed to be more vigorous than the other. Through long use it had taken on what might almost be called moral qualities of patience and determination, and Hippolyte preferred to rest his weight on it whenever he was given heavy work to do.

Since it was an equinus, Charles would have to cut the Achilles tendon, leaving the anterior tibial muscle to be taken care of later, to cure the varus, for he was afraid to risk two operations at once, and he was already trembling at the thought of getting into some important region he knew nothing about.

Ambrose Paré applying a ligature directly to an artery for the first time since Celsus had done it fifteen centuries before, Dupuytren about to cut into an abscess through a thick layer of the brain, Gensoul when he performed the first resection of the upper maxillary—none of of these men had such a pounding heart, such trembling hands or such a tense mind as Monsieur Bovary when he approached Hippolyte with his tenotomy knife in his hand. And, as in a hospital, beside him on a table lay a pile of lint, waxed thread and a great many bandages—a whole pyramid of bandages, the apothecary's entire stock. It was Monsieur Homais who, beginning early in the morning, had organized all these preparations, as much to dazzle the multitude as to delude himself. Charles pierced the skin; there was a sharp snap: the tendon was cut, the operation was over. Hippolyte was overcome with surprise; he bent over Bovary's hands and covered them with kisses.

"Come now, be calm," said the apothecary. "You can express your gratitude to your benefactor later."

And he went downstairs to announce the result to the five or six curious souls who were standing in the courtyard, expecting to see Hippolyte walk out without a limp. Charles buckled his patient into the apparatus and went home, where Emma was anxiously waiting for him at the door. She threw her arms around his neck; they sat down to table; he ate heartily and even asked for a cup of coffee with his dessert, a dissolute pleasure which he usually allowed himself only on Sundays when there was company.

They spent a delightful evening, full of intimate talk and shared dreams. They spoke of their future fortune, of the improvements they would make in their house. He saw his fame spreading, his prosperity growing, his wife loving him forever; and she was happy to refresh herself with a new, healthier, more commendable feeling: she now had a little affection for the poor man who loved her so. The thought of Rodolphe came into her mind for a moment, but then her eyes turned back to Charles and she noticed with surprise that his teeth were not at all bad-looking.

They were in bed when Monsieur Homais suddenly came into their bedroom, despite the cook's objections. He was holding a newly written sheet of paper in his hand: it was the article he had composed for the *Fanal de Rouen*. He had brought it for them to read.

"Read it to us," said Bovary.

He read:

" 'Despite the prejudices that still cover part of the face of Europe like a net, enlightenment is beginning to penetrate our rural areas. Thus on Tuesday our little town of Yonville was the scene of a surgical experiment that was also an act of lofty philanthropy. Monsieur Bovary, one of our most distinguished practitioners . . .' "

"Oh, that's too much, too much!" said Charles, choked with emotion.

"No it's not! Not at all! Don't be too modest. '. . . operated on a clubfoot . . .' I didn't use the scientific term, because in a newspaper, you know . . . everyone might not understand; the masses must be . . ."

"Yes, you're right," said Bovary. "Go on."

"I'll take it up where I left off," said the pharmacist. " 'Monsieur Bovary, one of our most distinguished practitioners, operated on a clubfoot. The patient was Hippolyte Tautain, stableboy for the past twenty-five years at the Lion d'Or inn, under the management of Madame Lefrançois, on the Place d'Armes. The novelty of the undertaking and the interest taken in the patient had drawn such a large gathering of people that there was a veritable crush in front of the establishment. The operation went off as though by magic, and only a few drops of blood appeared on the skin, as if to announce that the rebellious tendon had at last yielded to the surgeon's art. The patient, strangely enough (we report this from first-hand observation), gave no indication of pain. So far his condition leaves nothing to be desired. All evidence points to a short convalescence, and who knows?—perhaps at the next village festival we shall see our good Hippolyte taking part in Bacchic dances amid a chorus of joyous companions, thus proving to one and all, by his high spirits and his capers, that he has been completely cured. Hail to our magnanimous men of science! Hail to those tireless spirits who work day and night for the improvement or the relief of mankind! Hail, all hail! May we not now proclaim that the blind shall see, the deaf shall hear and the lame shall walk? What fanaticism promised to the elect in days gone by, science is now achieving for all men! We shall keep our readers informed about the successive phases of this remarkable cure.' "

Five days later, however, Madame Lefrançois rushed in panic-striken and cried, "Help! He's dying! It's driving me out of my mind!"

Charles immediately headed for the Lion d'Or, and the pharmacist, seeing him hurry across the square without a hat, abandoned his pharmacy. He too went to the inn; he arrived panting, flushed and worried, and he asked all the people he saw climbing the stairs, "What's wrong with our interesting taliped?"

The taliped was writhing in terrible convulsions; the apparatus enclosing his leg was pounding against the wall so violently that it threatened to break through.

Taking every precaution to avoid disturbing the position of the leg, Charles and the pharmacist took off the box and saw a horrible sight: the foot was a shapeless mass, so swollen that the entire skin seemed ready to burst, and it was covered with black and blue marks caused by the famous apparatus. Hippolyte had previously complained that it was hurting him, but no one had paid any attention to him; it was now obvious that his complaints had not been entirely unjustified, and he was allowed to keep his foot out of the box for several hours. But as soon as the swelling had gone down a little the two experts deemed it advisable to put the apparatus back on, and they fastened it more tightly than before, in order to speed things up. Finally, three days later, when Hippolyte could stand it no longer, they removed the box once again and were amazed at what they saw. A livid tumescence ran up the leg, and scattered over it were pustules from which a black liquid was oozing. The case had taken a serious turn. Hippolyte was beginning to despair, and Madame Lefrançois had him moved the little dining room beside the kitchen, so that he would at least have some distraction.

But the tax collector, who ate dinner there every day, complained bitterly about such company. Hippolyte was then carried into the billiard room.

He lay there groaning under his heavy blankets, pale, un-shaven and hollow-eyed, occasionally turning his sweaty head on the dirty pillow while flies swooped down on it from all sides. Madame Bovary came to see him now and then. She brought him linen for his poultices, comforted and encouraged him. He had no lack of company, especially on market-days, when peasants gathered around him to play billiards, fence with the cues, smoke, drink, sing and shout.

"How are you coming along?" they would ask, clapping him on the shoulder. "You don't look as if you're in very good shape. But it's your own fault! You should have . . ." And they would tell him stories about people who had been cured by remedies other than his; then, by way of consolation, they would add, "You're coddling yourself! Why don't you get up? You're pampering yourself like a king! Well, one thing is sure, you old rascal: you don't smell good!"

It was true: gangrene was mounting higher and higher. It made Bovary feel sick himself. He came in every hour, every few minutes. Hippolyte would look at him with eyes full of terror, sobbing and stammering, "When will I be well again? Oh, save me! I'm so miserable! So miserable!"

And the doctor always went away telling him to eat lightly.

"Don't listen to him, my boy," Madame Lefrançois would say. "They've made you suffer enough already! You mustn't get any weaker than you are now. Here, swallow this."

And she would give him some good bouillon, a slice of mutton or a piece of bacon, and sometimes a little glass of brandy, although he could not muster up enough strength to raise it to his lips.

Father Bournisien, having learned that he was getting worse, came and asked to see him. He began by telling him how sorry he was about his condition, but then he told him he ought to rejoice over it, since it was the Lord's will, and quickly take advantage of this opportunity to become re-conciled with heaven.

"After all," said the priest in a paternal tone, "you were neglecting your religious duties a little. You seldom came to divine services. How many years has it been since you last took Holy Communion? I can understand that your work and the whirl of other worldly activities may have distracted you from the salvation of your soul, but now is the time to give it serious thought. Don't fall into despair, however: I've known other great sinners who implored God's mercy when they were about to appear before Him—I realize you haven't come to that point yet—and who certainly died under the best conditions. Let's hope you'll give us as good an example as they have! What's to prevent you from saying an Ave Maria and the Lord's Prayer in the morning and at night, just as a precaution? Yes, you can do that! Do it as a favor to me. It's not hard. Will you promise?"

The poor devil promised. The priest came back on the following days. He would chat with the innkeeper and even tell stories interspersed with jokes and puns which Hippolyte did not understand. Then, at the first opportunity, he would turn the conversation to religion, taking on an expression appropriate to the subject.

His zeal was apparently effective, for soon the taliped expressed a desire to make a pilgrimage to Bon-Secours if he recovered, to which Father Bournisien replied that he could see nothing wrong with the idea: two precautions were better than one. "Might as well play safe," he added.

The apothecary indignantly condemned what he called "the priest's machinations"; they were hindering Hippolyte's recovery, he claimed, and he kept saying to Madame Lefrançois, "Leave him alone! Leave him alone! You're upsetting him with your mysticism!"

But the good woman would not listen to him. He was "the cause of everything." To defy him, she hung a full holy-water font and a sprig of boxwood at the head of Hippolyte's bed.

Meanwhile religion seemed to be helping him no more than surgery: the invincible gangrene continued to rise toward the belly. Different kinds of medicines and poultices were tried in vain: the muscles went on deteriorating from day to day, and finally Charles nodded in affirmation when Madame Lefrançois asked him whether, as a last resort, she shouldn't send to Neufchâtel for Monsieur Canivet, a famous doctor.

This colleague, a fifty-year-old M.D. of high standing and great self-assurance, laughed with undisguised contempt when he saw Hippolyte's leg, now gangrenous up to the knee. Then, having declared flatly that it would have to be amputated, he went to see the pharmacist and railed against the jackasses who had managed to reduce the poor man to such a state. Standing in the pharmacy and shaking Monsieur Homais by one of his coat buttons, he vociferated:

"Now there's a Paris invention for you! A brilliant idea from the capital! It's like strabotomy, chloroform and lithotricity—there ought to be a law against such atrocities! But some doctors want to be smart, so they use all sorts of remedies on their patients without worrying about the consequences. The rest of us aren't that smart, we're not scientists or dandies or fashionable fops—we're practitioners, healers, and we wouldn't dream of operating on someone who's in perfect health! Straightening a clubfoot! Whatever made anyone think such a thing could be done? It's like trying to straighten a hunchback!"

Homais suffered as he listened to this tirade, but he hid his discomfiture beneath an obsequious smile, for he judged it expedient to humor Monsieur Canivet, whose prescriptions sometimes reached Yonville. He therefore did not defend Bovary or make any comment at all; abandoning his principles, he sacrificed his pride to the more serious interests of his business.

It was quite an event in the village, that leg amputation by Dr. Canivet! Everyone rose earlier than usual that morning, and even though the main street was filled with people there was something sinister in the air, as though an execution were about to take place. Hippolyte's condition was discussed in the grocer's shop; none of the shops did any business and Madame Tuvache, the mayor's wife, was so eager to see the surgeon arrive that she never moved from her window.

He came in his gig, driving it himself. Through the years the right-hand spring had given way beneath the weight of his corpulent body, so the vehicle tilted slightly to one side as it rolled along, and beside him on the other cushion could be seen an enormous box covered with red leather, its three brass clasps gleaming majestically.

When he had drawn up like a whirlwind in front of the Lion d'Or, the doctor called loudly for someone to unharness his mare, then he went into the stable to see if she was eating her oats with a good appetite, for when he came to see a patient the first thing he did was always to take care of his mare and his gig. "Ah, that Canivet is a character!" people said. And they respected him much more for his unshakable self-possession. The whole world could have perished to the last man and he would not have changed a single one of his habits.

Homais came up to him.

"I'm counting on you," said the doctor. "Are you ready? Let's go."

But the apothecary, blushing, confessed that he was too sensitive to watch such an operation.

"When you're only a spectator," he said, "your imagination runs wild, you know! And besides, my nervous system is so—"

"Why, you look more like the apoplectic type to me!" interrupted Canivet. "And it doesn't surprise me, either, because you pharmacists are always cooped up in your kitchens and it must have a bad effect on your constitution sooner or later. Just look at me: I get up at four o'clock every morning, I shave with cold water (I never feel chilly), I don't wear flannels and I never catch a cold—I'm solid as a rock. I eat whatever happens to be in front of me, and I take the good with the bad, like a philosopher. That's why I'd just as soon carve up a Christian as a chicken. Once you get used to it . . ."

Then, with no consideration for Hippolyte, who was sweating between his sheets, the two gentlemen launched into a conversation in which the apothecary compared the cool-headedness of a surgeon to that of a general. The comparison pleased Canivet and he talked at length about the demanding nature of his profession, which he regarded as a sacred mission, even though it was dishonored by the *officiers de santé*. Finally, coming back to his patient, he inspected the bandages Homais had brought, the same ones that had appeared on the day of the clubfoot operation, and asked for someone to hold the leg for him. Lestiboudois was sent for, and, after rolling up his sleeves, Monsieur Canivet went into the billiard room. The apothecary stayed with Artémise and Madame Lefrançois, who were both whiter than their aprons, and the three of them kept their ears to the door.

Bovary, meanwhile, did not dare leave his house. He stayed downstairs in the parlor, sitting beside the empty fireplace with his chin on his chest, his hands folded, his eyes staring straight ahead. "What a disaster!" he was thinking. "What a disappointment!" And yet he had taken every possible precaution. Fate had taken a hand in it. Just the same, though, if Hippolyte should die later, it would be he who had murdered him. And then what reason could he give to his patients when they questioned him? Perhaps he *had* made some mistake after all. He tried to think what it might be, but found nothing. Even the greatest surgeons sometimes made mistakes. But no one would ever believe that! Everyone would laugh at him, slander him. The story would spread to Forges, to Neufchâtel, to Rouen, everywhere! It was even possible that some of his colleagues might publicly condemn him. There would be a controversy and he would have to write replies to the newspapers. Hippolyte himself might sue him. He saw himself dishonored, ruined, lost! And his imagination, assailed by a multitude of possibilities, was tossed back and forth like an empty barrel drifting in the sea and bobbing on the waves.

Emma, sitting opposite him, was looking at him. She did not share his feelings; she too was filled with humiliation, but it was of a different nature: it came from having imagined that such a man could amount to something, as though she hadn't clearly seen his mediocrity twenty times before!

Charles began to pace up and down the room. His boots creaked with each step.

"Sit down," she said, "you're getting on my nerves!"

He sat down again.

How could she have misjudged him so seriously once again, she who was so intellingent? Furthermore, what deplorable mania had driven her to ruin her life with constant self-sacrifice? She recalled all her yearnings for luxury, all the privations of her soul, the degradations of marriage and housekeeping, her dreams fallen into the mud like wounded swallows, everything she had desired, everything she had denied herself, everything she might have had! And why? Why?

In the midst of the silence that hung over the village, a piercing shriek suddenly rent the air. Bovary turned deathly pale. She frowned nervously, then resumed her thoughts. It was for him that she had made all those sacrifices, for that creature, that man who understood nothing, felt nothing. For he was sitting there calmly, totally unaware that from now on the ridicule attached to his name would disgrace her as well as him. And she had tried to force herself to love him, she had wept tears of repentance over having given herself to another man!

"But maybe it was a valgus!" suddenly exclaimed Bovary, who was now meditating.

At the unexpected impact of this remark, crashing into her mind like a lead bullet into a silver dish, Emma started and raised her head, trying to understand what he meant. They stared at each other in silence; they had both wandered so far away in their thoughts that each was almost amazed to see the other there. Charles looked at her with the clouded eyes of a drunken man as he listened to the amputee's last screams; they came in a succession of long, varied tones interspersed with short, fitful shrieks, like the howling of some animal being slaughtered far away. Emma bit her pale lips; rolling between her fingers a branch she had broken off the coral, she glared at Charles with blazing eyes that were like two fiery arrows ready to shoot forward. Everything about him exasperated her now: his face, his clothes, what he did not say, his entire person, his very existence. She repented of her past virtue as though it had been a crime, and what was still left of it was now collapsing under the furious onslaughts of her pride. She reveled in all the malicious ironies of triumphant adultery. The memory of her lover came back to her with intoxicating charm; her heart went out to him, swept along by a new surge of ardor; and Charles seemed as detached from her life, as permanently departed, as impossible and annihilated as though he were on the point of death, gasping his last before her eyes.

There was a sound of footsteps on the sidewalk. Charles looked out through the lowered jalousies and saw Dr. Canivet at the edge of the market shed in the bright sunlight, mopping his forehead with his handkerchief. Behind him was Homais, carrying a big red box, and they were both walking toward the pharmacy.

Then, suddenly filled with tenderness and despair, Charles turned to his wife and said, "Kiss me, darling!"

"Don't come near me!" she said, flushed with anger.

"What's wrong? What's wrong?" he asked, bewildered. "Be calm, pull yourself together! You know I love you! . . . Come . . ."

"Stop!" she cried in a terrible voice.

And she rushed from the room, slamming the door so violently that the barometer was shaken from the wall and shattered on the floor.

Charles sank into his chair, overwhelmed, wondering what could be wrong with her, imagining some sort of nervous malady, weeping and vaguely feeling that there was something ominous and incomprehensible in the air.

When Rodolphe arrived in the garden that night he found

his mistress waiting for him at the bottom of the steps. They embraced, and all their rancor melted like snow in the warmth of their kiss.

XII

Their love began anew. Often, in the middle of the day, she would suddenly write to him, then beckon through the window to Justin, who would quickly take off his apron and run to La Huchette; Rodolphe would come: she wanted to tell him she was bored, that her husband was odious and that life was horrible.

"What do you expect *me* to do about it?" he exclaimed impatiently one day.

"Oh, if only you would . . ."

She was sitting between his knees, with her hair hanging loose and a vague, dreamy look in her eyes.

"What could I do?" asked Rodolphe.

"We could go live somewhere else," she sighed, "in a place where . . ."

"You've really lost your mind!" he said, laughing. "You know that's impossible!"

She tried to discuss it with him; he seemed not to understand her and soon changed the subject. What he did not understand was why she should make such a fuss over such a simple thing as a love affair.

But she had a reason, a motive, something that reinforced her attachment to Rodolphe. Every day her love for him was increased by the repugnance she felt for her husband. The more completely she gave herself to the one, the more she loathed the other. Charles never seemed so disagreeable to her, his fingers never seemed so blunt, his mind so dull or his manners so crude as when she saw him after one of her meetings with Rodolphe. As she acted out her role of wife and virtuous woman, she would ardently think of her lover's black hair curling down over his tanned forehead, of his powerful yet elegant body, of his mature intelligence and hot-blooded temperament. It was for him that she filed her fingernails with the meticulous care of an engraver, faithfully rubbed her skin with cold cream and scented her handkerchiefs with patchouli. She wore all sorts of bracelets, rings and necklaces. On days when she expected him to come she would fill her two big blue glass vases with roses, arrange the whole room and adorn herself as though she were a courtesan awaiting a visit from a prince. The maid was kept busy washing lingerie; she was in the kitchen all day long, and young Justin watched her work there when he came in to keep her company for a while, as he frequently did.

With his elbow on the long ironing board, he would stare avidly at all the feminine garments spread out around him: dimity petticoats, fichus, collars and drawstring pantaloons, bulging voluminously at the hips and narrowing below.

"What's this for?" the boy would ask, running his hand over something made of crinoline, or a row of hook-and-eye fasteners.

"Haven't you ever seen anything?" Félicité would reply with a laugh. "I suppose your Madame Homais doesn't wear the same things!"

"Oh, Madame Homais . . ." And he would add thoughtfully, "Do you think she's a lady like Madame Bovary?"

But his constant visits were beginning to annoy Félicité. She was six years his elder, and Théodore, Monsieur Guillaumin's servant, was beginning to show an interest in her.

"Leave me alone!" she would say to him as she picked up her pot of starch. "Why don't you go grind your almonds, instead of always hanging around women? You're too young for that, little boy—you'd better wait till you get some whiskers on your chin."

"Don't be angry with me. I'll do her shoes for you."

And he would take Emma's shoes from the mantelpiece. They would always be caked with mud from her last meeting with Rodolphe. It would crumble to dust beneath his fingers and he would watch it slowly float upward in a ray of sunlight.

"You're so afraid of spoiling them!" the cook would say. She was not so careful when she cleaned them herself, because Madame always gave them to her as soon as they no longer looked new.

Emma had many pairs in her closet; she was always throwing them away and buying new ones, but Charles never ventured to make the slightest comment.

And he made no complaint about paying out three hundred

francs for a wooden leg which she felt they ought to give Hippolyte.

It was trimmed with cork and had spring joints, a complicated mechanism covered by a black trouser leg and ending in a black patent-leather shoe. But Hippolyte, reluctant to use such a beautiful leg every day, begged Madame Bovary to get him another one that would make him feel more at ease. Charles naturally paid for this one also.

The stableboy gradually resumed his work. He went all over the village as before, and Charles quickly turned in another direction whenever he heard the sharp tap of his stick on the cobblestones in the distance.

It was Monsieur Lheureux, the shopkeeper, who had taken care of the order; it gave him several opportunities to visit Emma. He talked with her about the latest items from Paris, about countless feminine novelties; he was extremely obliging and never asked for money. Emma abandoned herself to this easy way of satisfying all her whims. Thus, for example, when she decided to give Rodolphe a beautiful riding crop that was for sale in an umbrella shop in Rouen, Monsieur Lheureux laid it on her table the following week.

But the next day he came to her with a bill for two hundred and seventy francs, not counting the centimes. Emma did not know what to do: every drawer of the writing desk was empty, they owed Lestiboudois for two weeks of work, they had not paid Félicité for the past six months and they had many other debts besides. Bovary was impatiently awaiting a remittance from Monsieur Derozerays, who usually settled his account once a year, toward St. Peter's Day.

She managed to put Lheureux off for a while, but finally he lost patience: he was hard pressed for money, his capital was all tied up and if she did not pay him at least part of what she owed him he would be forced to take back all the items he had given her.

"Go ahead, take them!" said Emma.

"Oh, I was only joking," he replied. "The riding crop is really the only thing I'd like to get back. I'll ask your husband for it."

"No! No!" she cried.

"Aha, I've got you!" thought Lheureux.

And, sure of his discovery, he left her, saying softly, with his usual little hiss, "All right, we'll see. We'll see."

She was wondering how to get out of her predicament when

the cook walked in, put a little roll of blue paper on the mantel-piece and said, "It's from Monsieur Derozerays." Emma snatched it up and opened it. It contained fifteen napoleons: payment in full. She heard Charles on the stairs; she threw the gold coins into a drawer and took the key.

Lheureux came back three days later.

"I have an arrangement to suggest to you," he said. "If, instead of paying the sum we've agreed on, you'd be willing to take—"

"Here's the money!" she said, placing fourteen napoleons in his hand.

The shopkeeper was dumbfounded. Then, to conceal his disappointment, he showered her with apologies and offers of service, all of which she declined. When he was gone she stood for several minutes with her hand in her apron pocket, fingering the two five-franc coins he had given her as change. She promised herself she would economize, so that eventually she could pay back . . .

"Oh, what's the difference?" she said to herself. "He won't even think about it. . . ."

Besides the riding crop with the silver-gilt pommel, Rodolphe had received a signet ring with the motto *"Amor nel Cor,"* a scarf to be used as a muffler, and a cigar case almost exactly like the one belonging to the viscount, which Charles had picked up on the road and which Emma still kept. These presents humiliated him, however. Several times he refused to take them, but she always insisted and he finally gave in to her, inwardly complaining about the way she tyrannized him and interfered in his life.

And she had such silly ideas: "When the clock strikes midnight," she would say to him, "think of me." Then, if he admitted he had not thought of her, he would have to listen to a long series of reproaches, always ending with the eternal question: "Do you love me?"

"Of course I do."

"Very much?"

"Of course!"

"You never loved anyone before me, did you?"

"You don't think you deflowered me, do you?" he retorted, laughing.

Emma wept and he tried to comfort her, enlivening his protestations with puns.

"It's because I love you!" she said. "I love you so much I can't do without you. Do you really know that? Sometimes

I suddenly feel I have to see you, and my love makes me furious. 'Where is he?' I wonder. 'Maybe he's talking to some other woman. She's smiling at him, he's moving closer to her . . .' Oh, it's not true, is it? You're not interested in anyone else, are you? Some women are prettier than I am, but none of them could love you the way I do! I'm your servant and your concubine! You're my king, my idol! You're so good! So handsome! So intelligent! So strong!"

He had heard such things said to him so many times before that they no longer held any interest for him. Emma was like any other mistress; and the charm of novelty gradually fell away like a garment, revealing in all its nakedness the eternal monotony of passion, which always has the same form and speaks the same language. He, this man of great experience, could not distinguish dissimilarities of feeling beneath similarities of expression. Because lascivious or venal lips had murmured the same words to him, he now had little belief in their sincerity when he heard them from Emma; they should be taken with a grain of salt, he thought, because the most exaggerated speeches usually hid the weakest feelings—as though the fullness of the soul did not sometimes overflow into the emptiest phrases, since no one can ever express the exact measure of his needs, his conceptions or his sorrows, and human speech is like a cracked pot on which we beat out rhythms for bears to dance to when we are striving to make music that will wring tears from the stars.

But, with the shrewdness of those who hold themselves aloof in any relationship, Rodolphe saw other pleasures to be developed in his affair with Emma. He came to feel that all modesty was merely tiresome. He began to treat her coarsely, without consideration. He made her into something compliant and corrupt. She remained under the influence of a kind of idiotic infatuation, full of admiration for him and sensuality for herself, a blissful torpor; and her soul, sinking into that intoxication, shriveled and drowned like the Duke of Clarence in his butt of malmsey.

Her amorous activities changed her everyday behavior. Her glance grew bolder, her speech freer; she even had the audacity to walk with Rodolphe in public with a cigarette in her mouth, "as though she wanted to defy the whole world," people said. Finally even those who still had doubts lost them when she was seen stepping out of the Hirondelle one day wearing a tight, mannish-looking vest; and the elder Madame Bovary, who had come to take refuge in her son's house after a terrible scene with her husband, was by no means the least scandalized lady in town. There were many other things that displeased her: first of all, Charles had not followed her advice about forbidding Emma to read novels, and then she "didn't like the way the house was being run"; she took the liberty of making a few comments and there were quarrels, the most serious of which was touched off by Félicité.

The night before, as she was walking down the hall, the elder Madame Bovary had surprised her with a man, a man of about forty, with a fringe of dark whiskers around the lower part of his face, who had quickly run out of the kitchen when he heard her footsteps. Emma laughed when she heard about the incident, but the good lady flared up and said that unless one cared nothing about morals oneself, one ought to supervise those of one's servants.

"What social class do you come from?" said Emma, with such an impertinent look that her mother-in-law asked her if it wasn't really herself she was defending.

"Get out!" shouted Emma, leaping to her feet.

"Emma! Mother!" cried Charles, trying to reconcile them But they both stormed out of the room.

"Oh, what narrow-mindedness!" said Emma, stamping her foot. "What a peasant!"

He ran to his mother: she was beside herself with rage. "I've never seen such insolence!" she stammered. "She's an irresponsible fool, and maybe worse!"

She announced that she would leave immediately unless Emma came to her and apologized. Charles went back to his wife and begged her to give in; he knelt at her feet; she finally said, "All right! I'll do it!"

She held out her hand to her mother-in-law with the dignity of a marquise and said to her, "Excuse me, madame."

Then she went up to her room, threw herself face downward on the bed and wept like a child, with her head buried in the pillow.

She and Rodolphe had agreed that in case of an emergency she would fasten a little piece of white paper to her window blind, and that if he should happen to be in Yonville at the time he would hurry to the lane behind the house. She put up the signal; she had been waiting for three-quarters of an hour when she saw him at one corner of the market shed. She was tempted to open the window and call out to him, but he had already disappeared. She fell back on her bed in despair.

A short time later, however, she thought she heard someone walking on the footpath. She was sure it was Rodolphe. She went downstairs and crossed the courtyard. He was there, on the other side of the wall. She threw herself in his arms.

"Be careful!" he said.

"Oh, if you only knew what I've been through!" she replied. And she began to tell him the whole story, hurriedly, incoherently, exaggerating some facts, inventing others, and inserting so many parenthetical remarks that he had no idea of what she was trying to tell him.

"Come, darling, be brave! Cheer up! Be patient!"

"But I've been patient for four years now, and I've been suffering the whole time! A love like ours shouldn't have to be hidden from anyone! They're torturing me! I can't stand it any longer! Save me!"

She clung to him tightly. Her eyes, filled with tears, flashed like flames beneath a troubled sea; her panting breath made her chest heave rapidly. He loved her more than ever before, so much that he lost his head and said to her, "What should we do? What do you want?"

"Take me away!" she cried. "Take me with you! I beg you!"

And she pressed her lips to his, as though to seize the unexpected consent that he was now breathing out in a kiss.

"But . . ." he began.

"What?"

"What about your daughter?"

She thought for a few moments, then answered, "We'll just have to take her with us!"

"What a woman!" he said to himself as he watched her move away. She slipped back into the garden: someone was calling her.

During the days that followed, the elder Madame Bovary was amazed by her daughter-in-law's transformation. Emma was now docile, and she even carried deference to the point of asking her for a pickle recipe.

Was it in order to deceive Charles and his mother more thoroughly? Or was it that, with a kind of voluptuous stoicism, she wanted to feel more deeply the bitterness of the things she was about to leave behind? Actually, she was oblivious to everything around her, for she was completely absorbed in savoring her future happiness. It was the subject of endless conversations with Rodolphe. She would lean on his shoulder and murmur, "Just think what it will be like when we're in the stagecoach together! Can you imagine it?

When the carriage begins to move I think I'll feel as though
we're going up in a balloon, soaring up into the clouds. I
keep counting the days. . . . Do you?"

Madame Bovary had never been so beautiful as she was
now; she had that indefinable beauty which results from joy,
enthusiasm and success, and which is essentially a harmony
between temperament and circumstances. She had been gradually developed by her desires, her sorrows, her sensual
experience and her still-young illusions, as flowers are developed by manure, rain, wind and sun, and her entire nature
was now in bloom. Her eyelids seemed to have been made
expressly for those long amorous glances in which her pupils
were lost in profound reverie while her heavy breathing
dilated her thin nostrils and raised the fleshy corners of her
lips, with their delicate shadow of dark down. Her twisted
hair seemed to have been arranged by some artist skilled in
corruption; it lay coiled in a heavy mass, carelessly shaped
by the adulterous embraces that loosened it every day. Her
voice now took on softer inflections, and so did her body;
even the folds of her dress and the arch of her foot gave off a
kind of subtle, penetrating emanation. Charles found her exquisite and utterly irresistible, as in the first days of their
marriage.

When he came home in the middle of the night he did not
dare to wake her. The porecelain night lamp cast its round,
trembling glow on the ceiling, and the drawn curtains of the
little cradle made it look like a white hut swelling out in the
shadows beside the bed. Charles looked at his wife and
daughter. He thought he could hear the child's light breathing. She would be growing up rapidly from now on; each
season would bring changes. He saw her already coming
home from school at the end of the day, laughing, her blouse
stained with ink, her basket on her arm; then she would have
to be put in boarding school, which would be very expensive;
how would they manage? He pondered the question. He
thought of renting a small farm in the vicinity: he would be
able to supervise it himself every morning on his way to visit
his patients. He would put all the income from it into a sav-
ings account, then later he would invest the money in some
kind of securities. Besides, his practice would grow; he was
counting on it, because he wanted Berthe to have a good
education, to be an accomplished young lady, to take piano
lessons. How pretty she would be later, at fifteen! She would
look just like her mother, and they would both wear wide

straw hats in summer; from a distance they would look like two sisters. He pictured her working beside them in the evening, by lamplight; she would embroider slippers for him and help run the household; she would fill the whole house with her sweetness and gaiety. Finally they would think about her marriage: they would find her some fine young man with a good position; he would make her happy, and it would last forever.

Emma was not asleep, but only pretending to be; and while he sank into sleep beside her she lay awake, dreaming different dreams.

She and Rodolphe had been traveling for a week, drawn by four galloping horses toward a new country from which they would never return. They went on and on, their arms intertwined, without speaking. Often from the top of a mountain they would suddenly catch sight of some magnificent city, with domes, bridges, ships, forests of lemon trees and white marble cathedrals with storks' nests on their pointed steeples. The horses slowed to a walk as they approached, because of the large paving stones, and along the street there were bouquets of flowers being offered for sale by women in red bodices. They could hear the ringing of bells and the braying of mules, mingled with the strumming of guitars and the murmur of fountains whose flying spray cooled pyramids of fruit piled up at the feet of pale statues smiling through the jets of water. And then one night they would arrive in a fishing village where brown nets were drying in the wind along the cliff, in front of the cottages. This was where their journey would end; they would live in a low, flat-roofed house shaded by a palm tree, near the water at the end of a bay. They would ride in gondolas and swing in hammocks; their lives would be easy and relaxed, like their loose silk clothing, warm and starry like the soft nights they would contemplate together. Nothing specific, however, stood out in the vast expanse of the future as she imagined it: the days, all glorious, were as alike as the waves of the sea, and they stretched out endlessly to the farthest horizon, harmonious, blue, and bathed in sunlight. But then Berthe would cough in her cradle, or Charles would begin to snore more loudly, and Emma would not fall asleep until morning, when dawn was whitening the windowpanes and Justin, outside in the square, was already opening the shutters of the pharmacy.

She had sent for Monsieur Lheureux and said to him, "I need a cloak, a big one, with a long collar and a lining."

"Are you going on a trip?" he asked.

"No! But . . . Anyway, I can count on you to get one for me, can't I? And soon!"

He bowed.

"I'll also need a trunk," she went on. "Not too heavy . . . Easy to handle."

"Yes, yes, I know what you want: a trunk about three feet by a foot and a half, the kind they're making nowadays."

"And an overnight bag."

"She's had a quarrel with her husband, no doubt about it," thought Lheureux.

"Here, take this," said Madame Bovary, unfastening her watch from her belt. "You can sell it and take your payment out of what you get for it."

But the shopkeeper cried out that she was midjudging him; they knew each other, and he had complete confidence in her. What a foolish idea! But she insisted that he take at least the chain; he had already put it in his pocket and was on his way out when she called him back.

"Leave the trunk and the bag in your shop for the time being," she said. "As for the cloak"—she pretended to be trying to make up her mind—"don't bring it to me either; just give me the tailor's address and tell him to have it ready for me when I want it."

They had set their departure for the following month. She would leave Yonville as though going to do some shopping in Rouen. Rodolphe would have made reservations for them, taken out passports and even written to Paris so that they could have the whole coach to themselves as far as Marseilles, where they would buy a light carriage and continue along the road to Genoa without stopping. She would send her baggage to Lheureux's shop, from where it would be taken directly to the Hirondelle, so that no suspicion would be aroused. In all this there was never any mention of her child. Rodolphe avioded the subject; perhaps Emma had forgotten about her.

He said he needed two weeks in which to complete a few arrangements, then after the first one had gone by he said he needed two more; then he said he was ill; then he went off on a trip. The whole month of August passed. Finally, after all these delays, they decided they would leave without fail on September 4, a Monday.

At last Saturday came: only two more days! Rodolphe arrived earlier than usual that evening.

"Is everything ready?" she asked him.

"Yes."

They walked around a flower bed and sat down on the retaining wall of the terrace.

"You're sad," said Emma.

"No, I'm not; what makes you think so?"

And yet he looked at her in a strange, tender way.

"Are you sad because you're going away?" she asked. "Because you'll be leaving the things you love, the things that make up your life now? I can understand that. . . . But I have nothing, nothing at all! You're everything for me. And I'll be everything for you: your family, your country; I'll take care of you, I'll love you."

"You're so sweet!" he said, clasping her in his arms.

"Am I really?" she asked with a voluptuous laugh. "Do you love me? Swear you do!"

"Do I love you! What a question! I adore you, my angel!"

The moon, dark red and perfectly round, was just climbing above the horizon, beyond the meadows. It rose swiftly behind the poplars, whose branches partially hid it like a torn black curtain, then it appeared in all its elegant whiteness, lighting up the cloudless sky; finally, moving more slowly, it cast on the surface of the river a large patch of light which glittered like an infinity of stars; the silvery gleam seemed to writhe all the way to the bottom of the water like a headless serpent covered with luminous scales. It also resembled a monstrous candlestick with molten diamonds streaming down its sides. The soft night enveloped them; the spaces between the leaves of the trees were filled in with dark shadows. Emma, her eyes half closed, breathed in the cool breeze with deep sighs. Lost in reverie, they did not speak. The sweetness of earlier days returned to their hearts, as abundant and silent as the flowing river, soft as the fragrance of the lilacs, and it projected into their memories longer and more melancholy shadows than those cast on the grass by the motionless willows. Often some prowling nocturnal animal, a hedgehog or a weasel, would rustle through the foliage, and occasionally they heard the sound of a ripe peach dropping from one of the trees along the wall.

"What a beautiful night!" said Rodolphe.

"We'll have others!" replied Emma. Then, as though talking to herself, she went on: "Yes, it will be good when we're traveling. . . . And yet, why is my heart so sad? Is it fear of the unknown? Or uneasiness over leaving everything I'm used to? Or is it . . . No, it's only because I'm too happy! I'm so weak! Forgive me!"

"There's still time to change your mind!" he cried. "Think it over—you may regret it."

"Never!" she replied impetuously. She moved closer to him and said, "What do I have to fear? There's no desert, no precipice, no ocean that I wouldn't cross with you! The longer we live together the more it will be like an embrace that grows tighter and more complete every day! There'll be nothing to bother us, nothing for us to worry about, nothing to stand between us! We'll be alone, all to ourselves, forever and ever! . . . Say something, answer me."

He answered at regular intervals: "Yes . . . Yes . . ."

She had put her fingers in his hair, and, in a childish voice, despite the big tears welling up in her eyes, she said over and over, "Rodolphe! Rodolphe! Oh, Rodolphe, my darling Rodolphe!"

Midnight struck.

"Midnight!" she said. "It's tomorrow already! One more day!"

He stood up to leave, and as though this movement were the signal for their flight, Emma's face suddenly brightened.

"Do you have the passports?" she asked.

"Yes."

"You haven't forgotten anything?"

"No."

"Are you sure?"

"Of course."

"You'll be waiting for me at the Hôtel de Provence at noon, won't you?"

He nodded.

"Till tomorrow, then!" said Emma, caressing him one last time.

And she watched him walk away.

He did not look back. She ran after him and called out to him, leaning over the water among the bushes, "Till tomorrow!"

He was already on the other side of the river, walking swiftly across the meadow.

After several minutes he stopped, and when he saw her, in her white dress, gradually vanishing in the shadows like a phantom, his heart began to pound so wildly that he leaned against a tree to steady himself.

"What a fool I am!" he exclaimed, swearing violently. "Just the same, though, she was a pretty mistress!"

And Emma's beauty, along with all the pleasures of their love, rushed back into his mind. For a moment he was deeply moved, then he rebelled against her.

"After all," he cried, gesticulating, "I can't go into exile and saddle myself with a child!" He told himself these things to strengthen his resolution. "And besides, all that trouble and expense . . . Oh, no! No, by God! That would be too stupid!"

XIII

As soon as he reached home, Rodolphe brusquely sat down at his desk, beneath the stag's-head trophy hanging on the wall. But when he had his pen between his fingers he could think of nothing to write; he leaned on his elbows and pondered. Emma seemed to have receded into the remote past, as though the decision he had made had abruptly put a great distance between them.

In order to recapture some feeling of her, he went to the wardrobe at the head of his bed and took out the old Reims cookie box in which he kept most of the letters he had received from women. A smell of damp dust and withered roses floated up from it. The first thing he saw was a handkerchief covered with pale little stains. It was one of Emma's: she had once had a nosebleed while they were out walking together; he had forgotten all about it. Rattling around inside the box was the miniature she had given him; the clothes she was wearing in the picture struck him as pretentious, and her sidelong glance, meant to be seductive, seemed merely pitiful. Then, as he stared at the portrait, trying to evoke the memory of the model, Emma's features became confused in his mind, as though the living face and the painted one were rubbing together and wearing each other away. Finally he read some of her letters; they were full of details concerning their trip, as short, practical and urgent as business letters. He wanted to read the long ones, the early ones; to take them from the bottom of the box he had to push aside everything on top of them, and automatically he began to go through the pile of letters and other objects. He found, all jumbled together, a number of bouquets, a garter, a black mask, pins, and locks of hair—locks of hair! Brunette and blond . . . Some of them had caught on the metal fittings of the box and broken when he opened it.

As he rummaged among his souvenirs, he examined the handwriting and style of the letters, as varied as their spelling. There were tender, jovial, facetious and melancholy ones; some of them asked for love and others for money. Some words brought back the memory of a face, a gesture, the sound of a voice; sometimes, however, he remembered nothing.

Those women, all rushing into his mind at once, got in each other's way and grew smaller, as though compressed to a common level of love. Picking up handfuls of mingled letters, he amused himself for several minutes by letting them cascade from one hand to the other. Finally, bored and drowsy, he put the box back into the wardrobe and said to himself, "What a lot of nonsense!"

This summed up his opinion, for his amorous pleasures, like children in a schoolyard, had so trampled his heart that nothing green could grow in it; they were still more casual than children, for they had not even left their names on the walls.

"All right," he said to himself, "let's go to work."

He wrote:

> You must have courage, Emma, courage! I won't let myself ruin your life . . .

"After all," he thought, "it's true: I'm acting in her interest; I'm doing the honorable thing."

> Have you given serious thought to your decision? Are you aware of the abyss into which I was about to drag you, poor angel? No, I don't think so. You were going straight ahead, confidently and blindly, firmly believing in happiness and the future. . . . Oh, how wretched we are, how senseless!

He stopped at this point, trying to think of a good excuse. "I could tell her I've lost all my money," he said to himself. "No, that won't do; and besides, she wouldn't let that stop her. I'd just have to go through the whole thing later. Why is it so hard to make women like her listen to reason?"

He reflected a while longer, then went on writing:

> I'll never forget you, believe me; and I'll always be deeply devoted to you. But some day, sooner or later, our ardor would certainly have cooled—such is the fate of all human passions. We would have begun to have moments of weariness, and who knows—I might even have had the terrible pain of witnessing your remorse, and sharing it, since I would have been the cause of it. I'm tortured by the very thought of the suffering you're about to undergo, Emma! Forget me! Why did we ever meet? Why were you so beautiful? Was it my fault? Oh no, dear God, no! Only fate is to blame!

"There's a word that always makes an impression," he said to himself.

> Ah, if you had been a frivolous-hearted woman like so many others, the adventure we planned would have held no danger for you, and I might very well have plunged into it from entirely selfish motives. But the depth of your feelings, which is both your charm and your torment, prevented you, adorable woman that you are, from realizing the falsity of our future position. At first I gave it no thought either: I was resting in the shadow of that ideal happiness as in the shade of the poisonous manchineel tree, without foreseeing the consequences.

"Maybe she'll think I'm breaking off with her out of stinginess. . . . Well, what do I care? She can think whatever she likes, I just want to get this over with!"

> The world is cruel, Emma. It would have pursued us everywhere, no matter where we went. You would have had to submit to indiscreet questions, slander, scorn, perhaps even insult. You, insulted, you whom I would have liked to place on a throne! I will carry your memory with me like a talisman, for I am punishing myself with exile for all the harm I have done you. I am going away. Where? I have no idea, my reason has left me! Adieu! Be as kind as you have always been: don't forget the wretched man who has lost you. Teach my name to your child, and tell her to include me in her prayers.

The flames of the two candles were flickering. Rodolphe stood up and closed the window. When he sat down again he said to himself, "Well, I suppose that's all. . . . No, I'd better add this, to keep her from coming here and making a scene:"

> I shall be far away when you read these sad lines, for I want to flee as quickly as possible to avoid the temptation to see you again. I must not be weak! I shall come back, and perhaps some day we shall meet again and calmly talk of our past love. Adieu!

Then he wrote still another adieu, this one separated into two words—*"A Dieu"*—which he judged to be in excellent taste.

"Now how shall I sign it?" he wondered. " 'Devotedly'? No . . . 'Your friend'? Yes, that's it."

> Your friend.

He read over his letter. It seemed good to him.

"Poor woman!" he thought with emotion. "She's going to think my heart is made of stone. There ought to be a few tearstains on the paper, but I can't weep, it's not my fault." He filled a glass with water, dipped his finger in it and let a large drop fall on the page, making a pale blot on the ink. Looking around for something with which to seal the letter, the first thing he came across was the signet ring with the motto *"Amor nel Cor."*

"That's hardly appropriate in this case. . . . Oh well, what's the difference?"

He then smoked a pipe and went to bed.

When he got up the next day (it was about two in the afternoon—he had slept late), Rodolphe had some apricots picked and placed in a basket. He hid his letter at the bottom, beneath some vine leaves, and ordered Girard, his plowboy, to deliver the basket discreetly to Madame Bovary. He had been using this means of corresponding with her for some time, sending her either fruit or game, according to the season.

"If she asks about me," he said, "tell her I've gone off on a trip. Make sure she takes the basket from you personally, don't give it to anyone else. . . . Go there right now, and don't make any mistakes!"

Girard put on his new smock, tied his handkerchief over

the apricots and set out for Yonville, plodding along in his heavy hobnailed boots.

When he arrived at Madame Bovary's house, she and Félicité were piling up linen on the kitchen table.

"Here," said the plowboy, "this is from my master."

Emma was suddenly seized with apprehension, and as she fumbled in her pocket for some change she stared wildly at the peasant, who looked back at her in bewilderment, unable to understand how such a present could cause so much emotion. Finally he left. Félicité remained. Emma was beside herself with anxiety; she hurried into the parlor as if to set down the apricots there, turned the basket upside down, pulled away the leaves, found the letter and opened it; then, as though there were a terrible conflagration behind her, she began to flee panic-stricken toward her room.

Charles was there; she saw him; he spoke to her, but she understood nothing and continued to run up the stairs, panting, distraught, reeling, still holding that horrible piece of paper, which rattled between her fingers like a sheet of tin. When she reached the third floor she stopped in front of the closed attic door.

She tried to calm herself; she remembered the letter; she had to finish it, but she did not have the courage. Besides, where could she read it? How? She would be seen.

"No, I'll be all right in here," she thought. She opened the door and went in. The heat given off by the slate roof was so intense that it seemed to press against her temples, and she could scarcely breathe. She dragged herself over to the dormer window, whose shutters were closed; she drew back the bolt and dazzling sunlight burst into the room.

Outside, beyond the rooftops, the countryside stretched away as far as she could see. Below her the village square was empty; the pebbles in the footpath glittered, the weathervanes on the houses stood motionless; from one of the lower floors of a house at the corner came a droning sound with strident modulations: Binet was working at his lathe.

Leaning against the window frame, she read the letter through to the end, with a contemptuous, angry little laugh now and then. But the more she tried to concentrate her mind on it, the more confused her thoughts became. She saw him again, heard his voice, put her arms around him; and the palpitations of her heart, striking her under the breast like the crushing blows of a battering ram, came faster and faster, at irregular intervals. She glanced around her, longing for the whole earth to crumble. Why not end it all? What was to stop her? She was free. She leaned forward, looked down at the pavement and said to herself, "Go ahead! Go ahead!"

The rays of light reflected straight up to her from below pulled the weight of her body toward the abyss. The surface of the village square seemed to rock back and forth and rise up along the walls of the houses while the attic floor slanted downward like the deck of a pitching ship. She was now at the very edge of the window, almost suspended in mid-air, surrounded by a vast emptiness. The blue of the sky penetrated her, the wind invaded her hollow head; all she had to do now was to surrender, let herself go; and the lathe droned on, like a furious voice calling to her.

"Emma! Emma!" cried Charles.

She stopped.

"Where are you? Come down!"

The thought that she had just escaped death nearly made her faint in terror; she closed her eyes, then she started when she felt a hand touch her sleeve: it was Félicité.

"Monsieur is waiting for you, madame. The soup is on the table."

She had to go downstairs and take her usual place at table!

She tried to eat. Each mouthful choked her. She unfolded her napkin as though to examine the darns, then she made a genuine effort to concentrate her attention on counting the threads of the cloth. Suddenly the memory of the letter came back to her. Had she lost it? Where could she find it? But her mind felt so weary that she was unable to invent an excuse for leaving the table. And she had become cowardly: she was afraid of Charles; he knew everything, she was sure of it! As if to confirm this, he remarked in a singular tone, "I gather we won't be seeing Monsieur Rodolphe for quite a while."

"Who told you that?" she exclaimed with a start.

"Who told me?" he said, surprised by her abrupt reaction. "Why, Girard told me—I met him just now in the Café Français. Monsieur Rodolphe is going to take a trip; he may have left already."

A sob burst from her throat.

"What's so surprising about that? He goes off on pleasure trips every once in a while, and I think he's perfectly right to do it. After all, when a man's a bachelor and has money . . . And our friend Rodolphe really knows how to enjoy himself! He's quite a playboy! Monsieur Langlois once told me . . ."

He stopped short out of respect for decorum, because the maid had just entered the room.

She picked up the apricots scattered over the top of the cabinet and put them back in the basket. Without noticing that his wife had turned crimson, Charles asked Félicité to bring them to him, took one and bit into it.

"Oh, perfect!" he said. "Here, try one."

He held out the basket to her; she gently pushed it back.

"Just smell—what an odor!" he said, moving it back and forth under her nose several times.

"I'm suffocating!" she cried, leaping to her feet.

But she overcame her spasm with an effort of will and said, "It's nothing, nothing! Just nerves. Sit down, don't stop eating!"

She was afraid he would question her, try to make her feel better, stay with her.

Charles obediently sat down again and began dropping the apricot pits on his plate, after first spitting them in his hand.

Suddenly a blue tilbury crossed the square at a fast trot. Emma cried out, fell backward and lay on the floor, unconscious.

After a great deal of thought, Rodolphe had decided to go to Rouen. Since the Yonville road is the only one between La Huchette and Buchy, he was forced to pass through the village, and Emma had recognized him in the glow of the lanterns which cut through the twilight like a flash of lightning.

The pharmacist ran into the house when he heard the commotion. The table had been overturned and all the dishes were on the floor; the room was littered with gravy, meat, knives, the salt cellar and the cruet stand; Charles was calling for help; Berthe, frightened, was shrieking; and Félicité, with trembling hands, was unlacing Madame, whose whole body was shaken by convulsions.

"I'll run over to my laboratory for some aromatic vinegar," said the apothecary.

And when she opened her eyes with the flagon under her nose he said, "I knew it would work—it would wake up a corpse!"

"Speak to us!" said Charles. "Speak to us! Pull yourself together! It's me, your Charles, who loves you! Do you recognize me? Look, here's your little girl—give her a kiss!"

The child put out her arms to hug her mother around the neck, but Emma turned her head away and said in a broken voice, "No, no . . . No one!"

She fainted again. She was carried to her bed.

She lay with her mouth open, her eyes closed and her hands flat, as motionless and white as a wax statue. Two streams of tears flowed slowly from her eyes to the pillow.

Charles stood in the alcove, at the foot of the bed, and the pharmacist stood beside him, observing the thoughtful silence appropriate to the serious occasions of life.

"Don't worry," he said, nudging Charles with his elbow, "I think the paroxysm is past."

"Yes, she's resting a little now," replied Charles, watching her sleep. "Poor Emma! . . . Poor Emma! . . . She's had a relapse!"

Homais asked how the accident had occurred. Charles answered that she had been suddenly overcome while eating apricots.

"Amazing!" said the pharmacist. "The apricots may have been what made her faint! Some natures are so sensitive to certain odors! It would be a good question to study, as a matter of fact, from a pathological as well as a physiological point of view. The priests know how important it is—they've always aromatics in their ceremonies. They do it to stupefy the understanding and bring on a state of trance, which is easy to do with women, because they're more delicate than men. Some women have been known to faint from the smell of burnt horn, or fresh bread. . . ."

"Be careful not to wake her!" said Charles softly.

"And animals as well as human beings are subject to such anomalies," continued the apothecary. "For instance, I'm sure you know about the extraordinary aphrodisiac effect produced on the feline race by *nepeta cataria,* commonly known as catnip; and, to cite another example, one whose authenticity I can personally vouch for, an old friend of mine by the name of Bridoux, who's now in business on the Rue Malpalu, has a dog that goes into convulsions if you hold out a snuffbox in front of him. Bridoux often performs the experiment for his friends, in his house in Bois-Guillaume. Would you believe that a simple sternutatory could work such havoc in the organism of a quadruped? It's an extremely curious case, isn't it?"

"Yes," said Charles, who was not listening.

"It illustrates one of the countless irregularities of the nervous system," said the pharmacist with a smile of benign self-satisfaction. "As for Madame, I confess that she's always seemed to me a real sensitive. That's why, my good friend, I advise you not to use any of those so-called remedies which claim to attack the symptoms but actually attack the temperament. No, no useless medication! A proper regimen is all that's needed! Sedatives, emollients, antacids. And then, don't you think it might be a good idea to stimulate her imagination?"

"How?" asked Bovary. "What would do it?"

"Ah, that's just it!" replied Homais. "That's the problem! 'That is the question,' " he said in English, "as I read in the paper recently."

At this point Emma awoke and cried out, "The letter! Where is it?"

They thought she was delirious, and from midnight on she was: brain fever had set in.

Charles stayed with her for forty-three consecutive days. He abandoned all his patients; he never went to bed; he was constantly feeling her pulse and applying mustard plasters or cold compresses. He sent Justin to Neufchâtel for ice; the ice melted on the way; he sent him back. He called in Dr. Canivet for consultation; he sent to Rouen for Dr. Larivière, his old teacher; he was desperate. What alarmed him most was Emma's extreme prostration: she did not speak, heard nothing, and even seemed to be in no pain, as though both her body and her soul were resting from all their agitation.

Toward the middle of October she was able to sit up in bed with pillows behind her. Charles wept when he saw her eat her first piece of bread and jam. Her strength returned; she got out of bed for a few hours every afternoon, and one day when she was feeling better he persuaded her to take his arm and go out for a stroll in the garden. The gravel on the paths was almost entirely covered by dead leaves; she walked slowly, dragging her slippers, leaning on his shoulder and smiling the whole time.

They went to the far end of the garden, near the terrace. She drew herself up slowly, shaded her eyes with her hand and looked into the distance, as far as she could see; but there was nothing on the horizon except big grass fires smoking on the hills.

"You mustn't get too tired, darling," said Bovary. He tried to guide her gently into the arbor. "Sit down on the bench, you'll feel better."

"Oh, no! Not there! Not there!" she said in a faltering voice.

She had a dizzy spell, and that night her illness began again, this time with more erratic and complex symptoms. Sometimes her heart would pain her, then it would be her chest, her head or her limbs; she had fits of vomiting which Charles regarded as the first signs of cancer.

And, aside from all this, the poor man had money worries!

XIV

First of all, he did not know how he would ever manage to pay Monsieur Homais for all the medicaments he had taken from the pharmacy. As a doctor, he might have been exempted from any payment, but the obligation embarrassed him nevertheless. And then the household expenses were becoming alarming, now that the cook was in charge of everything; there was a steady stream of bills; the tradesmen were all grumbling; Monsieur Lheureux, especially, was harassing him: at the height of Emma's illness, taking advantage of the circumstances to pad his bill, he had quickly delivered the cloak, the overnight bag, two trunks instead of one, and a number of other things. Charles vainly protested that he had no use for them: the shopkeeper arrogantly replied that all those articles had been ordered from him and that he would not take them back; besides, it would mean upsetting Madame during her convalescence; Monsieur ought to think it over. In short, he was determined to take the matter to court rather than give up his rights and take back the merchandise. Shortly thereafter Charles told Félicité to have everything sent back to the shop, but she forgot; having other things on his mind, he gave it no further thought. Monsieur Lheureux came back; alternately threatening and groaning, he maneuvered Charles into signing a promissory note due six months later. But almost as soon as he signed it a bold idea came to him: why not borrow a thousand francs from Monsieur Lheureux? So he timidly asked if it was possible, adding that the loan would be for one year and at whatever interest Lheureux might see fit to charge. Lheureux hurried to his shop, came back with the money and dictated another promissory note whereby Bovary agreed to pay him 1,070 francs on September first of the following year; combined with the 180 francs already stipulated, this made a total of 1,250. Thus, lending at six per cent, plus his commission, and adding a mark-up of at least one-third to the cost of his merchandise, the whole transaction would yield a profit of 130 francs in twelve months; and he hoped the matter would not stop there, that Charles would be unable to pay the notes and would therefore have to renew them, and that finally his poor money, having been nourished in the doctor's house as in a sanitorium, would come back to him considerably plumper, fat enough to burst the bag.

Everything he did was turning out well these days. He had been awarded a contract to supply the Neufchâtel hospital with cider; Monsieur Guillaumin had promised him some shares in the peatery at Grumesnil; and he was thinking of beginning a new stagecoach line between Arcueil and Rouen, which would soon drive the Lion d'Or's old rattle trap out of business, and, being faster and cheaper and carrying greater loads, it would put the entire Yonville trade in his hands.

Charles wondered several times how he would be able to pay back such a large sum the following year. He racked his brain and thought of a number of expedients, such as asking his father to help him or selling something. But his father would turn a deaf ear to him and he had nothing to sell. He foresaw such overwhelming difficulties that he put the unpleasant subject out of his mind. He reproached himself with having forgotten Emma because of it, as though all his thoughts belonged to her and he could not stop thinking about her for a moment without being guilty of stealing something from her.

It was a severe winter. Emma's convalescence was slow. When the weather was good, her armchair was pushed over to the window, the one overlooking the square, for she now had an aversion to the garden, and the blinds on that side of the room were always drawn. She insisted that her horse be sold; things she had once liked now displeased her. All her thoughts seemed to be limited to taking care of herself. She ate light meals in bed and rang for the maid to ask about her tisanes, or just to talk with her. Meanwhile the snow on the roof of the market shed cast its steady white reflection into her room; then the rainy season began. And every day she waited with a kind of anxiety for the infallible recurrence of commonplace events which actually meant nothing to her. The most notable of them was the arrival of the Hirondelle every evening; Madame Lefrançois would shout and other

voices would answer her while Hippolyte's lantern stood out
in the darkness like a star as he looked for baggage under
the tarpaulin. At noon Charles would come home, then he
would leave again; she would drink her bouillon; and toward
five o'clock, when it was getting dark, the children on their
way from school, dragging their wooden shoes on the sidewalk, would all hit the catches of the shutters with their
rulers, one after the other.

It was at this time that Father Bournisien usually came to
see her. He would ask about her health, tell her the latest
news and exhort her to greater piety in an affectionate, gar-
rulous manner that was not without charm. She was comforted by the mere sight of his cassock. One day at the
height of her illness, when she thought she was dying, she
had asked for Communion, and as preparations for the sacrament were made in her room—the dresser, its top cluttered
with medicine bottles, was transformed into an altar, and
Félicité strewed dahlia blossoms over the floor—Emma felt
something strong pass over her, ridding her of all pain, all
perception, all feeling. Her unburdened body stopped thinking, another life was beginning; it seemed to her that her
spirit, rising up to God, was about to be annihilated in this
love, like burning incense dissolving in smoke. The sheets of
the bed were sprinkled with holy water; the priest took the
white Eucharistic host from the sacred pyx; and she was overcome with celestial bliss when she advanced her lips to receive the body of the Saviour. The curtains of her alcove
swelled out gently around her like clouds, and the rays of
light given off by the two wax tapers burning on the dresser
seemed to be dazzling aureoles. She let her head fall back,
thinking she heard the music of angelic harps coming to her
through boundless space; and on a golden throne in an azure
sky, amid saints holding green palm branches, God the Father
appeared in all His majesty, motioning angels with wings of
flame to descend to earth and bring her back in their arms.

This splendid vision remained in her memory as the most
beautiful dream possible, and she kept trying to recapture
the original sensation; its profound sweetnees had not diminished, but never again did it fill her mind so completely.
Her soul, exhausted and aching from so much pride, was at
last resting in Christian humility; and, savoring the pleasure
of being weak, she watched the inner destruction of her will,
which would no doubt clear a wide path for the entrance of
divine grace. She now saw that there was a bliss greater than

worldly happiness, and a different kind of love transcending all others, a constant, endless love that would grow through all eternity! Among the illusions of her hope, she glimpsed a state of purity floating above the earth, merging into the sky, and she longed to attain it. She resolved to become a saint. She bought rosaries and wore holy medals; she wished she could have an emerald-studded reliquary at the head of her bed so that she could kiss it every night.

The priest was amazed by her new attitude, although he felt that her piety, by its very fervor, might eventually border on heresy or even madness. But not being very well versed in such matters once they went beyond a certain point, he wrote a letter to Monsieur Boulard, the bishop's bookseller, asking him to send him "something especially good for a lady with a first-rate mind." As indifferently as though he were shipping trinkets to African savages, the bookseller packed up a collection of everything current in the religious book trade at the time: little question-and-answer manuals, pamphlets written in a haughty tone, in the manner of Monsieur de Maistre, and what might be called novels, in pink bindings and sugary style, concocted by troubadour seminarians or reformed bluestockings. There were such titles as *Think It Over Carefully; The Man of the World at the Feet of Mary, by Monsieur de* —————, *Holder of a Number of Decorations; The Errors of Voltaire, for the Use of Young People;* etc.

Madame Bovary's mind was not yet clear enough to enable her to apply herself seriously to anything; and besides, she undertook this reading much too precipitately. She was annoyed by the rules laid down for worship; the arrogance of the polemical writings displeased her because of their relentlessness in attacking people she had never heard of; and the secular stories with a religious tinge impressed her as having been written in such ignorance of the world that they gradually led her away from the truths of which she was hoping to be convinced. She persisted, however, and each time the book she was reading fell from her hands she believed herself plunged into the most exquisite Catholic melancholy an ethereal soul could conceive of.

As for the memory of Rodolphe, she had pushed it down to the bottom of her heart, and it lay there as still and solemn as the mummy of a pharaoh in an underground burial chamber. This great embalmed love gave off a fragrance which seeped through everything and perfumed with tenderness the

immaculate atmosphere in which she was striving to live.
When she knelt on her Gothic *prie-dieu* she addressed the
Lord in the same sweet words she had formerly murmured to
her lover in the ardor of adultery. She did it in the hope that
it would bring faith into her heart, but no rapture ever
descended upon her from heaven, and she would stand up
with aching limbs and a vague feeling that she had been
taken in by an immense fraud. Her search, she thought, was
only an added merit, and in the pride of her devotion she
likened herself to those great ladies of the past whose glory
she had dreamed of while contemplating a portrait of La Vallière and who, majestically trailing the ornate trains of their
long gowns, had withdrawn into solitude to shed at the feet
of Christ the tears of a heart wounded by life.

She plunged into excessive charity. She sewed clothes for
the poor; she sent firewood to women in childbed; and one
day when Charles came home he found three tramps eating
soup at the kitchen table. She had her little girl, whom
Charles had sent off to the wet-nurse during her illness,
brought back to the house. She tried to teach her to read, and
no matter how much Berthe cried she never lost her temper.
She was unshakably set on resignation and universal indulgence. She used lofty terms with regard to everything. "Has
your stomach-ache gone away, my angel?" She would say to
her child.

Charles's mother found nothing to condemn in Emma's
conduct, except, perhaps, her mania for knitting undershirts
for orphans instead of mending her own dish towels. Harassed
by domestic quarrels, the good woman enjoyed visiting her
son's peaceful home; she stayed there until after Easter, in
fact, in order to avoid the sarcastic remarks of her husband,
who never failed to order pork sausage on Good Friday.

In addition to the company of her mother-in-law, who
strengthened her good resolutions by the soundness of her
judgment and the gravity of her demeanor, Emma received
almost daily visits from other ladies: Madame Langlois,
Madame Caron, Madame Dunbreuil, Madame Tuvache and,
regularly from two o'clock to five, the excellent Madame
Homais; she, at least, had never believed a word of the gossip
about her neighbor. The Homais children also came to see
her, and Justin always accompanied them. He would go up to
her room with them and stand near the door, motionless and
silent. Madame Bovary, oblivious of his presence, would often
set about rearranging her hair. She would begin by removing

her comb and vigorously shaking her head, and the first time the poor boy saw her mass of black hair fall in ringlets down to her knees, it was like the sudden apparition of something wondrous and new whose splendor frightened him.

Emma probably never noticed his silent eagerness or his timidity. She did not even suspect that love, which had vanished from her life, was palpitating there beside her, beneath that coarse shirt, in that adolescent heart open to the emanations of her beauty. Furthermore, she was now so indifferent to everything, her words were so sweet, her glance was so haughty and her whole conduct was so changeable that it was no longer possible to distinguish selfishness from charity in her, or corruption from virtue. One night, for example, she flew into a rage against her maid, who was asking permission to go out and stammering as she tried to think of an excuse. Then Emma suddenly asked her, "Do you really love him?" And without waiting for the blushing Félicité to answer, she added softly, "Go on, hurry to meet him! Enjoy yourself!"

Early in spring she had the garden transformed from one end to the other, despite Bovary's objections; he was glad, however, to see her finally asserting her will about something. She asserted it more and more as she recovered her strength. First of all, she ordered Madame Rollet to stay away from the house: during her convalescence the wet-nurse had formed the habit of coming too often to the kitchen with her two babies and her boarder, who was more ravenous than a cannibal. Then she disengaged herself from the Homais family, got rid of all her other visitors one after the other and even began going to chuch less frequently, which won the apothecary's approval. "You were starting to get a little sanctimonious," he said to her amicably.

Father Bournisien continued to stop by every day after catechism class. He preferred to stay outside in the fresh air, in the "grove," as he called the arbor. It was the time of day when Charles usually came home. He and the priest would both be hot; Félicité would bring them cider and they would drink to Madame's complete recovery.

Binet would also be there, a little below them, beside the terrace wall, fishing for crayfish. Bovary would invite him to have a drink; he knew all there was to know about uncorking jugs.

"You have to hold the bottle straight up on the table," he would say, looking around with self-satisfaction and extending his gaze as far as the horizon. "Then, after you've cut the strings, you pry up the cork a little at a time, gently, the way they open bottles of Seltzer water in restaurants."

But during these demonstrations the cider would often spurt into their faces; the priest would laugh heavily and unfailingly make this little jest: "Its goodness strikes the eye immediately!"

He was a good-natured man; he was not even scandalized one day when the pharmacist advised Charles to give his wife a pleasant diversion by taking her to the opera in Rouen to hear the famous tenor Lagardy. Homais was surprised by his silence and asked his opinion; the priest declared that he regarded music as less dangerous to morals than literature.

The pharmacist sprang to the defense of letters. The theater, he said, was useful because it ridiculed prejudice, and under the guise of entertainment it taught virtue.

"*Castigat ridendo mores*, Monsieur Bournisien! Look at most of Voltaire's tragedies, for example: they're skillfully sprinkled with philosophical remarks that make them a real school of morality and politics."

"I once saw a play called 'The Paris Urchin,'" said Binet. "There's one very good character in it: an old general. A rich young man seduces a working girl and the general really gives him what's coming to him! In the end the girl—"

"Of course," continued Homais, "there's bad literature, just as there's bad pharmacy; but, in my opinion, making a blanket condemnation of the most important of the fine arts is sheer stupidity, a barbarous idea worthy of the abominable era when Galileo was thrown into prison."

"I know very well," objected the priest, "that there are good literary works and good authors. But all those people of different sex gathered in a luxurious room decorated with all sorts of worldly splendor, and the pagan disguises, the make-up, the bright lights, the effeminate voices—those things alone are enough to create a licentious frame of mind and give rise to evil thoughts and impure temptations. At least that's the opinion of all the Fathers of the Church. . . . And if the Church condemned the theater," he added, suddenly assuming a mystical tone as he rolled himself a pinch of snuff, "she must have had good reasons for it. We must submit to her decrees."

"Why," asked the apothecary, "does the Church excommunicate actors? They used to take part openly in religious ceremonies. That's right, they used to act in churches, right in the middle of the choir—they performed farcical plays called mysteries, in which the laws of decency were often violated."

The priest contented himself with groaning and the pharmacist went on: "That's also true of the Bible: it has more than one . . . spicy passage, you know; some of the things in it are really . . . quite strong!" When Monsieur Bournisien made a gesture of irritation he added, "Ah, I'm sure you'll agree it's not a book to give to a young girl! I'd be very upset if Athalie—"

"But *we're* not the ones who recommend the Bible!" cried the priest impatiently. "It's the Protestants!"

"Just the same," said Homais, "I'm surprised that in an enlightened age such as ours, there are still people who stubbornly go on forbidding a form of intellectual diversion that's harmless, morally beneficial, and sometimes even good for the health—isn't that right, doctor?"

"I suppose so," replied Charles casually, either because he was of the same opinion but did not want to offend anyone, or because he had no opinion at all.

The conversation was apparently at an end when the pharmacist saw fit to make one final thrust:

"I've known priests who sometimes put on secular clothes and went to watch dancers wiggle their legs on the stage."

"Come now!" said the priest.

"That's right, I've known some!" And, stressing each syllable, Homais repeated, "I—have—known—some!"

"Then they were wrong," said Bournisien, resigned in advance to everything he expected to hear.

"Oh, that's not all they do, either!" exclaimed the apothecary.

"Monsieur!" said the priest with such a fierce look in his eyes that Homais was intimidated.

"I only meant to say," he replied in a gentler tone, "that tolerance is the surest way of drawing souls into religion."

"Oh, that's true, that's true," conceded the priest, sitting down in his chair again.

But he remained there only a few minutes. When he was gone, Monsieur Homais said to the doctor, "Now that was what I call an argument! You saw how I mopped up on him! I really . . . Well, anyway, follow my advice and take Madame to the opera, if only to make a priest foam at the mouth for once in your life! If there were anyone who could replace me here, I'd go with you myself. Hurry! Lagardy will give only one performance—he's already booked in England for enor-

mous fees. From what I've heard about him, he's a holy terror! He's rolling in money! He takes three mistresses and a
cook with him wherever he goes! All those great artists burn
the candle at both ends; they have to lead a wild kind of life
to stimulate their imagination. But they die in the poorhouse,
because they never have sense enough to save up some money
when they're young. Well, enjoy your dinner. See you
tomorrow!"

The idea of going to the opera quickly took root in
Bovary's mind, and he told his wife about it as soon as he
saw her. She refused at first, pleading fatigue and objecting to
the trouble and expense; but Charles was so sure the diversion
would do her good that for once he did not give in. He saw
nothing to stop them from going: his mother had sent them
three hundred francs he had stopped counting on, their
present debts were nothing enormous, and the dates when
Monsieur Lheureux's notes would have to be paid were so
far off that there was no need to think about them. Feeling
that she was refusing only out of excessive tact, he insisted
still more strongly, until finally he harassed her so much that
she consented to go. At eight o'clock the next morning they
bundled themselves into the Hirondelle.

The apothecary, who had nothing to keep him in Yonville
but believed himself forced to stay there constantly, sighed
when he saw them leave.

"Well, have a good trip, you lucky people!" he said to
them. Then, addressing himself to Emma, who was wearing
a blue silk dress with four flounces, he added, "You look
pretty as a picture! You'll cause a sensation in Rouen!"

The stagecoach let them off at the Hôtel de la Croix-Rouge,
on the Place Beauvoisine. It was one of those inns such as
one finds on the outskirts of provincial towns, with big stables and little bedrooms, and chickens pecking oats under the
muddy gigs of traveling salesmen in the yard—good old
lodgings with worm-eaten wooden balconies that creak in the
wind on winter nights, constantly full of people, commotion
and food, their black tables made sticky by spilled coffee
laced with brandy, their thick windowpanes yellowed by flies,
their damp napkins stained by cheap wine; they always have
an air of the village about them, like farmhands wearing
town clothes, and they have a café facing the street and a
vegetable garden facing the open country in back. Charles
immediately went off to get tickets. He confused the stage
boxes with the balconies, the other boxes with the orchestra;

he asked for explanations, did not understand them, was sent from the ticket seller to the manager, went back to the inn, returned to the box office, and in this way he covered the entire length of the town several times, from the theater to the boulevard.

Madame bought herself a hat, some gloves and a bouquet. Monsieur was terribly worried about missing the beginning; and, without having time to swallow a cup of bouillon, they arrived in front of the theater before the doors were open.

XV

The crowd was standing along the wall, lined up symmetrically between the railings. At the nearby street corners there were gigantic posters repeating in complicated letters: *"Lucia di Lammermoor* . . . Lagardy . . . Opera . . . etc. It was a clear night; everyone was hot; curls were wet with perspiration, handkerchiefs were taken out to mop red foreheads; and from time to time a warm wind coming from the river gently stirred the edges of the twill awnings over the café doors. A little further away, however, people were cooled off by a current of icy air which smelled of tallow, leather and oil: it was the exhalation of the Rue des Charrettes, which is lined with big, dark warehouses in which barrels are rolled across the floor.

For fear of appearing ridiculous, Emma insisted on taking a stroll along the waterfront before going into the theater. Charles cautiously held the tickets in his hand, which he kept in his trousers pocket, pressed up againt his stomach.

Her heart began to pound as soon as she entered the lobby. She involuntarily smiled with self-satisfaction when she saw the crowd hurrying off to the right along another corridor while she climbed the stairs leading to the first tier. She took childish pleasure in pushing the wide upholstered doors with her fingertip; she deeply breathed in the dusty smell of the corridors, and when she sat down in her box she arched her back with the casual ease of a duchess.

The seats were beginning to fill; opera glasses were taken out of their cases and subscribers exchanged nods as they spotted one another in the distance. They had come to let art distract them from the cares of buying and selling, but they did not forget business: they still discussed cottons, proof spirits or indigo. There were old men with placid, expressionless faces whose whitish hair and skin made them look like silver medals tarnished by lead vapor. The young dandies strutted around in the orchestra, displaying pink or apple-green cravats in the openings of their vests; and Madame Bovary admired them from above as they pressed the taut palms of their yellow gloves against the gold knobs of their walking sticks.

Meanwhile the musicians' candles were lighted and the chandelier was lowered from the ceiling; the glitter of its facets filled the theater with sudden gaiety. Then the musicians came in one after another and there was a long din of rumbling cellos, squeaking violins, blaring cornets and peeping flutes and flageolets. Finally three loud thumps came from the stage; the kettledrums rolled, the brasses struck a series of chords and the curtain rose, revealing a landscape.

It was a crossroad in the forest, with a fountain to the left, shaded by an oak. A group of peasants and noblemen with plaid cloaks over their shoulders sang a hunting song, then a captain came in and evoked the spirit of evil, raising his arms to heaven; another man appeared; he and the captain left and the huntsmen resumed their song.

Emma found herself back in the books she had read as a girl, immersed in the world of Sir Walter Scott. She seemed to hear the sound of Scottish bagpipes echoing across the heather in the mist. Her memory of the book made it easier for her to understand the libretto, and she followed the plot word by word while the elusive thoughts that came back into her mind were quickly dispersed by the overwhelming flow of the music. She abandoned herself to the soaring melodies and felt herself vibrating to the depths of her being, as though the violin bows were being drawn across her nerves. She feasted her eyes on the costumes, the sets, the characters, the painted trees which quivered whenever someone walked on the stage, the velvet toques, the cloaks, the swords—all those fanciful things moving in harmony as though in the atmosphere of another world. A young woman stepped forward, tossing a purse to a squire dressed in green. She stood alone and a flute began to play, making a sound like the tinkle of a fountain or the warbling of a bird. Lucia solemnly began her cavatina in G major; she complained of the sufferings of love and asked for wings. Emma, too, longed to flee from life, to fly away in an embrace. Suddenly Edgar Lagardy appeared.

He had one of those magnificently pale complexions which impart the majesty of a marble statue to the ardent races of the south. His robust chest was tightly encased in a brown doublet, a small chased dagger hung loosely over his left thigh and he rolled his eyes languorously, flashing his white teeth. It was said that a Polish princess, hearing him sing one night on the beach at Biarritz, where he used to repair the hulls of boats, had fallen in love with him and ruined herself for him. He had then left her for other women, and his fame as a seducer did not fail to enhance his artistic reputation. A shrewd ham actor, he always saw to it that his advertising contained a few poetic words about his personal charm and the sensitivity of his soul. A fine voice, imperturbable self-confidence, more temperament than intelligence, more pomposity than lyricism—such were the defining characteristics of this admirable charlatan, in whom there was something of both a hairdresser and a toreador.

He enraptured the audience from the very first scene. He clasped Lucia in his arms, left her, came back to her and seemed desperate; he had outbursts of anger, followed by plaintive moans of infinite sweetness, and the notes that poured from his bare throat were full of sobs and kisses. Emma leaned forward to see him better, scratching the velvet of her box with her fingernails. She filled her heart with the melodious laments as they slowly floated up to her accompanied by the strains of the double basses, like the cries of a castaway in the tumult of a storm. She recognized all the ecstasy and anguish that had once nearly brought on her death. Lucia's voice seemed only the echo of her own heart, and the illusion that was now holding her in its spell seemed a part of her own life. But no one on earth had ever loved her with such a love. Unlike Edgar, *he* had not wept during their last night together, when, in the moonlight, they had said to each other, "Till tomorrow! Till tomorrow . . ." The theater was bursting with shouts of "Bravo!" The whole stretto was repeated; the lovers spoke of the flowers on their graves, of vows, exile, fate and hope, and when they gave voice to their last farewell, Emma uttered a sharp cry which was swallowed up in the vibrations of the final chords.

"Why is that nobleman treating her so badly?" asked Bovary.

"He's not," she replied. "He's her lover."

"But he was swearing to take vengeance on her family, and the other man, the one that came on a while ago, said 'I love Lucia and I believe she loves me.' Besides, he walked off arm in arm with her father. That *was* her father, wasn't it: the ugly little man with the rooster feather in his hat?"

Despite Emma's explanations, when, at the beginning of the two-part recitative in which Gilbert describes his abominable machinations to his master Ashton, Charles saw the false engagement ring which was to deceive Lucia, he believed it to be a token of love sent by Edgar. He confessed that the whole story was unclear to him, in fact, because of the music, which made it very hard to follow the words.

"What's the difference?" said Emma. "Be quiet!"

"But I like to know what's going on, you know that," he replied, leaning on her shoulder.

"Be quiet! Be quiet!" she said impatiently.

Lucia came forward, half supported by her maids, wearing a wreath of orange blossoms in her hair and paler than the white satin of her gown. Emma thought of her wedding day and saw herself walking to the church along the narrow path between the wheatfields. Why had she not resisted and supplicated, like Lucia? But she had actually been joyful, unaware of the abyss into which she was plunging herself. . . . Oh, if only in the freshness of her beauty, before the defilement of marriage and the disillusionment of adultery, she had been able to rest her life on some noble, stalwart heart! Virtue, tenderness, sensuality and duty would have been merged, and she would never have fallen from such a lofty pinnacle of bliss. But that kind of happiness was no doubt only a lie invented to make one despair of all desires. She was now acquainted with the pettiness of the passions exaggerated by art. Forcing herself to take her mind off her sorrows, she tried to see in this reproduction of them nothing but a visual fantasy designed for her enjoyment, and she even smiled inwardly with scornful pity when a man wearing a black cloak appeared from behind the door curtain at the back of the stage.

One of his gestures sent his broad Spanish hat flying from his head, and the instruments and singers immediately launched into the sextet. Edgar, flashing fury, dominated all the others with his clearer voice; Ashton flung his murderous challenges at him in low notes; Lucia uttered her shrill lament; Arturo modulated his asides in a medium-pitched voice; and the minister's basso rumbled like an organ while the women's voices repeated his words in a delightful chorus. Everyone on the stage was now gesticulating in a single line, and anger, vengeance, jealousy, terror, compassion and amazement poured simultaneously from their half-open mouths. The outraged lover was brandishing his drawn sword; his point-lace collar rose and fell abruptly with the movements of his chest, and he strode back and forth, rattling the silver-gilt spurs attached to his soft flaring boots. He must have inexhaustible depths of love, she thought, to be able to pour it out so abundantly on the audience. All her determination to disparage the emotions vanished in the poetry that swept over her, and, drawn to the man by the illusion of his role, she tried to imagine what his life was like, that radiant, extraordinary, glorious life which she herself could have led if chance had willed it. They would have met and fallen in love! With him she would have traveled through all the kingdoms of Europe, from capital to capital, sharing his fatigue and his pride, gathering up the flowers that were thrown to him, embroidering his costumes with her own hands; and every evening, sitting at the back of a theater box, behind the gold trellis, she would have received, open-mouthed, the outpourings of his soul as he sang for her alone; he would have looked at her during every performance. A mad idea came over her: he was looking at her now, she was sure of it! She longed to rush into his arms, to take refuge in his strength as in the incarnation of love itself, to say to him, cry out to him, "Carry me off, take me with you, far away! All my passion and all my dreams are yours, yours alone!"

The curtain fell.

The smell of gas mingled with the breath of the audience; the currents of air set in motion by the fans made the atmosphere still more stifling. Emma stood up to leave; the corridors were jammed with people and she sank back into her chair, her heart palpitating so violently that she felt as though she were suffocating. Charles, afraid she might be about to faint, hurried to the refreshment stand to get her a glass of orgeat.

He had great difficulty in returning to the box, for people kept bumping against his elbow at every step, because of the glass he was holding in his hand; he spilled three-quarters of it, in fact, on the shoulders of a Rouen lady in short sleeves; feeling the cold liquid running down her back, she screamed like a peacock, as though she were being murdered. Her husband, a spinning-mill owner, angrily reprimanded the awkward passer-by, and while she wiped the stains off her beautiful cherry-red taffeta gown with her handkerchief he sullenly muttered the words "damages," "cost," and "reimbursement." At last Charles made his way back to his wife and said to her, out of breath, "Oh, I thought I'd never make it! There's such a crowd! Such a crowd!"

Then he added, "Guess who I ran into upstairs: Monsieur Léon!"

"Léon?"

"That's right! He's going to come here and pay his respects to you."

Just as he finished his sentence the former Yonville law clerk entered the box.

He held out his hand with aristocratic casualness, and Madame Bovary automatically held out hers, yielding, no doubt, to the attraction of a stronger will. She had not felt it since that spring evening when the rain was falling on the green leaves and they had told each other good-by, standing beside the window. But, quickly remembering the demands of decorum in the situation, she made an effort to shake off the torpor of her memories and began to stammer rapidly:

"Oh, good evening. . . . Imagine seeing you here!"

"Quiet!" cried a voice from the orchestra, for the third act was beginning.

"So you're living in Rouen now?"

"Yes."

"Since when?"

"Quiet! Quiet!"

People were turning around to glare at them; they stopped speaking.

But from then on she was no longer listening to the opera; the chorus of guests, the scene between Ashton and his valet, the great duet in D major—for her, everything took place as though at a distance, as though the instruments had become softer and the singers more remote. She recalled the card games in the pharmacist's house and the walk to the wet-nurse's house, the time they had spent reading to each other in the arbor, their intimate talks beside the fire—the whole course of their poor love, so calm and so long, so discreet, so tender. And yet she had forgotten it. Why had he come back to her? What combination of events had placed him in her life again? He was sitting behind her, leaning one shoulder against the wall, and from time to time she quivered when she felt his warm breath on her hair.

"Are you enjoying this?" he asked, leaning over so close to her that the tip of his mustache grazed her cheek.

She replied nonchalantly, "No, not very much."

He suggested that they leave the theater and go somewhere for an ice.

"Oh, not yet!" said Bovary. "Let's stay! Her hair is hanging loose now—it looks as if something tragic is going to happen."

But the mad scene did not interest Emma, and she felt that Lucia was overacting.

"She shrieks too loudly," she said, turning to Charles, who was listening attentively.

"Yes . . . maybe . . . a little . . ." he replied, torn between his undeniable enjoyment and the respect in which he held his wife's opinions.

Then Léon said, smiling, "It's so hot in here . . ."

"Yes, it's unbearable!"

"Are you uncomfortable?" asked Bovary.

"Yes, I'm suffocating. Let's go."

Monsieur Léon delicately spread her long lace shawl over her shoulders and the three of them went to the waterfront and sat down at an outdoor table in front of a café. First of all they spoke of her illness, although she interrupted Charles now and then, for fear, she said, of boring Monsieur Léon; then the latter told them he had come to Rouen to spend two years in a large law office in order to familiarize himself with the kind of business carried on in Normandy, which was different from what one encountered in Paris. He asked about Berthe, the Homais family and Madame Lefrançois; then, since he and Emma had nothing more to say to each other in front of her husband, the conversation soon came to an end.

People coming from the opera walked past along the sidewalk, humming or bawling at the top of their lungs, *"O radiant angel, my Lucia!"* Léon began talking about music, to show off his knowledge. He had seen Tamburini, Rubini, Persiani and Grisi; compared to them, Lagardy was nothing at all, no matter how loudly he sang.

"Still," interrupted Charles, who was nibbling a rum sherbet, "they say he's really magnificent in the last act; I'm sorry we left before the end—I was beginning to enjoy it."

"Well, he'll be giving another performance soon," said the clerk.

But Charles replied that they were leaving the following day. "Unless you'd like to stay here alone," he added, turning to his wife.

Changing his tactics in view of the unexpected opportunity that had just been offered to his hopes, the young man began to sing the praises of Lagardy in the final scene. He was superb, sublime! Charles insisted:

"You can come home Sunday. Come on, make up your mind to stay! You'd be wrong not to if you feel there's any chance it would do you good."

Meanwhile the tables around them were emptying; a waiter came over and discreetly stood near them; Charles understood the hint and took out his purse; the clerk gripped his arm to stop him, paid the bill himself and even left two silver coins as a tip, clinking them loudly on the marble table top.

"I'm terribly embarrassed," murmured Bovary, "about the money you . . ."

Léon made a friendly gesture which indicated that the matter was of no importance, took his hat and said, "Then it's agreed? Tomorrow at six?"

Charles protested once again that he could not stay away any longer than he had planned; but there was no reason why Emma shouldn't . . .

"It's just that—I'm not too sure whether—" she stammered with a strange smile.

"Well, then, think it over. We'll sleep on it tonight and decide tomorrow. . . ." Then he said to Léon, who was walking with them, "Now that you're back in our part of the world, I hope you'll come to our house for dinner every once in a while."

The clerk declared that he would certainly do so, especially since he needed to go to Yonville for a business matter. They parted in front of the Passage Saint-Herbland just as the cathedral clock struck half-past eleven.

Part Three

While studying law, Monsieur Léon had managed to spend
a considerable amount of time in the Chaumière, where he
had been quite successful with the young working girls, who
found him "distinguished-looking." He was a model student:
he wore his hair neither too long nor too short, he did not
spend in one day the money that was supposed to last him
for an entire quarter, and he kept on good terms with his
professors. As for any kind of excess, he had always avoided
it, as much from lack of courage as from refinement.

Often, when he stayed in his room to read, or when he was
sitting beneath the linden trees in the Jardin du Luxembourg,
he would drop his law book and the memory of Emma would
come back to him. But his feeling for her was gradually
weakened and overlaid by new desires, although they never
completely destroyed it, for he never gave up all hope: there
was always an uncertain promise dangling in the future like
a golden fruit hanging from some fantastic bough.

Then, on seeing her again after three years of separation,
his passion was rekindled. The time had at last come, he
decided, when he must firmly resolve to possess her. Some
of his timidity had been worn away by the loose women he
had frequented, and furthermore he was now back in the
provinces, despising all women who did not walk along the
Paris boulevards in patent-leather shoes. In the presence of
a Parisian lady adorned with lace, in the drawing room of

some illustrious physician with medals on his chest and a private carriage at his orders, the poor clerk would no doubt have trembled like a child, but here in Rouen, before the wife of this insignificant doctor, he felt at ease, sure in advance that he would dazzle her. A man's self-assurance depends on his surroundings: one speaks differently on a mezzanine and in an attic, and a rich woman seems to have all her banknotes around her, like a cuirass beneath her corset, to protect her virtue.

After taking leave of Monsieur and Madame Bovary the previous night, Léon had followed them at a distance in the street; then, having seen them enter the Croix-Rouge, he had retraced his steps and spent the entire night working out a plan.

The next day, toward five o'clock, he walked into the kitchen of the inn; his throat was tight, his cheeks were pale and he had the unshakable resolution of a coward who will stop at nothing.

"Monsieur Bovary isn't here," a servant informed him.

This was probably a good sign. He went upstairs.

She was not at all flustered when he appeared; she even apologized for having forgotten to tell him where they were staying.

"Oh, I guessed!" said Léon.

"How?"

He claimed to have been guided to her without any knowledge of where she was, by instinct. She smiled, and to repair the damage done by his blunder he quickly told her he had spent the whole morning looking for her, going from one hotel to another.

"So you've decided to stay?" he asked.

"Yes, and it's a mistake," she said. "It's wrong to let yourself get used to impractical pleasures when you're surrounded by all sorts of obligations . . ."

"Oh, I can imagine . . ."

"No, you can't, because you're not a woman."

But men also had their sorrows, and the conversation got under way with a few philosophical reflections. Emma spoke at length about the wretchedness of earthly affections and the isolation in which the heart must remain forever.

Either in order to impress her or because he spontaneously shared her melancholy, the young man declared that he had been prodigiously bored and annoyed during the whole time he had studied law. Legal procedures irritated him, he felt drawn toward other vocations, and his mother kept tormenting him in every letter she wrote to him. He and Emma became more and more specific about the causes of their sorrow, and they were both carried away by their confidences as they talked. They occasionally stopped short, leaving the statement of a thought incomplete and trying to find words that would express it in another way. She did not confess her passion for another man; he did not tell her he had forgotten her.

Perhaps he no longer remembered his suppers after fancy-dress balls, with women wearing longshoremen's costumes; and she probably no longer remembered her meetings with her lover, when she had run through the grass to his château in the morning. The sounds of the city reached them only faintly, and the room seemed small, expressly designed to enclose them more intimately in their solitude. Emma, wearing a dimity dressing gown, pressed her chignon against the back of the old armchair; the yellow wallpaper was like a golden background behind her; her bare head was reflected in the mirror, with the white line of her part running down the middle and the tips of her ears protruding from the smooth surface of her hair on each side.

"But forgive me, I shouldn't be talking like this: I'm boring you with my endless complaints."

"Oh, no! Not at all!"

"If you only knew all the things I've dreamed of!" she said, raising her lovely tear-filled eyes to the ceiling.

"It's the same with me! Oh, I've suffered so much! Often I used to go out and wander aimlessly along the river, hoping that the noise of the crowd would drown out my thoughts, but I was never able to drive away the obsession that was pursuing me. In the shop of a print dealer on the boulevard there's an Italian engraving of one of the Muses. She's draped in a tunic and she's looking up at the moon; her hair is hanging loose and there are forget-me-nots in it. Something kept driving me there again and again; I used to stand there for hours at a time." Then, in a quavering voice, he added, "She looked a little bit like you."

Madame Bovary turned her head away to hide the smile she could not prevent her lips from forming.

"I often wrote you letters," he said, "but I always tore them up."

She made no reply. He went on:

"I sometimes imagined we'd meet by chance. I used to

think I recognized you on some street corner, and every time I looked at the window of a cab and saw a shawl or a veil like yours, I'd run after it . . ."

She seemed determined to let him speak without interrupting him. Crossing her arms and lowering her head, she stared at the bows of her slippers, occasionally moving her toes beneath the satin.

"The most pitiful fate of all," she sighed at length, "is to go on dragging out a futile life, the way I do. Don't you think so? If our misery were at least useful to someone, we could console ourselves with the thought of sacrifice!"

He began to praise virtue, duty and uncomplaining sacrifice, for he too had a terribly strong need for selfless devotion which he could not satisfy.

"I'd love to be a nun in a hospital," she said.

"Alas," he replied, "there aren't any sacred missions like that for men, and I can't think of any kind of work . . . unless it's the medical profession . . ."

Emma shrugged slightly and interrupted him to complain of the illness that had nearly killed her. What a pity it hadn't! Her suffering would now be over. Léon immediately expressed his longing for "the peace of the grave"; one night he had even written his will, asking to be buried in the beautiful velvet-striped bedspread he had received from her. This was how they wished they had been: each was creating an ideal into which he was now fitting his past life. Speech is a rolling mill which always stretches out the feelings that go into it.

"Why?" she asked when she heard the story he had invented about the bedspread.

"Why?" He hesitated. "Because I was in love with you!"

Congratulating himself on having gotten past the difficulty, Léon watched her face out of the corner of his eye.

It was like the sky when a gust of wind drives away the clouds. The mass of sad thoughts which had been darkening her blue eyes seemed to withdraw from them, and her whole face became radiant.

He waited. Finally she replied:

"I always suspected it . . ."

They then went over all the details of that faraway period whose pleasures and sorrows they had just evoked with a few words. They recalled the bower of clematis, the dresses she had worn, the furniture of her bedroom, her entire house.

"And what about our poor cactuses? Where are they?"

"The cold killed them last winter."

"Oh, I've thought about them a lot, you know! I've often imagined them the way they used to look on summer mornings when the sun was shining on the blinds . . . and I saw your bare arms moving among the blossoms."

"Poor boy!" she said, holding out her hand to him.

Léon quickly pressed his lips to it. Then, after taking a deep breath, he said, "In those days you were some sort of mysterious force that cast a spell over my whole life. Once, for example, when I came to see you . . . But you probably don't remember, do you?"

"Yes," she said. "Go on."

"You were downstairs in the hall, ready to go out, standing on the bottom step. . . . I even remember your hat: it had little blue flowers on it. You didn't ask me to go with you, but I couldn't help it. I felt more and more foolish as I walked along beside you. I didn't dare to follow you all the way, yet I didn't want to leave you. When you went into a shop I stayed outside in the street; I looked in through the window and saw you take off your gloves and count the change on the counter. Then you rang Madame Tuvache's bell and went inside. I stood there like an idiot in front of the big heavy door after it had closed behind you."

As she listened to him, Madame Bovary was amazed at how old she was; all these things that were reappearing to her seemed to broaden her life, as though she were looking back over vast expanses of emotional experience; and from time to time, with half-closed eyes, she said softly, "Yes, that's true . . . I remember . . . Yes . . ."

They heard eight o'clock struck by several clocks in the Beauvoisine quarter, which is full of boarding schools, churches and large deserted mansions. They had stopped speaking, but as they looked at each other they seemed to hear a kind of humming inside their heads, as though something audible were escaping from their motionless eyes. They had just joined their hands, and the past, the future, their reminiscences, their dreams—everything merged in the sweetness of their ecstasy. Night was darkening the walls, on which could still be seen the garish colors of four prints representing four scenes from *La Tour de Nesle*, with captions beneath in French and Spanish. Through the sash window they could see a patch of dark sky between pointed rooftops.

She stood up, lit two candles on the dresser, then came back and sat down again.

"Well . . ." said Léon.

"Well . . ." she replied.

And he was trying to think of a way to resume their interrupted conversation when she said to him, "Why is it that no one ever expressed such feelings to me before?"

The clerk eagerly explained that idealistic natures were nearly always misunderstood. He, however, had fallen in love with her at first sight, and he was filled with despair at the thought of the happiness that would have been theirs if fate had brought them together sooner, for they would now be indissolubly united.

"I've thought about that sometimes," she said.

"What a dream!" murmured Léon. Then, gently fingering the blue border of her long white belt, he added, "What's to prevent us from beginning again?"

"No, my friend," she replied. "I'm too old . . . You're too young . . . Forget me! Other women will love you . . . You'll love them . . ."

"Not the way I love you!" he cried.

"You're such a child! Come, let's be sensible. I insist!"

She explained all the things that made their love impossible and told him they would have to restrict themselves to friendship, like brother and sister, as in the past.

Was she speaking seriously when she said this? She herself probably did not know, engrossed as she was in the charm of seduction and the need to protect herself from it; looking fondly at the young man, she gently repelled the timid caresses his trembling hands were attempting.

"Oh, forgive me!" he said, drawing back.

And Emma was seized by a vague terror in the face of this timidity, more dangerous for her than Rodolphe's boldness when he had moved toward her with outstretched arms. No other man had ever seemed so handsome to her. He had an exquisite candor about him. His long, curved, delicate eyelashes were lowered. The smooth skin of his cheek was flushed—she thought—with desire for her, and she felt an almost irresistible longing to put her lips to it. Leaning toward the clock, as though to see the time, she said, "Good heavens, look how late it is! How we've been chattering!"

He took the hint and picked up his hat.

"I even forgot all about the opera!" she said. "And poor Bovary left me here expressly to see it! Monsieur Lormeaux and his wife, who live on the Rue Grand-Pont, were supposed to take me there."

And the opportunity was lost, for she was leaving the next day.

"Really?" said Léon.

"Yes."

"But I must see you again," he said, "there's something I must tell you . . ."

"What is it?"

"It's something . . . important and serious. No! You mustn't leave! You can't! If you only knew . . . Listen to me . . . Haven't you understood what I've been trying to say? Haven't you guessed?"

"I think you speak quite clearly," said Emma.

"Oh, don't make fun of me! Enough! Have pity on me, let me see you again . . . Once, just once!"

"Well . . ." She stopped; then, as though changing her mind, she said, "No, not here!"

"Wherever you like."

"Will you . . ." She seemed to reflect for a moment, then she said tersely, "Eleven o'clock tomorrow, in the cathedral."

"I'll be there!" he cried, seizing her hands. She drew them away from him.

They were both standing, he behind her, she with lowered head; he leaned forward and gave her a long kiss on the back of the neck.

"You're mad! Oh, you're mad!" she said with short little bursts of laughter as he kissed her again and again.

Then, leaning his head over her shoulder, he seemed to seek consent in her eyes, but when they turned toward him they were filled with icy majesty.

He took three steps backward and prepared to leave. He stood in the doorway for a time, then said in a faltering whisper, "Tomorrow!"

She replied with a nod and disappeared like a bird into the next room.

That night Emma wrote the clerk an endless letter canceling their appointment; everything was all over now, and, for the sake of their own happiness, they must not meet again. But she was perplexed when she finished the letter, for she realized she did not know his address. "I'll give it to him in person when he comes," she thought.

The next morning, humming to himself on his balcony in front of the open window, Léon gave his low-cut shoes several coats of polish. He put on a pair of white trousers, fine socks and a green tail coat; he sprinkled his handkerchief with every kind of perfume he possessed, then, having had his hair curled, he uncurled it to give it more natural elegance.

"It's still too early!" he thought, looking at the hairdresser's cuckoo clock, whose hands pointed to nine.

He read an old fashion magazine, went out, smoked a cigar, strolled up three streets, decided it was time and began to walk briskly toward the Parvis Notre-Dame.

It was a beautiful summer morning. Silver-plate articles were gleaming in the windows of jewelry shops, and the sunlight slanting down on the cathedral sparkled on the rough edges of the gray stones; a flock of birds was wheeling in the blue sky, around the trefoiled pinnacles; the square, echoing with cries, smelled of the flowers that bordered its pavement: roses, jasmine, carnations, narcissus and tuberoses spaced out irregularly by patches of damp catnip and chickweed; the fountain in the center was gurgling, and under broad umbrellas, amid pyramids of cantaloups, bareheaded flower-women were wrapping pieces of paper around bouquets of violets.

The young man bought one. It was the first time he had ever bought flowers for a woman; when he smelled them his chest swelled with pride, as though this tribute intended for someone else had turned back upon himself.

But he was afraid of being seen; he resolutely entered the church.

The uniformed verger was standing in the left-hand doorway, beneath the picture of Salome dancing before Herod; with his plumed hat on his head, his rapier hanging down to his calf and his staff in his hand, he was more majestic than a cardinal, and he shone like a holy pyx.

He walked toward Léon and said to him with the unctious, benign smile of a priest questioning a child, "Is Monsieur a stranger in our city? Does Monsieur wish to see the points of interest in the church?"

"No," said Léon.

He went inside and walked around the side aisles. Then he came back out and looked over the square. Emma was nowhere in sight. He went up to the choir.

The nave was mirrored in the full holy-water fonts, with the bottoms of the ogives and a few portions of the stained-glass windows, and the reflections of the paintings, after breaking sharply over the marble, continued further, on the stone floor, like a many-colored carpet. Bright sunlight streamed into the church in three enormous shafts through the three open portals. Now and then a sacristan walked across the far end, making the oblique genuflection of the hurried pious when he passed in front of the altar. The crystal chandeliers hung motionless. A silver lamp was burning in the choir, and from the side chapels and shadowy parts of the church came occasional sighing sounds, and the clanging of metal grilles falling shut echoed beneath the high vaults.

Léon walked solemnly along the walls. Life had never seemed so good to him before. She would soon come in, charming, agitated, looking around to see if anyone was watching her, with her flounced dress, her gold lorgnette, her dainty shoes, all sorts of elegance which he had not yet savored, and the ineffable seductiveness of succumbing virtue. The church would spread out around her like a gigantic boudoir, the vaults would bend down to receive the confession of her love in the shadows, the stained glass would shine in all its splendor to illuminate her face, and the censers would burn so that she could make her appearance like an angel, in a cloud of perfume.

But she still had not come. He sat down on a chair and his eyes rested on a section of blue stained glass representing boatmen carrying baskets. He stared at it for a long time, counting the scales on the fish and the buttonholes in the doublets, while his thoughts wandered in search of Emma.

The verger, standing off to one side, was inwardly indignant at this young man who was taking the liberty of admiring the cathedral alone. It seemed to him that he was behaving monstrously, robbing him in a way, and almost committing a sacrilege.

Then there was a rustle of silk on the stone floor, the edge of a hat, a black hooded cape—it was she! Léon stood up and ran to meet her.

She was pale. She was walking swiftly.

"Read this!" she said to him, holding out a piece of paper. "Oh, no!"

She abruptly drew back her hand and went into the Chapel of the Virgin, where she knelt against a chair and began to pray.

At first Léon was annoyed by this pious whim, then he found a certain charm in seeing her lost in prayer, like a

Spanish marchioness, in the middle of an amorous rendezvous; but he was soon annoyed again, for it began to seem to him that she would never stop.

Emma was praying, or rather trying to pray, in the hope that sudden resolution might descend on her from heaven; and, to hasten divine aid, she filled her eyes with the splendors of the tabernacle, breathed in the fragrance of the white rocket flowers standing full-blown in tall vases and listened intently to the silence of the church, which only increased the tumult of her heart.

She stood up. They were about to leave when the verger eagerly came up to them and said, "Is Madame a stranger in our city? Does Madame wish to see the points of interest in the church?"

"Oh, no!" cried the clerk.

"Why not?" she asked.

Feeling her virtue collapsing, she tried to steady herself by clutching at the Virgin, the sculpture, the tombs and any opportunity that might present itself.

In order to "do things right," the verger led them to the entrance near the square and pointed out to them, with his staff, a large circle of black paving stones without carvings or inscriptions.

"There," he said majestically, "is the circumference of the magnificent Amboise bell. It weighed forty thousand pounds. There was nothing like it anywhere else in Europe. The workman who cast it died of joy . . ."

"Let's go," said Léon.

The verger moved on; then, when they had returned to the Chapel of the Virgin, he put out his arm in a broad gesture and said to them more proudly than a provincial landowner showing a visitor his espaliered fruit trees: "This simple slab of stone covers Pierre de Brézé, Seigneur of La Varenne and Brissac, Grand Marshal of Poitou and Governor of Normandy, killed in the Battle of Monthéry on July 16, 1465."

Léon bit his lips, beside himself with patience.

"And to your right, that steel-clad gentleman on a rearing horse is his grandson, Louis de Brézé, Seigneur of Breval and Montchauvet, Count of Maulevrier, Baron of Mauny, Royal Chamberlain, Knight of the Order and also Governor of Normandy. He died on July 23, 1531, a Sunday, as the inscription says. And below, that figure of a man ready to descend into the tomb represents exactly the same person. I think you'll agree that you couldn't see a more perfect representation of human mortality anywhere."

Madame Bovary raised her lorgnette to her eyes. Léon stood still and looked at her, so discouraged by this double assault of chatter and indifference that he did not even try to say a word or make a move.

The never-ending guide went on:

"Beside him, that kneeling, weeping woman is his wife, Diane de Poitiers, Countess of Brézé, Duchess of Valentinois, born in 1499, died in 1565; and to the left, the woman holding a child is the Holy Virgin. Now turn this way: here are the tombs of the Amboises. They were both cardinals and archbishops of Rouen. That one was one of King Louis XII's ministers. He did a great deal for the cathedral. In his will he left thirty thousand gold *écus* to the poor."

And without pausing or interrupting the flow of his speech, he pushed them into a chapel cluttered with railings. He moved some of them aside to reveal a kind of block which looked as though it might once have been a badly carved statue.

"This statue," he said with a long sigh, "once adorned the tomb of Richard the Lion-Hearted, King of England and Duke of Normandy. It was the Calvinists, monsieur, who reduced it to its present condition. Out of sheer malice, they buried it in the ground beneath the bishop's throne. That door over there, by the way, is the one the bishop uses to go back to his residence. And now let's move on to the gargoyle windows."

But Léon quickly took a silver coin from his pocket and gripped Emma's arm. The verger stood dumbfounded, puzzled by this untimely munificence when the stranger still had so many things to see. He therefore called after him: "Monsieur! The spire! The spire!"

"No, thank you," said Léon.

"You're wrong not to see it, monsieur! It's going to be four hundred and forty feet high, only nine feet lower than the Great Pyramid of Egypt. It's made entirely of cast iron, it . . ."

Léon was fleeing, for it seemed to him that his love, which had been held as motionless as the stones in the church for nearly two hours, was now going to vanish like smoke up that truncated pipe, that long cage, that openwork chimney which rises so boldly and grotesquely above the cathedral, like the wild invention of some whimsical ironsmith.

"Where are we going?" she asked.

He made no reply and continued to stride swiftly toward the exit; she was already dipping her finger in the holy water when they heard, behind them, the sound of heavy breathing interspersed at regular intervals by the tapping of a staff. Léon turned around.

"Monsieur!"

"What?"

He saw the verger coming toward him, carrying a stack of about twenty thick paperbound volumes pressed against his stomach. They were books which "told about the cathedral."

"Idiot!" growled Léon, dashing out of the church.

An urchin was playing in the square.

"Go get me a cab!"

The child ran off down the Rue des Quatre-Vents with the speed of a bullet; they were left alone together for a few minutes, face to face and a little embarrassed.

"Oh, Léon . . . Really . . . I don't know . . . if I ought to . . ." She simpered as she spoke these words; then she took on a serious expression and said, "It's very improper, you know."

"What's improper about it?" retorted the clerk. "Everybody does it in Paris!"

Like an irrefutable argument, this remark decided her.

But still there was no cab. Léon was afraid she might go back into the church. Finally a cab appeared.

"At least go past the north portal," shouted the verger, standing in a doorway, "so you can see the Resurrection, the Last Judgment, Paradise, King David, and the souls of the damned in the flames of hell!"

"Where does Monsieur wish to go?" asked the driver.

"Anywhere you like!" said Léon, pushing Emma into the cab.

And the heavy vehicle set off.

It rolled down the Rue Grand-Point, crossed the Place des Arts, the Quai Napoléon and the Pont Neuf, then it stopped short in front of the statue of Pierre Corneille.

"Keep going!" said a voice from inside.

The cab set off again. After rolling swiftly along the downgrade beginning at the Carrefour de Lafayette, it entered the railroad station at a gallop.

"No, straight ahead!" cried the same voice.

The cab emerged through the gates, soon reached the tree-lined avenue and went on at a gentle trot between the elms.

The driver wiped his forehead, put his leather hat between his legs, turned his cab and drove beyond the side streets to the grass-covered waterfront.

The cab went along the river on the cobbled towpath for a long time in the direction of Oyssel, past the islands.

But suddenly it rushed through Quatremares, Sotteville, the Grande-Chaussée, the Rue d'Elbeuf, and made its third stop, in front of the Jardin des Plantes.

"Keep moving!" cried the same voice, more furiously this time.

The cab immediately started up again; it went through Saint-Sever, along the Quai des Curandiers and the Quai aux Meules, over the bridge again, and across the Place du Champ-de-Mars; it passed behind the gardens of the hospital, where old men in black jackets were strolling in the sunshine on a terrace green with ivy, then went up the Boulevard Bouvreuil, along the Boulevard Cauchoise and all the way across Mont-Riboudet to the hill at Deville.

It turned back, then began to wander aimlessly. It was seen at Saint-Pol, Lescure, Mont Gargan, La Rouge-Mare and the Place du Gaillardbois, the Rue Malandrerie, the Rue Dinanderie, in front of the churches of Saint-Romain, Saint-Vivien, Saint-Maclou and Saint-Nicaise, in front of the customs house, at the Basse-Vieille-Tour, Trois-Pipes and the Cimetière Monumental. From his seat the driver occasionally cast desperate glances at the taverns he passed. He could not imagine what mania for movement was keeping these people from ever wanting to stop. He tried now and then, but there was always an immediate outburst of angry exclamations behind him; he would lash his two sweating nags more vigorously and set off again, paying no attention to bumps in the road and sideswiping things here and there; he was indifferent to everything around him, demoralized and almost weeping from thirst, fatigue and despair.

On the waterfront, among the drays and the barrels, and along the streets, standing beside the curbstones, the bourgeois stared wide-eyed at that sight so extraordinary in the provinces: a carriage with drawn blinds which kept appearing and reappearing, closed as tightly as a tomb and rocking like a ship.

Once, in the middle of the day, as the cab was crossing a stretch of open countryside and the blazing sunlight was flashing on its old silver-gilt lanterns, a bare hand emerged from beneath the little yellow cloth curtains and threw out some torn scraps of paper which scattered in the wind and fluttered down further on, like white butterflies, in a field of flowering red clover.

Finally, toward six o'clock, the cab stopped on a small street in the Beauvoisine quarter and a woman with her veil down stepped out of it. She walked away without looking back.

II

When Madame Bovary reached the inn she was surprised to see that the stagecoach was not there. Hivert had finally driven off after waiting fifty-three minutes for her.

Nothing was really forcing her to leave, but she had given her word she would return that evening. Besides, Charles was expecting her; and already she felt in her heart that abject docility which, for many women, is both the punishment and the expiation of their adultery.

She quickly packed her bag, paid the bill, hired a gig in the yard and, after telling the driver to hurry, urging him on and constantly asking him what time it was and how many miles they had covered, she managed to catch up with the Hirondelle on the outskirts of Quincampoix.

She closed her eyes almost as soon as she had sat down in her corner and did not open them again until they were at the bottom of the hill, where, in the distance, she saw Félicité awaiting her arrival in front of the blacksmith's house. Hivert stopped the horses, and the cook, standing on tiptoe to speak through the window, said mysteriously, "Madame, you must go to Monsieur Homais' house right away. It's for something urgent."

The village was silent as usual. On the street corners there were little pink mounds steaming in the air, for it was jam-making time and all the families of Yonville always made their supply on the same day. In front of the pharmacy, for everyone's admiration, rose a much larger mound: it surpassed all the others with the superiority which a laboratory ought to have over a housewife's kitchen, public need over an individual whim.

She went in. The big armchair was overturned, and even

the *Fanal de Rouen* was lying on the floor, spread out between the two pestles. She opened the hall door. In the middle of the kitchen, among the brown earthenware jars filled
with stemmed red currants, the grated sugar, the lump sugar,
the scales on the table and the pans on the fire, she saw all
the Homais', big and small, wearing aprons that came up to
their chins and holding forks in their hands. Justin was
standing with his head bowed and the pharmacist was shouting, "Who told you to go get it from the depository?"

"What's the matter? What's wrong?"

"What's wrong?" replied the apothecary. "We're making
jam; it was cooking, but it was about to boil over, so I
ordered another pan. And Justin here, out of sheer laziness,
went to my laboratory and took the key to the depository
that was hanging on a nail there!"

"The depository" was the apothecary's name for a little
room under the eaves filled with the utensils and merchandise of his profession. He often spent long hours alone there,
labeling, decanting and repackaging, and he regarded it not as
an ordinary storeroom, but as a veritable sanctuary from
which issued all sorts of pills, boluses, decoctions, lotions
and potions which he had made with his own hands and
which would spread his fame throughout the countryside. No
one else in the world ever set foot in it, and he held it in
such great respect that he always swept it out himself. The
pharmacy, open to anyone who cared to enter, was the place
where he displayed his pride, but the depository was the
refuge in which, selfishly withdrawing from the world, he
could revel in the pursuit of his favorite occupations. Justin's
carelessness therefore struck him as monstrous irreverence.

"That's right: the key to the depository!" he went on, his
face redder than the currants. "The key that locks in the
acids with the caustic alkalis! He went in there and took
one of my spare pans! A pan with a lid! One I may never
use! Everything has its own importance in the delicate
operations of our art! You've got to make distinctions! You
can't use pharmaceutical equipment for ordinary household
work! It's like carving a chicken with a scalpel, it's as if a
judge—"

"Be calm!" said Madame Homais.

And Athalie pulled on his coat and said, "Papa! Papa!"

"No, leave me alone!" cried the apothecary. "Leave me
alone! Good God! I might as well become a grocer! Go
ahead, don't respect anything! Smash everything, break it to

bits! Let the leeches loose! Burn the marshmallow paste! Make pickles in the medicine jars! Tear up the bandages!"

"But I was told that you—" began Emma.

"Just a minute," said Homais. And to Justin: "Do you know the risk you were taking? Didn't you see anything in the corner on the left, on the third shelf? Answer me, talk, say something!"

"I— I— don't know . . ." stammered the boy.

"Ah! You don't know! Well, *I* know! You saw a blue glass bottle sealed with yellow wax, with white powder in it, on which I've written the word 'Dangerous'! And do you know what was in that bottle? Arsenic? And you went in there and took a pan sitting right beside it!"

"Right beside it!" cried Madame Homais, clasping her hands. "Arsenic? You might have poisoned us all!"

And the children began to scream as though they already felt excruciating pains in their entrails.

"Or you might have poisoned a patient!" continued the pharmacist. "Did you want me to be arrested and tried as a criminal? Did you want to see me dragged to the scaffold? Don't you know how carefully I handle everything in my work, even though I've been doing it for years and years? Sometimes it terrifies me when I think of my responsibilities, because the government persecutes us, and the absurd legislation that governs us is like a sword of Damocles hanging over our heads!"

Emma had by now given up all thought of asking him why he wanted to see her. He went on breathlessly:

"So that's how you show your gratitude for all the kindness you've received! That's how you reward me for the fatherly care I've given you! Where would you be if it weren't for me? What would you be doing? Who is it that gives you food, clothing, education and everything else you need in order to take up an honorable position in society some day? But if you want to succeed you're going to have to pull hard on your oar, get some callouses on your hands, as the saying goes. *Fabricando fit faber, age quod agis.*"

His fury had driven him to quote in Latin, and he would have quoted in Chinese and Greenlandic if he had known those languages, for he was undergoing one of those crises in which the entire soul indistinctly shows what it contains, just as, in a storm, the sea fleetingly opens to reveal everything from the seaweed on its shore to the sand of its greatest depths.

And he went on:

"I'm beginning to regret bitterly that I ever took you into my care! I should have left you to wallow in the poverty and filth you were born into. You'll never be good for anything except looking after cattle! You don't have the slightest aptitude for science! You're hardly even capable of sticking a label on a bottle! And you live like a king, here in my house, stuffing yourself like a hog!"

Emma turned to Madame Homais and said, "I was told to come here—"

"Oh, yes!" interrupted the good lady sadly. "How can I tell you? Something terrible has happened!"

She went no further, for the apothecary thundered: "Empty it! Scour it out! Take it back! Hurry!"

And as he shook Justin by the collar of his smock, a book fell from its pocket. The boy bent down, but Homais was quicker. Having picked up the volume, he looked at it with his eyes wide open and his jaw hanging down.

"Conjugal—Love!" he said, slowly separating the two words. "Ah! Very good! Very good! Delightful! And with illustrations, too! . . . Oh, this is too much!"

Madame Homais stepped forward.

"No, don't touch it!"

The children asked to see the pictures.

"Leave the room!" he said imperiously.

And they left.

He paced back and forth for a time, holding the volume open between his fingers, rolling his eyes, choking, his face swollen and apoplectic. Then he walked straight up to his apprentice and stood in front of him with his arms folded.

"So, apparently you have every vice imaginable, you little wretch! You'd better watch your step, because you're on a downward path! . . . Didn't it ever occur to you that this abominable book might fall into my children's hands? That it might set their blood on fire, soil Athalie's purity, corrupt Napoléon? He's already a man, from a physical point of view. Are you sure they haven't read it? Can you guarantee me that—"

"Excuse me, monsieur," said Emma impatiently, "didn't you have something to tell me?"

"Yes, that's true, madame. . . . Your father-in-law is dead."

The elder Monsieur Bovary had died two days before, from a sudden attack of apoplexy at the end of a meal; and Charles, excessively concerned for Emma's sensibilities, had asked Monsieur Homais to break the horrible news to her gently.

He had pondered his little speech, rounded it, polished it and developed its cadences; it was a masterpiece of caution and transition, of delicate phrasing and tact. But anger had swept away his rhetoric.

Making no attempt to learn further details, Emma left the pharmacy, for Monsieur Homais had resumed his vituperations. He was becoming calmer, however, and was now grumbling in a fatherly tone as he fanned himself with his fez:

"It's not that I entirely disapprove of the book! The author was a doctor. It deals with certain scientific aspects which it does no harm for a man to know; in fact, I'll go so far as to say that a man *ought* to know them. But later, later! At least wait till you're a man yourself, till your nature is completely developed."

When Emma rapped on the door with the knocker, Charles, who had been waiting for her, met her with open arms and said to her with tears in his voice, "Oh, my darling . . ."

He bent down gently to kiss her, but at the touch of his lips the memory of the other man seized her and she passed her hand over her face with a shudder.

She answered, however: "Yes, I know . . . I know."

He showed her the letter in which his mother told of the event without any sentimental hypocrisy. She regretted only that her husband had not received the aid of religion: he had died in the street at Doudeville, just outside a café, after a patriotic banquet with a group of former army officers.

Emma handed back the letter; then, at dinner, for the sake of form, she made some effort to pretend that she had no appetite. But when he urged her she resolutely began to eat while he sat opposite her, motionless and bowed down with grief.

From time to time he would raise his head and look at her for a long time, his eyes filled with distress. Once he sighed, "I wish I could have seen him again!"

She made no reply. Finally realizing that she had to say something, she asked, "How old was your father?"

"Fifty-eight!"

"Oh."

And that was all.

Several minutes later he said, "My poor mother! What's to become of her now?"

She made a gesture of ignorance.

Seeing her so taciturn, Charles believed her to be deeply affected; he was touched by her grief and forced himself to remain silent in order not to intensify it. After a time, however, he shook off his own grief and asked her, "Did you have a good time yesterday?"

"Yes."

When the tablecloth was removed, Bovary did not stand up. Neither did Emma; and as she looked at him the monotony of the sight gradually drove all compassion from her heart. He seemed to her contemptible, weak and insignificant, a poor man in every sense of the word. How could she get rid of him? What an endless evening! She felt numb, as though she had been overcome by opium fumes.

From the vestibule they heard the sharp tap of a stick on the floorboards. It was Hippolyte bringing Madame's bags.

To set them down, he painfully described a quarter-circle with his wooden leg.

"He doesn't even think about it any more!" she said to herself, looking at the poor devil, whose coarse red hair was dripping sweat.

Bovary took a small coin from his purse. Apparently not realizing the humiliation implicit in the very presence of the man who was now standing there like a living reproach to his incurable ineptitude, he said to Emma, having noticed Léon's violets on the mantelpiece, "Oh, you have a pretty bouquet!"

"Yes," she said casually, "I bought it this afternoon . . . from a beggar woman."

Charles picked up the violets, refreshed his tear-reddened eyes with them and sniffed them delicately. Emma quickly took them from his hand and went off to put them in a glass of water.

The next day the elder Madame Bovary arrived. She and her son wept for a long time. Emma disappeared, saying there were household matters that required her attention.

On the following day they had to hold a consultation about the details of mourning. The ladies took their sewing boxes and the three of them went out to sit in the arbor beside the river.

Charles thought about his father and was surprised to feel so much affection for him—up till now he had thought he loved him only very moderately. The elder Madame Bovary thought about her husband. Her worst days in the past now seemed enviable to her. Everything else faded away before instinctive sorrow over having lost something to which she had been accustomed for so long; and from time to time, as she plied her needle, a large tear would run down her nose and hang there for a moment.

Emma was thinking that less than forty-eight hours ago they had been together, far from the world, enraptured, avidly feasting their eyes on each other. She tried to recapture the most minute details of that vanished day. But she was hindered by the presence of her mother-in-law and her husband. She wished she could hear nothing, see nothing, so that she would be free to evoke her love undisturbed; despite all her efforts, it was slowly being driven away by external sensations.

She was ripping out the lining of a dress whose scraps lay scattered around her; the elder Madame Bovary kept working her squeaking scissors without ever looking up; Charles, in his cloth slippers and the old brown frock coat which he used as a dressing gown, sat with his hands in his pockets and remained as silent as the two ladies; and near them, wearing a little white apron, Berthe was scraping the gravel of the path with her shovel.

Suddenly they saw Monsieur Lheureux, the dry-goods dealer, walk in through the gate.

He had come to offer his services, "in view of the sad occasion." Emma replied that she could do without them. The shopkeeper did not acknowledge defeat.

"Please excuse me," he said, "but I'd like to speak to you in private." Then he lowered his voice: "It's about that matter. . . . You know what I mean, don't you?"

Charles blushed to the roots of his hair and said, "Oh, yes . . . Yes, I know." He turned to his wife and said, ill at ease, "Darling, would you please . . ."

She seemed to understand, for she stood up; and Charles said to his mother, "It's nothing! Probably some trivial household detail."

He did not want her to know about the note, for he dreaded her comments.

As soon as he was alone with Emma, Monsieur Lheureux congratulated her rather pointedly on the forthcoming inheritance, then he began to talk of extraneous matters: fruit trees, crops and his own health, which was still "just so-so, not too good, not too bad." He was always working like a horse, and yet, no matter what people said about him, he hardly made enough money to buy butter for his bread.

Emma let him talk. She had been so prodigiously bored for the past two days!

"And now you're completely well again?" he went on. "Your poor husband was in quite a state, you know! He's a fine man, even though we've had a little trouble between us."

She asked what he was referring to, for Charles had told her nothing about his dispute over the things Lheureux claimed she had ordered.

"Why, you know!" exclaimed Lheureux. "It was about those things you wanted me to get for you, those trunks . . ."

He had pulled his hat down over his eyes; with his hands behind his back, smiling and whistling softly, he stood staring at her in an insufferable way. Did he suspect something? She was overcome by all sorts of apprehensions. Finally he went on:

"We're on friendly terms again now, and I've come to propose another arrangement."

It was to renew the note signed by Bovary. Monsieur could do as he pleased, of course, but there was no need for him to worry about it, especially since he was now going to be bothered by so many other things.

"In fact, he'd do better to let someone else handle it for him—you, for example. With a power of attorney it would be quite simple, and then you and I could take care of our little affairs together . . ."

She did not understand. He let the matter drop. Then, turning the conversation to his merchandise, he declared that Madame simply must order something from him. He would send her twelve yards of black barège, enough to make a dress.

"The one you have on is all right for the house, but you need another one to wear when you go out. I saw that right away, as soon as I came in. I have very sharp eyes!"

He did not send the cloth: he brought it. Then he came back to measure it; he returned on other pretexts, striving each time to be agreeable and helpful, making himself her flunky, as Homais would have put it, and always slipping in a few words of advice about the power of attorney. He never mentioned the promissory note. She gave it no thought; Charles had said something to her about it at the beginning of her convalescence, but her mind had been so agitated that she had forgotten. Besides, she had no desire to open a discussion of financial matters. Charles's mother was surprised by her change of attitude and attributed it to the religious sentiments she had acquired during her illness.

But as soon as she was gone, Emma amazed Bovary with her practical common sense. They would have to make inquiries, check on the mortgages, see if there were grounds for liquidation or a public auction.

She used technical terms at random, uttered impressive words such as "order," "the future" and "foresight," and constantly exaggerated the difficulties of the inheritance, until finally one day she showed him the draft of a general authorization to "manage and administer all his affairs, negotiate all loans, sign and endorse all promissory notes, pay all sums," etc. She had profited from Lheureux's lessons.

Charles naïvely asked her where the document had come from.

"From Monsieur Guillaumin," she replied; then, with the greatest coolness imaginable, she added, "I don't trust him too much. Notaries have such a bad reputation! Perhaps we ought to consult . . . We don't know anyone except . . . No, we don't know anyone."

"Unless Léon . . ." said Charles thoughtfully.

But it would be difficult to work things out by correspondence, so she offered to make the trip. He thanked her but said it would not be necessary. She insisted. For a time they vied with each other to see who could show the most consideration. Finally she cried out in a tone of mock rebellion, "Don't say any more about it! I'll go!"

"How good you are!" he said, kissing her on the forehead.

The next day she boarded the Hirondelle to go to Rouen and consult Monsieur Léon. She stayed there for three days.

III

They were three full, exquisite, wonderful days, a real honeymoon.

They stayed at the Hôtel de Boulogne, on the waterfront. They lived there behind closed shutters and doors, with flowers on the floor, sipping the iced fruit drinks they began to order as soon as they got up in the morning.

Toward evening they would hire a covered boat and go to have dinner on an island.

It was the time of day when one hears the sound of caulkers' mallets striking against hulls in the shipyards. Tar smoke floated up through the trees, and on the surface of the river there were large oily patches undulating irregularly in the crimson glow of the sun, like plaques of Florentine bronze.

They moved downstream amid moored vessels whose long slanting cables grazed the top of their boat.

The noises of the city slowly faded away: the rumble of carts, the tumult of voices, the barking of dogs on the decks of ships. She untied her hat and they landed on their island.

They sat down at a table in a low-ceilinged restaurant with black fishnets hanging in front of it. They ate fried smelt, cream and cherries. Then they lay down on the grass in a secluded place and kissed beneath the poplars. They wished they could live forever, like two Robinson Crusoes, in that little spot which seemed to them, in their bliss, the most magnificent one on earth. It was not the first time they had ever seen trees, blue sky and grass, or heard water flowing and a breeze rustling the leaves, but they had never admired all that before, as though nature had not existed till then, or had begun to be beautiful only after the gratification of their desires.

At nightfall they returned. The boat followed the shoreline of the islands. They sat inside it, hidden by the shadows, without speaking. The square-tipped oars struck regularly against the iron oarlocks, marking the silence like the beat of a metronome, while the rope trailing from the stern kept up its gentle splashing in the water.

One night the moon came out, and they did not fail to make eloquent comments about how melancholy and poetic it was; she even began to sing:

"One night—do you remember?—we were sailing . . ."

The sound of her sweet, frail voice was soon lost as it floated out over the waves; the wind carried away the notes and Léon heard them pass like the fluttering of wings.

She was sitting opposite him, leaning against the side of the boat while the moon shone on her through one of the open shutters. Her black dress, whose folds spread out around her like a fan, made her look thinner and taller. Her head was raised, her hands were joined and she was looking up at the sky. Now and then she was hidden by the shadow of a willow, then she would suddenly reappear in the moonlight, like a vision.

Léon, sitting beside her on the bottom of the boat, picked up a bright red silk ribbon which he had happened to touch with his hand.

The boatman examined it for a time, then said, "Oh, yes! It was probably left by one of those people I took out the other day. They were a lively bunch of men and women, and they really enjoyed themselves—they had pastry, champagne, trumpets, the whole works! There was one of them, especially, that kept everybody laughing—a tall, handsome man with a little mustache. They were always saying, 'Come on, tell us a story, Adolphe!' Or maybe it was 'Dodolphe' they called him, I don't remember for sure."

She shuddered.

"Is anything wrong?" asked Léon, moving closer to her.

"Oh, it's nothing—probably just the cold night air."

"And I think *he* does all right for himself with women, too," the old sailor added softly, intending his remark as a compliment to Léon. Then he spat on his hands and took up his oars again.

But finally they had to part. Their farewells were sad. She told him to write to her in care of Madame Rollet, and she gave him such precise instructions with regard to the double envelopes he was to use that he greatly admired her amorous guile.

"Are you sure everything's all right?" she asked as they kissed for the last time.

"Yes, of course!" he replied.

"But why," he wondered as he walked back alone through the streets, "is she so set on getting that power of attorney?"

IV

Léon soon took on an air of superiority in front of his colleagues, spurned their company and completely neglected his work.

He waited for her letters and read them over and over. He

wrote to her. He evoked her presence with all the strength of his desire and his memories. Instead of being diminished by absence, his longing to see her again grew steadily more intense, until finally one Saturday morning it drove him from his office.

When, from the top of the hill, he looked down into the valley and saw the church steeple with its tin flag turning in the wind, he felt that delightful mixture of triumphant pride and egotistic sentimentality which a millionaire must feel when he revisits the humble village of his childhood.

He prowled around outside her house. There was a light shining in the kitchen. He watched for her shadow behind the curtains. Nothing appeared.

Madame Lefrançois uttered loud exclamations when she saw him. She found him "taller and thinner"; Artémise, on the other hand, found him "heavier and darker."

He had dinner in the small dining room, as in the past, but alone, without the tax collector, for Binet, "tired of waiting for the Hirondelle," had permanently set his mealtime an hour earlier: he now dined on the stroke of five, and even so he usually claimed that "the rusty old clock was slow."

Léon finally got up the courage to go and knock on the doctor's door. Madame was in her room and did not come down until a quarter of an hour later. Monsieur seemed delighted to see him again; but he stayed home all evening, and all next day.

He was not able to see her alone until the second night, very late, in the lane behind the garden—the same lane in which she had once met Rodolphe! It was a stormy night, and they talked together beneath an umbrella, their faces illuminated by the lightning.

The thought of their separation became unbearable to them.

"I'd rather die!" said Emma.

She twisted her body in anguish, clinging to his arm and weeping.

"Good-by! . . . Good-by! . . . When will I see you again?"

They ran back together for another kiss, and it was then that she promised him she would soon find some way for them to see each other in complete freedom at least once a week. She was sure she would succeed. Furthermore, she was filled with hope by the money that would soon come in from Charles's inheritance.

She therefore bought, for her bedroom, a pair of broad-

striped yellow curtains which Monsieur Lheuheux had rec-
ommended as a bargain. When she said she would like a
carpet, he assured her it "wouldn't be hard to arrange" and
obligingly promised to find one for her. She was no longer
able to do without his services. She sent for him a dozen
times a day, and he would always drop whatever he was doing without so much as a murmur of protest. The people of
Yonville were also unable to understand why Madame Rollet
had lunch at her house every day, and even visited her in
private.

It was at about this time, toward the beginning of winter,
that she apparently developed a great ardor for music.

One evening when Charles was listening to her, she started
the same piece over again four times, growing more and
more annoyed, while Charles, without noticing any difference,
kept crying out, "Bravo! Very good! . . . You shouldn't stop!
Keep going!"

"No! It's disgusting! My fingers are rusty."

The next day he asked her to "play him something again."

"All right, if you really want me to."

And he admitted that she had gotten a little out of practice.
She struck wrong notes, fumbled and hesitated; then she
stopped short and said, "No more! I ought to take lessons,
but . . ." She bit her lip and added, "Twenty francs a lesson—
it's too expensive."

"Yes, you're right, it is a little . . ." said Charles, laughing
foolishly. "I think we might be able to find a teacher for
less, though, because there are a lot of musicians who don't
have a big reputation but are better than the celebrities."

"Well, find one of them," said Emma.

When he came home the next day he gave her a sly look
and finally blurted out, "You're so opinionated sometimes!
I went to Barfeuchères today, and Madame Liégeard told me
that her three girls—they're all at La Miséricorde now—used
to take lessons for two and a half francs an hour, and from
a wonderful teacher, too!"

She shrugged her shoulders and left her instrument closed
from then on.

But whenever she walked past it she would sigh (if Bovary
happened to be there), "Ah, my poor piano!"

And when she had visitors she never failed to inform them
that she had abandoned her music and could not go back
to it now, for reasons beyond her control. Everyone pitied
her. It was a shame! She had such talent! Some people even

spoke to Bovary about it. They made him feel ashamed, especially the pharmacist:

"You're making a mistake! We should never let natural faculties lie fallow. Besides, my friend, don't you realize that by encouraging Madame to study now, you'll save money later on your child's musical education? I think mothers ought to educate their children themselves. That's an idea of Rousseau's; it may be a little new now, but I'm sure it will triumph in the end, like breast feeding by mothers, and vaccination."

And so Charles brought up the question of the piano again. Emma answered bitterly that it would be better to sell it. But that poor old piano had given his pride such satisfaction that to see it go would have been almost like watching Emma kill part of herself.

"If you want to . . ." he said. "After all, a lesson now and then wouldn't really make us go bankrupt."

"But lessons don't do any good," she replied, "unless you take them regularly."

It was thus that she obtained her husband's permission to go to the city once a week to see her lover. And by the end of the first month everyone found that she had made considerable progress.

V

It was on Thursdays that she made her trips. She always got up and dressed silently in order not to wake Charles, who would have commented on her getting up too early. Then she paced back and forth and stood in front of the windows, looking out at the square. The first light of morning shone between the pillars of the market shed; and on the pharmacist's house, whose shutters were still closed, the capital letters of his shop sign were beginning to stand out in the soft-colored glow of dawn.

When the clock showed a quarter past seven she went to the Lion d'Or, where Artémise, yawning, opened the door for her and, so that Madame could warm herself, dug out the smoldering coals buried beneath the ashes. Emma was then left alone in the kitchen. Now and then she stepped outside. Hivert was harnessing the horses at a leisurely pace, at the same time listening to Madame Lefrançois, who, still wearing her nightcap, had put her head through a window and was giving him detailed instructions about his errands in a way that would have bewildered anyone else. Emma tapped her foot on the paving stones of the yard.

Finally, when he had eaten his soup, put on his overcoat, lighted his pipe and picked up his whip, he calmly installed himself on the driver's seat.

The Hirondelle set off at a gentle trot, and for the first two miles or so it kept stopping every few minutes to take on passengers who were watching for it along the road, standing in front of courtyard gates. Those who had given notice the day before were not ready on time; some of them, in fact, were still in bed; Hivert would call, shout and curse, then climb down from his seat and knock loudly on the door while the wind whistled through the cracked windows of the coach.

Meanwhile the four benches were filling up, the coach rolled along, rows of apple trees moved steadily past, and the road stretched forth between two long ditches full of yellow water, narrowing as it approached the horizon.

Emma was intimately acquainted with it from one end to the other; she knew that after this pasture there was a road sign, then an elm tree and a barn, or a roadmender's cabin; sometimes she even closed her eyes to give herself a little surprise. But she was always clearly aware of how far she still had to go.

At last the brick houses began to move closer together, the road was hard beneath the wheels and the Hirondelle glided between gardens in which, through the iron fence, one could see statues, a mound of earth surmounted by a vine arbor, clipped yew trees and a swing. Then, all at once, the city came into view.

Sloping downward like an amphitheater and drowned in fog, it expanded in confusion beyond its bridges. Then the countryside rose monotonously on the other side until it joined the indistinct base of the pale sky. Thus seen from above, the whole landscape looked static, like a painting; the ships at anchor were huddled together in one corner, the river traced out its curve at the foot of green hills, and its oblong islands were like enormous black fish floating motionless on the surface of the water. From the factory chimneys emerged great plumes of brown smoke whose tips were swept away by the wind. The roar of foundries could be heard along with the clear chiming of bells from the churches that rose high into the mist. The leafless trees along the boulevards formed purple thickets among the houses, whose rooftops, shiny with rain, gleamed with unequal brilliance, according to the elevation of the various quarters of the city. Now and then the clouds would be blown toward the Sainte-Catherine hill, like aerial waves soundlessly breaking against a cliff.

For Emma, there was something intoxicating in the sight of that vast concentration of life, and her heart swelled as though the hundred and twenty thousand souls palpitating there had all sent her a breath of the passions she attributed to them. Her love expanded in that space, and filled itself with tumult from the vague clamor that floated up from below. She poured it out over the squares, the promenades, the streets; and in her eyes the old Norman city stretched out like an immense metropolis, like a Babylon which she was about to enter. She leaned out the window, bracing herself with both hands, and drew the wind into her lungs as the three horses galloped along. The wheels ground over stones in the mud, the coach swayed and Hivert called out to carts ahead of him in the road, while middle-class citizens who had spent the night in their country houses in Bois-Guillaume calmly rolled down the hill in their little family carriages.

The coach stopped briefly at the city gate. Emma took off her overshoes, changed her gloves and straightened her shawl; then, twenty yards further on, she alighted from the Hirondelle.

The city was now coming to life. Clerks in fezzes were wiping off shop windows, and on the street corners women with baskets on their hips were uttering loud cries at regular intervals. Emma walked along with her eyes lowered, keeping close to the walls and smiling with pleasure beneath the black veil that hung over her face.

For fear of being seen, she usually avoided the shortest route. She would plunge into dark alleys and come out, perspiring, at the lower end of the Rue Nationale, near the fountain, in the theater district, which is also full of taverns and prostitutes. Often a cart would roll past, laden with quivering stage sets. Waiters in aprons were sprinkling sand over the pavement between green bushes. There was a smell of absinthe, cigars and oysters.

She turned a corner and recognized him by the curly hair hanging down below his hat.

Léon walked on along the sidewalk. She followed him to the hotel; he climbed the stairs, opened the door, went in. . . . What an embrace!

Then, after the kisses, words came pouring out. They told each other of their sorrows during the week, of their forebodings, of their worries about the letters; but now everything was forgotten, and they looked at each other face to face, laughing voluptuously and calling each other tender names.

The bed was a large mahogany one, shaped like a boat. Red silk curtains, curved at the bottom, hung down very low from the ceiling beside the flaring headboard; and there was nothing in the world so lovely as her dark hair and white skin against that crimson background when, in a gesture of modesty, she brought her bare arms together and hid her face in her hands.

The warm room, with its discreet carpet, its whimsical ornaments and its tranquil light, seemed expressly designed for the intimacies of passion. The arrow-tipped curtain rods, the brass curtain hooks and the big knobs on the andirons would all begin to gleam whenever the sun shone in. On the mantelpiece, between the candlesticks, were two of those large pink shells in which you can hear the ocean when you hold them to your ear.

How they loved that friendly, cheerful room, despite its rather faded splendor! They always found each piece of furniture in its place, and sometimes, beneath the pedestal of the clock, there were hairpins she had forgotten the Thursday before. They had lunch beside the fire, on a little table inlaid with rosewood. Emma carved, showering him with all sorts of endearments as she put the pieces on his plate; and she laughed loudly and wantonly when the champagne foamed over the brim of her thin glass and onto the rings on her fingers. They were so completely lost in the possession of each other that they felt as though they were in their own house, where they would spend their whole lives together as eternally young newlyweds. They spoke of "our bedroom," "our carpet," "our chairs"; and she even said "our slippers," referring to a pair which Léon had bought her in response to a whim. They were made of pink satin, trimmed with swansdown. When she sat on his lap her legs, too short to touch the floor, swung in the air, and the dainty slippers, open down to the tips, hung lightly from the toes of her bare feet.

He now savored for the first time the ineffable delicacies of feminine refinements. Never before had he encountered this grace of language, this modesty of attire, these languid, dovelike poses. He admired the exaltation of her soul and the lace on her petticoat. Furthermore, was she not a "lady" and a married woman—in short, a real mistress?

With the diversity of her moods—by turns mystic, joyous, loquacious, taciturn, passionate or nonchalant—she awakened a thousand desires in him, aroused his instincts and memories. She was the amorous heroine of all novels and plays, the vague "she" of all poetry. He saw on her shoulders the amber skin of the "Bathing Odalisque"; she had the long-waisted figure of a feudal chatelaine; she also resembled the "Pale Woman of Barcelona," but above all she was an angel!

When he looked at her it often seemed to him that his soul rushed out to her, flowed like a wave around the contours of her head and was drawn down into the whiteness of her bosom.

He would sit on the floor in front of her with his elbows on his knees and look at her smilingly, his face upturned. She would lean toward him and murmur, as though choking with rapture, "Oh, don't move! Don't talk! Keep looking at me! There's something so sweet in your eyes, and it does me so much good!"

She called him "child": "Do you love me, child?"

And his lips would rise to hers so quickly that she scarcely heard his answer.

On the clock there was a little bronze cupid simpering and curving his arms beneath a gilded wreath. They often laughed at him; but when it was time to part, everything seemed serious to them.

Facing each other motionlessly they would say over and over, "Till Thursday! Till Thursday . . ."

She would abruptly take his head between her hands, quickly kiss him on the forehead, cry out "Good-by!" and run downstairs.

She would go to the hairdresser's shop on the Rue de la Comédie to have her hair arranged. Night was falling; the gas was being lighted in the shop.

She could hear the theater bell calling the actors to the performance, and across the street she saw white-faced men and shabbily dressed women going through the stage door.

It was warm in that low-ceilinged little room with its stove purring amid the wigs and pomades. The smell of the curling irons and the touch of the soft hands working on her head soon made her drowsy and she dozed a little as she sat there in her dressing gown. Often, as he arranged her hair, the hairdresser would ask her if she wanted tickets to the masked ball.

Then she left. She walked through the streets to the Croix-Rouge, took out her overshoes, which she had hidden under a bench that morning, and squeezed herself into her seat among the impatient passengers. The others got out of the coach when it began to climb the hill, leaving her alone inside.

At each bend in the road she could see more of the city's lights, whose reflections formed a luminous haze above the solid mass of houses. She would kneel on the cushions and let her eyes wander over that bright glow. She would sob, call out to Léon and send him sweet words and kisses that were lost in the wind.

There was a poor devil who roamed up and down the hill with his stick, in the midst of the coaches. His shoulders were covered by a mass of rags, and a battered old beaver hat, rounded into the shape of a basin, hid his face; but when he took it off he revealed two bloody, gaping sockets in place of eyelids. The flesh was falling away in crimson shreds, and from it oozed liquids which hardened into green scabs down to the nose, whose black nostrils were always sniffling convulsively. Whenever he spoke to anyone he would throw back his head and laugh idiotically, and his bluish eyeballs would then roll constantly, pushing against the exposed flesh near his temples.

As he followed the coaches he sang a little song:

> The heat of the sun on a summer day
> Warms a young girl in an amorous way.

The other verses were filled with birds, sunlight and green leaves.

Sometimes he would suddenly appear behind Emma, bareheaded. She would draw back with a cry. Hivert would joke with him, urging him to rent a booth at the Saint-Romain fair, or laughingly ask him how his mistress was.

Often, while the coach was in motion, he would abruptly thrust his hat in through a window, holding fast with his other hand as he stood on the footboard between the wheels, which spattered him with mud. His voice, low and wailing at first, would grow shrill and linger in the darkness like the indistinct lamentation of some vague distress; and as Emma heard it through the jingling of the bells, the murmur of the trees and the hollow rumble of the coach, it had a faraway sound that troubled her deeply. It descended into the depths of her soul, like a whirlwind in an abyss, and swept her into realms of boundless melancholy. But then Hivert, noticing that the coach was being weighed down on one side, would begin striking at the blind man with his whip. The lash would snap against his open sores and he would fall into the mud with a shriek.

Finally the Hirondelle's passengers would all fall asleep, some with their mouths open, others with their chins lowered, leaning on their neighbor's shoulder, or with one arm in the strap, swaying steadily with the movement of the coach; and the glow of the lantern, swinging above the rumps of the shaft horses outside and shining in through the chocolate-colored calico curtains, cast blood-red shadows on all those inert figures. Emma, intoxicated with sadness, would shiver beneath her clothes as her feet grew colder and colder and she felt icy despair gripping her heart.

Charles would be waiting for her at home; the Hirondelle was always late on Thursdays. At last Madame would arrive! She would hurriedly kiss her little daughter. Dinner would not be ready, but it didn't matter! She always excused the cook. It had begun to seem that Félicité could do no wrong.

Her husband often noticed her pallor and asked her if she felt ill.

"No," she would reply.

"But you're acting so strangely tonight!"

"Oh, it's nothing! It's nothing!"

There were even days when she went up to her room almost as soon as she came in. Justin would be there; he would silently move around the room, serving her more expertly than a skilled maid. He would lay out matches, a candlestick, a book and her bed jacket, then open her bed.

"All right, that's good," she would say to him. "You can leave now."

For he would be standing there with his arms hanging loosely and his eyes wide open, as though he had suddenly become enmeshed in the countless strands of an intricate reverie.

The next day was always horrible, and the days that followed were still more unbearable because of her impatience to seize her happiness again; it was a fierce desire, inflamed by remembered images, and on the seventh day it burst forth freely under Léon's caresses. His ardor was hidden beneath outpourings of wonderment and gratitude. Emma savored his love discreetly yet intensely, stimulated it with every artifice inspired by her passion, and was always a little afraid that some day she might lose it.

She often said to him, with melancholy sweetness in her voice, "Oh, you'll leave me, I know that! . . . You'll get married . . . You'll be like the others."

"What others?"

"Other men—all other men," she replied. Then, pushing him away with a languid gesture, she added, "You're all treacherous!"

One day when they were philosophically discussing the disillusionments of life she told him (wishing to test his jealousy, or perhaps yielding to an overpowering need to confide in him) that she had loved someone else before him. "Not the way I love you!" she quickly added; and she swore on her daughter's life that "nothing had happened."

He believed her, but he questioned her about the other man nevertheless.

"He was a sea captain, darling."

By giving him this answer, was she not preventing him from making any inquiries, and at the same time placing herself in an exalted position by claiming to have captivated a man who was presumably of a bellicose nature and accustomed to dominating others?

The clerk now felt the lowliness of his own position; he longed for epaulettes, medals and titles. Judging from her spendthrift ways, she must have a liking for such things.

Emma was silent about a number of her extravagant desires, however; to take her to Rouen, for example, she dreamed of owning a blue tilbury drawn by an English horse and driven by a groom wearing top-boots. It was Justin who had inspired her with this caprice, by begging her to take him into her service as a valet. Being deprived of her tilbury did not diminish her pleasure in arriving for a rendezvous, but it certainly increased the bitterness of her return to Yonville.

Often, when they had been speaking of Paris, she would murmur, "Oh, how happy we'd be if we were living there!"

"Aren't we happy here?" the young man would ask softly, stroking her hair.

"Yes, of course! I'm talking foolishly. Kiss me!"

She was more charming than ever to her husband; she made him pistachio custards and played waltzes for him after dinner. He regarded himself as the luckiest of mortals, and she never worried about him until suddenly one evening he asked her, "It's Mademoiselle Lempereur who gives you lessons, isn't it?"

"Yes."

"Well, I saw her today," said Charles, "in Madame Liégeard's house. I talked to her about you: she doesn't know you."

It was like a thunderbolt. However, she answered in a natural tone, "She must have forgotten my name."

"Or maybe there are several piano teachers named Lempereur in Rouen," said the doctor.

"Maybe so." Then she quickly added, "Anyway, I have my receipts: here, look!"

She went to the writing desk, rummaged through all the drawers, mixed up all the papers and finally became so frantic that Charles strongly urged her not to go to so much trouble for those wretched receipts.

"Oh, I'll find them!" she said.

True enough, on the following Friday, as Charles was putting on one of his boots in the dark little room where he kept his clothes, he felt a piece of paper between the leather and his sock; he pulled it out and read: *"Received the sum of sixty-five francs, for three months of lessons, plus various supplies. Félicie Lempereur, Music Teacher."*

"How the devil did this get into my boot?"

"It probably fell down from that old box full of bills on the shelf," she replied.

From then on her whole life was a tissue of lies which she wrapped around her love like a veil, to hide it.

Lying became a need, a mania, a pleasure; so much so that if she said she had walked down the right side of a street the day before, it was almost certain that she had walked down the left.

One morning just after she had left, rather lightly dressed as usual, it suddenly began to snow; and as Charles was looking out the window at the weather, he saw Father Bournisien on his way to Rouen in Monsieur Tuvache's buggy. He hurried outside with a heavy shawl and asked the priest to give it to Madame when he reached the Croix-Rouge. As soon as he entered the inn, Bournisien asked where the Yonville doctor's wife was. The innkeeper replied that she was seldom there. That evening, when he saw Madame Bovary in the Hirondelle, the priest told her about his little difficulty, although he apparently attached no importance to it, for he immediately began to sing the praises of a preacher who was having a phenomenal success in the cathedral, where all the ladies flocked to hear him.

But while he had not asked her for any explanation, others might be less discreet in the future; she therefore decided it would be useful to take a room at the Croix-Rouge each time, so that the good people of her village would see her on the stairs there and suspect nothing.

One day, however, Monsieur Lheureux met her as she was leaving the Hôtel de Boulogne on Léon's arm. She was frightened, for she was sure he would talk. But he was not foolish enough to do that. Three days later he walked into her room, closed the door and said, "I need money."

She declared that she could not give him any. Lheureux moaned and reminded her of all the things he had done to oblige her.

Emma had paid off only one of the two notes which Charles had signed. As for the second one, the shopkeeper had agreed, at her request, to replace it with two others, and these had in turn been renewed for a very long term. He now took from his pocket a list of unpaid items which he had delivered to her: the curtains, the carpet, the cloth for the armchairs, several dresses and various toilet articles; the total came to about two thousand francs.

She bowed her head.

"If you don't have any cash," he said, "at least you have some property."

And he mentioned a dilapidated little house at Barneville, near Aumale, which was bringing in very little money. It had once been part of a small farm that Charles's father had sold. Lheureux knew everything about it, from the acreage to the neighbors' names.

"If I were you," he said, "I'd sell the place and pay off my debts. You'd still have money left over."

She objected that it would be difficult to find a buyer; he assured her that one could probably be found; she then asked him what she would have to do to be able to sell.

"You have a power of attorney, haven't you?"

These words came to her like a breath of fresh air.

"Leave your bill with me," she said.

"Oh, that's not necessary," replied Lheureux.

He came back the following week and boasted that, after a great deal of difficulty, he had discovered a man by the name of Langlois who had been eyeing the property for a long time without ever saying how much he would be willing to pay for it.

"I don't care about the price!" she exclaimed.

But he said they ought to wait and sound the man out. It was worth making a trip for, and since she could not make it he said he would go to see Langlois in person. When he returned he announced that the buyer had offered four thousand francs.

Emma was overjoyed at this news.

"Frankly," he added, "it's a good price."

She received half of the sum immediately, and when she was about to pay his bill he said to her, "Really, it hurts me to see you give up so much money all at once."

She looked at the banknotes and thought of the endless series of rendezvous those two thousand francs represented. "What—what do you mean?" she stammered.

"Oh," he replied with a good-natured laugh, "you can put anything you like on a bill! I know how it is with married couples!"

And he looked at her pointedly, holding two long pieces of paper in his hand and sliding them back and forth between his fingertips. Finally he opened his billfold and spread out on the table four promissory notes, each for a thousand francs.

"Just sign these," he said, "and you can keep all the money!"

She uttered an exclamation of shocked surprise.

"But if I give you the balance," said Monsieur Lheureux impudently, "won't I be doing you a favor?"

He picked up a pen and wrote at the bottom of his bill: *"Received from Madame Bovary the sum of four thousand francs."*

"What's there to worry about? In six months you'll have the rest of the money for your house, and the last note won't be due till after you've been paid."

Emma became a little confused in her calculations, and her ears were ringing as though gold coins were bursting open their bags and raining down on the floor all around her.

Lheureux finally explained that he had a friend named Vinçart, a banker in Rouen, who would discount the four promissory notes, after which he himself would bring Madame the balance of the actual debt.

But instead of two thousand francs he brought her only eighteen hundred, for his friend Vinçart (as was "only right") had taken out two hundred as commission and discount.

Then he casually asked for a receipt.

"You understand . . . In business . . . sometimes . . . And write down the date, please, the date."

A whole horizon of realizable whims opened up before Emma. She was sensible enough to put aside three thousand francs with which she paid the first three bills when they fell due; but the fourth one happened to come to the house on a Thursday, and Charles patiently waited for her return to ask her for an explanation.

She hadn't told him about that note because she didn't want to bother him with household details; she sat on his lap, caressed him, cooed lovingly and gave him a long list of all the indispensable things she had bought on credit.

"You must admit it's not too much money for so many things," she said.

Charles, at his wits' end, soon resorted to the ever-present Lheureux, who swore he would smooth things over if Monsieur would sign two notes, one for seven hundred francs payable in three months. Charles wrote his mother a desperate letter asking her to help him. Instead of sending a reply she came herself; and when Emma asked him if he had gotten anything out of her he answered, "Yes, but she wants to see the bill."

The next day at dawn, Emma hurried to Monsieur Lheureux and begged him to make out another note for not more than a thousand francs, because if she were to show the one for four thousand she would have to say she had already paid two-thirds of it and therefore admit she had sold the house; the shopkeeper had handled the transaction quite skillfully, and it did not become known until later.

Despite the low price of each article, the elder Madame Bovary made it plain that she considered the purchases extravagant.

"Couldn't you have gotten along without a carpet? Why did you have to re-cover the armchairs? In my day there was only one armchair in a house, and that was for old people—at least that's how it was in my mother's house, and she was a respectable woman, I can tell you that. Everybody can't be rich! Nobody has so much money that it can't all be squandered away! I'd be ashamed to pamper myself the way you do, even though I'm old now and need to take care of myself. . . . Just look at all those fancy things! What! Silk for linings at two francs, when you can get along perfectly well with jaconet that sells for fifty centimes, or even as low as forty?"

Emma, stretched out on the settee, replied with great calm, "Enough, madame, enough . . ."

Charles's mother went on preaching to her, predicting that they would end up in the poorhouse. Besides, it was Bovary's fault. It was a good thing he had promised to revoke that power of attorney . . .

"What!"

"Oh yes, he gave me his word," the good woman replied.

Emma opened the window and called Charles inside; the poor man was forced to confess the promise his mother had wrung from him.

Emma disappeared, then quickly returned and majestically handed her a large sheet of paper.

"Thank you," said the old woman.

And she threw the power of attorney into the fire.

Emma began to laugh loudly, shrilly and continuously: she was having a fit of hysterics.

"Oh, my God!" cried Charles. "You're in the wrong, too! Why did you have to come here and make a scene with her?"

His mother shrugged her shoulders and said that Emma's conduct was "all put on."

But Charles, rebelling against her for the first time in his life, came to his wife's defense; as a result, the elder Madame Bovary decided to go back home. She left the next day. As she was walking out of the house he tried to persuade her to stay, but she replied, "No, no! You love her more than you do me, and you're right—that's the way it ought to be. Anyway, you're the one that's going to suffer, you'll see! . . . Well, good-by and good luck. . . . And you can be sure of one thing: it'll be a long time before I come back and 'make a scene with her' again, as you put it."

Charles nevertheless behaved very sheepishly toward Emma, and she did not conceal her resentment over the lack of confidence he had shown in her; he had to beg her many times before she would consent to accept a power of attorney again, and he even went with her to have Monsieur Guillaumin draw up another one exactly like the first.

"I can understand why you want her to have it," said the notary. "A man of science can't be bothered with the practical details of life."

And Charles felt relieved by this unctuous remark, which gave his weakness the flattering appearance of lofty preoccupation.

What wild rejoicing there was with Léon in their hotel room the following Thursday! She laughed, wept, sang, danced, sent for sherbets and insisted on smoking cigarettes; she seemed giddy to him, but adorable and superb.

He did not understand the deep-seated reaction that was now driving her into a still more reckless pursuit of sensual pleasure. She was becoming more and more excitable, greedy and voluptuous; and she walked with him in the street with her head high, unafraid, she said, of compromising herself. Sometimes, however, she shuddered at the sudden thought of meeting Rodolphe, for it seemed to her that, although they had parted forever, she was still not completely free of his domination.

One night she did not return to Yonville. Charles nearly lost his head, and little Berthe, unwilling to go to bed without her mama, was sobbing as though her chest were about to burst. Justin had gone off down the road, not knowing what else to do, and Monsieur Homais had even left his pharmacy.

Finally at eleven o'clock, unable to go on waiting any longer, Charles harnessed his horse to his buggy, leapt into it, cracked his whip and reached the Croix-Rouge at two in the morning. She was not there. It occurred to him that Léon might have seen her; but where did he live? Fortunately he remembered the address of his employer; he went there as fast as he could.

The first light of dawn had appeared in the sky. He saw several brass plaques above a door; he knocked. Without opening the door, someone shouted the information he had requested, along with a number of angry remarks about people who disturbed other people in the middle of the night.

The house the clerk lived in had neither bell, knocker nor doorman. Charles pounded the shutters with his fists. He saw a policeman coming toward him, became frightened and went away.

"I'm losing my mind," he told himself. "Monsieur and

Madame Lormeaux probably insisted on her staying for dinner."

The Lormeaux family no longer lived in Rouen.

"She must have stayed to take care of Madame Dubreuil . . . No, Madame Dubreuil died ten months ago! . . . Where can she be?"

An idea came to him. He went into a café, asked for the directory and quickly looked up Mademoiselle Lempereur's name: she lived at 74 Rue de la Renelle-des-Maroquiniers.

Just as he turned into this street, Emma herself appeared at the other end of it. He ran to her, crushed her in his arms and cried out, "Why didn't you come home?"

"I was ill."

"What was wrong? Where were you? What . . ."

She passed her hand over her forehead and replied, "I was in Mademoiselle Lempereur's house."

"I was sure of it! I was just going there!"

"Well, there's no use going there now," said Emma. "She went out a little while ago. But in the future, try to be a little calmer. I can't feel free if I know you're going to get upset like this whenever I'm the slightest bit late."

It was her way of giving herself permission to indulge in her escapades without restraint. She used it freely and fully. Whenever she felt like seeing Léon she would invent some pretext or other and go off to Rouen, and since he would not be expecting her that day, she would call for him at his office.

They were both overjoyed the first few times, but soon he no longer hid the truth from her, namely, that his employer was complaining strongly about his absences.

"Oh, come on anyway!" she would say.

And he would slip out again.

She insisted that he dress entirely in black and grow a little pointed beard, so that he would look like the portraits of Louis XIII. She asked to see his apartment and found it rather drab; he blushed, but she did not notice. She advised him to buy curtains like hers. When he objected that they would be too expensive she laughed and said, "Oh, I see! You like to keep your money in your pocket!"

Each time they met, Léon had to tell her everything he had done since their last rendezvous. She asked for poetry, poetry written for her, "love poems" in her honor; he could never find a rhyme for the second line, so he always ended up copying a sonnet from a keepsake album.

He did this less out of vanity than for the sole purpose of pleasing her. He never argued against her ideas; he accepted all her tastes; he was becoming her mistress more than she was his. His soul was carried away by her sweet words and kisses. Where had she learned that depravity, so profound and so artfully concealed that it was almost intangible?

VI

On his trips to see her, Léon had often dined at the pharmacist's house, and he felt that politeness required him to invite him in return.

"With pleasure!" replied Monsieur Homais. "It's about time I had a little diversion: I'm getting rusty here. We'll go to the theater and eat in a restaurant—we'll really make a night of it!"

"Oh, my dear!" murmured Madame Homais tenderly; she was alarmed by the vague perils to which he was preparing to expose himself.

"What's wrong with that? Don't you think I ruin my health enough, constantly breathing in drug fumes? That's how women are: they're jealous of Science, and then they oppose the most innocent kind of amusement. Never mind, though, you can count on me: I'll turn up in Rouen one of these days and we'll paint the town red."

In the past, the apothecary would never have used such an expression, but he was now intent on giving himself a jaunty Parisian air which he considered quite fashionable, and, like his neighbor Madame Bovary, he eagerly questioned the clerk about life in the capital; he even talked slang in order to dazzle his bourgeois listeners, using such words as *turne, bazar, chicard* and *chicandard*, referring to the Rue de Bréda in English as "Breda Street," and saying *"Je me la casse"* for *"Je m'en vais."*

And so one Thursday in the kitchen of the Lion d'Or, Emma was surprised to see Monsieur Homais in traveling garb; that is, he was wrapped in an old cloak that no one had ever seen him wear before, and holding a suitcase in one hand and the foot-warmer from his shop in the other.

He had kept his plans a secret, fearing his absence might alarm the public.

He was apparently excited by the thought of revisiting the places where he had spent his youth, for he kept talking all the way. Then as soon as they arrived he leapt from the coach and went off in search of Léon. The clerk struggled, but in vain: Monsieur Homais dragged him into the spacious Café de Normandie, where he entered majestically without taking off his hat, regarding it as extremely provincial to uncover oneself in a public place.

Emma waited for Léon three-quarters of an hour. Finally she hurried to his office; then, lost in all sorts of conjectures, accusing him of indifference and reproaching herself for her weakness, she spent the afternoon with her forehead pressed against the windowpanes of their room.

At two o'clock Léon and Homais were still sitting across the table from each other. The big dining room was becoming empty; the stovepipe, made in the shape of a palm tree, spread its gilded branches over the white ceiling; and near their table, in the bright sunlight behind the net window curtain, a little fountain was gurgling in a marble basin in which, among watercress and asparagus, three lobsters were sluggishly stretching out toward a pile of quail lying on their sides.

Homais was blissfully happy. Although he was more intoxicated with luxury than with fine food and drink, the Pommard wine did go to his head a little, and when the rum omelet appeared he advanced a number of immoral theories about women. It was *chic* that captivated him more than anything else. He adored an elegantly dressed woman in a tastefully furnished room; and as for physical attributes, he was not averse to "a pretty little morsel."

Léon kept looking at the clock in despair while the apothecary went on drinking, eating and talking.

"You must feel quite a lack here in Rouen," he said abruptly, "although your sweetheart doesn't really live too far away."

Léon blushed.

"Come now, be frank!" continued Homais. "You can't deny that in Yonville . . ."

The young man stammered something.

"In Madame Bovary's you used to court . . ."

"Whom?"

"The maid!"

He was not joking. But Léon's vanity overcame his
prudence and he protested vigorously in spite of himself.
Besides, he liked only brunettes.

"You're quite right," said the pharmacist, "they're more
passionate." And, leaning close to his friend's ear, he told
him the signs by which one can recognize whether or not
a woman is passionate. He even launched into an ethno-
graphical digression: German women were moody, French
women lascivious, Italian women fiery.

"What about Negro women?" asked the clerk.

"Artists often have a taste for them," said Homais.
"Waiter! Two demitasses!"

"Shall we go?" asked Léon, completely out of patience
by now.

"*Yes,*" replied Homais, in English.

But, before leaving, he insisted on seeing the manager and
offering him his congratulations.

To get rid of him, the young man said he had an appointment.

"Ah! I'll go with you," said Homais.

And as they walked through the streets together, he talked
about his wife, his children, their future and his pharmacy,
describing the wretched condition in which he had found
it and the peak of perfection to which he had brought it.

When they reached the Hôtel de Boulogne, Léon brusquely
took leave of him, ran upstairs and found his mistress in
a state of intense anxiety.

When she heard the pharmacist's name she flew into a
rage. He defended himself ably, however; it wasn't his fault
—didn't she know how Monsieur Homais was? Surely she
didn't believe he preferred his company to hers! But she
turned away from him; he drew her back; and, sinking to
his knees, he put his arms around her waist and clung
to her in a disconsolate pose full of desire and supplication.

She stood looking solemnly down at him, her big eyes
blazing in a way that was almost frightening. Then they were
clouded over by tears; she lowered her pink eyelids and
abandoned her hands to him. He was about to press them
to his lips when a servant came to say that someone was
asking for Monsieur.

"Will you come back?" she asked.

"Yes."

"But when?"

"Right away."

"You seemed annoyed about your appointment," said the pharmacist when he saw Léon, "so I used this little trick to get you away from it. Let's go see Bridoux and have a glass of liqueur."

Léon swore he had to go back to his office. The apothecary made a few jokes about paper work and legal procedures.

"Why the devil can't you forget about Cujas and Bartole for a while? What's to stop you? Are you a man or a mouse? Let's go to Bridoux's house! You'll see his dog there—it's very interesting!"

And when the clerk stubbornly continued to refuse he said, "All right, then, I'll go to your office with you. I'll read a newspaper while I wait for you, or look through a law book."

Stunned by Emma's anger, Monsieur Homais' chatter, and perhaps also by the heavy lunch he had eaten, Léon hesitated, as though struggling against the pharmacist's spell.

"Let's go to Bridoux's house!" the latter said again. "It's only a few steps from here, on the Rue Malpalu."

Finally, out of cowardice, stupidity and that indefinable feeling which sometimes pushes us into the very actions that are most repugnant to us, Léon let Homais lead him to Bridoux's house. They found him in his little courtyard supervising three workmen who were panting as they turned the big wheel of a machine for making Seltzer water. Homais gave them several pieces of advice and embraced Bridoux; then they had their liqueur. Léon tried to leave a dozen times, but Homais always held him by the arm and said, "Just a minute, I'll come with you! We'll go to the *Fanal de Rouen* and see everybody there. I'll introduce you to Thomassin."

Eventually, however, he managed to get away without him. He ran to the hotel. Emma was gone.

She had just left in a fury. She now hated him. His failure to keep his word about their rendezvous seemed to her an outrage, and she sought other reasons for breaking off their affair: he was incapable of heroism, weak, commonplace, spineless as a woman, and stingy, too, and cowardly.

Then she grew calmer and decided she was probably being unjust to him. But disparaging those we love always detaches us from them to some extent. It is better not to touch our idols: the gilt comes off on our hands.

From then on they talked more often about things irrelevant to their love, and the letters she wrote to him were

largely concerned with flowers, poetry, the moon and the
stars—naïve expedients of a weakened passion trying to
stimulate itself by external means. She always assured herself that her next trip would bring her profound bliss, but
afterward she would have to admit that she had felt nothing
extraordinary. Her disappointment would soon be wiped
away by new hope, and she would come back to him
more ardent and avid than ever. She would eagerly throw
off her clothes, pulling her thin corset string so violently
that it hissed like a snake winding itself around her hips.
After she had tiptoed barefoot to the door to make sure
once again that it was locked, she would let all her clothes
fall in a single movement; then, pale, silent and solemn,
she would fling herself on his chest and a long tremor
would run through her body.

And yet, in that forehead covered with beads of cold sweat,
in those stammering lips, those wild eyes and those clutching
arms, Léon felt the presence of something mad, shadowy
and ominous, something that seemed to be subtly slipping
between them, as though to separate them.

He did not dare to question her, but, seeing how experienced she was, he told himself that she must have gone
through all the extremes of suffering and pleasure. What
had once fascinated him now frightened him a little.
Furthermore, he rebelled against the steadily increasing absorption of his personality. He resented her continuous victory
over him. He even tried to force himself to stop loving
her, but as soon as he heard her footsteps he would feel
helplessly weak, like a drunkard at the sight of liquor.

She never failed, it is true, to shower him with all sorts
of attentions, from rare, delicate foods to seductive clothes
and languourous glances. She brought roses from Yonville in
her bosom and cast them at his face, she showed concern
over his health, gave him advice about his conduct and, to
bind him more tightly to her, hoping, perhaps, that heaven
might come to her aid, she hung a medal of the Virgin
around his neck. Like a virtuous mother, she inquired about
his friends and acquaintances. She sometimes said to him,
"Don't see them, don't go out, don't think about anything
but us; love me!"

She would have liked to keep an eye on everything he
did, and she conceived the idea of having him followed in
the streets. Near the hotel there was always a kind of tramp

who accosted travelers; he would not refuse to . . . But her pride rebelled.

"Let him deceive me! Why should I care? He doesn't mean that much to me!"

One day when they had parted earlier than usual and she was walking back along the boulevard alone, she saw the walls of her convent. She sat down on a bench in the shade of the elms. How peaceful her life had been in those days! How she had longed for the ineffable sentiments of love which she had tried to imagine from her books!

The first months of her marriage, her rides in the forest, her waltzes with the viscount, Lagardy singing—everything passed before her eyes. . . . And Léon suddenly appeared to her as remote as the others.

"But I do love him!" she said to herself.

No matter: she was not happy, and never had been. Why was life so unsatisfying? Why did everything she leaned on instantly crumble into dust? . . . But if somewhere there existed a strong, handsome man with a valorous, passionate and refined nature, a poet's soul in the form of an angel, a lyre with strings of bronze intoning elegiac nuptial songs to the heavens, why was it not possible that she might meet him some day? No, it would never happen! Besides, nothing was worth seeking—everything was a lie! Each smile hid a yawn of boredom, each joy a curse, each pleasure its own disgust; and the sweetest kisses only left on one's lips a hopeless longing for a higher ecstasy.

A grating metallic sound hovered in the air and the convent clock struck four. Four o'clock! It seemed to her that she had been there on that bench for all eternity. But an infinity of passions can be contained in a minute, like a crowd in a little space.

Emma's passions absorbed her completely; she was as unconcerned about money as an archduchess.

One day, however, a bald, sickly-looking, red-faced man came to her house and told her he had been sent by Monsieur Vinçart, of Rouen. He pulled out the pins fastening the side pocket of his long green frock coat, stuck them into his sleeve and politely handed her a document.

It was a promissory note for seven hundred francs, signed by her, which Lheureux, despite all his assurances, had made over to Vinçart.

She sent her maid for Lheureux. He could not come.

The stranger, who had remained standing, his bushy blond eyebrows dissimulating the curious glances he cast right and left, now asked her innocently, "What answer shall I give Monsieur Vinçart?"

"Well," replied Emma, "you can tell him . . . that I don't have . . . It will have to be next week . . . Tell him to wait . . . Yes, next week."

And the man left without a word.

But the next day at noon she received a protest of non-payment, and she was so frightened by the sight of the stamped document, bearing the words "Maître Hareng, Bailiff at Buchy" several times in big letters, that she hurried to the dry-goods dealer immediately.

She found him in his shop, tying up a package.

"What can I do for you?" he said. "I'm at your service."

He nevertheless went on with his task, aided by a slightly hunchbacked girl of about thirteen who worked for him as both clerk and cook.

Then, after clattering across the floor of the shop in his wooden-soled shoes, he led Madame up to the second floor and showed her into a narrow office where several ledgers were lying on a big fir desk, held down by an iron bar padlocked across them. A safe could be partially seen against the wall, beneath some pieces of calico: judging from its size, it surely contained something besides promissory notes and cash—pawnbroking was one of Monsieur Lheureux's activities, and it was there that he had put Madame Bovary's gold chain, along with the earrings he had received from poor old Tellier, who, finally forced to sell his establishment, had bought a little grocery store in Quincampoix, where he was slowly dying of his catarrh, his face yellower than his tallow candles.

Lheureux sat down in his wide straw-bottomed armchair.

"What's new?"

"Look at this."

And she showed him the document.

"Well? What can I do about it?"

She angrily reminded him that he had promised not to transfer her notes; he admitted it.

"But I had no choice: my own creditors were holding a knife to my throat."

"And what's going to happen now?" she asked.

"Oh, it's quite simple: a court judgment, then a seizure; there's nothing more to be done now!"

Emma had to restrain herself from hitting him. She asked him gently if there might not be some way to pacify Monsieur Vinçart.

"What! Pacify Vinçart? You don't know him: he's more ferocious than an Arab."

Even so, Monsieur Lheureux would have to do something.

"Listen, it seems to me I've been pretty good to you so far." He opened one of his ledgers. "Look." He moved his finger up the page. "Let's see now . . . let's see . . . August 3: two hundred francs . . . June 17: a hundred and fifty . . . March 23: forty-six . . . In April . . ."

He stopped short, as though afraid of making some foolish mistake.

"And I won't even mention the notes signed by Monsieur, one for seven hundred and the other for three hundred! As for your little payments on account, and the interest, the whole thing's nothing but an endless mess. I won't have anything more to do with it!"

She wept; she even called him "my dear Monsieur Lheureux." But he kept laying the blame on "that rascal Vinçart." Besides, he didn't have a franc to his name; everyone had stopped paying him; if things went on that way much longer he would lose the shirt off his back; a poor shopkeeper like himself couldn't advance money to anyone.

Emma said nothing; Monsieur Lheureux, chewing on the quill of a pen, was no doubt worried by her silence, for he finally added, "Unless one of these days some money should happen to come in . . . Then I could . . ."

"Anyway," she said, "as soon as I get the rest of the money for the house at Barneville . . ."

"What?"

He seemed surprised to learn that Langlois had not yet paid. A moment later he said blandly, "Then I take it you'd be willing to . . ."

"Oh, anything you say!"

He closed his eyes for a moment to reflect and wrote down a few figures; then, after declaring that he was making great difficulties for himself, taking a grave risk and "bleeding himself white," he dictated four promissory notes for one hundred and fifty francs each, payable at one-month intervals.

"If only Vinçart will listen to me! Anyway, you can count

on me to tell you exactly how things stand; there's nothing two-faced about me."

He casually showed her some of his new merchandise, but none of it, in his opinion, was worthy of Madame.

"Just think of it: dress cloth like this sells for seven sous a yard, and it's guaranteeed not to fade! And people believe it! I don't do anything to make them believe differently, either, you can be sure of that." He made this admission of treachery toward others in order to convince her thoroughly of his honesty toward her.

He then called her back to show her four yards of point lace which he had recently acquired at a public auction. "Isn't it beautiful?" he said. "It's being used a lot these days for antimacassars; it's the latest style."

And, as deftly as a sleight-of-hand artist, he wrapped the lace in blue paper and handed it to Emma.

"At least let me know . . ."

"Oh, we'll talk about that later!" he said, turning away from her.

That evening she insisted that Bovary write to his mother and ask her to send the balance of the inheritance immediately. Her mother-in-law replied that there was nothing left: the liquidation was finished, and, not counting Barneville, they would have a yearly income of six hundred francs, which she would send to them punctually.

Emma then sent bills to two or three patients, and before long she was making extensive use of this practice, which succeeded quite well. She was always careful to add a postscript: "Don't mention this to my husband—you know how proud he is. Please excuse me. Your humble servant." There were a few complaints; she intercepted them.

To raise money she began to sell her old gloves, her old hats and various old household articles; and her peasant blood drove her to bargain rapaciously. Then she decided to buy knickknacks each time she made a trip to the city, sure that she could resell them to Monsieur Lheureux, if no one else. She bought ostrich feathers, Chinese porcelains and wooden chests; she borrowed from Félicité, from Madame Lefrançois, from the landlady of the Croix-Rouge, from everyone, everywhere. With the money she finally received from Barneville, she paid off two notes; the remaining fifteen hundred francs slipped between her fingers. She signed more notes, and so it continued!

Sometimes, it is true, she tried to make a few calculations, but she always ended with such exorbitant figures that she could not believe them; she would then begin all over again, quickly become confused, drop the whole matter and forget about it.

The house now took on an air of sadness. Tradesmen were seen leaving it with angry faces. There were handkerchiefs lying around on the stoves, and little Berthe had holes in her stockings, which scandalized Madame Homais. If Charles timidly ventured a comment, Emma would retort angrily that it wasn't *her* fault.

Why these fits of temper? He imputed everything to her old nervous malady; and, reproaching himself with having taken her infirmities for faults, he accused himself of selfishness and felt like running up to her and kissing her. But then he said to himself, "No, I'd only annoy her!" And he stayed where he was.

After dinner he would walk alone in the garden; then he would take little Berthe on his lap, open his medical journal and try to teach her to read. But the child, who never studied, would soon open her eyes wide in despair and begin to weep. He would comfort her and fill the watering can for her so that she could make little rivers in the gravel, or break off privet branches for her to plant as trees in the flower beds, which did little to spoil the appearance of the garden, since it was already overgrown with tall grass and weeds—they owed so many days' pay to Lestiboudois! Finally the child would begin to feel chilly and ask for her mother.

"Call the maid," Charles would say. "You know mama doesn't like to be disturbed."

Autumn had set in and already the leaves were falling—the same as when she had been ill, two years before. When would it all end? And he would go on walking, with his hands behind his back.

Madame was in her room, where no one else ever went. She would stay there all day long, listless and scarcely dressed, occasionally lighting one of the conical pieces of incense she had bought in an Algerian shop in Rouen. In order not to have Charles lying asleep beside her at night, she had made such an obvious show of displeasure that she finally succeeded in banishing him to the third floor; and she would stay up all night reading lurid novels full of orgiastic scenes and bloody deeds. Often, seized with terror, she would utter a cry. Charles would come running in, but she would say to him, "Oh, go away!"

At other times, burned more intensely than usual by that inner flame fanned by adultery, panting, trembling, consumed with desire, she would open her window and breathe in the cold air, letting the wind ruffle the heavy mass of her hair as she looked up at the stars and wished she were loved by a prince. Then she would think of him, of Léon. At such moments she would have given anything for one of those meetings with him which sated her desire.

The days she spent with him were her gala days, and they had to be glorious! When he could not pay for everything himself, she would liberally make up the difference, and this happened nearly every time. He tried to convince her that they would be just as well off somewhere else, in a more modest hotel, but she raised objections.

One day she opened her bag, took out six little silver-gilt spoons (her father's wedding present) and asked him to go and pawn them for her immediately. Léon obeyed, but with reluctance—he was afraid he might compromise himself.

On thinking it over, he decided that his mistress was beginning to act quite strangely, and that those who wanted him to stop seeing her might be right.

For someone had sent his mother a long anonymous letter warning her that he was "ruining himself with a married woman"; and the good lady instantly had visions of the eternal bugaboo of respectable families: the shadowy, pernicious creature, the siren, the fabulous monster dwelling in the depths of love. She wrote to Maître Dubocage, his employer, who handled the matter perfectly. He talked to Léon for three-quarters of an hour, trying to open his eyes and warn him of the abyss into which he was plunging. Such an affair would damage his career later. He begged him to break it off, and if he would not make the sacrifice in his own interest, he should at least make it for him, Dubocage!

Léon had finally sworn never to see Emma again, and he reproached himself for not having kept his word, considering all the difficulties and lectures he would probably have to face because of her, not to mention the jokes his colleagues made about him every morning around the stove. Besides, he was about to be promoted to head clerk; it was time to settle down and work hard. He therefore gave up the flute, exalted sentiments and flights of fancy—for every bourgeois, in the heat of his youth, if only for a day or a minute, has believed himself capable of stormy passions and lofty enterprises. The most mediocre libertine has dreamed of Oriental queens; every notary bears within himself the remains of a poet.

He was now bored whenever Emma suddenly burst out sobbing on his chest; and, like those who can stand only a certain amount of music, his heart grew drowsy and indifferent amid the tumult of a love whose more delicate nuances he could no longer distinguish.

They knew each other too well to feel that breathless wonder which makes the joy of possession a hundred times more intense. She was as satiated with him as he was tired of her. She was beginning to find in adultery all the dullness of marriage.

But how could she bring herself to give it up? Although she felt humiliated by the baseness of her satisfactions, she continued to cling to them out of habit or depravity; and every day she pursued them with greater determination, destroying all chance of happiness by insisting on too much of it. She blamed Léon for her disappointed hopes, as though he had betrayed her; and she even wished for a catastrophe that would bring about their separation, since she did not have the courage to take any action herself.

She went on writing him love letters nevertheless, on the principle that a woman must always write to her lover.

But, as she wrote, she saw another man, a phantom composed of her most ardent memories, her strongest desires and the most beautiful things she had read. He finally became so real, so accessible, that she was thrilled and amazed, even though she was never able to imagine him clearly, for his form, like that of a god, was lost in the abundance of his attributes. He lived in that nebulous realm where silk ladders swing from balconies bathed in moonlight and the fragrance of flowers. She felt him near her; he was about to come and sweep her away entirely in a kiss. Then she would fall back to earth, shattered, for these vague amorous raptures tired her more than the wildest orgies.

She was now living in a state of profound and constant

lassitude. She often received writs, documents bearing official stamps, but she scarcely even looked at them. She wished she could stop living entirely, or sleep continuously.

One Thursday she did not return to Yonville. It was the night of the mid-Lent festivities, and she went to a masked ball. She wore velvet knee breeches, red stockings, a wig tied with a ribbon at the back, and a cocked hat over one ear. She danced all night to the furious sound of the trombones; there was always a circle of admirers around her; and when morning came she found herself under the portico of the theater with five or six masked revelers dressed as longshoremen or sailors; they were friends of Léon's, and they were talking about going somewhere to eat.

The nearby cafés were all full. On the waterfront they found a shabby-looking restaurant whose owner showed them into a small private room on the fifth floor.

The men whispered in a corner, no doubt discussing the expense. There was a clerk, two medical students and a salesman—what company for her! As for the women, she quickly realized, from the sound of their voices, that most of them must be of the lowest class. Suddenly feeling afraid, she pushed back her chair and lowered her eyes.

The others began to eat. She did not; her forehead was flushed, her eyelids were smarting and her skin was icy cold. In her head she could still feel the ballroom floor quaking to the rhythmic pounding of a thousand dancing feet. Then the smell of punch and cigar smoke made her dizzy. She fainted and was carried to the window.

Day was beginning to break, and a wide band of crimson was spreading across the pale sky in the direction of Sainte-Catherine. The pale river was shivering in the wind; there was no one on the bridges; the street lamps were going out.

Meanwhile she regained consciousness. She thought of Berthe, sleeping in the maid's room back in Yonville. But a cart laden with long strips of iron went by, throwing a deafening metallic vibration against the walls of the houses.

She left abruptly, took off her costume, told Léon she had to go home and was finally left alone in the Hôtel de Boulogne. Everything, including herself, seemed unbearable to her. She wished she could fly away like a bird and make herself young again somewhere in the vast purity of space.

She left the hotel and walked across the boulevard, the

Place Cauchoise and the outskirts of the city until she came to an open street overlooking a series of gardens. She walked swiftly; the fresh air calmed her; and gradually the faces of the crowd, the costumed dancers, the quadrilles, the chandeliers, the restaurant, those women—everything vanished like mist blown away by the wind. Then, when she reached the Croix-Rouge, she threw herself on the bed in her little third-floor room with its pictures of the Tour de Nesle. Hivert awakened her at four in the afternoon.

When she came home, Félicité showed her a sheet of gray paper that had been placed behind the clock. She read:

"By virtue of a written instrument, in execution of a judgment . . ."

What judgment? She did not know that another document had been brought to the house the day before; she was therefore dumbfounded to read these words:

"Madame Bovary is hereby ordered by the king, the law and the court . . ."

Then, skipping several lines, she saw:

"Within twenty-four hours at the latest." What was this? *"Pay the total amount of eight thousand francs."* And further on: *"She will be constrained thereto by due process of law, notably, by the seizure of all her personal property and effects."*

What was to be done? Within twenty-four hours—by tomorrow! Lheureux, she thought, was probably trying to frighten her again; for all his maneuvers had suddenly become clear to her, and she now realized why he had been so obliging to her. What reassured her was the exorbitance of the sum.

However, as a result of buying, not paying, borrowing, signing promissory notes and then renewing them, so that they grew larger each time they fell due, she had finally built up a capital for Monsieur Lheureux, and he was now eager to have it to use in his speculations.

She walked into his office with a casual air.

"Do you know what's happened to me? It must be some kind of joke!"

"No, it's not."

"What do you mean?"

He slowly turned away from her, crossed his arms and said, "My dear lady, did you think I was going to go on being your supplier and banker till the end of time, out of charity? I have to get back the money I've laid out for you, that's only fair!"

She protested about the debt.

"There's no use talking about it—the court has upheld it and handed down a judgment! You've been notified! Anyway, it's not my doing, it's Vinçart's."

"Couldn't you . . ."

"No, I couldn't do anything!"

"But . . . even so . . . let's talk it over."

And she began to stammer incoherently; she had known nothing about it . . . it had come as a complete surprise to her . . .

"Whose fault is that?" said Lheureux, bowing ironically. "While I work like a slave, you're out having a good time for yourself."

"Never mind preaching to me!"

"It never does any harm," he retorted.

She was abject: she pleaded with him and even put her long, pretty white hand on his knee.

"Stop that! You act as though you're trying to seduce me!"

"You're disgusting!" she cried.

"My, my, how you do go on!" he said, laughing.

"I'll let everybody know what kind of a man you are! I'll tell my husband . . ."

"In that case I'll show him something!"

And Lheureux took from his safe a receipt for eighteen hundred francs which she had given him after Vinçart had discounted her note.

"Do you think the poor, dear man won't see how you arranged your little theft?"

She collapsed as though she had been stunned by a blow on the head. He paced back and forth between the window and the desk, saying over and over, "I'll show him, all right . . . I'll show him . . ."

Then he came up to her and said softly, "It's not pleasant, I know that; but it's never killed anyone, and since it's the only way you have left to pay me what you owe me . . ."

"But where can I get any money?" said Emma, wringing her hands.

"Oh, that shouldn't be hard—after all, you have friends!"

And he gave her such a knowing, terrible look that she shuddered to the depths of her being.

"I promise," she said, "I'll sign . . ."

"I've got enough of your signatures already!"

"I can still sell . . ."

"Come, come!" he said, shrugging his shoulders. "You have nothing left to sell."

And he called through the peephole that opened into his shop: "Annette! Don't forget those three pieces of number fourteen."

The servant came in; Emma understood the hint and asked how much money it would take to stop all the proceedings.

"It's too late!"

"But what if I brought you several thousand francs—a quarter of the amount, a third, almost all of it?"

"No! It's useless!"

He pushed her gently toward the stairs.

"I beg you, Monsieur Lheureux: just a few days more!"

She was sobbing.

"Ah! Now come the tears!"

"You're destroying my last hope!"

"What do I care?" he said, closing the door.

VII

She was stoical the next day when Maître Hareng, the bailiff, came to the house with two witnesses to make an official inventory for the seizure.

They began with Bovary's consulting room and did not include the phrenological head, which was considered as "an instrument of his profession;" but in the kitchen they counted the plates, pots, chairs and candlesticks, and in her bedroom all the knickknacks on the whatnot. They examined her dresses, the linen and everything in her dressing room; her whole existence, down to its most intimate details, was laid open like a dissected corpse before the eyes of those three men.

Maître Hareng, buttoned into a thin black tail coat, with a white cravat and tight shoestraps, kept saying from time to time, "Allow me, madame. Allow me." And often he exclaimed, "Charming! Very pretty!" Then he would begin to write again, dipping his pen in the inkhorn he held in his left hand.

When they had finished with all the other rooms, they went up to the attic.

She kept Rodolphe's letters locked in a desk there. She had to open it.

"Ah, letters!" said Maître Hareng with a discreet smile. "But please allow me—I must make sure the box doesn't contain anything else."

And he tilted the sheets of paper gently, as though trying to make gold coins slide out from between them. She was filled with indignation when she saw that big red hand, its fingers as soft as slugs, touching those pages that had once made her heart pound with emotion.

At last they left! Félicité came in. Emma had sent her to watch for Bovary and keep him away. They quickly installed the guard in the attic, and he promised to stay there.

Charles seemed worried to her that evening. She kept glancing at him anxiously, thinking she saw accusations in the wrinkles of his face. Then, when her eyes fell on the fireplace adorned with Chinese screens, on the broad curtains, the armchairs—in short, on all the things that had helped to alleviate the bitterness of her life—she was overcome with remorse, or rather with profound regret, which, far from obliterating her passion, aroused it all the more. Charles was placidly stirring the fire, with his feet on the andirons.

At one point the guard—bored, no doubt, in his hiding-place—made a slight noise.

"Is someone walking up there?" asked Charles.

"No!" she replied. "One of the dormer windows was left open and the wind is banging it."

The next day, Sunday, she went to Rouen to see all the bankers whose names she knew. Most of them were either in the country or traveling. She did not lose heart, however; she asked for loans from those she succeeded in seeing, telling them she had to have some money and promising to pay it back. Some of them laughed in her face; they all refused.

At two o'clock she hurried to Léon's house and knocked on his door. No one came to open it. Finally he appeared.

"What brings you here?"

"Do you mind?"

"No . . . but . . ."

And he confessed that his landlord didn't like him to have "women visitors."

"I must talk to you," she said.

He took out his key. She stopped him.

"No, not here! Let's go to *our* room."

And they went to their room in the Hôtel de Boulogne. She drank a large glass of water when she arrived. She was very pale. She said to him, "Léon, there's something you must do for me." She clutched his hands tightly and shook them. "Listen: I need eight thousand francs!"

"You must be out of your mind!"

"Not yet!"

She quickly told him about the seizure and the desperateness of her situation: Charles was ignorant of everything, her mother-in-law hated her and her father was unable to help; but she knew that he, Léon, would go out and find her the money she needed . . .

"How do you expect me to . . ."

"You're acting like a coward!" she cried.

"Things aren't as bad as you think," he said stupidly. "If you give your man three thousand francs or so he may calm down."

All the more reason for trying to do something: surely they could manage to scrape together three thousand francs. Besides, Léon could sign promissory notes for her.

"Go ahead! Try! You must! Hurry! Oh, try, do your best! I'll love you so much for it!"

He left, came back an hour later and said solemnly, "I went to see three people. No luck."

They sat facing each other on either side of the fireplace, silent and motionless. Emma shrugged her shoulders and tapped her foot. He hear her murmur, "If I were in your place, *I'd* find some money!"

"Where?"

"In your office!"

And she looked at him.

Demoniac resolution blazed from her eyes, and she narrowed them in a lascivious and encouraging look; the young man felt himself weakening before the silent will of this woman who was urging him to commit a crime. Fear gripped his heart, and to keep her from explaining herself more clearly he clapped his hand to his forehead and exclaimed:

"Morel is supposed to come back tonight! He won't refuse

me, I hope!" (Morel was one of his friends, the son of a very
rich businessman.) "I'll bring you the money tomorrow."

Emma did not appear to welcome this hope as joyfully
as he had thought she would. Did she suspect his lie? He
added, blushing, "But if I don't come by three o'clock, don't
wait for me any longer, darling. I have to go now, excuse
me. Good-by!"

He pressed her hand, but it was limp and inert. She no
longer had strength enough for any feeling.

The clock struck four; she stood up to go back to Yonville,
yielding to the force of habit like an automaton.

It was a beautiful day—one of those clear, crisp March
days when the sun glows brightly in a white sky. Contented-
looking local citizens were out strolling in their Sunday best.
She reached the square in front of the cathedral. Vespers
had just ended; the crowd was flowing out through the three
portals like a river beneath the three arches of a bridge, and
in the middle, steadfast as a rock, stood the verger.

She remembered the day when, full of anxiety and hope,
she had entered that great nave, her love soaring higher
than its lofty vaults; and she walked on, weeping beneath
her veil, dazed, unsteady on her feet, almost fainting.

"Look out!" cried a voice from a courtyard whose gate
was opening.

She stopped; a black horse, prancing between the shafts
of a tilbury, passed in front of her, driven by a gentleman in
sable. Who was he? She knew him . . . The tilbury leapt
forward and disappeared.

The viscount! That's who it was! She turned and looked
down the street: it was empty. She suddenly felt so crushed,
so heartsick, that she leaned against a wall to keep from
falling.

Then she told herself she had been mistaken. In any
case, she could not be sure. Everything inside her, and
everything around her, was abandoning her. She felt lost, as
though she were tumbling blindly into some indescribable
abyss; and when she reached the Croix-Rouge she was almost
glad to see good old Homais watching a big box full of
pharmaceutical supplies being loaded onto the Hirondelle;
in his hand, wrapped in a silk handkerchief, he was holding
six *cheminots* for his wife.

Madame Homais was very fond of these heavy turban-
shaped rolls which are eaten with salted butter during Lent;
a remnant of Gothic fare, they go back perhaps to the time

of the Crusades, when the stalwart Normans gorged themselves on them, seeing them on the table, by the light of
the yellow torches, between the pitchers of spiced wine and
the gigantic slabs of pork, as so many Saracen heads to be
devoured. Like them, the pharmacist's wife bit into her
cheminots heroically, despite the wretched state of her teeth;
and when Monsieur Homais made a trip to the city he never
failed to bring some back to her, always buying them from
the best baker, on the Rue Massacre.

"Delighted to see you!" he said, holding out his hand to
help Emma climb into the Hirondelle.

Then he put the *cheminots* in the baggage net and sat,
with bare head and folded arms, in a thoughtful, Napoleonic
pose.

But when the blind man appeared, as usual, at the foot of
the hill, he cried out, "I can't understand why the authorities
still tolerate such shameful occupations! All those unfortunate
people ought to be put away somewhere, and forced to do
some kind of work. Yes, progress is moving at a snail's
pace! We're still floundering in barbarism!"

The blind man held out his hat, and it bobbed up and
down at the edge of the window like a loose section of
upholstery.

"There," said the pharmacist, "is a scrofulous disease!"

And although he was well acquainted with the poor devil,
he pretended to be seeing him for the first time; he murmured
the words "cornea," "opaque cornea," "sclerotic" and "fa-
cies," then he asked in a paternal tone, "How long have
you had that terrible infirmity, my friend? Instead of getting
drunk in a tavern, you'd do better to follow a diet."

He urged him to drink good wine and good beer, and eat
good roast meat. The blind man went on singing; in general,
he seemed to be almost idiotic. Finally Monsieur Homais
opened his purse.

"Here's a sou—give me change for half of it and keep
the other half for yourself. And don't forget my advice: it
will do you good."

Hivert took the liberty of expressing some doubt about
its efficacy, but the apothecary guaranteed that he could cure
the man's blindness himself, with an antiphlogistic salve of
his own composition, and he gave him his address: "Monsieur
Homais, near the market shed—anyone can direct you."

"Now," said Hivert, "show your appreciation by doing
your act."

The blind man squatted on his haunches, tilted back his head, rolled his greenish eyes, stuck out his tongue, rubbed his stomach with both hands and let out a kind of muffled howl, like a starving dog. Emma, overcome with disgust, tossed him a five-franc coin over her shoulder. It was her entire fortune. Throwing it away like that seemed to her a noble gesture.

The coach was moving again when Monsieur Homais suddenly leaned out the window and shouted, "No farinaceous foods or dairy products! Wear wool next to your skin! Expose the diseased parts to the smoke of juniper berries!"

The sight of familiar objects filing past before her eyes gradually took Emma's mind off her sorrow. She was oppressed by an unbearable fatigue, and by the time she reached home she was dazed, apathetic and almost asleep.

"From now on I don't care what happens!" she said to herself.

And then, who could tell? Why couldn't something extraordinary occur at any minute? Lheureux might even die.

She was awakened at nine o'clock the next morning by the sound of voices in the square. A crowd was gathering around the market shed to read a large notice posted on one of the pillars. She saw Justin climb up on a curbstone and begin tearing down the notice, but then the village policeman laid his hand on his shoulder. Monsieur Homais came out of the pharmacy, and Madame Lefrançois, standing in the middle of the crowd, seemed to be making a speech.

"Madame! Madame!" cried Félicité, bursting into the room. "It's an outrage!"

And the poor girl, all upset, handed her a sheet of yellow paper which she had just torn off the door. Emma read at a glance that all her personal property was for sale.

They looked at each other in silence. There were no secrets between the servant and her mistress. Finally Félicité said with a sigh, "If I were you, madame, I'd go to see Monsieur Guillaumin."

"Do you think so?"

This question meant: "You know Monsieur Guillaumin's manservant, so you know what goes on in his house; does he sometimes talk about me?"

"Yes, go ahead; it's a good idea."

She put on her black dress and her bonnet with jade beads; and, to avoid being seen (there was still a large crowd in the square), she took the path running alongside the river, outside the village.

She was out of breath when she arrived at the notary's gate; the sky was dark and it was snowing a little.

She rang the bell. Théodore, wearing a red vest, appeared in the doorway; he came out and opened the gate for her almost familiarly, as though she were a friend of his, and showed her into the dining room.

A wide porcelain stove was purring beneath a niche occupied by a cactus plant, and against the oak-colored wallpaper hung two pictures in black wooden frames: Steuben's *Esmeralda* and Schopin's *Potiphar*. The table, already set, the two silver chafing dishes, the crystal door-knobs, the floor, the furniture—everything gleamed with meticulous English cleanliness; the windows were adorned at each corner with panes of colored glass.

"This is the kind of dining room I ought to have," thought Emma.

The notary came in, pressing his dressing gown, decorated with palm-leaf designs, against his body with his left hand, while with his right he took off his brown velvet skullcap and then quickly put it on again; he pretentiously wore it tilted over his right ear, and from it protruded the ends of three strands of blond hair which, beginning at the back, were combed over his bald skull.

After offering her a chair he sat down to eat, apologizing profusely for his discourtesy.

"Monsieur," she said, "I'd like to ask you . . ."

"What is it, madame? I'm listening."

She began to tell him of her predicament.

Monsieur Guillaumin already knew about it, for he was secretly allied with the dry-goods dealer, who was always ready to put up capital for the mortgage loans he was asked to arrange.

He therefore knew (and better than she) the long story of her promissory notes, for small sums at first, bearing the names of various people as endorsers, made out for long terms, falling due on different dates and continually being renewed until the day when Lheureux, having gathered all the protests of nonpayment, asked his friend Vinçart to institute the necessary legal proceedings in his name, not wishing to be regarded as a shark by his fellow townsmen.

She interspersed her story with recriminations against

Lheureux, to which the notary occasionally made some vague reply. As he ate his cutlet and drank his tea, his chin pushed down against his sky-blue cravat, which was held in place by two diamond stickpins attached to either end of a little gold chain, and there was a strange, bland, ambiguous smile on his lips. Then, noticing that her shoes were damp, he said to her, "Move closer to the stove . . . Put your feet up higher, against the porcelain."

She was afraid of dirtying it. The notary said gallantly, "Pretty things never spoil anything."

She tried to arouse his compassion; growing emotional herself, she told him of her straitened circumstances, her torments, her needs. He understood very well—an elegant woman like her! Without interrupting his eating, he had turned around to face her; his knee grazed her shoe, whose sole was curling and steaming against the stove.

But when she asked him for three thousand francs he pinched his lips and said he was very sorry he hadn't had the management of her capital in the past, for there were dozens of convenient ways in which even a lady could put her money to work. She could have made profitable and almost risk-free investments in the Grumesnil peateries or building sites in Le Havre, for example; and he let her burn with rage at the thought of the fantastic sums she would surely have made.

"Why is it that you never came to me?" he asked.

"I don't know exactly," she said.

"Why didn't you come? Were you afraid of me? *I'm* the one who ought to complain, though! We hardly know each other! But I'm already very fond of you—I hope you don't have any doubts about that."

He put out his hand, took hers and kissed it greedily, then he kept it on his knees and gently fondled her fingers as he showered her with compliments.

His flat voice murmured on like the sound of a running brook; his eyes sparkled through the reflections of his glasses, and his hands moved up her sleeve to caress her arm. She felt his panting breath on his cheek. She was filled with loathing and embarrassment.

She leapt to her feet and said, "Monsieur, I'm waiting!"

"For what?" asked the notary, suddenly turning extremely pale.

"For that money."

"But . . ." Then, yielding to an overpowering surge of desire: "Yes! Yes!"

He dragged himself toward her on his knees, heedless of his dressing gown.

"Please stay! I love you!"

He seized her by the waist.

A wave of crimson rushed to her face. She stepped back with a terrible look and cried out, "You're insolently taking advantage of my distress, monsieur! I'm to be pitied, but I'm not for sale!"

And she walked out.

The notary was thunderstruck. He stood staring at his beautiful carpet slippers. They had been given to him by one of his mistresses. The sight of them finally comforted him. Anyway, he thought, such an affair would have involved him too deeply.

"What a vile, disgusting, contemptible man!" Emma said to herself as she fled feverishly beneath the aspens lining the road. Disappointment at having failed reinforced the indignation of her outraged modesty; it seemed to her that Providence was relentlessly persecuting her. Her pride swelled: never before had she felt such esteem for herself or such contempt for others. And she was exalted by a feeling of belligerency. She wished she could attack all men, spit in their faces, grind them into the dust. She walked swiftly along the road, pale, trembling and furious, scanning the empty horizon with tear-filled eyes and almost delighting in the hatred that was choking her.

When she finally came within sight of her house she suddenly felt numb. She could not walk toward it any further, and yet she had to; besides, where could she flee?

Félicité was waiting for her at the door.

"Well?"

"No!" said Emma.

And for a quarter of an hour they tried to think of everyone in Yonville who might be willing to help her. But each time Félicité named someone, Emma would reply, "Impossible! They wouldn't do anything!"

"And Monsieur will be home any minute now!"

"I know . . . You can go now, I want to be alone."

She had tried everything. There was nothing more to be done; when Charles came in she would say to him, "Stop! That rug you're walking on is no longer ours. Not one stick of furniture in your house belongs to you now, not one pin, not even a wisp of straw, and I'm the one who's ruined you, poor man!"

A great sob would burst from his throat, and tears would stream from his eyes; then, when he had recovered from his surprise, he would forgive her.

"Yes," she murmured, clenching her teeth, "he'll forgive me—but even if he offered me a million francs I wouldn't forgive *him* just for having met me! Never! Never!"

She was infuriated by the thought of Bovary's superior moral position. But, whether she confessed or not, he was sure to learn of the disaster sooner or later, today or tomorrow; she would therefore have to wait for that horrible scene and bear the weight of his magnanimity. She had an impulse to go back to Lheureux; but what good would it do? To write to her father; but it was too late. And she was perhaps beginning to regret not having yielded to the notary when she heard a horse trotting in the lane. It was Charles. He opened the gate, his face whiter than the plaster on the wall. She ran downstairs and quickly slipped out into the square. The mayor's wife, chatting with Lestiboudois in front of the church, saw her go into the tax collector's house.

She hurried off to Madame Caron's house to tell her the news. The two ladies went up to the attic, where, hidden by some laundry that had been hung up to dry, they took up a position from which they could easily see into Binet's house.

He was alone in his garret, engaged in making a wooden replica of one of those carved ivory objects that defy description, composed of crescents and spheres hollowed out inside each other, the whole thing as straight as an obelisk and utterly useless. He was just beginning the last piece—the end was in sight! In the mingled light and shadow of his workshop the yellow sawdust flew from his lathe like a spray of sparks from the hooves of a galloping horse; the two wheels were spinning and purring; Binet was smiling with his chin lowered and his nostrils spread wide; he was apparently lost in that utter bliss found only, perhaps, in humble occupations which divert the mind with easy difficulties and provide the satisfaction of accomplishing something which cannot be improved upon.

"Ah! There she is!" said Madame Tuvache.

But the sound of the lathe made it almost impossible to hear what she was saying.

Finally the two ladies thought they heard the word "francs," and Madame Tuvache whispered, "She's asking him to let her put off paying her taxes."

"Probably so," replied Madame Caron.

They saw her pacing back and forth, looking at the napkin rings, candlesticks and staircase knobs lined up along the wall while Binet stroked his beard with satisfaction.

"Could she have come to order something from him?" said Madame Tuvache.

"But he doesn't sell anything!" objected Madame Caron.

The tax collector seemed to be listening, staring as though he did not understand. She went on speaking, apparently in a gentle and supplicating tone; then she moved closer to him; her chest was heaving; they were both silent.

"Is she making advances to him?" said Madame Tuvache.

Binet was blushing to the roots of his hair. She took his hands in hers.

"Oh! This is too much!"

She was no doubt making some abominable proposition, for, even though he was a brave man who had fought at Bautzen and Lützen, taken part in the French campaign and even been under consideration for the Legion of Honor, the tax collector suddenly recoiled as though he had seen a snake and cried out, "Madame! You can't be serious!"

"Women like that ought to be horsewhipped!" said Madame Tuvache.

"Where is she now?" asked Madame Caron.

For Emma had disappeared while these words were being spoken. Then the two ladies saw her hurry down the main street of the village and turn right, as though heading for the cemetery, and they became lost in conjectures.

"Madame Rollet!" she cried when she reached the wet-nurse's house. "Unlace me! I can't breathe!"

She fell onto the bed, sobbing. Madame Rollet covered her with a petticoat and remained standing beside her. Then, getting no reply to her questions, she walked away, took up her wheel and began spinning flax.

"Oh! Stop it!" murmured Emma, thinking she was hearing Binet's lathe.

"What's bothering her," wondered the wet-nurse. "Why did she come here?"

She had been driven there by a kind of terror which made it impossible for her to go home.

Lying motionless on her back, she stared at the things around her, but she was able to see them only vaguely, despite the idiotic persistence with which she focused her attention on them. She contemplated the flaking plaster on the wall, two logs smoking end to end in the fireplace, and a slender spider crawling along a crack in the beam over her head. Finally she began to collect her thoughts. She remembered . . . One day with Léon . . . Oh, how long ago it was! . . . The sun had been shining on the river, the air had been filled with the fragrance of clematis. . . . Then, swept along in her memories as in a seething torrent, she soon came to a recollection of the day before.

"What time is it?" she asked.

Madame Rollet stepped outside, raised the fingers of her right hand to the brightest part of the sky, slowly came back inside and said, "Almost three o'clock."

"Ah! Thank you! Thank you!"

For he was going to come, she was sure of it! He had found some money for her. But he was perhaps about to arrive at her house without knowing she was at Madame Rollet's; she ordered the wet-nurse to go there immediately and bring him back.

"Hurry!"

"I'm going, dear lady, I'm going!"

She was now amazed that she had not thought of him in the first place: he had given her his word the day before and he would not fail to keep it; she could already see herself in Lheureux's office, spreading out the three banknotes on his desk. Then she would have to invent some story to explain things to Bovary. What could she say?

Meanwhile the wet-nurse was taking a long time to return. But since there was no clock in the cottage, Emma was afraid she might be exaggerating the length of time that had gone by. She began to walk slowly around the garden, step by step; she walked down the path alongside the hedge, then hurried back, hoping Madame Rollet had returned by some other route. Finally, weary of waiting, assailed by suspicions which she tried to put out of her mind, no longer knowing whether she had been there for a century or a minute, she sat down in a corner, closed her eyes and put her hands over her ears. The gate creaked; she leapt to her feet; before she could speak, Madame Rollet said to her, "He's not there."

"What!"

"That's right: he's not there. And Monsieur is crying. He keeps calling you. Everybody's looking for you."

Emma made no reply. She was gasping and staring wildly around her; the peasant woman, frightened by her face, stepped back instinctively, thinking she had gone mad. Suddenly she clapped her hand to her forehead and uttered a cry, for the memory of Rodolphe had just burst into her mind like a great flash of lightning in a dark night. He was so good, so sensitive, so generous! And even if he should hesitate to help her she could easily make him change his mind by reminding him with a single glance of their lost love. And so she set out for La Huchette, not realizing that she was now rushing off to offer herself to the same thing that had made her so furious only a short time before, totally unaware that she was about to prostitute herself.

VIII

"What am I going to say?" she wondered as she walked along. "How shall I begin?" Drawing nearer to La Huchette, she recognized the bushes, the trees and the gorse on the hill; then she saw the château in the distance. The sensations of her first love came back to her, and her poor oppressed heart swelled amorously in them. A warm wind was blowing in her face; melting snow was dripping from the buds of the trees to the grass.

She entered, as she had done in the past, by the little park gate, then she came to the main courtyard, bordered by a double row of dense linden trees whose long branches were swaying and rustling. All the dogs in the kennel barked, but no one came out at the sound of their voices.

She climbed the broad, straight, wooden-banistered staircase that led up to a hall with a dusty flagstone floor. Opening onto it were a number of bedrooms laid out in a straight line, as in a monastery or an inn. Rodolphe's room was at the far end, on the left. When she touched the door handle her strength abandoned her. She was afraid he would not be there; she almost wished he would not be, and yet he was her only hope, her last chance of salvation. She stopped for a moment to calm herself; then, plucking up her courage with the thought of her desperate need, she went in.

He was sitting in front of the fire, smoking a pipe with his feet propped up against the edge of the fireplace.

"Oh! It's you!" he said, quickly standing up.

"Yes, it's I. . . . Rodolphe, I want to ask you for some advice."

Despite all her efforts, she was unable to go on.

"You haven't changed—you're still as charming as ever!"

"Oh," she said bitterly, "my charms must not be worth much, judging from the way you scorned them."

He began to apologize and make vague excuses for his conduct, unable to invent anything better.

She let herself be taken in by his words, and still more by the sound of his voice and the sight of his face; she pretended to believe—or perhaps she actually did believe—the reason he gave for having broken off their affair: it was a secret involving the honor and even the life of a third person.

"Just the same," she said, looking at him sadly, "I suffered terribly."

He replied philosophically, "That's how life is!"

"Has it been good to you, at least, since we parted?" she asked.

"Oh, not too good . . . and not too bad, either."

"Perhaps it would have been better if we hadn't parted."

"Yes . . . perhaps."

"Do you think so?" she asked, moving closer to him. And she sighed: "Oh, Rodolphe! If you only knew! . . . I loved you so much!"

She took his hand, and for a time their fingers were intertwined—as they had been that first day, at the fair! Out of pride, he struggled against his feelings; but she pressed up against his chest and said:

"How did you expect me to live without you? Once you've known happiness it's impossible to get used to not having it. I was desperate! I thought I was going to die! I'll tell you all about it, you'll see. . . . And you—you stayed away from me!"

He had been carefully avoiding her for the past three years, out of that natural cowardice which characterizes the stronger sex; and Emma went on, moving her head in winsome little gestures, more affectionate than an amorous cat:

"You have other women now, admit it! Oh, I understand

them! I don't blame them—you seduced them the way you seduced me. You're a real man! You have everything it takes to make a woman love you. But we'll begin all over again, won't we? We'll love each other! Look, I'm laughing—I'm happy! . . . Say something!"

And she was ravishing to see, with tears quivering in her eyes like raindrops in the blue chalice of a flower after a storm.

He drew her onto his lap and, with the back of his hand, caressed her smooth hair, on which a last sunbeam was gleaming like a golden arrow in the twilight. She bent down her forehead; after a time he kissed her on the eyelids, gently, his lips scarcely touching them.

"But you've been crying!" he said. "Why?"

She burst out sobbing. He thought it was an explosion of love; she did not answer, and he interpreted her silence as due to her expiring modesty.

"Oh, forgive me!" he cried. "You're the only woman who means anything to me. I've been stupid and cruel! I love you, I'll always love you! What's the matter? Tell me!"

He was on his knees.

"All right, I'll tell you: I'm ruined, Rodolphe! You must lend me three thousand francs!"

"But . . . but . . ." he said, slowly standing up, his face taking on a grave expression.

"You know," she went on quickly, "my husband gave a notary all his money to invest for him—the notary has disappeared. We borrowed; the patients weren't paying their bills. The liquidation isn't finished yet: we'll have more money later. But today, if we don't raise three thousand francs, everything we own is going to be seized, right now, at this very moment! I've come to you because I knew I could count on your friendship."

"Ah!" thought Rodolphe, suddenly turning very pale. "So that's why she came!"

A few moments later he said calmly, "My dear lady, I don't have it."

He was not lying. If he had had the money he would no doubt have given it to her, even though such noble actions are usually disagreeable, for of all the winds that blow on love, none is so chilling and destructive as a request for money.

She looked at him in silence for a long time.

"You don't have it!" She repeated it several times: "You

don't have it! . . . I should have spared myself this last shame. You've never loved me! You're no better than the rest!"

She was betraying herself, no longer aware of what she was saying.

Rodolphe interrupted her, protesting that he was "hard up" himself.

"Ah, I pity you!" said Emma. "Yes, I really pity you. . . ." Her eyes fell on a damascened rifle gleaming in a collection of weapons on the wall. "But when a man's as poor as you say you are, he doesn't put silver on the stock of his rifle! He doesn't buy a clock inlaid with tortoise-shell," she went on, pointing to his Boulle clock, "or silver-gilt whistles for his whip"—she touched them—"or charms for his watch chain! Oh, you don't lack anything! You even have a liqueur stand in your bedroom. You take good care of yourself, you live well, you have a château, farms, forests; you go hunting, you make trips to Paris. . . . Even things like this," she cried, taking his cuff links from the mantelpiece, "the least of your little bagatelles, could be turned into money! . . . Oh, I don't want them! Keep them!"

And she threw the cuff links against the wall, breaking their gold chain.

"But *I* would have given you everything, I'd have sold everything, worked with my hands, begged in the streets, just for a smile or a look, just to hear you say 'Thank you.' And you sit there calmly in your chair, as if you hadn't made me suffer enough already! I could have been happy if it hadn't been for you! Nobody forced you to pursue me. Why did you do it? Was it a bet? You did love me, though; or at least you said so. . . . And you said it again just now. . . . Oh, you'd have done better to send me away! My hands are still warm from your kisses, and there on the rug is the place where you swore on your knees that you'd love me forever. You made me believe it: you led me on for two years in a sweet, wonderful dream. . . . Remember our plans for going away together? Oh, your letter, your letter! It tore my heart out! You're rich, happy and free, and yet when I come back to beg you for a favor that anyone else would do for me, when I come to you humbly, bringing you all my love, you reject me, because it would cost you three thousand francs!"

"I don't have three thousand francs," replied Rodolphe with that perfect calm which resigned anger draws over itself as a shield.

She left. The walls were trembling, the ceiling pressed down on her head; and she walked back down the long lane, stumbling against piles of dead leaves that were being scattered by the wind. At last she came to the ditch in front of the gate; she opened the latch in such haste that she broke her fingernails on it. Then, a hundred yards further on, out of breath, ready to drop, she stopped. She turned around and took one last look at the impassive château, at its park, its gardens, its three courtyards and all the windows along its façade.

She was in a stupor, conscious of her own existence only from the throbbing of her arteries, which she heard as deafening music filling the whole countryside. The ground felt like water beneath her feet, and the furrows appeared to her as enormous, dark, breaking waves. The memories and thoughts in her mind all gushed out at once, like the countless sparks of a fireworks display. She saw her father, Lheureux's office, their room in the hotel, another landscape. She had begun to drift into madness; she suddenly felt afraid and managed to regain control of herself, although her thoughts were still in disorder, for she no longer remembered the cause of her horrible state: the question of money. She was now suffering only through her love, and she felt her soul slipping away in the memory of it, just as a wounded man, as he lies dying, feels his life flowing out through the bleeding gash.

Night was falling and crows were flying overhead.

Suddenly it seemed to her that fiery little balls were bursting in the air like exploding bullets, and whirling around and around until they melted in the snow among the branches of the trees. She saw Rodolphe's face at the center of each of them. They multiplied, moved close together and penetrated her; then everything vanished. She recognized the lights of the houses shining in the distance, through the mist.

Her situation now appeared before her like an abyss. She was panting as though her lungs would burst. Then, in a surge of heroism that made her almost joyous, she ran down the hill, across the cow plank, along the path and the lane and through the market shed. She stopped in front of the pharmacist's shop.

It was empty. She was about to go in, but she realized that the sound of the bell might bring someone. She slipped under the gate and, holding her breath, groped her way along the walls until she came to the door of the kitchen, in which a candle was burning on the stove. Justin, in his shirt sleeves, was carrying a dish out of the room.

"Ah, they're having dinner," she thought. "I'll wait."

Justin returned. She tapped on the windowpane. He came out.

"The key! The one for upstairs, where the—"

"What!"

He stared at her, amazed by the pallor of her face, which stood out white against the black background of the night. She looked extraordinarily beautiful to him, and majestic as a phantom; without understanding what she wanted, he had a foreboding of something terrible.

She went on quickly, in a low, sweet, insinuating voice: "I want it! Give it to me."

The wall was so thin that they could hear the forks clinking on the plates in the dining room.

She claimed she needed to kill some rats that were keeping her awake at night.

"I'll have to tell Monsieur."

"No! Stay here!" She added casually, "Don't bother to go to him now—I'll tell him later. Come on, light the way for me."

She entered the hall onto which the laboratory opened. Hanging on the wall was a key labeled "Depository."

"Justin!" shouted the apothecary impatiently.

"Let's go up!"

He followed her.

The key turned in the lock and she went straight to the third shelf, so well did her memory guide her, seized the blue bottle, pulled out the stopper, plunged in her hand and drew it out full of white powder which she began to eat immediately.

"Stop!" cried Justin, rushing toward her.

"Be quiet! Someone will come . . ."

He was frantic; he wanted to call for help.

"Don't breathe a word about this, or all the blame will fall on your master!"

She went home, suddenly at peace, feeling what was almost the serenity of a duty well done.

When Charles came home, overwhelmed by the news of the seizure, Emma had just left. He shouted, wept and fainted, but she did not return. Where could she be? He sent Félicité to Homais' house, to Monsieur Tuvache's, to Lheureux's, to the Lion d'Or, everywhere; and each time his frenzy subsided a little he saw his reputation ruined, all their money gone, Berthe's future destroyed! What was the cause of it all? . . . Not a word! He waited till six o'clock in the evening. Finally, unable to bear it any longer, he decided she must have gone to Rouen; he went out, walked along the highway for over a mile without meeting anyone, waited a while and came back to the house.

She was there.

"What happened? . . . Why? . . . Tell me . . ."

She sat down at her desk, wrote a letter, sealed it slowly and added the date and the hour. Then she said in a solemn tone, "Read this tomorrow. Till then, please don't ask me any questions—not a single one!"

"But . . ."

"Oh, leave me alone!"

And she stretched out on her bed.

She was awakened by an acrid taste in her mouth. She caught a glimpse of Charles and closed her eyes again.

She observed herself with interest to see if she was in any pain. No—nothing yet! She heard the ticking of the clock, the crackling of the fire and the sound of Charles's breathing as he stood beside her bed.

"Ah, death is no great matter!" she thought. "I'll just go to sleep and everything will be over!"

She took a sip of water and turned toward the wall.

There was still that horrible taste of ink.

"I'm thirsty! . . . Oh, I'm so thirsty!" she sighed.

"What's the matter with you?" asked Charles, handing her a glass.

"It's nothing . . . Open the window! . . . I'm choking!"

And she was seized with a fit of nausea so sudden that she scarcely had time to snatch her handkerchief from under the pillow.

"Take it!" she said vehemently. "Throw it away!"

He questioned her; she did not answer. She lay still, fearing that the slightest agitation would make her vomit. Meanwhile she felt an icy cold rising from her feet to her heart.

"Ah! It's beginning!" she murmured.

"What did you say?"

She rolled her head from side to side in a slow, anguished movement, constantly opening her jaws as though she had something very heavy on her tongue. At eight o'clock the vomiting began again.

Charles observed that there was a kind of fine white gravel at the bottom of the basin, sticking to the porcelain.

"That's strange!" he said several times. "Very unusual!"

But she said loudly, "No, you're mistaken!"

Delicately, almost caressingly, he moved his hand over her stomach. She uttered a shrill cry. He drew back, frightened.

Then she began to moan, weakly at first. Her shoulders were shaken by a violent shudder and she turned as pale as the sheet into which she was digging her tensed fingers. Her pulse was now irregular and almost imperceptible.

Beads of sweat were oozing from her bluish face, which looked as though it had been hardened in some sort of metallic vapor. Her teeth were chattering, her wide-open eyes stared vaguely around her, and to all his questions she replied only with a nod; she even smiled two or three times. Little by little, her groans became louder. A muffled scream escaped from her; she claimed she was feeling better and that she would get up in a little while. But she was seized with convulsions, and she cried out, "Oh, God! It's horrible!"

He fell to his knees beside her bed.

"Speak to me! What have you eaten? Answer me, in the name of God, answer me!"

And in his eyes she saw a love such as she had never seen before.

"All right, there . . . over there . . ." she said in a faltering voice.

He rushed to the writing desk, broke open the seal and read aloud: *"No one is to blame . . ."* He stopped, passed his hand over his eyes and went on reading.

"What? Help! Help!"

And he could say only this word, over and over: "Poisoned! Poisoned!" Félicité ran to Homais, who exclaimed it loudly in the square; Madame Léfrançois heard it in the Lion d'Or; several people got out of bed to repeat it to the neighbors, and the village was awake all night.

Distraught, stammering, nearly fainting, Charles walked in circles around the bedroom. He stumbled against the furniture and tore his hair; the pharmacist would never have believed there could be such a frightful spectacle.

He went back home to write to Monsieur Canivet and Dr. Larivière. He lost his head and had to begin the letters fifteen times before he finished them. Hippolyte set out for Neufchâtel, and Justin spurred Bovary's horse so relentlessly that he left it on the hill at Bois-Guillaume, foundered and half dead.

Charles tried to consult his medical dictionary but he could not read; the lines danced before his eyes.

"Be calm!" said the apothecary. "All we have to do is administer some powerful antidote. What poison is it?"

Charles showed him the letter. It was arsenic.

"All right," said Homais, "we'll have to make an analysis."

For he knew that an analysis must be made in all cases of poisoning; and Charles, who did not understand, replied, "Make one, then, go ahead! Save her!"

He went over to her, sank down on the carpet and began to sob, leaning his head on the edge of the bed.

"Don't cry!" she said. "Soon I'll stop tormenting you forever!"

"Why? What made you do it?"

"I had to, my dear," she answered.

"Weren't you happy? Is it my fault? I did everything I could!"

"Yes . . . that's true . . . *You've* always been good!"

She slowly passed her hand through his hair. The sweetness of her touch brought his grief to a climax; he felt his whole being collapsing in despair at the thought of having to lose her just when she was confessing more love for him than ever before. And he could think of nothing to do; he no longer knew anything or dared to try anything: the need for immediate action had thrown him into a state of utter bewilderment.

Now, she thought, she was through with all the betrayals, infamies and countless desires that had tortured her. She hated no one, now; a twilight confusion was settling down over her mind, and of all the sounds of the earth she heard only the spasmodic lamentations wrung from poor Charles's heart, gentle and indistinct, like the last echoes of a fading symphony.

"Bring me my little girl," she said, raising herself on one elbow.

"You're not feeling any worse, are you?" he asked.

"No, no!"

The child was brought in by the maid; her bare feet showed beneath her long nightgown, and she had a serious expression on her face, having scarcely emerged from her dreams. She stared in astonishment at the disorderly room and blinked her eyes, dazzled by the candles that had been placed on various pieces of furniture. They reminded her, no doubt, of New Year's Day or Mid-Lent, when she was always awakened in the same way, by candlelight, and brought to her mother's bed to receive her presents, for she asked, "Where is it, mama?"

Everyone remained silent.

"I don't see my little shoe!"

Félicité held her over the bed, but she kept looking toward the fireplace.

"Did nurse take it away?" she asked.

At the word "nurse," which brought back memories of her adultery and her calamities, Madame Bovary turned her head away, as though revolted by another, stronger poison rising to her mouth. Meanwhile Berthe had been set down on the bed.

"Oh, how big your eyes are, mama! You're so pale! You're sweating . . ."

Her mother looked at her.

"I'm afraid!" said the little girl, shrinking back.

Emma took her hand to kiss it; she struggled.

"Enough! Take her away," said Charles, who had been sobbing near the bed.

The symptoms stopped for a moment; she seemed less agitated; and with each insignificant remark, with each breath of her calmer chest, his hope grew stronger. When Canivet finally arrived he threw himself in his arms, weeping.

"Ah, it's you! Thank you! It's so kind of you! But she's better now. Look at her . . ."

His colleague was not at all of this opinion; without "beating around the bush," as he himself put it, he prescribed an emetic, to empty the stomach completely.

A short time later she was vomiting blood. Her lips were pressed together more tightly. Her limbs were tense, her body was covered with brown blotches and her pulse slipped beneath the doctor's fingers like a taut wire, like a harp string ready to snap.

Then she began to shriek, horribly. She cursed the poison, vilified it, begged it to hurry and pushed away with her stiffened arms everything that Charles, in greater agony than herself, tried to make her drink. He stood holding his handkerchief to his lips, moaning, weeping, choked by sobs that shook him from head to toe; Félicité was rushing around the room; Homais, motionless, sighed loudly from time to time; and, although he still maintained his self-possession, Monsieur Canivet was beginning to feel uneasy.

"What the devil . . . But she's purged, and since the cause has been removed . . ."

"The effect must cease," said Homais. "It's self-evident."

"But you've got to save her!" exclaimed Bovary.

Without listening to the pharmacist, who was venturing the hypothesis that "this may be a beneficial paroxysm," Canivet was about to administer a dose of theriaca when the crack of a whip was heard from outside; all the windowpanes rattled and a stagecoach, drawn by three mud-spattered horses straining against their breast straps, burst into the square at one corner of the market shed. It was Dr. Larivière.

The sudden appearance of a god would not have aroused greater emotion. Bovary raised his hands, Canivet stopped short and Homais took off his fez long before the doctor entered the room.

He belonged to that great surgical school engendered by Bichat, to that generation, now vanished, of philosophical practitioners who cherished their art with fanatical love and exercised it with enthusiasm and wisdom. Everyone in his hospital trembled when he became angry, and his students held him in such veneration that as soon as they set up their own practices they tried to imitate him as much as possible; as a result, in all the surrounding towns there were doctors who wore copies of his long, quilted merino overcoat and his loose black tail coat, whose unbuttoned cuffs partially covered his fleshy hands—magnificent hands, always ungloved, as though to be constantly ready to come to grips with suffering. Disdainful of decorations, titles and academies, hospitable, generous, a father to the poor, practicing virtue without believing in it, he might almost have passed for a saint if the keenness of his mind had not made everyone fear him like a demon. His glance, as sharp as his lancet, plunged deep into your soul, through all pretense and reserve, and laid bare any lies hidden there. Everything about him was impregnated with the good-natured majesty imparted to him by the consciousness of his great abilities, his wealth, and forty years of hard work and irreproachable conduct.

He frowned in the doorway when he saw Emma's cadaverous face; she was lying on her back with her mouth open. Then, seeming to listen to Canivet, he passed his forefinger back and forth beneath his nostrils and said at intervals, "Yes . . . Yes . . ."

But he slowly shrugged his shoulders. Bovary noticed it and they looked at each other; despite his long habituation to the sight of suffering, Dr. Larivière could not keep a tear from dropping on his shirt front.

He asked Canivet to step into the next room with him. Charles followed him.

"She's in bad condition, isn't she? Do you think poultices would help? Or anything else? You must be able to think of something—you've saved so many other lives!"

Charles put his arms around him and looked at him beseechingly, terror-stricken and half collapsing against his chest.

"Come, my poor boy, be brave! There's nothing more to be done."

And Dr. Larivière turned away.

"You're leaving?"

"I'll be back."

He went outside, as though to tell the coachman something, with Monsieur Canivet, who was no more eager than he to see Emma die under his care.

The pharmacist joined them in the square. He was temperamentally incapable of staying away from famous men. He therefore begged Monsieur Larivière to do him the signal honor of coming to his house for lunch.

Madame Homais quickly sent for pigeons from the Lion d'Or, all the cutlets in the butcher's shop, cream from Tuvache and eggs from Lestiboudois; the apothecary himself helped with the preparations while she pulled on the strings of her house jacket and said, "I hope you'll excuse us, monsieur—in our poor little village, if we're not notified the day before . . ."

"The wine glasses?" whispered Homais.

"If we lived in the city, we'd at least have stuffed pigs' feet to fall back on."

"Be quiet! . . . Have a seat, doctor."

After the first few mouthfuls he saw fit to give a few details of the catastrophe.

"First there was a sensation of dryness in the pharynx, then unbearable pains in the epigastrium, superpurgation and coma."

"How did she poison herself?"

"I don't know, doctor; I can't even imagine where she managed to get that arsenious oxide."

Justin, who was then bringing in a pile of plates, was seized with a fit of trembling.

"What's the matter with you?" asked the pharmacist.

At this question, the young man dropped everything on the floor with a great clatter.

"Idiot!" cried Homais. "Clumsy oaf! Blockhead! Numbskull!"

Then, quickly controlling himself, he said, "I decided to try an analysis, doctor, so first I carefully inserted a tube . . ."

"You'd have done better to insert your fingers in her throat," said the surgeon.

His colleague remained silent, having been severely reprimanded in private, a short time before, about his emetic; as a result, the worthy Canivet, so arrogant and verbose during the clubfoot incident, was now extremely modest and unassuming, and there was a constant smile of approval on his face.

Homais' pride blossomed as he played host to his distinguished guests, and the thought of Bovary's suffering contributed vaguely to his pleasure when he selfishly considered his own situation. Furthermore, he was carried away by the presence of Dr. Larivière. He displayed his erudition, making jumbled references to the cantharides, the poison of the upas and manchineel trees, the viper . . .

"And I've even read about several people who were poisoned, doctor, laid low as though they'd been struck by lightning, from eating blood sausages that had been subjected to excessive fumigation! At least that's what it says in an excellent report written by one of our pharmaceutical celebrities, one of our masters, the illustrious Cadet de Gassicourt!"

Madame Homais reappeared, carrying one of those rickety contraptions that are heated with alcohol, for Homais insisted on making his coffee at table, having already roasted, ground and blended it himself.

"*Saccharum*, doctor?" he asked, offering him the sugar.

Then he had all his children come downstairs, eager to have the surgeon's opinion on their constitutions.

Finally, when Monsieur Larivière was about to leave, Madame Homais asked him for a consultation about her husband: he was making his blood too thick by falling asleep every evening after dinner.

"Oh, his *blood* isn't too thick!"

And, smiling a little at his unnoticed joke, the doctor opened the door. But the pharmacy was packed with people, and he had a hard time getting rid of Monsieur Tuvache, who was afraid his wife might get pneumonia because of her habit of spitting into the ashes; and then there was Monsieur Binet, who sometimes had fits of violent hunger; Madame Caron had prickly sensations, Lheureux had dizzy spells, Lestiboudois had rheumatism and Madame Lefrançois had heartburn. He finally rolled away in his three-horse coach, and the consensus of opinion was that he had not been very obliging.

The attention of the public was distracted by the appearance of Father Bournisien, walking through the market shed with the holy oils.

Homais, faithful to his principles, compared priests to carrion crows attracted by the odor of death; the sight of a priest was disagreeable to him personally, because a cassock made him think of a shroud, and his aversion to the former was due in part to his fear of the latter.

Nevertheless, he did not shrink from what he called his "mission"; he went back to the Bovary house with Canivet, whom Monsieur Larivière, before leaving, had urged to remain with the patient. If it had not been for his wife's protests, Homais would even have taken his two sons with him, to accustom them to dire situations and provide them with a lesson, an example, a solemn spectacle that they would remember later.

When they entered the bedroom it was filled with ominous solemnity. On the sewing table, which had been covered with a white napkin, there were five or six little balls of cotton in a silver dish, near a large crucifix, between two lighted candelabra. Emma lay with her chin on her chest, her eyes open inordinately wide; and her poor hands were moving feebly over the sheets in that appalling gesture of the dying, who seem to be trying to cover themselves with their shrouds already. Pale as a statue, his eyes as red as burning coals, Charles, no longer weeping, stood facing her at the foot of the bed, while the priest, with one knee on the floor, mumbled softly.

She slowly turned her face and seemed overjoyed when she suddenly saw the purple stole, no doubt recapturing, in this moment of extraordinary peace, the lost ecstasy of her first mystical transports, along with the first visions of eternal bliss.

The priest stood up and took the crucifix; she stretched forth her neck as though she were thirsting, pressed her lips to the body of the God-Man and imprinted on it, with all her fading strength, the most ardent kiss of love she had ever given. Then he recited the *Miseratur* and the *Indulgentiam,* dipped his right thumb in the oil and began the anointments: first her eyes, which had so fiercely coveted all earthly luxury; then her nostrils, so avid for warm breezes and amorous scents; then her lips, which had opened to speak lies, cry out in pride and moan in lust; then her hands, which had taken such pleasure in sensuous contacts; and finally the soles of her feet, once so swift in hurrying to gratify her desires, and now never to walk again.

The priest wiped his fingers, threw the oil-soaked wads of cotton into the fire, came back to the dying woman, sat down beside her and told her she must now join her sufferings to those of Jesus Christ and surrender herself to divine mercy.

As he finished his exhortations he tried to place in her hands a blessed candle, symbol of the celestial glories that would soon surround her. Too weak to close her fingers, she would have dropped it on the floor if it had not been for Father Bournisien.

She was now less pale, however, and her face wore an expression of serenity, as though the sacrament had cured her.

The priest did not fail to point this out; he even explained to Bovary that the Lord sometimes prolonged people's lives when He judged it desirable for their salvation, and Charles recalled that other day when she had been close to death and had received Communion.

"Maybe I shouldn't lose all hope," he thought.

For she was now looking around her, slowly, like someone awakening from a dream; then, in a clear voice, she asked for her mirror and remained leaning over it for some time, until great tears began to flow from her eyes. She raised her head with a sigh and fell back on the pillow.

Her chest immediately began to heave rapidly. Her whole tongue emerged from her mouth; her eyes rolled and grew dim, like the globes of two lamps about to go out, and she would have seemed dead already if it had not been for the frightful movement of her ribs, shaken by furious, constantly quickening gasps, as though her soul were struggling to break away. Félicité knelt before the crucifix, and even the pharmacist flexed his knees a little, while Monsieur Canivet stared vaguely out into the square. Father Bournisien had begun to pray again, with his face bowed over the edge of the bed and his long black cassock trailing on the floor behind him. Charles was kneeling on the other side, his arms stretched out toward Emma. He had taken her hands and was now squeezing them, quivering with each beat of her heart, as with the tremors of a falling ruin. As the death rattle grew louder, the priest accelerated his prayers; they mingled with Bovary's stifled sobs, and at times everything seemed to fade into the steady murmur of Latin syllables as they rolled on like the tolling of a bell.

Suddenly, from outside, came the sound of heavy wooden

shoes and the scraping of a stick on the sidewalk, then a voice rose up, a raucous voice singing:

> *The heat of the sun on a summer day*
> *Warms a young girl in an amorous way.*

Emma sat up like a galvanized corpse, her hair hanging loosely, her eyes fixed and gaping.

> *To gather up the golden stalks*
> *After the scythe has cut the wheat,*
> *Nanette bends down and slowly walks*
> *Along the furrows at her feet.*

"The blind man!" she cried.

And she began to laugh, a horrible, frenzied, desperate laugh, imagining that she could see the wretched beggar's hideous features looming in the shadows of eternity like the face of terror itself.

> *The wind was blowing hard that day*
> *And Nanette's petticoat flew away.*

A convulsion threw her back down on the mattress. Everyone moved toward her. She had ceased to exist.

IX

The sight of death is always followed by a kind of stupefaction, so difficult is it to understand this sudden advent of nothingness and resign oneself to accepting it. But when Charles saw how still she was lying he threw himself on her and cried out, "Good-by! Good-by!"

Homais and Canivet drew him out of the room.

"You must control yourself!"

"All right," he said, struggling, "I'll be reasonable, I won't do anything wrong—but let me stay! I want to see her! She's my wife!"

And he wept.

"That's right, weep," said the pharmacist. "Let nature take its course: it will make you feel better."

Helpless as a child, Charles let himself be led downstairs to the parlor. Monsieur Homais soon went home.

He was accosted in the square by the blind man, who, having dragged himself to Yonville in the hope of being cured by the antiphlogistic salve, was now asking every passer-by where the apothecary lived.

"That's just fine! As though I didn't have enough on my mind already! You're out of luck, my friend—you'll have to come back later."

And he hurried into the pharmacy.

He had to write two letters, prepare a sedative for Bovary, invent a lie to cover up the suicide, turn it into an article for the *Fanal* and give it out to the people who were waiting to ask him for information. When they had all heard his story about the arsenic she had mistaken for sugar while making a vanilla custard, Homais once again returned to Bovary.

He found him alone (Monsieur Canivet had just left), sitting in the armchair near the window and staring dazedly at the parlor floor.

"You'll have to set a time for the ceremony," said the pharmacist.

"Why?" asked Charles. "What ceremony?" Then he stammered in a frightened voice, "Oh, no! I don't have to, do I? I want to keep her."

To hide his uneasiness, Homais picked up a carafe from the whatnot and began to water the geraniums.

"Oh, thank you!" said Charles. "You're so kind!"

He stopped short, choked by the flood of memories brought back to him by the pharmacist's action.

Then, to distract him, Homais decided it would be a good idea to talk about horticulture for a while. The plants were in need of moisture. Charles nodded in agreement.

"Anyway, we'll be having some warm weather before long."

"Ah!" said Bovary.

Having run out of ideas, the apothecary began slowly drawing back the sash curtains.

"Ah, there goes Monsieur Tuvache!"

Charles repeated like a machine: "There goes Monsieur Tuvache."

Homais could not bring himself to say anything more about the funeral arrangements; it was the priest who finally persuaded Charles to take action.

He shut himself in his consulting room, took up a pen and, after sobbing a while, began to write:

> I want her to be buried in her wedding gown, with white shoes and a wreath. Her hair is to be spread over her shoulders. Three coffins: one oak, one mahogany, one lead. No one has to say anything to me, I will have the strength to go through with it. Cover her with a big piece of green velvet. This is what I want. Do it.

Homais and the priest were amazed at Bovary's romantic ideas; the pharmacist immediately said to him, "That velvet seems superfluous to me, and besides, the expense . . ."

"Is it any of your business?" cried Charles. "Leave me alone! You didn't love her! Go away!"

The priest took him by the arm and led him into the garden for a walk, discoursing on the vanity of earthly things. God was great and good; we ought to submit to His decrees without complaint; in fact, we ought even to thank Him.

Charles burst into blasphemy.

"I hate your God!"

"The spirit of rebellion is still in you," sighed the priest.

Charles had moved away from him and was walking swiftly past the espaliered fruit trees along the wall, grinding his teeth and casting curses up to heaven with his eyes but he was not answered by so much as the stirring of a leaf.

A fine rain was falling. His chest was bare and he finally began to shiver; he went back inside and sat down in the kitchen.

At six o'clock there was a clatter in the square: the Hirondelle was arriving. He stood with his forehead against the windowpane, watching all the passengers get out one after the other. Félicité put down a mattress for him in the parlor; he threw himself on it and went to sleep.

Despite his philosophy, Monsieur Homais respected the dead. And so, holding no grudge against poor Charles, he came back that night to sit up with the body. He brought three books with him, and a portfolio, so that he could take notes.

Father Bournisien was there, and two large candles were burning at the head of the bed, which had been moved out of the alcove.

The silence weighed down on the apothecary; he soon made a few sorrowful remarks about "this unfortunate young woman," and the priest replied that there was nothing left to do but pray for her.

"But," said Homais, "either she died in a state of grace (as the Church puts it), in which case she has no need of our prayers, or else she died impenitent (I believe that's the correct ecclesiastical term), and in that case . . ."

Bournisien interrupted him, replying curtly that they ought to pray for her just the same.

"But," objected the pharmacist, "since God knows all our needs, what good can prayer do?"

"What!" exclaimed the priest. "Prayer? Aren't you a Christian?"

"I beg your pardon!" said Homais. "I admire Christianity. First of all, it freed the slaves, and it gave the world a moral code . . ."

"That's not the point! All the texts . . ."

"Oh! Oh! If you want to talk about the texts, open your history book—everybody knows they were falsified by the Jesuits."

Charles came in, walked over to the bed and slowly drew back the curtains.

Emma's head was turned toward her right shoulder. The corner of her mouth, which remained open, was like a black hole at the bottom of her face; both thumbs were bent inward toward the palms; her eyelashes were sprinkled with a kind of white dust; and her eyes were beginning to disappear in a viscous pallor that was like a fine web, as though spiders had been spinning on her face. The sheet sagged from her breasts to her knees, rising again at the tips of her toes; and it seemed to Charles that an infinite mass, an enormous weight, was pressing down on her.

The church clock struck two. They could hear the low murmur of the river flowing past in the darkness at the end of the terrace. Father Bournisien loudly blew his nose from time to time, and Homais' pen was scratching on his paper.

"Come, my friend," he said, "go to bed: this sight is torturing you!"

Once Charles was gone, and pharmacist and the priest resumed their arguments.

"Read Voltaire!" said the one. "Read d'Holbach, read the Encyclopedia!"

"Read the *Letters of Some Portuguese Jews!*" said the

other. "Read the *Truth of Christianity*, by Nicolas, a former magistrate!"

They became excited and flushed; they both spoke at once, without listening to each other; Bournisien was shocked by such audacity; Homais was amazed at such stupidity; and they were not far from insulting each other when Charles suddenly reappeared. Drawn by a kind of fascination, he kept coming back upstairs.

He stood at the foot of the bed, to see her better, and became lost in contemplation so profound that it was no longer painful.

Recalling stories about catalepsy and miracles of magnetism, he told himself that by concentrating all his will power he might be able to bring her back to life. Once he even leaned toward her and called out softly, "Emma! Emma!" The force of his breath made the candles flicker against the wall.

The elder Madame Bovary arrived at dawn; Charles had another fit of weeping when he embraced her. She tried, as the pharmacist had done, to make a few remarks about the expenses of the funeral. He flew into such a rage that she dropped the subject; he even told her to go to the city immediately and buy what was needed.

He was alone all afternoon; Berthe had been placed in Madame Homais' care; Félicité stayed upstairs in the bedroom, with Madame Lefrançois.

That evening he received visits. He stood up to shake hands with his visitors, unable to speak, then each one sat down with the others, forming a large semicircle in front of the fireplace. Bowing their heads and swinging one leg crossed over the other, they sighed deeply from time to time; they were all inordinately bored, yet each was determined not to be the first to leave.

When Homais came back at nine o'clock (he seemed to have been constantly in the square for the past two days), he was laden with a supply of camphor, benzoin and aromatic herbs. He also brought a vase full of chlorine water, to drive away miasmas. When he arrived, the maid, Madame Lefrançois and the elder Madame Bovary were gathered around Emma, about to finish dressing her; they drew down the long, stiff veil which covered her all the way to her satin shoes.

Félicité sobbed: "Oh, my poor mistress! My poor mistress!"

"Look at her," said Madame Lefrançois with a sigh. "She's still so pretty! You'd swear she was about to get up!"

Then they bent over and put on her wreath.

They had to lift her head a little, and when they did so a flood of black liquid came from her mouth as though she were vomiting.

"Oh! Look out for her dress!" cried Madame Lefrançois. "Give us a hand!" she said to the pharmacist. "You're not afraid, by any chance, are you?"

"I, afraid?" he answered, shrugging his shoulders. "Don't be silly! I saw worse things than that in the hospital, when I was studying pharmacy! We used to make punch in the dissecting room! Death doesn't frighten a philosopher; in fact, as I've often said, I intend to leave my body to the hospitals, so that I can still be of service to Science after I'm gone."

When the priest arrived he asked how Monsieur was; and on hearing the apothecary's reply he said, "Yes, the blow is still too recent!"

Homais congratulated him on not being exposed, like other men, to the risk of losing a beloved wife, and this led to an argument about the celibacy of priests.

"It's unnatural for a man to be without women!" said the pharmacist. "There have been crimes . . ."

"But how in the name of common sense," cried the priest, "would you expect a married man to be able to keep the secrets of the confessional, for example?"

Homais attacked confession. Bournisien defended it; he expatiated on the restitutions it had brought about, citing various cases of thieves who had suddenly turned honest. Soldiers approaching the tribunal of penance had felt the scales fall from their eyes. In Fribourg there was a minister . . .

His listener had fallen asleep. Feeling slightly suffocated by the heavy atmosphere of the room, he opened the window; this woke the pharmacist.

"Here, have a pinch of snuff," he said to him. "Go on, take it—it will help you while away the time."

They could hear a continual barking coming from somewhere in the distance.

"Do you hear a dog howling?" asked the pharmacist.

"They say dogs can smell death," replied the priest. "It's the same with bees—they fly away from the hive whenever someone dies." Homais did not challenge these superstitions, for he had gone back to sleep.

Father Bournisien, more tenacious, went on moving his lips in a soft murmur for a time, then his chin slowly drooped, his big black book slipped from his hand and he began to snore.

They sat opposite each other, their stomachs thrust forward, their faces puffy and scowling, finally united in the same human weakness after so much dissension; and they were as motionless as the corpse lying beside them, as though asleep.

Charles did not wake them when he entered. This was the last time. He had come to bid her farewell.

The aromatic herbs were still smoking, and at the window the swirling, bluish vapor mingled with the mist that was drifting in. There were a few stars in the sky, and the night was mild.

Wax was dripping from the candles onto the bedsheets in large tears. Charles stared at the flames, tiring his eyes in their bright yellow glow.

Shimmering reflections played over the surface of Emma's satin gown, white as moonlight. She was invisible beneath it, and it seemed to him that she was spreading out beyond herself, merging into the things around her, into the silence, the night, the passing wind, the moist odors rising from the ground.

Then suddenly he saw her in the garden at Tostes, sitting on the bench beside the thorn hedge; or in the streets of Rouen, in the doorway of their house, in the farmyard at Les Bertaux. . . . He again heard the laughter of the light-hearted young men dancing beneath the apple trees; the bedroom was filled with the fragrance of her hair, and her dress rustled in his arms with the sound of flying sparks. It had been the same dress she was wearing now!

For a long time he was lost in memories of his past happiness, of her poses, her gestures, the sound of her voice. One surge of despair followed another, endlessly, like the waves of an incoming tide.

He was seized with a terrible curiosity: slowly, with the tips of his fingers, quivering, he lifted her veil. He uttered a cry of horror that woke the pharmacist and the priest. They led him downstairs to the parlor.

Then Félicité came up to tell them he was asking for a lock of hair.

"Cut some for him!" said the apothecary.

She could not bring herself to do it, so he stepped forward

himself, scissors in hand. He was trembling so violently that he pricked the skin of the temples in several places. Finally, stiffening himself against his feelings, he cut vigorously two or three times at random, leaving patches of white in her beautiful black hair.

He and the priest resumed their respective occupations, not without falling asleep now and then and reproaching each other for it each time they awoke. Then Father Bournisien would sprinkle the room with holy water and Homais would pour a little chlorine water on the floor.

Félicité had thoughtfully left a bottle of brandy, a cheese and a big brioche for them on top of the dresser. Toward four o'clock in the morning, unable to hold out any longer, the apothecary said with a sigh, "You know, I could use a little nourishment right now!"

The priest did not need any persuading; he went out, said his Mass and came back, then they ate and drank, clinking their glasses together and chuckling a little without knowing why, animated by that vague gaiety which comes over us after periods of gloom. With the last glass of brandy, the priest clapped the pharmacist on the shoulder and said to him, "We'll manage to get along with each other yet!"

Downstairs in the entrance hall they met the workmen arriving. For two hours Charles had to undergo the ordeal of hearing the hammer pounding on the planks. Then they brought her down in her oaken coffin, which they placed inside the two others; but the outer one was too wide and the spaces between had to be filled with wool from a mattress. Finally, when the three lids had been planed, nailed and soldered, it was placed in front of the door, the house was thrown open and the people of Yonville began to stream in.

Monsieur Rouault arrived. He fainted outside in the square when he saw the black cloth.

X

He had not received the pharmacist's letter until thirty-six hours after the event, and, to spare his feelings, Monsieur Homais had phrased it in such a way that it was impossible for him to know what to expect.

When he first read it he fell as though stricken by apoplexy. Then he gathered that she was not dead. But she might be . . . Finally he put on his smock, took his hat, attached a spur to his shoe and set off at a gallop; and he panted all the way, consumed with anxiety. Once he was forced to stop and get off his horse. He could see nothing, and he heard voices around him; he felt himself going mad.

At dawn he saw three black hens asleep in a tree; he shuddered, terrified at this omen. He promised the Holy Virgin he would donate three chasubles to the church and walk barefoot from the cemetery at Les Bertaux to the chapel in Vassonville.

When he rode into Maromme he shouted to the people in the inn, burst open the door with his shoulder, ran to the oat bag, poured a bottle of cider into the manger, climbed back on his little horse and set off in a shower of sparks.

He kept telling himself she would surely be saved: the doctors would find a remedy, no doubt about it. He recalled all the miraculous recoveries he had heard about.

Then he had a vision of her dead. She was there, in front of him, lying on her back in the middle of the road. He drew back on the reins and the hallucination vanished.

At Quincampoix, to brace himself, he drank three cups of coffee one after another.

It occurred to him that his name might have been put on the envelope by mistake. He felt for the letter in his pocket, found it, but did not dare to open it.

Next he began to imagine that it might be a practical joke, a way of getting even with him for something, or a prank concocted by someone who had been drinking too much; and besides, if she were dead he would know it! But no—there was nothing unusual about the countryside: the sky was blue, the trees were swaying; a flock of sheep passed by. He caught sight of the village; he was seen galloping in, hunched over his horse, beating it furiously with a stick while its saddle girths dripped blood.

When he had regained consciousness he fell weeping into Bovary's arms:

"My daughter! Emma! My child! Tell me . . ."

And Charles answered, sobbing, "I don't know, I don't know! It's a curse!"

The apothecary separated them.

"There's no use going into the horrible details. I'll tell Monsieur about it later. People are coming. You've got to show some dignity! Be philosophical!"

Poor Charles tried to appear strong; he said several times, "Yes . . . Be brave."

"All right, by God, I'll be brave!" cried the old man. "I'll stay with her to the end!"

The bell was tolling. Everything was ready. It was time to go.

Sitting beside each other in one of the choir stalls, they saw the three cantors continually walking back and forth in front of them, chanting. The serpent player was blowing with all his might. Father Bournisien, in full regalia, was singing in a shrill voice; he bowed to the tabernacle, raised his hands and stretched forth his arms. Lestiboudois was walking around the church with his whalebone staff. The coffin was near the lectern, between four rows of candles. Charles restrained an impulse to stand up and blow them out.

He tried to arouse religious feelings inside himself, to seize on the hope of a future life in which he would see her again. He tried to imagine that she had gone off on a long trip, a long time ago. But when it came back to him that she was really there inside the coffin, and that everything was over, that she was soon going to be put into the earth, he was overcome with fierce, black, desperate rage. At times it seemed to him that he could no longer feel anything, and he relished this softening of his grief, at the same time calling himself a faithless scoundrel.

He heard what sounded like the sharp, even tapping of a metal-tipped cane. It came from the far end of the church, and it stopped abruptly in one of the side aisles. A man wearing a coarse brown jacket knelt painfully. It was Hippolyte, the stableboy of the Lion d'Or. He had put on his new leg.

One of the cantors walked around the nave, taking up the

collection, and the ten-centime coins clattered into the silver plate one after the other.

"Hurry up! I can't hold out much longer!" cried Charles, angrily tossing him a five-franc coin.

The churchman thanked him with a lengthy bow.

They went on singing, kneeling and rising—it was endless! He remembered that once, in the early days of their marriage, they had gone to Mass together and sat on the other side, to the right, against the wall. The bell began to toll again. There was a great moving of chairs. The pallbearers slipped three poles under the bier and everyone left the church.

At that moment Justin appeared in the doorway of the pharmacy. He suddenly turned and staggered back inside, his face white.

People were looking out their windows to see the procession go by. Charles walked erect at the head of it. He put up a brave front nodding to those who came out of lanes and doorways to join the crowd. The six men, three on each side, walked along with short steps, breathing rather heavily. The priests, the cantors and the two choirboys recited the *De Profundis;* the sound of their voices floated out over the countryside, rising and falling in waves. Sometimes they disappeared around a bend in the path, but the great silver cross could always be seen high up among the trees.

The women followed, wearing black cloaks with turned-down hoods; each held a big lighted candle in her hand, and Charles felt himself grow faint in the midst of that steady procession of prayers and flames, those cloying odors of wax and cassocks. A cool breeze was blowing; the rye and rapeseed were green in the fields; dewdrops quivered on the thorn hedges along the path. All sorts of joyous noises filled the air: the rattle of a cart bouncing along the ruts in the distance, the repeated crowing of a rooster, the hoofbeats of a colt that could be seen galloping away beneath the apple trees. The pure sky was dotted with pink clouds; trails of bluish smoke swirled down over thatched-roof cottages covered with iris. Charles recognized all the farmyards as he passed; he remembered leaving them on mornings like this, after visiting some patient or other, and then going home to her.

The black pall, with its white tear-shaped decorations, billowed up now and then, revealing the coffin beneath. The tired pallbearers were slowing down, and it moved forward in a steady series of jerks, like a boat pitching with every wave.

They arrived.

The pallbearers continued down to where the grave had been dug in the sod.

The others gathered around it; and while the priest spoke, the red earth that had been thrown up around the sides kept trickling silently down at the corners.

Then, when the four ropes were in position, the coffin was pushed over them. He watched it being lowered. It went down and down.

Finally there was a thud; the ropes scraped as they were pulled up. Bournisien took the spade Lestiboudois held out to him; sprinkling holy water with his right hand, with his left he vigorously pushed in a large spadeful of earth. The stones striking the wooden coffin made that awesome sound which seems to us the reverberation of eternity.

The priest handed the holy-water sprinkler to the man standing beside him. It was Monsieur Homais. He shook it solemnly, then held it out to Charles, who sank on his knees in the loose earth and threw handfuls of it into the grave, crying out, "Good-by!" He blew kisses to her and dragged himself toward the grave as though to plunge into it with her.

He was led away; and he soon grew calmer, perhaps feeling vaguely relieved, like everyone else, that it was all over.

On the way back, Monsieur Rouault placidly smoked his pipe, which Homais privately judged to be improper. He also noticed that Monsieur Binet had not appeared, that Tuvache had "sneaked away" after the Mass, and that Théodore, the notary's servant, was wearing a blue coat, "as though he couldn't find a black one, since it's the custom, for heaven's sake!" And he went from one group to the other to communicate these observations. Everyone was deploring Emma's death, especially Lheureux, who had not failed to attend the funeral.

"Poor little lady! What a blow to her husband!"

"If it hadn't been for me, you know," said the apothecary, "he would have tried to take his own life!"

"Such a good woman! When I think that only last Saturday she was in my shop . . ."

"I didn't have time," said Homais, "to prepare a little speech to say over her grave."

When he came home, Charles changed clothes. Monsieur Rouault put on his blue smock again. It was new, and since he had often wiped his eyes with his sleeve during his ride to

Yonville, the dye had rubbed off on his face, which was covered with a layer of dust streaked by tears.

The elder Madame Bovary was with them. The three of them were silent for a time. Finally the old man sighed, "Do you remember, my friend, the time I came to Tostes after you'd lost your first wife? I tried to console you then! I thought of things to say. But now . . ." His chest heaved in a long groan. "Oh, this is the end for me! I've seen my wife go . . . then my son . . . and now my daughter!"

He insisted on going back to Les Bertaux immediately, saying he could not sleep in that house. He even refused to see his granddaughter.

"No, no! It would hurt me too much. But give her a big kiss for me. Good-by! You're a good boy! . . . And I'll never forget this," he said, slapping his thigh. "Don't worry, you'll always get your turkey!"

But when he reached the top of the hill he turned around, as he had once turned around after parting from her on the road to Saint-Victor. The sun was setting beyond the meadow, and the windows of the village were ablaze in its slanting rays. He shaded his eyes with his hand and saw, on the horizon, a walled enclosure in which dark clumps of trees were scattered among white stones; then he went on his way at a gentle trot, for his horse was limping.

Despite their fatigue, Charles and his mother stayed up very late that night, talking. They spoke of the past and the future. She would come to live in Yonville and keep house for him; they would never leave each other again. She was artful and loving, inwardly rejoicing at having recaptured his affection, which had eluded her for so many years. The clock struck midnight. The village was silent as usual, and Charles, still awake, thought constantly of her.

Rodolphe, who had roamed the woods all day to distract his thoughts, was sleeping peacefully in his château; and, in Rouen, Léon was also sleeping.

But there was someone else who was not asleep at that hour.

On the grave among the fir trees, a boy was kneeling in the darkness with tears in his eyes, his chest racked by sobs, his heart oppressed by an immense grief as tender as the moon and as unfathomable as the night. Suddenly the gate creaked. It was Lestiboudois coming to get the spade he had left there that day. He recognized Justin climbing over the wall. Now he knew who had been stealing his potatoes.

XI

The next day Charles had Berthe brought back to the house. She asked for her mother and was told that she had gone away on a trip and would bring her back some toys. Berthe mentioned her again several times, then eventually stopped thinking about her. The child's gaiety pierced Bovary's heart, and he also had to submit to the pharmacist's intolerable efforts to console him.

Money troubles soon began again. Monsieur Lheureux goaded his friend Vinçart as he had done before, and Charles signed notes for exorbitant sums, because he refused to sell any of *her* belongings. His mother was furious with him. His anger was even greater than hers. He had changed completely. She moved out of the house.

Then everyone began to take advantage of his situation. Mademoiselle Lempereur demanded payment for six months of lessons, even though Emma had never taken a single one, despite the receipted bills she had shown him; the two women had agreed on the scheme between themselves. The owner of the lending library demanded three years' subscription fees. Madame Rollet demanded payment for delivering twenty or so letters; and when Charles asked for an explanation she was tactful enough to answer, "Oh, I don't know anything about them! They were business letters."

Each time he paid a debt, Charles thought it was the last. But others kept cropping up.

He dunned patients for unpaid bills. They showed him the letters his wife had sent to them and he had to apologize.

Félicité now wore Madame's dresses, though not all of them, for he had kept a few for himself, and he sometimes shut himself up in her dressing room to look at them. Félicité was almost the same size as Emma, and often when he saw her from behind he would be seized by an illusion and cry out, "Oh, stay! Stay!"

But at Pentecost she fled from Yonville with Théodore, stealing everything that was left of Emma's wardrobe.

It was about this time that Madame Dupuis had the honor of announcing to him "the marriage of Monsieur Léon Du-

puis, her son, notary at Yvetot, and Mademoiselle Léocadie
Leboeuf, of Bondeville." In his letter of congratulations,
Charles wrote this sentence: "How happy this would have
made my poor wife!"

One day, wandering aimlessly around the house, he went
up to the attic. He felt a wad of thin paper beneath one of
his slippers. He opened it and read: *"You must have courage,
Emma, courage! I won't let myself ruin your life."* It was
Rodolphe's letter; it had fallen on the floor among some
boxes and stayed there, and the wind coming in through the
dormer window had just blown it toward the door. Charles
stood motionless and gaping, in the same spot where Emma,
desperate and still paler than he, had once longed for death.
Finally he discovered a small "R" at the bottom of the
second page. Who was it? He remembered Rodolphe's
friendly attentions, his sudden disappearance and his air of
embarrassment on the two or three occasions when they had
met since then. But he was deluded by the respectful tone of
the letter.

"Maybe they loved each other platonically," he thought.

Besides, Charles was not by nature one of those who go
to the root of things; he shrank back in the face of the evidence, and his uncertain jealousy was swallowed up in the
immensity of his grief.

Everyone must have adored her, he told himself. Certainly
every man who saw her had desired her. This made her seem
even more beautiful to him and gave him a constant, furious
desire for her which inflamed his despair and had no limits,
for now it could never be satisfied.

To please her, as though she were still alive, he adopted
her tastes and ideas. He bought patent-leather boots; he began
wearing white cravats and using perfumed mustache wax; he
signed promissory notes as she had done. She was corrupting
him from beyond the grave.

He was forced to sell the silverware piece by piece; next
he sold the parlor furniture. Eventually all the rooms were
bare, except for her bedroom, which remained the same. He
always went up to it after dinner. He pushed the round table
in front of the fire, moved her chair close to it and sat down
facing it. A tallow candle burned in one of the gilded candlesticks. Berthe, beside him, colored pictures.

It pained him, poor man, to see her so shabbily dressed,
with her unlaced shoes and her smock torn from the armhole
to the waist, for the cleaning woman took no care of her.

But she was so gentle, so sweet, and she tilted her little head so gracefully, letting her pretty blond hair fall over her rosy cheeks, that he was flooded with infinite delight, a pleasure mingled with bitterness, like those badly made wines which taste of resin. He repaired her toys, made cardboard puppets for her, or sewed up the torn stomachs of her dolls. But if his eyes happened to fall on the sewing box, a stray piece of ribbon, or even a pin that had remained in a crack in the table, his thoughts would begin to wander, and then he always looked so disconsolate that she became sad too.

No one came to see them now: Justin had run off to Rouen and gone to work in a grocery store, and the apothecary's children saw less and less of Berthe, for, in view of the difference between their respective social statuses, Monsieur Homais was not eager for them to continue their association.

The blind man, whom he had been unable to cure with his salve, had gone back to the hill at Bois-Guillaume, where he told everyone who passed along the road about the pharmacist's failure, so much so that Homais, each time he went to the city, hid behind the curtains of the Hirondelle to avoid seeing him. He hated him, and, wishing to get rid of him at any cost, for the sake of his reputation, he launched an undercover attack which revealed the depth of his cunning and the unscrupulousness of his vanity. For six consecutive months paragraphs such as the following appeared in the *Fanal de Rouen*:

> All those who journey toward the fertile regions of Picardy have no doubt noticed, on the hill at Bois-Guillaume, a poor wretch suffering from a horrible facial affliction. He molests travelers, harasses them and levies a veritable tax on them. Are we still in the monstrous days of the Middle Ages, when vagabonds were allowed to display in our public squares the leprosy and scrofula they had brought back from the Crusades?

Or:

> Despite the laws against vagrancy, the approaches to our large cities continue to be infested by bands of beggars. There are also some who prowl alone, and they are perhaps not the least dangerous. Are our municipal authorities incapable of action?

Homais also invented incidents:

> Yesterday, on the hill at Bois-Guillaume, a skittish
> horse . . .

Then followed the story of an accident caused by the blind
man's presence.

He finally managed to have the beggar locked up. But
he was released. He went on as before, and so did Homais.
It was a fight to the finish. Homais won: his enemy was sen-
tenced to spend the rest of his life in an asylum.

This success emboldened him; and from then on whenever
a dog was run over anywhere in the district, or a barn burned
down, or a woman beaten, he immediately reported it to the
public, always guided by love or progress and hatred of the
clergy. He made comparisons between the public and religious
schools, to the detriment of the latter; he recalled the Massacre of Saint Bartholomew with regard to every hundred-
franc allocation to the Church, denounced abuses and dealt
out sharp thrusts of wit, as he himself put it. His attacks were
subversive; he was becoming dangerous.

He felt stifled within the narrow limits of journalism, however; soon he had to have a book, a "work." He composed
his *General Statistics of the Canton of Yonville, Followed by
Climatological Observations*, and statistics led him into philosophy. He dealt with the great questions: the social problem,
raising the moral standards of the lower classes, fish-breeding,
rubber, railroads, etc. Finally he came to feel ashamed of
being a bourgeois. He affected bohemian ways—he even
smoked! He bought two fashionable statuettes in the Pompadour style, to decorate his parlor.

He did not abandon pharmacy, however; on the contrary,
he kept up with all the latest discoveries. He followed the
development of chocolate. He was the first to introduce into
the Department of the Seine-Inférieure the health-giving
Cho-Ca Flower and Revalentia Meal. He became an enthusiastic partisan of Pulver-macher Hydroelectric Chains; he
wore one himself, and at night, when he took off his flannel
undershirt, Madame Homais was always dazzled by the
golden spiral in which he was encased, and she felt her ardor
redouble for this man wrapped up like a Scythian and re-
splendent as a Persian priest.

He had brilliant ideas for Emma's tombstone. First he suggested a truncated column with drapery, then a pyramid, a
Temple of Vesta, a kind of rotunda, or "a mass of ruins."

In all his plans he firmly insisted on a weeping willow, which he regarded as the obligatory symbol of grief.

He and Charles went to Rouen together to look at some samples in the establishment of a tombstone contractor. They were accompanied by a painter named Vaufrylard, a friend of Bridoux's, who kept up a steady stream of puns. Finally, after examining a hundred designs, requesting an estimate and making a second trip to Rouen, Charles decided on a mausoleum whose two main sides were to bear "a spirit holding an extinguished torch."

As for the inscription, Homais could think of nothing else as beautiful as *"Sta viator,"* and there he stayed; he racked his brain, but he kept repeating *"Sta viator."* At last he came up with *"Amabilem conjugem calcas,"* and this was adopted.

Strangely enough, Bovary was forgetting Emma, despite the fact that he thought about her constantly. It made him desperate to feel her image fading from his memory while he struggled to hold it back. He dreamed of her every night, however; it was always the same dream: he approached her, but just as he embraced her she fell into decay in his arms.

He was seen going into the church every evening for a week. Father Bournisien called on him two or three times, then abandoned him. The priest was drifting into intolerance, into fanaticism, said Homais. He fulminated against the spirit of the times, and every other week, in his sermon, he was sure to describe the death throes of Voltaire, who died devouring his own excrement, as everyone knows.

Despite the frugality with which he was now living, Bovary was far from being able to pay off his old debts. Lheureux refused to renew any more notes. Seizure became imminent. He asked his mother for help; she agreed to let him mortgage her property, but she also included in her letter a great many accusations against Emma, and in return for her sacrifice she asked him for a shawl that had escaped Félicité's depredations. Charles refused to give it to her. They quarreled.

She made the first move toward a reconciliation by offering to take Berthe in to live with her: the child would be a help to her in the house. Charles consented. But just as she was about to leave, his courage failed him. This time he and his mother broke off completely and irrevocably.

As his ties with other people vanished, he clung more tightly to his love for his child. She worried him, however, for she sometimes coughed, and she had red spots over her cheekbones.

Opposite his house, Charles often saw the pharmacist's thriving, joyful family. Everything was now contributing to Homais' self-satisfaction. Napoléon helped him in the laboratory, Athalie embroidered him a fez, Irma cut out paper circles to cover the jam jars, and Franklin could recite the multiplication table without so much as a pause. He was the happiest of fathers, the most fortunate of men!

But no! He was gnawed by a secret ambition: he wanted the cross of the Legion of Honor. He had ample qualifications:

"First: During the cholera epidemic, was distinguished by boundless devotion to duty. Second: Have published, at my own expense, various works useful to the public, such as . . ." (And he referred to his treatise entitled "Cider: Its Manufacture and Effects," some observations on the wooly aphis that he had sent to the Academy, his volume of statistics, and even his pharmacist's thesis.) ". . . not to mention my membership in several learned societies." (He belonged only to one.)

"Why, my outstanding service in fire-fighting would be enough all by itself!" he exclaimed, performing a little pirouette.

He began to curry favor with the authorities. He secretly rendered great services to the prefect during an election campaign. In short, he sold himself, prostituted himself. He even addressed a petition to the sovereign in which he begged him to "do him justice"; he called him "our good king" and compared him to Henri IV.

And every morning the apothecary snatched up the newspaper in the hope of reading the news of his nomination, but it did not come. Finally, consumed with impatience, he had a star-shaped plot of grass laid out in his garden to represent the decoration, with two little strips of grass on top for the ribbon. He would walk around it with his arms folded, meditating on the incompetence of the government and the ingratitude of mankind.

Out of respect, or because of the almost sensual pleasure he took in dragging out his investigations, Charles had not yet opened the secret compartment in the rosewood desk Emma had always used. At last he sat down in front of it one day, turned the key and pushed the spring. All of Léon's letters were inside. This time there could be no doubt! He avidly read every one of them, then he rummaged in every corner, every piece of furniture, every drawer; he sounded the walls for hiding-places; he was sobbing, howling, frenzied, mad with pain. He discovered a box and kicked it open. Rodolphe's portrait leapt out at him amid a jumble of love letters.

Everyone was amazed at his despondency. He no longer went out or received visitors, and he even refused to visit his patients. People began to say he was "shutting himself up in his house to drink."

Now and then, however, some curious soul would peer over the garden hedge and be startled to see him with a long beard, wearing filthy clothes, staring wildly and weeping aloud as he paced up and down.

In summer he took his little girl to the cemetery every evening. They would come back after nightfall, when the only light on the square came from Binet's dormer window.

But he was still unable to savor his grief to the full, for there was no one around him who shared it. He sometimes visited Madame Lefrançois to talk about *her*, but the inn-keeper listened to him with only one ear because she had her own troubles: Monsieur Lheureux had finally established his stagecoach line, *Les Favorites du Commerce*, and Hivert, who enjoyed a great reputation as an errand-runner, was demanding a raise and threatening to go to work for "the competition."

One day at the market in Argueil, where he had gone to sell his horse, his last resource, Charles met Rodolphe.

They both turned pale when they saw each other. Rodolphe, who had merely sent a card after Emma's death, stammered a few excuses, then he grew bolder and even had the nerve (it was a hot August day) to invite him to have a bottle of beer in a tavern.

Sitting opposite him with his elbows on the table, he chewed his cigar as he talked, and Charles was lost in reverie before that face she had loved. It seemed to him that he was seeing something of her. He was overcome with wonder. He would have liked to be that man.

Rodolphe went on talking about farming, livestock and fertilizers, filling up with commonplace remarks all the gaps in the conversation through which an undesirable allusion might slip in. Charles was not listening to him; Rodolphe noticed it and began to read his thoughts in the changing expressions of his face. It slowly turned crimson; his nostrils were agitated

by his heavy breathing, his lips quivered; and once, filled with
somber fury, he glared at Rodolphe, who abruptly stopped
speaking, startled almost to the point of fear. But soon
Charles's features resumed their usual look of gloomy lassitude.

"I don't hold it against you!" he said.

Rodolphe remained silent. Charles put his head between
his hands and repeated dully, in the resigned tone of infinite
sorrow, "No, I don't hold it against you any more."

He even added a lofty philosophical remark, the only one
he had ever made in his life:

"Only fate is to blame."

Rodolphe, who had directed that fate, judged him to be
extremely meek for a man in his position—comical, even, and
a little contemptible.

The next day Charles sat down on the bench in the arbor.
The sun was shining in through the trellis; vine leaves cast
their shadows on the gravel, the jasmine filled the air with its
fragrance, the sky was blue, blister beetles were buzzing
around the blooming lilies, and Charles's aching heart was
swollen with vague amorous longings that made him suffer
like an adolescent boy.

At seven o'clock little Berthe, who had not seen him all
afternoon, came to call him to dinner.

His head was leaning back against the wall; his eyes were
closed, his mouth was open, and in his hands he held a long
lock of black hair.

"Papa! Come on!" she said.

Thinking he was playing, she gave him a little push. He fell
to the ground. He was dead.

Thirty-six hours later Monsieur Canivet arrived, at the
apothecary's request. He performed an autopsy but found
nothing.

When everything had been sold, there remained twelve
francs and seventy-five centimes, which paid for Mademoiselle
Bovary's trip to her grandmother's house. The good woman
died that same year, and since Monsieur Rouault was now
paralyzed, an aunt took charge of the child's upbringing. She
is poor and has put her to work in a cotton mill to earn her
living.

Since Bovary's death, three different doctors have tried to
establish themselves in Yonville, but they have all been swiftly
driven away by Monsieur Homais' vehement attacks. He now
has more patients than the devil himself could handle; the

authorities treat him with deference and public opinion supports him.

He has just been awarded the cross of the Legion of Honor.

Biographical
Sketch

BIOGRAPHICAL SKETCH

Gustave Flaubert was born on December 12, 1821, in Rouen, where his father was chief surgeon at the Hôtel-Dieu. His parents—Achille-Cléophas (1784-1846) and Anne-Justine-Caroline Fleuriot (1793-1872)—had six children, three of whom died in childhood. Flaubert's older brother Achille took over his father's post as chief surgeon after the latter's death; their youngest sister Caroline married Emile Hamard, one of Flaubert's friends, in 1845, and died in 1846.

Flaubert wrote abundantly during his years at the *collège* of Rouen (from 1832 to 1840) as well as during the brief time when he was enrolled as a law student in Paris. Among the works of this period are *Les Mémoires d'un fou* (1838), *Smarh* (1839), and especially *Novembre* (1842—translated by Frank Jellinek and edited by Francis Steegmuller, New York: Serendipity Press, 1967). In 1836, on the beach at Trouville, Flaubert met Mme Elisa Schlésinger, then 26, whom he loved—mainly at a distance—all his life. Mme Schlésinger was the principal inspiration behind the figure of Marie Arnoux in *L'Education sentimentale*. In 1844 Flaubert had his first attack of what was probably temporal lobe epilepsy. His father insisted that he give up his studies; Flaubert returned home, and in fact spent most of the rest of his life (living with his mother until her death) at the family property of Croisset, near Rouen.

The story of Flaubert's life is essentially the story of his work. In 1845 he finished the first *Education sentimentale* and, during a trip to Italy with his family, was deeply impressed by a Breughel painting in Genoa which was to inspire *La Tentation de saint Antoine*. In the fall of 1849 he read aloud the first version of *La Tentation* to his friends Louis Bouilhet and Maxime Du Camp, who advised him to throw the manu-

script away, to give up "diffuse" and "vague" themes, and to
try a "down-to-earth" subject. (The incident is related by the
sour and probably jealous Du Camp in his *Souvenirs littéraires*.) Flaubert then traveled with Du Camp in the Near East
for almost two years, and in September, 1851, three months
after his return to Croisset, he began *Madame Bovary*, which
he finished in the spring of 1856. The *Correspondence* during this period is particularly interesting, especially the letters
to his mistress, the minor poetess Louise Colet. Their rather
stormy affair lasted, not without interruptions, from 1846 to
1854. After the final break, most of the letters concerning
Madame Bovary are addressed to Bouilhet. In 1857 Flaubert
was brought to trial for the "immorality" and "irreligion" of
Madame Bovary; he was successfully defended by the Rouen
lawyer Marie-Antoine-Jules Sénard, to whom the novel is
dedicated.

In 1856 Flaubert revised the 1849 version of *La Tentation*.
Toward the end of 1857 he began to write *Salammbô* (at
first entitled *Carthage*). He interrupted his work with a two-
month research trip to North Africa in the spring of 1858;
the novel was finished in April, 1862. With *L'Education sentimentale*, written from 1864 to 1869, Flaubert came back to
a modern, "bourgeois" subject. The novel—considered by
many critics today as Flaubert's greatest work—was almost
unanimously panned. Flaubert returned again to *La Tentation de saint Antoine*, the third and final version of which he
finished in 1872 and published in 1874. At Croisset and in his
apartment in Paris, Flaubert, acclaimed as the head of the
new "realistic" school, received many of the leading literary
figures of the time: among others, Théophile Gautier, the
Goncourt brothers, George Sand, Turgenev, Zola and Maupassant. *Bouvard et Pécuchet*, which Flaubert never finished,
was begun in 1874; pressed for money, he interrupted work
on the novel for two years and in 1877 published the *Trois
contes* ("Un Coeur simple," "La Légende de saint Julien
l'Hospitalier," and "Hérodias"). Flaubert died of a stroke,
at Croisset, on May 8, 1880.

Critical
Supplement

THE NOVELIST ON HIS ART

Excerpts from Flaubert's Correspondence*

To Ernest Chevalier.[1]
(Rouen, December 31, 1830.)

. . . If you want us to get together to write, I would write comedies and you will write me your dreams; and since there is a lady who comes to see papa and always tells us silly things, I would write them down.

To Alfred Le Poittevin.
(Croisset, September, 1845.)

I notice that I hardly ever laugh any more and that I am no longer sad. I am ripe. You talk about my serenity, dear friend, and you envy me for it. Indeed, it is amazing. Ill, fretful, suffering a thousand times a day moments of excruciating anguish, without women, without activity, without any of the little trinkets of worldly existence, I grind away like a good workman who, with his sleeves turned up and his hair damp with sweat, bangs on his anvil, oblivious to rain or wind, hail or thunder. I have not always been like this. The change has come about naturally. My will has had something to do with it too. It will take me further, I hope. The only thing I am afraid of is that it may weaken, for there are days when my listlessness frightens me. However, I think I have discovered a truth, an important truth, which is that happiness for people like us lies in the *idea,* and nowhere

---

* Translated by Helen Weaver.
[1] One of Flaubert's childhood friends, born in 1820. Letter written when Flaubert was nine.

else. Discover your own true nature, and be in harmony with it. *"Sibi constat,"* says Horace. It is all there. I swear to you that I do not think about fame, and seldom even about Art. I am trying to spend my time in the way that is least tiresome, and I have found it. Follow my example: *break with the outside world,* live like a bear—a polar bear—send everything to the devil, everything and yourself with it, except your own intelligence. There is now such an enormous gap between me and the rest of the world that sometimes I am amazed to hear people say the simplest and most natural things. The most commonplace remark sometimes holds me rapt with admiration. There are gestures and tones of voice which utterly undo me, and stupidities which almost make me dizzy. Have you ever listened attentively to people talking a foreign language which you did not understand? That is the state I'm in. Because I want to understand everything, everything is a mystery. And yet it seems to me that this wonder is not foolishness. The bourgeois, for example, is for me something infinite. You cannot imagine how the *horrible* disaster of Monville[2] affected me. For a thing to be interesting, you need only look at it for a long time.

To Maxime du Camp.
(*Croisset, April, 1846.*)

When I consider everything that can happen, I do not see anything that might change me; I mean essentially, in my life, in the daily rhythm of existence; and then I am beginning to develop a habit of working for which I thank heaven. I read or write regularly from eight to ten hours a day; and if somebody disturbs me, I am quite sick about it. There are many days when I don't go to the end of the garden; the boat is not even afloat. I am thirsty for long study and hard work. That inner life which I have always dreamed about is at last beginning to emerge. All this may mean a decline in poetry, by which I mean inspiration, passion, the instinctive movement. I am afraid of drying up from too much learning, and yet from another point of view I am so ignorant that I blush for myself. It is remarkable how, since the deaths of my father and sister, I have lost all love for fame. The moments when I think about the future

---

[2] A town devastated by a tornado on August 19, 1845.

success of my career as an artist are the exceptional ones. I very often doubt that I shall ever publish a line. Do you know, I like the idea of a jolly fellow who would publish nothing until the age of fifty and who, all of a sudden, one fine day, would bring out his complete works and leave it at that? . . . An artist who would really be an artist and for himself alone, without concerning himself with anything, that would be fine; he might enjoy himself enormously. It is probable that the pleasure one can have strolling through a virgin forest or hunting tigers is marred by the idea that one must later make an artful description to please as many bourgeois people as possible.

To Louise Colet.
(Croisset, Friday, 10 P.M., September 18, 1846.)

Why are you always saying that I love tinsel, glitter, sequins! The poet of form! This is the great insult that utilitarians hurl at real artists. For my part, until someone has shown me how you can separate the form from the content in any given sentence, I shall maintain that these two words are devoid of meaning. There is no such thing as a beautiful idea without beautiful form, and vice versa. Beauty is secreted by form in the world of Art, as in our human world form gives rise to temptation and love. Just as you cannot separate from a physical body the qualities that make it up, that is, color, size, solidity, without reducing it to an empty abstraction, in other words, without destroying it, just so you cannot remove the form from the Idea, for the Idea exists only by virtue of its form. Imagine an idea that has no form, it is impossible; the same is true of a form that does not express an idea. Here is a heap of nonsense which is the bread and butter of criticism. People who write in a good style are condemned for overlooking the Idea, the moral purpose; as if the purpose of the doctor were not to cure, the purpose of the painter to paint, the purpose of the nightingale to sing, as if the purpose of Art were not Beauty above all!

To Maxime Du Camp.
(Croisset, Tuesday, October 21, 1851.)

I shall go and live in Paris this winter. I shall be a man like any other; I shall lead the worldly and sensual life. I shall have to go through with a great many things which will revolt me and which I regret in advance. Alas! Am I cut out for all this? You know me for a man of passionate enthusiasms and sudden depressions. If you only knew all the invisible nets of inaction that surround my body and all the mists that float in my brain! I often feel the most overwhelming fatigue at the idea of performing the smallest action, and it is only through great effort that I succeed in grasping the simplest idea. My youth steeped me in I know not what drug of apathy for the rest of my days. I detest life—there, the word is spoken, let it stand! Yes, life and everything that reminds me that I must endure it. It is torture to eat, to dress, to be on my feet. I have dragged this with me everywhere, through everything I have done—at school, in Paris, in Rouen, on the Nile, on our trip. You, with your clear and precise nature, have often rebelled against these vague *normandismes* which I apologized for so clumsily and you have not spared me your criticism!

To Louise Colet.
(Croisset, Friday evening, January 16, 1852.)

There are in me, from a literary point of view, two separate persons: one who is fond of bombast, lyricism, great eagle flights, all the musical power of language and the heights of abstract thought; another who burrows and digs out the truth as best he can, who likes to emphasize the small fact as forcefully as the great one, who would like to make you feel almost *physically* the things he reproduces; this person likes to laugh and delights in the animal nature of man.

*

*   *

What seems beautiful to me, what I would like to write, is a book about nothing, a book without any external support, which would be held together only by the inner strength of its style, the way the earth hangs suspended in space, a book which would have almost no subject, or at least in which the subject would be almost invisible, if that is possible. The most beautiful works are those in which there is the least matter; the closer the expression comes to the thought, the more perfectly the language clings to the idea

and disappears, the more beautiful the style. I believe that
the future of Art lies in this direction. I see Art, as it has
developed over the years, becoming more and more ethereal,
from the pylons of Egypt to the Gothic lancets, and from
the twenty-thousand verse poems of the Indians to the flights
of Byron. Form, as it becomes more skillful, is attenuated;
it abandons all liturgy, all law, all measure; it deserts the
epic for the novel, poetry for prose; it rejects all orthodoxy
and is as free as the individual will that creates it. This
liberation from materiality can be found in everything, for
example, in the way governments have evolved, from oriental
despotisms to the socialist states of the future.

This is why there are neither beautiful nor ugly subjects
and why you could almost establish as an axiom, from the
point of view of pure Art, that there is no such thing as
subject, since style itself is an absolute way of seeing things.

To Louise Colet.
(Croisset, Saturday night, 1 A.M., March 20-21, 1852.)

For the moment I am up to my neck in girlish daydreams.
I am almost annoyed you advised me to read the memoirs
of Mme. Lafarge,[3] for I shall probably follow your advice
and I am afraid of being carried too far. The whole value
of my book, if it has any, will be to have succeeded in
treading a hairline between the two abysses of lyricism and
vulgarity (which I want to fuse in a narrative analysis).
When I think about what it could be, I become dizzy. But
then when I think that so much beauty has been entrusted
to *me,* I have such spasms of terror that I want to run and hide.
I have been working like a mule for fifteen long years.
I have lived all my life a slave to this maniacal stubbornness,
to the exclusion of my other passions, which I locked up
in cages and visited now and then solely for diversion. Oh!
If I ever write a good book, I will really have earned it. I
wish to God that that blasphemous remark of Buffon's were
true![4] I would be sure of being among the first.

---

[3] Suspected of having poisoned her husband, Mme. Lafarge was sen-
tenced to life imprisonment. She obtained a pardon in 1852, after more
than ten years in prison, but died in 1853. The three volumes of her
Heures de prison appeared in 1853.

[4] "Genius is a long patience."

To Louise Colet.
(Croisset, Saturday evening, April 24, 1852.)

If I have not replied sooner to your doleful and despondent letter, it is because I was in the midst of a great fit of work. The day before yesterday I went to bed at five o'clock in the morning and yesterday at three. Since last Monday I have put aside everything else, and have spent the whole week slaving away at my *Bovary* and annoyed with myself for not getting on with it. I have now arrived at my party which I shall begin Monday. I hope that will go better. Since you saw me, I have done twenty-five pages all told (twenty-five pages in six weeks). They were hard going. I shall read them to Bouilhet tomorrow. As for my own opinion, I have worked on them so much, copied them over, changed them, handled them, that for the moment I can't see them at all. I believe, however, that they will stand up. You speak of your discouragements: if you could only see mine! Sometimes I wonder why my arms don't fall off my body from fatigue, and why my brain doesn't turn to porridge. I lead a harsh life, stripped of all external pleasure and in which I have nothing to sustain me but a kind of permanent rage which sometimes weeps with impotence, but which never leaves me. I love my work with a frenetic and perverse love, as the ascetic loves the hairshirt which scrapes his belly. Sometimes, when I find myself empty, when the words refuse to come, when, after scrawling pages on end, I discover that I have not written a single sentence, I fall on my couch and lie there dazed in a private swamp of misery.

I hate myself and I blame myself for this lunacy of pride which makes me pant after the unattainable. A quarter of an hour later, everything is changed; my heart pounds with joy. Last Wednesday, I had to get up and find my pocket handkerchief; tears were streaming down my face. I had moved myself while writing, I was experiencing the most exquisite pleasure, from the emotion of my idea, from the words that expressed it, and from the satisfaction of having found the words. At least I think all this entered into that emotion which was, after all, largely a matter of nerves. There are loftier emotions of this kind; they are those in which the tangible element is totally absent, and which surpass virtue in moral beauty, so independent are they of any personal element, of any human relation. Sometimes, in moments of great illumination, in the glow of an enthusiasm that made me tremble from head to foot, I have caught a glimpse of just such a spiritual state, superior to life, for which fame would be nothing, and even happiness futile. If everything that surrounds you, instead of automatically and eternally conspiring to drag you down into the mire, instead sustained you in a healthy regime, who knows whether it might not be possible to recreate for aesthetics what Stoicism invented for ethics? Greek art was not an art; it was the fundamental constitution of a whole people, of a whole race, of the land itself. The mountains in Greece had a completely different shape and were made of marble for sculptors, etc.

*

*   *

Getting back to *Graziella*.[5] There is a paragraph that goes on for a whole page all in infinitives: "to get up in the morning," etc. The man who adopts constructions of this kind is tone-deaf; he is not a writer. Not one of those old sentences with taut, bulging muscles whose hooves ring on the pavement. But *I* have a certain style in mind: a style that would be beautiful, which someone will create some day, in ten years or ten centuries, and which would be as rhythmical as poetry, as precise as the language of the sciences, and would have undulations, the mellow throb of the 'cello, plumes of fire; a style that would pierce your mind like a stiletto, and allow your thoughts to sail over polished surfaces, the way you skim along in a boat with a fair wind. Prose is in its infancy; this is what we must tell ourselves. Verse is the form *par excellence* of ancient literatures. All the prosodic combinations have been invented; but the forms of prose remain to be discovered.

To Louise Colet.
(Croisset, Saturday evening, midnight, May 8-9, 1852.)

If *Bovary* has any value, this book will not be lacking in human feeling. And yet it seems to me that irony dominates life, Why is it that when I wept I often went and looked in the mirror to see my own face? This tendency to hover over oneself is perhaps the source of all virtue. It frees you from

---

[5] By Lamartine; an episode in his *Confidences* (1849).

personality, far from binding you to it. The comic carried
to the extreme, the comic that does not arouse laughter,
the poetry of the joke is for me everything I desire most as
a writer. The two elements of human nature are there.

To Louise Colet.
(Croisset, Monday-Tuesday night, 2 A.M., July 5-6, 1852.)

Passion does not make poetry, and the more personal you
are, the less effective you will be. I myself have always
sinned in that direction; I have always put myself into everything I have done. Instead of Saint Anthony, for example,
it's I who am there; the *Temptation* was for me and not for
the reader. *The less one feels a thing, the better one is able
to express it as it is* (as it is intrinsically, in its generality
and freed from all its ephemeral accidents). But one must
have the faculty *to make oneself feel it*. This faculty is nothing
other than genius: to be able to *see*, to have the model in
front of you, posing.

To Louise Colet.
(Croisset, Thursday, 4 P.M., July 22, 1852.)

What hellish thing prose is! It's never finished; there's
always something to do over. Still, I believe it can be given
the consistency of poetry. A good sentence should be like a
good line of poetry, *unchangeable*, just as rhythmic, just as
resonant. That, at least, is my ambition (there is one thing
I am sure of, and that is that nobody has ever contemplated
a kind of prose more perfect than what I have in mind;
but as for the execution, my God, what weaknesses!). Nor
does it seem to me impossible to give psychological analysis
the speed, precision, and excitement of a purely dramatic
narrative. This has never been attempted and would be beautiful. Have I succeeded in this to some extent? I have no
idea. At this moment I have no clear opinion of my work.

To Louise Colet.
(Croisset, Monday evening, midnight, September 13, 1852.)

Divorce yourself more and more, as you write, from what
is not pure Art. Always keep your eye on the model, and
nothing else. You have the ability to go far; this I promise
you. Have faith, have faith. I want (and I intend) to see

you become excited about a caesura, a phrase, an enjamb-
ment, about form itself, in short, apart from the subject, the
way you used to become excited about feeling, the heart,
the passions. Art is representation; we must put everything
else out of our minds. The mind of the artist must be like
the sea, so vast that the boundaries are invisible, so clear
that the stars are reflected to the very bottom.

To Louise Colet.
(Croisset, Saturday, 1 A.M., October 9, 1852.)

For two or three days now it's been going well. I'm working on a conversation between a young man and a young
lady on literature, the sea, the mountains, music—in short,
every poetic subject there is. It could be taken seriously and
I intend it to be totally absurd. I believe this will be the
first time a book has ever made fun of its leading lady and
its leading man. Irony in no way diminishes pathos; on the
contrary, it exaggerates it . . .

In my third part, which will be full of farcical things, I
want the reader to weep.

To Louise Colet.
(Croisset, Thursday, 1 P.M., December 9, 1852.)

The author, in his book, must be like God in the universe,
everywhere present and nowhere visible. Art being a second
nature, the creator of this nature must employ analogous
procedures. The reader must feel in every atom, on every
surface, a concealed and infinite indifference. The effect for
the spectator must be a species of amazement. How was all
this done? he must wonder, and he must feel overwhelmed
without knowing why. Greek art was based on the same
principle, and to achieve the effect more quickly, it chose
characters whose social conditions were exceptional, kings,
gods, demi-gods. The writers did not speak to you about
yourself; they aimed for the divine.

To Louise Colet.
(Croisset, Thursday night, 1 o'clock, December 17, 1852.)

. . . I sometimes have an uncontrollable urge to rail at
the human race and I'll do it some day, ten years from now,
in a long novel with a large canvas; meanwhile, an old idea

came to me again, namely, my *Dictionary of Received Ideas* (did I tell you about it?). I am particularly excited about the preface, and the way I conceive of it (it would be a whole book), I would be safe from the law although I would attack everything. It would be the glorification, down through history, of everything that is accepted. In it I would demonstrate that majorities have always been right and minorities have always been wrong. I would sacrifice the great men to all the idiots, the martyrs to all the executioners, and this in an extravagant, bombastic style. Thus, in the field of literature, I would have no trouble establishing the fact that mediocrity, being within reach of all, is alone justifiable, and that we must therefore revile every species of originality as dangerous, absurd, etc. This apology for human vileness in all its forms, ironic and shrill from beginning to end, full of examples, proofs (which would prove the opposite), and appalling quotations (that would be easy) is intended, I would say, to put an end, once and for all, to eccentricity of every kind. Thus I would fall in with the modern democratic idea of equality, and Fourier's remark that great men will become useless; and it is to this end, I would say, that the book was written. Thus it would contain, in alphabetical order, on all possible subjects, *everything one should say in society to be a respectable and agreeable man* . . .

For example:

> *Artists:* are all disinterested.
> *Crayfish:* the female lobster.
> *France:* needs to be ruled with an iron hand.
> *Bossuet:* the eagle of Meaux.
> *Fénelon:* the swan of Cambrai.
> *Negro women:* are more amorous than whites.
> *Erection:* said only in speaking of monuments, etc.

I believe that the overall effect would be formidable for sheer weight. It would be necessary that in the entire book there not be one word of my own invention, and that once people had read it they would no longer dare open their mouths for fear of unintentionally using one of the expressions that are in it. Certain subjects would lend themselves admirably to development, such as Man, Woman, Friend, Politics, Manners, Magistrate. I could also describe types in a few lines, and show not only what one should *say*, but how one should *look*.

To Louise Colet.
(Croisset, Monday, 5 o'clock, December 27, 1852.)

. . . I believe my *Bovary* is going to work; but I am having trouble with the metaphorical sense, which decidedly preoccupies me too much. I am riddled with comparisons like a man with lice, and I spend all my time squashing them; my sentences crawl with them.

To Louise Colet.
(Croisset, Saturday afternoon, 3 o'clock, January 15, 1853.)

I spent *five days writing one page*, last week, and I had put aside everything else to write—Greek, English; I did only that. What torments me in my book is the comic element, which is mediocre. There is a lack of event. I myself hold that *ideas* are events. It is more difficult to make ideas interesting, I know, but then the style is to blame. I now have fifty consecutive pages in which there is not a single event. It is a sustained portrait of a bourgeois life and an inactive love; a love which is all the more difficult to describe because it is both timid and profound, but alas! without inner turmoil, because my gentleman is of a quiet nature. I have already had something similar in the first part: my husband loves his wife in somewhat the same way as my lover. They are two mediocrities in the same milieu who must, however, be differentiated. If I succeed in doing this it will, I think, be very strong, for it means laying one color over another that is very close to it, which is not easy. But I am afraid that all these subtleties will be tiresome and that the reader would just as soon see more action. Well, one must be true to one's original conception. If I tried to introduce action into it, I would be following a program and I would spoil everything. One must sing in one's own voice; and mine will never be dramatic or arresting. Besides, I am convinced that everything is a matter of style, or rather of shape, the outward appearance of sentences.

To Louise Colet.
(Croisset, Sunday night, 1:30, February 27-28, 1853.)

We must write more *coldly*. Let us beware of that overheated state which is called inspiration and which often consists more of nervous emotionalism than muscular strength. At this moment, for example, I feel I am at the top of my form, my forehead is burning, the words flow easily, I've been meaning to write you for two hours now and the work keeps pulling me back. Instead of one idea I have six, and where I need the simplest exposition my mind produces a metaphor. I am sure I could keep going until tomorrow noon without fatigue. But I know these masked balls of the imagination from which one returns with death in the heart, exhausted, having seen nothing but falsity and uttered nothing but nonsense. Everything must be done coolly, deliberately.

To Louise Colet.
(Croisset, Sunday, 4 o'clock, March 27, Easter Day, 1853.)

As for myself, the more difficulty I have in writing, the more audacious I become (this is what saves me from pedantry, into which I would no doubt otherwise fall). I have enough plans for books to keep me busy the rest of my life, and if I sometimes have bitter moments which make me almost scream with rage, so keenly do I feel my impotence and weakness, there are others when I can hardly contain myself for joy. Something profound and supremely voluptuous is gushing out of me in rapid bursts, like an ejaculation of the soul. I feel transported and completely inebriated with my own thought, as if a gust of warm perfumed air were reaching me through some inner passageway. I shall never go very far, I know my limitations. But the task I am undertaking will be completed by someone else. I shall have shown the way to someone more gifted and more spontaneous. To want to give prose the rhythm of poetry (at the same time leaving it unmistakably prose) and to write about ordinary life the way you write a history or an epic (without distorting the subject) may be an absurdity. I sometimes wonder about this. But it may also be a noble effort and a very original one! I am quite aware of where I fall short. (Ah! If only I were fifteen!) No matter, whatever happens, I shall have had some value, if only because of my stubbornness. And then, who knows? Perhaps someday I shall find a good *motif*, a melody completely within my range, neither above nor below it. No matter what happens, I shall have spent my life in a noble and often delightful way.

There is a saying of La Bruyère's which I like: "A good writer believes in writing reasonably." That is all I ask, to write reasonably, and that alone is a great ambition. Nevertheless it does make me sad to see how easily great men achieve their effects without regard to Art. What could be more badly constructed than many things by Rabelais, Cervantes, Molière and Hugo? But what sudden thrusts! What power in a single word! We lesser men must painstakingly add one little pebble at a time to make our pyramids which are less than one hundredth the size of theirs, which are hewn out of a single block. But to try to imitate the methods of these geniuses would be disastrous. They are great precisely because they *have* no methods. Hugo has many, that is what diminishes him. He lacks variety, he has more height than breadth.

To Louise Colet.
(Croisset, Wednesday evening, midnight, April 6, 1853.)

The reason I proceed so slowly is that nothing in this book is drawn from me; never will my own personality have been so useless. Perhaps in the future I may be able to write things that are better (I hope I will), but I find it difficult to believe that I will compose anything more skillful. Everything has come out of my *head*. If it doesn't come off, it will still have been a good exercise for me. What is natural to me is what is unnatural for others—the extraordinary, the fantastic, the metaphysical, mythological roar. *Saint Anthony* did not require a quarter of the mental tension that *Bovary* causes me. It was an outlet; I experienced nothing but pleasure in its writing, and the eighteen months I spent writing its five hundred pages were the most profoundly voluptuous of my whole life. Imagine, then, I must every minute get inside of human beings who are antipathetic to me. For six months now I have been making Platonic love, and at the moment I feel a Catholic exaltation at the sound of church bells, and I long to go to confession!

* *

Literature will increasingly adopt the methods of science; it will be above all *educational,* which does not mean didactic. We must present a picture, show nature as it is, but it must be a complete picture, we must paint the underside as well as the surface.

To Louise Colet.
(Croisset, Saturday night, 1 o'clock, May 21-22, 1853.)

This book, all calculation and stylistic tricks, is not in my blood, it does not come from my guts, I feel that coming from me it is artificial, contrived. It may turn out to be a *tour de force* which certain people—and only a few at that—will admire; others will find in it some truth of detail and observation. But air, air! The high style, the great sweeping periods rolling like rivers, the teeming metaphors, the dazzling effects of language, in short, everything I love, will be absent.

To Louise Colet.
(Croisset, Saturday night, 1 o'clock, June 25-26, 1853.)

If the book which I am writing with so much difficulty comes out well, I will have established by the mere fact of its execution these two truths, which are axioms for me, namely: first of all, that poetry is purely subjective, that in literature there are no beautiful or artistic subjects, and that therefore Yvetot[6] is as good as Constantinople; and that consequently one subject is just as good as another. *The artist must elevate everything;* he is like a pump, he has in him a great tube which goes down into the bowels of things, into the deepest layers. He draws up and causes to leap into the light in giant fountains what was lying under the ground and what could not be seen.

To Louise Colet.
(Croisset, Thursday night, 1 o'clock, July 7-8, 1853.)

The ability to create an effect of three-dimensionality springs from a profound understanding, a *penetration, of the objective world;* for external reality, if we are to reproduce it well, must enter us until we almost scream.

To Louise Colet.
(Croisset, Friday night, 1 o'clock, July 22, 1853.)

. . . Today I had a great triumph. As you know, yesterday *we* were *honored* by a visit from Monsieur Saint-Arnaud.[7] Well, this morning in the Rouen newspaper, I found a sentence

---

[6] Small French town in Normandy.
[7] The Minister of War; in a speech to the people of Rouen, he assured them of Napoleon the Third's concern for their agricultural prosperity.

of the mayor's in a speech to him which I had the night before written *word for word* in *Bovary* (in a prefect's speech at the agricultural fair). Not only did it have the same idea and the same words, but the same stylistic assonance. I won't hide the fact that this sort of thing gives me pleasure. When literature arrives at the precision of an exact science, it's staggering. Anyway, I'll bring you this official speech and you'll see whether I know how to sound like a civil servant and a shameless hypocrite.

To Louise Colet.
(Croisset, Sunday, 10 o'clock, November 6, 1853.)

The idea of your memoirs, written later on when we have some time to ourselves, touched me. I, too, have often had this vague intention. But we must save this sort of thing for our old age, when the imagination is exhausted. Let us always remember that impersonality is the sign of strength. Let us absorb objective reality and allow it to circulate within us and then reproduce itself externally, without betraying anything about this marvelous chemistry. Our hearts must be sensitive in order to feel the passions of others. Let us be magnifying mirrors of external truth.

To Louise Colet.
(Croisset, Friday night, 2 o'clock, December 23, 1853.)

Unless I loved you I could not write you this evening, for I am *exhausted*. There is an iron band around my brain. Since two in the afternoon (except for about twenty-five minutes for dinner) I have been working on *Bovary*, I am . . . right in the thick of it; they're sweating and their throats are tight. This has been one of the rare days in my life that I have spent in illusion, completely and without interruption. A little while ago, at six o'clock, just as I was writing the phrase *attack of nerves*, I was so carried away, I was shouting so loud and feeling so deeply what my little woman was going through, that I was afraid I might have one myself. I got up from my desk and opened the window to calm myself. My head was spinning. I now have severe pains in the knees, the back, and the head. I am like a man who has . . . too much (if you will forgive the expression), that is, in a kind of drunken lethargy. And since I am *immersed in love* it is only fitting that I do not go to sleep without sending you a caress, a kiss, and all the thoughts I have left. Will it be good? I have no idea (I am hurrying a little so I'll have a complete section to show Bouilhet when he comes). All I know is that it's been going quickly for the past week. If only it continues! for I am tired of my slowness. But I dread the awakening, the disillusionment of revision! No matter, well or ill, it is a delightful thing to write, to cease to be *oneself*, to flow through the whole creation of which one speaks. Today, for example, man and woman at the same time, lover and mistress at once, I rode horseback through a forest on an autumn afternoon under the yellow leaves, and I was the horses, the leaves, the wind, the words they said to each other and the red sun that beat down on their eyelids, heavy with love, and made them droop. Is this pride or piety? Is it the inane outpouring of egotism, or a vague and noble religious instinct? When I think it over, after experiencing these delights, I would be tempted to offer a prayer of gratitude to God, if I were sure he could hear me.

To Louise Colet.
(Croisset, Thursday night, March 2-3, 1854.)

I spent two execrable days, Saturday and yesterday. It was impossible for me to write a line. How I cursed, wasted paper and stamped with rage, no one will ever know. I had to write a psychological-nervous passage of the subtlest possible kind, and I kept wandering off into metaphors instead of stating the facts. This book, which is all style, is constantly threatened by the style itself. The phrase goes to my head and I lose sight of the idea. If the entire universe were to hiss at me I could not be more overwhelmed with shame than I am at times. Who has not experienced these feelings of impotence, when you feel as if your brain is coming apart like a bundle of dirty laundry? And then the breeze starts up again and the sail fills. This evening, in one hour, I wrote all of half a page. I might even have finished it if I had not heard the clock strike and thought of you.

To Louise Colet.
(Croisset, Friday evening, midnight, April 7, 1854.)

I have just finished making a clean copy of everything I have done since New Year's Day, or more precisely, since the middle of February, for on my return from Paris I burned

everything. It comes to thirteen pages, no more, no less—
thirteen pages in seven weeks. Well, at least they are done, I
think, and as perfect as I can make them. I have left only
two or three repetitions of the same word to eliminate and
two sentences to differentiate where the rhythm is too similar.
But at last I have something finished. It was a difficult passage; I had to bring the reader gradually from psychology to
action without his noticing it. I am about to start on the
dramatic and eventful part. Another two or three important
developments and the end will be in sight. By July or August
I hope to begin the denouement. What a struggle it will have
been, my God! what a struggle! What back-breaking work,
what discouragements! Yesterday I spent the whole evening
plunged in a frenzied study of surgery. I am doing research
on the theory of club feet. In three hours I devoured an entire volume of this interesting literature and took notes. There
were some very beautiful things: "The breast of the mother
is an impenetrable and mysterious sanctuary where," etc. And
a fine study, too! If only I were young, how I would work!
One must know everything in order to write. Hacks that we
are, we are all monstrously ignorant, and yet what a wealth
of ideas and comparisons all this knowledge would provide!
It is *marrow* that most of us lack! The books which have
given rise to entire literatures,—Homer, Rabelais—are en-
cyclopedias of their times. They knew everything, those good
men; and we, we know nothing. There is in Ronsard's poetics
a curious precept: he advises the poet to study the arts and
crafts—blacksmith, goldsmith, locksmith, etc.,—as a source
of *metaphors*. There, indeed, is the material for a rich and
varied language. The sentences in a book must stir like the
leaves in a forest, all similar but no two alike.

To Mlle. Leroyer de Chantepie.[8]
(Paris, March 18, 1857.)

With a reader such as yourself, Madame, and as sympa-
pathetic as you are, candor is a duty. I shall therefore answer your questions: *Madame Bovary* has no truth in it. The
story is *totally invented*; I put nothing into it either of my own

---

[8] Marie-Sophie Leroyer de Chantepie (1800-1885) had written to Flaubert to congratulate him for having been brought to trial and acquitted
in 1857. Although they wrote to each other rather regularly, they never
met.

feelings or of my own life.[9] The illusion (if there is one) comes, on the contrary, from the *impersonality* of the book. It is one of my principles that a writer should not *write himself*. The artist must be in his work the way God is in the creation, invisible and all-powerful; he should be felt everywhere but seen nowhere.

And then, Art must rise above personal inclinations and nervous susceptibilities! It is time that, by a ruthless method, Art achieved the precision of the physical sciences! The fundamental problem for me nevertheless remains style, form, the indefinable Beauty *which results from the conception itself* and which is the splendor of Truth, as Plato said.

To George Sand.
(Croisset, Monday evening, April 3, 1876.)

I do not share the severity of Turgenev's criticism of *Jack* nor the immensity of his admiration for *Rougon*.[10] One has charm and the other has strength. But neither of the two is *primarily* concerned with what for me is the end of Art, namely, Beauty. I remember my heart beating wildly, and experiencing a violent pleasure on contemplating a wall of the Acropolis, a completely bare wall (the one that is on the left when you walk up to the Propylaea). Well! I wonder whether a book could not produce the same effect, independently of what it says. In the precision of the structure, the rarity of the elements, the polish of the surface, the harmony of the whole, is there not an intrinsic value, a species of divine force, something as eternal as a principle? (I speak as a Platonist.) For instance, why is there a necessary connection between the right word and the musical word? Why does one always end by writing a line of poetry when one condenses one's thought too much? Thus the law of numbers governs feelings and images, and what seems to be the exterior is purely and simply the interior. If I carried this argument much further I would

---

[9] On the other hand, René Descharmes, in *Flaubert: sa vie, son caractère et ses idées avant 1857* (Paris, 1909), p. 103, writes: "A person who knew Mlle. Amélie Bosquet, Flaubert's correspondent, very intimately was recently telling me that when Mlle. Bosquet asked the novelist where he had found the character of Mme. Bovary, he apparently answered very clearly, and repeated several times: '*In myself! I* am Mme. Bovary!' ('Mme. Bovary, *c'est moi!—D'après moi!*')"

[10] *Jack:* a novel by Alphonse Daudet (1876). Zola's *Son Excellence Rougon* had just been published.

really put my foot in it, for from another point of view Art must be down to earth. Or rather, Art is whatever we can make it: we are not free. Everyone follows his own path, in spite of his own will. In short, your Cruchard doesn't have a single solid idea in his head.

Contemporary
Views

CONTEMPORARY VIEWS

Gustave Flaubert*
by Emile Zola

My first visits to Flaubert were a great disillusionment, almost an ordeal. I arrived with a complete image of Flaubert already in my head, an image based on his work of a Flaubert who was the pioneer of the century, the portrayer and philosopher of our modern world. I saw him as clearing a new path, founding an orderly state in the province conquered by romanticism, marching into the future with strength and confidence. In short, I went expecting to find the man of his books, and I encountered a shameless joker, a paradoxical thinker, an impenitent romantic who made my head spin for hours with a deluge of astonishing theories. . . .

For example, how could anybody listen without surprise to what he said about *Madame Bovary?* He swore that he had written this book only to "annoy" the realists, Champfleury and his friends; he wanted to show them that it was possible to be at the same time an accurate portrayer of the modern world and a great stylist. And this was said so straightforwardly that you found yourself wondering whether he had been aware of his achievement, whether he had foreseen the evolution it was going to produce in literature. To tell the truth, today I doubt it; many creative geniuses are like this, they are unaware of the new era that they bring about. All his theories contradicted the doctrine that we, his juniors, had found in *Madame Bovary*.

---

* From *Les Romanciers naturalistes* (1881). Translated by Helen Weaver. [Footnotes added by the Editor.]

Thus, he would declare in his thundering voice that there is no such thing as the modern, that there were no modern subjects; and when, dismayed by this statement, we urged him to explain what he meant, he would add that Homer was just as modern as Balzac. If he had said human, we would have understood each other; but modern remained unacceptable. Furthermore, he seemed to deny evolutions in literature. I argued twenty times with him on this subject without being able to make him admit, even when confronted by the evidence, that writers do not appear as isolated phenomena; they influence each other, they form a chain which brings about certain developments, according to the climate of the times. He, like the fanatical individualist he was, would shout outrageous things at me: that he didn't give a damn (substitute another word), that it was all nonsense, that every writer was independent, that society had nothing to do with literature, that you had to write in a beautiful style, and that was all. Naturally, I agreed that it would be idiotic to try to found a school; but I added that schools arise spontaneously and that we might as well accept them. But this disagreement continued between us right to the end; no doubt he thought I would like to impose rules on temperament, whereas I was simply performing one of the tasks of criticism, by ascertaining the periods which had developed in the past and which continue to develop before our eyes. When he became infuriated by labels, by *isms*, I would answer that we have to have words to take note of facts; indeed, often these words are invented and circulated by the public, which needs to make sense of the artistic productions of its time. In short, we agreed on the free development of originality, we had the same philosophy and the same aesthetic, the same likes and dislikes in literature; our disagreement appeared only if I tried to push him further by tracing the writer back to the group, by trying to find out where our literature came from and where it was going.

If I am not very clear on this subject, it is because to tell the truth I have never fully understood the overall scheme of his ideas on literature. They impressed me as very disconnected, they would suddenly appear in the conversation with a paradoxical rigidity and a stentorian brilliance, usually full of contradictions and surprises. Perhaps I was guilty of wanting to make too logical a connection between the thinker and the writer in Flaubert. I would have wished the author of *Madame Bovary* to like the modern world, I would have wished him to be aware of the trend of which he was one of the most powerful agents; and it distressed me to find instead a romantic who "railed" against railroads, newspapers, and democracy, an individualist for whom the writer was an absolute, a mere phenomenon of rhetoric. The day of our terrible argument on Chateaubriand, as he was maintaining that in literature all that mattered was the well-made sentence, I infuriated him by saying, "There is something else besides well-made sentences in *Madame Bovary,* and it is because of this something else that the book will live. You can say what you like, the fact remains that you dealt romanticism its first blow." Well, he screamed that *Madame Bovary* was s - - -, that people were driving him mad with that book, that he would gladly exchange it for one sentence by Chateaubriand or Hugo. He absolutely refused to see anything other than literature in the novels of others and even in his own; he denied that they had anything to do with, I won't say the progress of ideas, but even with the history of ideas; beautiful language, nothing more. And his individualism, his horror of groups, sprang from an enormous pride. One of his favorite comments, when someone explained his principles in a preface and allied himself with some movement or other, was "Come now, have more pride!" To make correct and superb sentences, and to make them in his own corner, like a monk who dedicates his entire life to his task: such was his literary ideal.

I mentioned his hatred for the modern world. This hatred burst out in everything he said. He had acquired it during his intimacy with Théophile Gautier; for last year when I read the volume of reminiscences published by M. Bergerat[1] on his father-in-law, I was amazed to find the Flaubert I knew in the inexhaustible paradoxes of the author of *Mademoiselle de Maupin.*[2] Here was the same love for the East, the passion for travel, far from this loathsome Paris, so bourgeois and confining. Flaubert used to say that he was born to live down there, in a tent: the smell of coffee gave him hallucinations of caravans on the march; he ate the vilest dishes religiously, provided they had beautiful, exotic-sounding names. Here were the same diatribes against all our inventions; the mere sight of a machine threw him into a rage, a fit of nervous revulsion.

---

[1] The prolific writer Emile Bergerat (1845-1923) had married Gautier's second daughter.
[2] A novel by Gautier, published in 1835.

To be sure, he took the train to go to Rouen, only to save time, he said; but he grumbled incessantly throughout the trip. Here, too, were the same contempt for the new manners and the new arts, a continual regret for the old France, to use his expression, a kind of self-imposed blindness to the future and a veiled fear of it; to hear him talk, there would be no tomorrow, we were walking toward a bottomless abyss; and when I would state my belief in the twentieth century, when I would say that our vast scientific and social movement was destined to lead to a flowering of humanity, he would look at me fixedly with his large blue eyes and shrug his shoulders. Ultimately these were general questions which did not concern him; he preferred to confine himself to literary technique. But above all he reserved his fits of rage for the press; the hullabaloo of the newspapers, their self-importance, the nonsense they inevitably print in the haste with which they are issued, provoked him to fury. He talked about abolishing them all at once. He was particularly wounded by the details they sometimes gave about his personal life. He found this unseemly, he said that the writer alone belonged to the public. I was very badly received one day when I ventured to tell him that, after all, the critic who concerned himself with the way he dressed and ate was doing for him the same work of analysis that he, as a novelist, did for the characters whose appearance he observed in life. This logic upset him terribly, never would he agree that everything is related and that the press is the little sister, very badly groomed if you will, of *Madame Bovary*. And yet this ferocious man who talked about hanging all journalists was moved to tears when the meanest pen-pusher wrote a squib about him. He found him talented, he carried the clipping around in his pocket. . . .

This charming simplicity sprang from a total lack of critical faculty. Make no mistake, he was a very good judge of his own work, and he had a very wide erudition; but in his opinions of others he lacked a sense of proportion, his gullibility led him to singular indulgences, whereas his stubborn insistence on never generalizing, on ignoring the history of ideas, plunged him into the severities of a pure rhetorician. Thus he sometimes expressed enthusiasms which surprised us, especially since he could be revoltingly unfair in the case of talents with which he was out of sympathy. . . . Add that when he became aroused in an argument, he reached the point where he denied everything that was not style; and then he would make statements that dismayed us: the characters did not exist in a book, truth was a joke, notes were of no use at all, a single well-made sentence was enough to make a man immortal; words that were all the more disturbing because he recognized that he himself was foolish enough to waste his time collecting documents and to want to people his books only with accurate and living characters. What a strange and profound mystery, the author of *Madame Bovary* and *Sentimental Education* despising life, despising the truth, and ending by killing himself in a more and more tormented obsession with the perfection of style! This will help to explain his literary infatuations and aversions. He knew by heart sentences of Chateaubriand and Victor Hugo which he would declaim with extraordinary vehemence. Goncourt used to say with a laugh that advertisements, delivered in this tone, would have sounded sublime. And Flaubert insisted on his sentences, in his eyes all of Chateaubriand and all of Hugo were there. Naturally, for the same reasons, he held Mérimée in low esteem, and he loathed Stendhal. He called the latter Monsieur Beyle, the way he called Musset Monsieur de Musset. For him, the poet was merely an amateur who had had the bad taste to mock the language and to abandon prosody. As for Stendhal, was he not that arrogant wit who had boasted that he read a page of the Code[3] every morning to get the right tone? We knew this great psychologist, to use M. Taine's[4] expression, to be so antipathetic to Flaubert that we avoided even pronouncing his name. I shall add here that it became very difficult to have a discussion with Flaubert when you did not agree with him; for he did not debate calmly, like a man who has arguments to present and who consents to listen to those of his adversary in order to be informed; he proceeded by means of violent declarations and lost his temper almost immediately if you did not give in to him. So, to keep from upsetting him, to spare him the risk of an attack, we either agreed with him or held our tongues. It was absolutely futile to try to convince him.

Fortunately, along with the impeccable stylist, the rhetorician obsessed with perfection, there is a philosopher in Flaubert. He is the most sweeping negator that we have had in our literature. He professes the true nihilism—an *ism* that would

---

[3] The *Code Civil*, the document which embodies the private law of France, promulgated by Napoleon I in 1804.

[4] Hippolyte Adolphe Taine (1828-93): French critic and historian whose ideas became the theoretical basis for the naturalistic school.

have thrown him into a rage; he did not write a page in which he did not deepen our sense of nothingness. The strangest part is, I repeat, that this portrayer of human failure, this bitter sceptic, was at bottom so tender-hearted and naive a man. One would be greatly mistaken if one imagined him as a Jeremiah lamenting the perennial corruption of the world. Among his intimates he rarely raised these questions; he sometimes cursed the minor miseries of existence, but without lyricism. A good man, that's how to describe him. His very special brand of humor would also require study. Stupidity held a kind of fascination for him. When he had discovered a document of consummate folly it was a glorious event for him, he talked about it for weeks. I remember his having procured a collection of verses written solely by doctors; he forced us to listen to selections, which he read in his most resounding voice, and he was astonished when we did not join in his uproarious laughter. One day he remarked sadly, "It's strange, I now laugh at things that nobody else laughs at." At Croisset, he had a strange collection of the official reports of rural policemen, excerpts from unusual trials, childish and stupid pictures, all the evidence of human imbecility that he had been able to find. Note that his books are all there, that he has never done anything but study this imbecility, even in the splendid visions of *The Temptation of Saint Anthony*. He simply flung his admirable style over human folly, and I mean the lowest, the most vulgar, with occasional vistas of the wounded poet. His humor is not the fine wit of the last century, the sly and malicious laugh, the jab that stings; but a humor that goes back to the sixteenth century, whose blood is thicker and whose touch heavier, good-natured and brutal at the same time, leaving a wound. This also explains his lack of success in the drawing room and with women. People found his humor crude, like that of a traveling salesman. In private he was terrible when he dropped his formality.

*

*   *

When he set himself to write, he began by rather rapidly writing a passage, a whole episode, five or six pages at the most. Sometimes, when a word would not come, he would leave the space blank. Then he would attack the passage again; and there would follow two or three weeks, sometimes more, of intense work on those five or six pages. He wanted them perfect, and I assure you that his perfection did not come easily. He weighed every word, examining not only the sense, but the structure. Avoiding repetitions, rhymes, roughness—that was just the coarse part of the job. He reached the point where he did not want the same syllables to occur in a sentence; often one letter exasperated him, he tried to find words in which it did not appear; or else he needed a certain number of *r's* to make the period roll. He did not write for the eye, for the reader who reads silently to himself by the fireside; he wrote for the reader who declaims, who pronounces the sentences in a loud voice; indeed, this is the key to his whole working method. To test his sentences he would "bellow" them, alone at his desk, and he was not satisfied with them until they had come out of his mouth with the sound he wanted them to have. At Croisset this method was well known, the servants had been ordered not to disturb themselves when they heard Monsieur shouting; however, local citizens would stop on the road out of curiosity, and many called him "the lawyer," no doubt thinking that he was practicing oratory. Nothing, in my opinion, is more characteristic than this need for harmony. One does not know Flaubert's style until one has "bellowed" his sentences the way he did. It is a style made to be declaimed. When this is done, the sonorousness of the words, the sweep of the rhythm give an amazing power to the idea, sometimes by lyrical amplification, sometimes by comic opposition. For instance, he excelled in describing idiots with an organ roll that overwhelmed them.

I cannot here give even an idea of his meticulousness in regard to style. One would have to deal with language on a microscopic level. Punctuation was a matter of major importance. He wanted movement, color, music, and all this by means of those dead words in the dictionary which he had to bring to life. And yet he was not a grammarian, for he was not above using a word incorrectly when it made a sentence denser and more thunderous. Moreover, he moved further every day in the direction of economy, of the definitive word, for perfection is the enemy of abundance. I often thought, without telling him so, that he was carrying on the work of Bolieau[5] on the language of romanticism, encumbered as it was with new expressions and new constructions. He castrated

---

[5] Nicolas Boileau-Despréaux (1636-1711): literary critic and poet, one of the principal spokesmen of seventeenth-century classicism, revered as a literary lawgiver.

himself, he sterilized himself, he ended by being afraid of words, turning them a hundred ways, rejecting them when they did not enter into his idea on his page. . . .

When he was at his desk, looking at a page of first draft, he would hold his head in his hands and stare at the page for minutes on end as if he had mesmerized it. He would drop his pen, he would not speak, but remain absorbed, lost in the search for an elusive word or a construction whose mechanism escaped him. Turgenev, who had seen him this way, said that it was touching. And he must not be disturbed, and he had the patience of an angel, he who was ordinarily so impatient. He was very gentle in the presence of the language, he did not swear, but waited until it was good enough to accommodate him. He said that he had spent months searching for certain words. . . .

I shall quote another sentence which Flaubert wrote recently to a friend: "I have admired Balzac very much, but the desire for perfection has gradually separated me from him." Here is the essence of Flaubert. I am just collecting notes here, I am not discussing a literary theory. But I would like to add that this desire for perfection was, in the novelist, a real sickness which exhausted and immobilized him. If we follow him carefully, from this point of view, from *Madame Bovary* to *Bouvard et Pécuchet,* we shall see him gradually become preoccupied with form, reduce his vocabulary, dedicate himself more and more to method, increasingly limit the humanity of his characters. To be sure, this endowed French literature with perfect masterpieces. But it was sad to see this powerful talent relive the ancient fable of the nymphs who were changed to stone. Slowly, from the legs to the waist, then to the head, Flaubert turned to marble.

Essay on Gustave Flaubert*
by Guy de Maupassant

When *Madame Bovary* appeared, the public, accustomed to the unctuous sweetness of fashionable novels, as well as to

---

* From an essay written for the Quantin edition of Flaubert's work, published in 1885; reprinted in the Conrad edition. Translated by Helen Weaver. [Footnotes added by the Editor.]

the improbabilities of novels of adventure, classified the new writer among the realists. This is a gross error and a total absurdity. Gustave Flaubert was no more a realist because he was a careful observer of life than M. Cherbuliez[1] is an idealist because he is a poor one.

A realist is a writer who concerns himself with the bald fact alone without understanding its relative importance or noting its repercussions. For Gustave Flaubert, a fact by itself signified nothing. He explains himself as follows in one of his letters:

> . . . You can complain that the events are not varied: that is the complaint of a realist, and anyway, what do you know about it? One must examine them more closely. Have you ever believed in the existence of things? Is not everything an illusion? The only truth is in relationships, that is, in the way in which we perceive objects.

Even so, no observer was more conscientious; but none tried harder to understand the causes which bring about the effects.

His work method, his artistic method relied much more on penetration than on observation.

Instead of expounding the psychology of his characters in explanatory dissertations, he simply showed it by their actions. Thus the interior was revealed by the exterior, without any psychological argumentation.

First he imagined types: then, proceeding by deduction, he made these persons perform those characteristic actions which they must inevitably perform with an absolute logic, given their temperaments.

Thus the life which he studied so scrupulously served him merely as information.

Never does he announce events; while reading him, one would swear that the facts themselves come forward to speak, so much importance does he attach to the tangible appearance of people and things.

It was this rare quality of theatrical director, of impassive conjurer, which caused him to be labeled a realist by super-

---

[1] Victor Cherbuliez (1829-1899): witty, cosmopolitan novelist, critic, aesthetician. Wrote for the *Revue des Deux Mondes,* to which he contributed much discussed political articles under the name of G. Valbert. Elected to the Académie française in 1881.

ficial minds which cannot understand the profound meaning of a book unless it is expounded in philosophical terms.

He was greatly irritated by this epithet of realist which had been hung on him and claimed to have written his *Bovary* only out of hatred for the school of M. Champfleury.[2]

In spite of his great friendship for Emile Zola and his great admiration for his powerful talent which he described as genius, he did not forgive him for his *naturalism*.

One need only read *Madame Bovary* intelligently to realize that nothing could be further from realism.

The method of the realistic writer consists simply in recounting actions that have taken place and have been performed by ordinary characters whom he has known and observed.

In *Madame Bovary*, each character is a type, that is, the essence of a series of persons belonging to the same intellectual order.

The country doctor, the dreamy provincial woman, the pharmacist, a kind of Prudhomme,[3] the priest, the lovers, and even all the minor figures are types, endowed with a three-dimensionality that is all the more effective because in them the writer has distilled quantities of related observations, and all the more lifelike because they represent the most typical examples of their class.

But Gustave Flaubert had grown up during the height of the romantic movement; he had been weaned on the ringing phrases of Chateaubriand and Victor Hugo, and he felt in his heart a lyrical impulse which could not find adequate outlet in precise books like *Madame Bovary*.

Here is one of the most unusual aspects of this great man: this innovator, this discoverer, this pioneer was, until his death, under the dominant influence of romanticism. It was almost in spite of himself, almost unconsciously, driven by the irresistible force of his genius, by the creative force locked inside of him, that he wrote these novels so new in manner, so personal in tone. His own preference was for epic subjects which unfold in song-like forms similar to operatic tableaus.

---

[2] Pseudonym of Jules Husson (1821-1889): novelist, critic, author of scholarly studies on ceramics, best known as head of the realistic school in France.

[3] Joseph Prudhomme: a character in the works of Henri Monnier (1805-1872). Came to be referred to as an exemplary figure of self-satisfied bourgeois mediocrity.

Indeed, the language of *Madame Bovary*, like that of the *Sentimental Education*, though forced to render common things, often has flights, resonances, tones above the subjects it expresses. It soars, as if tired of being contained, of serving this dullness, and to express the stupidity of Homais or the foolishness of Emma, it becomes stately or brilliant, as if it were translating the motifs of poetry.

*

*   *

He had a conception of style which embraced all the qualities that constitute both a thinker and a writer. And when he declared, "There is nothing but style," we must not think that he meant, "There is nothing but the sound or the harmony of the words."

"Style" is generally understood as the manner of presenting his thought peculiar to a given writer. By this definition, style differs according to the man—dazzling or restrained, rich or concise, depending on his temperament. Gustave Flaubert believed that the personality of the author must vanish into the originality of the book and that the originality of the book must never arise from the peculiarity of its style.

For he did not think of "styles" as a series of individual moulds each of which carries the mark of a writer and into which all his ideas are poured; he believed in *style*, that is, in a unique, absolute manner of expressing a thing in all its color and intensity.

For him, form was the work itself. Just as, in human beings, the blood nourishes the flesh and even determines its shape, its outward appearance, according to race and family, so, for him, in the work of art the material inevitably imposes the unique and right expression, the measure, the rhythm, all the elements of form.

He could not conceive that content could exist without form, or form without content.

Style should therefore be impersonal, so to speak, and should derive its qualities only from the quality of the thought and the power of the vision.

Obsessed by this absolute belief that there exists only one way of expressing a thing, one noun to name it, one adjective to qualify it and one verb to set it in motion, he engaged in a superhuman labor in order to discover for each sentence that noun, that epithet, and that verb. Thus he believed in a mysterious harmony of language, and when a suitable term did not seem to him euphonious, he searched for another with an unconquerable patience, certain that he did not have the true, the unique word.

Gustave Flaubert*
by Henry James

. . . *Madame Bovary* has a perfection that not only stamps it, but that makes it stand almost alone; it holds itself with such a supreme unapproachable assurance as both excites and defies judgment. For it deals not in the least, as to unapproachability, with things exalted or refined; it only confers on its sufficiently vulgar elements of exhibition a final unsurpassable form. The form is in *itself* as interesting, as active, as much of the essence of the subject as the idea, and yet so close is its fit and so inseparable its life that we catch it at no moment on any errand of its own. That verily is to *be* interesting—all round; that is to be genuine and whole. The work is a classic because the thing, such as it is, is ideally *done,* and because it shows that in such doing eternal beauty may dwell. A pretty young woman who lives, socially and morally speaking, in a hole, and who is ignorant, foolish, flimsy, unhappy, takes a pair of lovers by whom she is successively deserted; in the midst of the bewilderment of which, giving up her husband and her child, letting everything go, she sinks deeper into duplicity, debt, despair, and arrives on the spot, on the small scene itself of her poor depravities, at a pitiful tragic end. In especial she does these things while remaining absorbed in romantic intention and vision, and she remains absorbed in romantic intention and vision while fairly rolling in the dust. That is the triumph of the book as the triumph stands, that Emma interests us by the nature of her consciousness and the play of her mind, thanks to the reality and beauty with which those sources are invested. It is not only that they represent *her* state; they are so true, so observed and felt, and especially so shown, that they represent the state, actual or potential, of all persons like her, persons romantically determined. Then

* From *Notes on Novelists, With Some Other Notes,* New York: Charles Scribner's Sons, 1914.

sensibility, Flaubert's treatment is like that of other realists. But where the fantasy of *Don Quixote* took the form of a vanishing heroism, which the heroine did not jeopardize with her presence, the feminine outlook of *Madame Bovary* is consistently belied by its masculine characters. Where romance, to Cervantes, signified knightly adventure, to Flaubert—more narrowly and intensively—it signifies passionate love. The means of exposure, which put Cervantes' realism on a solid and genial basis, was an appeal to the common sense of the bourgeoisie. That would have been, for Flaubert, almost as evanescent and fantastic as romanticism itself. Hence he often seems to have taken the realistic method and turned it inside out. "Realism seems to me with *Madame Bovary* to have said its last word," commented Henry James, with a sigh of somewhat premature relief.

In sharpest contradistinction to Don Quixote, whose vagaries were intellectual, Emma Bovary's are emotional. Hence they are counterweighted by no earthbound Sancho Panza, but by the intellectually pretentious M. Homais. The comic relief that he injects into Emma's tragedy is later to be elaborated into the unrelieved comedy of *Bouvard and Pécuchet*. Because it is herself that she misconceives, where Don Quixote's misconception of actuality could be corrected by reference to his fellow-men, she remains incorrigibly tragic. This narcissistic attitude of Emma's, this self-hallucination induced by over-reading, this "habit of conceiving ourselves otherwise than as we are," is so epidemic that Jules de Gaultier[2] could diagnose the weakness of the modern mind as *Bovarysme*. The vicarious lives that film stars lead for shopgirls, the fictive euphoria that slogans promise and advertisements promote, the imaginary flourishes that supplement daily existence for all of us, are equally Bovaristic. If to Bovarize is simply to daydream, as everyone does to a greater or lesser extent, its criterion is not how much but whether our daydreams are egoistic like Emma's or altruistic like Don Quixote's. Every epoch depends upon some verbal medium for its conception of itself: on printed words and private fictions, if not on public rituals and collective myths. The trouble came when, instead of the imitation of Christ or the venera-

---

[2] French essayist whose book entitled *Le Bovarysme* was published in 1892.

tion of Mary, readers practised the emulation of Rastignac[3]
or the cult of Lélia. Yet, whatever their models, they roman-
ticized a reality which would otherwise have been formless and
colorless; for when nature has established norms of conduct,
art is called upon to publicize them. "There are people who
would not fall in love if they had never heard of love," said
La Rochefoucauld. Denis de Rougemont[4] has more recently
tried to substantiate that epigram by arguing that the erotic
motive was superimposed upon the West through medieval
romance. And Paolo might never have loved Francesca, in
Dante's memorable episode, had not the book of Galeotto
acted as a go-between.

But the writer, unlike the reader, cannot afford to be swept
off his feet by emotions involved in his story. Thus Flaubert,
in his first *Sentimental Education*, describes the youthful reading of his poet, Jules:

> He reread *René* and *Werther* and was disgusted with
> life; he reread Byron and dreamed of the solitude of his
> great-souled heroes; but too much of his admiration was
> based on personal sympathy, which has nothing in com-
> mon with the disinterested admiration of the true artist.
> The last word in this kind of criticism, its most inane ex-
> pression, is supplied to us every day by a number of
> worthy gentlemen and charming ladies interested in litera-
> ture, who disapprove of this character because he is crude,
> of that situation because it is equivocal and rather smutty
> —discovering, in the last analysis, that in the place of
> such a person they would not have done the same thing,
> without understanding the necessary laws that preside
> over a work of art, or the logical deductions that follow
> from an idea.

It follows that Emma Bovary and her censors, though their
ethics differed, shared the same aesthetic approach. Jules on
the other hand would learn, as did Flaubert, to differentiate a
work of art from its subject matter and the artist from his
protagonist. The anecdote of Cervantes on his deathbed, iden-
tifying himself with his hero, has its much quoted Flaubertian
parallel: *Madame Bovary c'est moi*. But this equivocal state-

---

[3] One of the principal characters in Balzac's *Comédie humaine*.
[4] In *Love and the Western World*.

ment was not so much a confession as a cautious disclaimer
of certain resemblances which Madame Delamare's neighbors,
without indulging in unwarranted gossip, might have suspected. In so far as Flaubert lived the part, as any novelist
enters into his fully realized characterizations, it was a *tour
de force* of female impersonation. The identification was not
nearly so close as it had been with Saint Anthony or would
become with Frédéric Moreau. It is true that, on summer days,
he worked in the arbor where he stages trysts between Emma
and Rodolphe; that the cigar case, the seal inscribed *Amor
nel cor*, and other relics actually commemorate his own affair
with Louise Colet; that Louise may well have suggested aspects
of Emma, and Emma's husband and lovers may have embodied aspects of Gustave. But the very first premise of the
book was the suppression of his own personality, and his later
pronouncements adhere with stiffening conviction to the principle of *ne s'écrire*.[5] Empathy is seasoned with antipathy whenever he writes about Emma to Louise; he repeatedly complains
that the bourgeois vulgarity of his material disgusts and nause-
ates him. He would much prefer to write a book without a
subject; or rather, he would like to abolish the transitions and
obstacles between thought and expression, and he prophesies
that literary convention, like the Marxian concept of the state,
will some day wither away.

Flaubert had chosen the theme of the *Temptation of Saint
Anthony* in accordance with his personal predilections. Baudelaire, who preferred the more imaginative work, explained
Madame Bovary as a sort of wager. "The budding novelist
found himself facing an absolutely worn-out society—worse
than worn-out, brutal and greedy, fearing nothing but fiction
and loving nothing but property." Deliberately choosing the
drabbest setting, the pettiest characters, the most familiar plot,
he undertook to create a masterpiece out of them: to turn
their shapeless ugliness into formal beauty. He did not quite
succeed in assimilating the psychology of his heroine, according to Baudelaire: "Madame Bovary has remained a man."
Now it may be—it is, in fact, Dorothy Richardson's hypothesis
—that no masculine novelist can ever quite penetrate the
feminine mind. Nevertheless, as Matthew Arnold perceived,
Tolstoy's portrayal of Anna Karenina could be more warmly
sympathetic than the "petrified feeling" that went into Flau-

---

[5] Not writing about oneself.

bert's portraiture. In attaching his narrative to his heroine,
Flaubert was detaching himself from those whom she repudiated and from those who repudiated her. Thereby he ostensibly
gave up, to the indignation of his critics, the moralistic preroga-
tives of the narrator. He replaced sentiment, so Brunetière[6]
charged, with sensation. He developed the technical device
that handbooks term "point of view" by adapting the rhythms
of his style to the movement of his character's thoughts. By
limiting what has more precisely been termed the "centre of
consciousness" to the orbit of a single character—and, with
Henry James, a peculiarly limited character—purists could
intensify the focus of the novel still further. *Madame Bovary*
begins, prologue-wise, in the first person; then it switches from
an anonymous classmate to Charles Bovary; through his eyes
we first glimpse Emma's fingernails and gradually experience
his delayed reaction; thereafter the action is mainly, though
by no means exclusively, circumscribed within her range
of perception. But towards the end the perspective opens up
and detaches itself from Emma more and more; her pantomime interview with the tax collector is reported as wit-
nessed by a chorus of townswomen; and Flaubert's account
of her funeral terminates with the various night-thoughts of
the men that have loved her.

And there are such moments as when, having escorted his
lovers into a curtained cab, Flaubert draws back a tactful
distance and projects a rapid sequence of long-range shots, so
that—instead of witnessing their embrace—we participate in
a tour of the city of Rouen, prolonged and accelerated to a
metaphorical climax. The invisible omnipresence that stage-
manages these arrangements is normally expressed by *on*,
initially by *nous*, but never by *je*. The author's commentary
is to be inferred from his almost cinematographic manipula-
tion of detail: the close-up of a religious statuette, for example, which falls from the moving-wagon into fragments on
the road between Tostes and Yonville. This comment is trans-
posed to a scientific key when, after the unsuccessful operation, Emma slams the door on Charles and breaks his barometer. Henceforth the incongruous memento of his failure is the
patent leather shoe attached to the artificial limb of his patient,
the no longer club-footed stableboy. A silly cap which characterizes Charles on his first appearance, a pocketknife which

---

[6] See selected bibliography.

betokens his coarseness in Emma's eyes—nothing is mentioned that does not help to carry the total burden of significance. Hence every object becomes, in its way, a symbol; and the novelist seeks not merely the right word but the right thing. Charles's first marriage is tellingly summed up by a bouquet of withered orange blossoms in a glass jar, while the handsome cigar case retains the aroma of fashionable masculinity that Emma has inhaled at the ball. Such effects are governed by a rigorous process of selection, far removed from the all-inclusiveness with which Balzac accumulated background. The atmosphere, for Flaubert, is the story; the province is both his setting and his subject—the colorlessness of local color. The midland that he describes is a bastard territory, somewhere along the borders of Normandy, Picardy, and Ile-de-France, where the speech has no accent, the landscape no character, the soil no richness. Even the cheese thereabouts is lacking in savor. Everything seems, like Charles's conversation, "as flat as a sidewalk."

To render flatness flatly, however, is to risk the stalemate that confronted Pope when he tried to excoriate dullness without being dull. Flaubert, deploying his full stylistic resources, relieves the ennui by colorful allusion and invidious comparison. What is literally boring he renders metaphorically interesting. The river quarter of Rouen, at first sight, is "a small, ignoble Venice." The names of famous surgeons are mock-heroically sounded in connection with Charles's professional activities. Similies, ironically beautiful, frequently serve to underline ugly realities: thus the pimples on the face of his first wife had "budded like spring." Occasionally Flaubert seems to set thousands of miles between himself and the situation at hand, as when—with anthropological objectivity—he notes the similarity between a statue of the Virgin in the village church and an idol from the Sandwich Islands. Despite his more usual closeness to his *dramatis personae*, he austerely dissociates himself from their subjective opinions, and italicizes certain expressions which their lack of fastidiousness has forced him to use. He manages to approximate their points of view, while retaining the detachment of the third person and avoiding the formality of indirect discourse, through his mastery of *le style indirect libre*. Though this term seems to have no English equivalent, it denotes a kind of grammatical figuration, a modulation of tenses, and a dropping of pronominal antecedents which, thanks primarily to Flaubert, are now employed in most of our novels and short stories. *"Elle aban-donna la musique, pourquoi jouer? qui l'entendrait?"*[7] Di-verging from Balzac, whose descriptions are like introductory stage directions, Flaubert introduces objects as they swim into the ken of his personages. His personages, since they are the fluid receptacles of sense-impressions, are much less numerous and more complex than the clear-cut types from the facile Balzacian mint. His technique of characterization, as he formu-lated it to Taine, was "not to individualize a generality like Hugo or Schiller, but to generalize a particularity like Goethe or Shakespeare."

He forwarded this large intention by deciding to portray a particular individual who also happened to be a universal type. She had actually existed in the ill-fated Madame Dela-mare; and, as Zola remarked, her sisters went on existing throughout France. Even while Flaubert was writing his novel, her misadventures were being enacted by the wife of his friend, the sculptor Pradier. Strangely enough, her fate was later paralleled by that of the novel's English translator, Eleanor Marx-Aveling. American readers recognize Emma's kinship with Carol Kennicott, the capricious wife of Sinclair Lewis's country doctor in *Main Street*, and are struck by re-current features of small-town existence which abridge the spatial and temporal intervals between Gopher Prairie and Yonville-l'Abbaye. Flaubert's preoccupation with his heroine's environment is emphasized by his subtitle, *Provincial Cus-toms*. His social observation, which of course is more precise and analytic than Balzac's, concentrates upon a much smaller terrain and thoroughly exhausts it. His fiction starts from and returns to fact: when he read in a newspaper the very phrase that he had put into his imaginary orator's mouth, he con-gratulated himself that literature was being reduced to an ex-act science at last. When *Madame Bovary* appeared, it was blandly saluted[8] by the critic Duranty as "a literary applica-tion of the calculus of probabilities." Though that is a far cry from any classical doctrine of probability, it looks beyond mere particularizing towards some meaningful pattern into which all the particulars must fit, a result which is predictable from the data, the logical deductions that follow from an idea. The concrete details that Flaubert selects, we have noticed,

---

[7] She gave up music. Why play? Who would listen?
[8] In the magazine *Réalisme*.

are always typical and often symbolic. We notice too his tendency to multiply the specific instance into a generalization. In his treatment of crowds, at the wedding or the exhibition, traits which were individually observed are collectively stated. Similarly, the plural is applied to immediate experiences which have become habitual, as in this summary of the doctor's routine:

> He ate omelets on farmhouse tables, poked his arm into damp beds, felt the warm spurts of blood-letting in his face, listened for death rattles, examined basins, turned over a good deal of dirty linen; but every evening he found a blazing fire, a laid-out table, comfortable chairs, and a well-dressed wife, so charming and sweet-smelling that it was hard to say whence the odor came, or whether her skin were not perfuming her chemise.

The second half of this highly Flaubertian sentence brings us home to Emma, balances the attractions of her day against the revulsions of Charles's, and registers the incompatibility of their respective ways of life. A sequence of vividly physical manifestations, ranging through the clinical towards the sensual, unfolds itself for us as it did for Charles. Strain is compensated by relaxation; pain and suffering give place to comfort and well-being; but, contrasted with the grim concreteness of his own sensations and the tangible solidity of his cases, there is something elusive and possibly deceptive in the person of Emma, which is vaguely hinted by her ambiguous perfume. More commonly we see the uxorious husband, from her vantage point, as the thick-skinned personification of plodding mediocrity: the medical man well suited to the village of Tostes, whose competence is strained by the town of Yonville. From his earliest entrance into the schoolroom he falters between the comic and the pathetic; his solitary youth and loveless first marriage prepare him for the ungrateful role of the cuckold; on his visit to the château he seems indeed to be playing the bourgeois gentleman. His very schoolmates have found him too unromantic, yet his love is the most devoted that Emma finds—as Flaubert expressly states in his worksheets, adding: "This must be made very clear." His own devotion to his motherless niece is doubtless reflected in Charles's tenderness towards his daughter, Berthe. In the final retrospect—the counterpart of that weary reunion which rounds out the *Sentimental Education*—Charles, over a bottle of beer with his wife's lover, Rodolphe, forgives him and blames the whole affair on "fatality." Rodolphe, though he has blamed fatality in his farewell letter to Emma, was scarcely a fatalist when he took the initiative; while Emma has enjoyed, as long as it lasted, the poetic illusion of liberty. Now that it has yielded to necessity, and the probable has become the inevitable, Charles is left to bear—and it kills him—the unpoetic truth.

The issue is poised between his materialistic plane, which is vulgar but real, and her ideal of refinement which is illusory. "Charles conjugal night: plans for his career. his child. Emma: dreams of travel. the lover. villa on the seashore. until dawn . . ." This bare notation was expanded by Flaubert into two of his most luminous pages—pages which reveal not only the nocturnal reveries of the doctor and his wife, her Italianate fancies and his Norman calculations, but the conflict within Flaubert's dual personality between lyricism and criticism—or, to use his synonym, "anatomy." To anatomize Emma's imagination is succinctly to recapitulate the romantic movement itself, moving from the primitive idyll of *Paul and Virginie* through the highly colored mysticism of Chateaubriand's *Spirit of Christianity* towards the vicarious passions of George Sand and Balzac. Emma's sentimental education, accompanied by the excitations of music and perfumed by the incense of religiosity, is traced back to the convent where she has been schooled. From the drab milieu she has known as a farmer's daughter, her extracurricular reading conjures up the allurements of escape: steeds and guitars, balconies and fountains, medieval and oriental vistas. Dreaming between the lines, she loses her identity in the heroines of the novels she peruses, the mistresses to whom verses are inscribed, the models in the fashion magazines. The ball at the Château lends a touch of reality to her fictitious world, which Flaubert likened —in a discarded metaphor—to "a drop of wine in a glass of water." When she discovers a kindred soul in the young law clerk Léon, the only person in the community who seems comparably sensitive to boredom and yearning and the arts, their friendship is "a continual traffic in books and romances." And when a neighboring landowner, the sportsman-philanderer Rodolphe, assists her to fulfill her sexual desires, fantasy and actuality seem to merge in the realization: "I have a lover!"

But adultery ends by reasserting "the platitudes of marriage," and neither condition teaches Emma the meaning of "the words that looked so fine in books: felicity, passion, and intoxication." Here, more explicitly than in *Don Quixote* itself, language is of the essence; the basic misunderstanding, since it is verbal, is regulated by the flow and ebb of Flaubert's prose; and his rhetoric is constantly expanding into purple passages which are trenchantly deflated by his irony. The resulting style, he feared, might read like "Balzac *chateaubrianisé.*" Yet if that compound means eloquent banality rather than banal eloquence, it is not too inept a summary of what Flaubert attempted and achieved; and those literary auspices are not inappropriate for the incongruity between Emma's high-flown sentiments and Charles's pedestrian bumblings. If we ever forgot that the book was about an ill-matched pair, we should be reminded by the way sentences double back upon themselves and episodes are paired off against each other. The two turning points of the first part, the fourth and eighth chapters, frame a significant contrast between the peasantry and the aristocracy. The garish colors of the rustic wedding, the fresh haircuts of the farmers, the lengthened communion dresses of the girls, the boisterous jokes and substantial viands in the manner of Brueghel, are pointedly offset by the grand entertainment at the Château de Vaubyessard, where the stately dancers show "the complexion of wealth, that fair complexion which is enhanced by the pallor of porcelain, the shimmer of satin, the veneer of fine furniture." In the second part a similar pairing occurs which even more fatally brings out the variance between Charles and Emma: the operation versus the opera. On the one hand his surgical incompetence, the gangrenescent cripple, and the amputated foot are portents of Emma's relapse. On the other the romantic libretto from Scott, the flamboyant tenor, and the dazzling spectacle would corrupt purer souls than hers—notably Natasha's in *War and Peace*.

The two antithetical strains are juxtaposed in the central chapters of the book, where the agricultural exhibition takes place in the public square while Rodolphe flirts with Emma in the privacy of the deserted neo-Greek town hall. His amorous pleas are counterpointed by the official slogans of the political orators outside; a prize for the highest quality of manure is awarded at the delicate moment when he grasps her hand; the bifurcation is so thoroughgoing that the national guard and the fire brigade refuse to march together; and the series of anticlimaxes culminates when nightfall brings a fizzle of dampened fireworks. Now Flaubert built up this scene by writing out continuous speeches for both sets of characters, which he thereupon broke down and rearranged within the larger framework of the situation. By such means he caught that interplay of cross-purposes which is increasingly stressed through the third and last part, above all in the cathedral and at the deathbed. He told Louise Colet that the method of *Madame Bovary* would be biographical rather than dramatic; yet biography seems to branch out into drama at all the crucial stages of Emma's career; and these in turn furnish the novel with its six or eight major scenes—several of which are overtly theatrical or, at any rate, ceremonial. Their relation to the rest of the book, and to his ambivalent purpose, may be gathered from his further remark that "dialogue should be written in the style of comedy, narrative in the style of epic." Mock-epic would probably be a more accurate clasisfication of Flaubert's tone, as differentiated from the various inflections he reproduces, and softened by lyrical interludes when he is Emma. The many contrasting strands of discourse are so closely interwoven that the texture is uniformly rich, although it varies from one chapter to the next. Each of them advances the narrative a single step, scores a new point and captures another mood, much as a well-turned short story does in the hands of Flaubert's recent emulators.

The chapter, as Flaubert utilizes it, is in itself a distinctive literary genre. Its opening is ordinarily a clear-cut designation of time or place. Its conclusion habitually entails some striking effect; a pertinent image, an epigrammatic twist, a rhetorical question, a poignant afterthought. "She had loved him after all." The succession of episodes, like the articulation of a rosary, shapes the continuity of the work. The three-part structure allows the novelist, with a classicism seldom encountered in novels, to give his conception a beginning, a middle and an end: to study first the conditions of Emma's marriage, then her Platonic romance and her carnal affair, and finally the train of consequences that leads to her death. Different leading men play opposite her, so to speak, in these three successive parts: Charles in the first, Rodolphe in the second, Léon in the third. The setting broadens with her aspirations, starting from the narrowest horizon, Tostes, proceeding to the main locale, Yonville, and ultimately reaching the provincial capital, Rouen. Not that she wished to stop there. "She wanted simultaneously to die and to live in Paris," Flaubert reminds us in a characteristic zeugma, and he seems to have toyed with the notion of granting that two-edged wish. But he wisely decided to confine her to the province, reserving his study of the metropolis for the fortunes of Frédéric Moreau. The chronology of *Madame Bovary*, which spans the decade from 1837 to 1847, roughly corresponds with the period of the *Sentimental Education*, stopping just short of the mid-century crisis. Each of its subdivisions, conforming to a rough but Dantesque symmetry, covers slightly more than three years. The pivotal date for the story is 1843, the year in which Emma commits adultery with Rodolphe. Up to that stage, her illusions mount with manic fervor; after that, with steady disillusionment, she sinks towards her last depression. It will be recalled, for what it may be worth, that Flaubert's own career pivoted around his personal crisis in 1843.

Between the autumn of 1851 and the spring of 1856 his concentrated labor was the writing of *Madame Bovary*. For those who hold—with André Gide—that the gestation of art is more interesting than the finished product, no record could be more fascinating than Flaubert's correspondence during those four and a half years. The parallel lives of the author and the heroine, daily, weekly, monthly, yearly, charge the novel with their emotional tension. Imaginative effort was reinforced by documentation when Flaubert sought the proper shading for Emma's hallucinations by immersing himself in *Keepsakes* and other feminine periodicals. By plying his brother with queries about surgery and toxicology, he filled in the peculiar symptoms his outline required: "Agony precise medical details 'on the morning of the twenty-third she had vomiting spells again . . .'" He familiarized himself with the children of his brain by drawing a map of Yonville and keeping files on its citizens. He controlled his plot—or should we say he calculated his probabilities?—by carefully drafting and firmly reworking scenarios. The embryonic material for his novel embodied 3600 pages of manuscript. The demiurgic function of reducing that mass to its present form might be likened to the cutting of a film, and—rather than speak of Flaubert's "composition" in the pictorial sense—we might refer, in kinetic terms, to montage. To watch him arranging his artful juxtapositions, or highlighting one detail and discarding another, is a lesson in artistic economy. To trace his revision of a single passage, sometimes through as many as twelve versions, is the hopeful stylist's *gradus ad Parnassum*. It is therefore a boon to students of literature that Flaubert's drafts and variants have been printed. But to reincorporate them into a composite text of *Madame Bovary*, interpolating what he excised, amplifying what he condensed, and thereby undoing much of what he did —as has latterly been done—is a doubtful service, to say the very least. Flaubert might have preferred Bowdlerization.

He did protest against expurgations when the novel was published serially in the *Revue de Paris;* but Du Camp and his fellow editors had not expurgated enough to appease the prudery of the imperial police; and Flaubert, together with the publisher and the printer, was prosecuted for outraging civic and religious morality. The outrage—so the prosecution alleged —was worse than pornography, it was blasphemy; Flaubert's offense was less a concern with sex than an attempt to link sex with religion. It mattered little that the linkage had been effected on the naive level of Emma's confused motivation; or that his analysis could be corroborated, by such sympathetic clerics as Bishop Dupanloup, from their first-hand remembrance of country confessionals. The ruse of citing passages out of context figured heavily in the trial, and the government staked much of its case on the passage where Emma receives extreme unction. It was a precarious example, since by definition this sacrament hovers ambiguously between the worlds of sense and spirit: shift the emphasis, as Joyce does in *Finnegans Wake*, and it becomes an apology for the flesh. Flaubert's defense, by warily refusing to admit the ambiguity, was able to claim the support of orthodox sanctions, along with the precedent of such diverse French writers as Bossuet and Sainte-Beuve. It argued that *Madame Bovary* as a whole, far from tempting its readers to sensualism, offered them an edifying object lesson. Considerable stress was laid *ad hominem* on the bourgeois respectability of the Flaubert family. Won by such arguments, the judge acquitted Flaubert and his accomplices, with a parting disquisition on taste and a fatherly warning against "a realism which would be the negation of the beautiful and the good." Six months later, when *Flowers of Evil* was condemned, Flaubert must have wondered whether he or Baudelaire was the victim of judicial error. Meanwhile, in April 1857, when *Madame Bovary* came out as a book, its intrinsic ironies were enhanced by a preliminary dedication to Flaubert's lawyer and an appended transcript of the court proceedings.

Great books have their proverbial fates, among which banning and burning may not be the hardest, since they involve straightforward conflicts of principle. It may be harder for the serious artist—be he Flaubert or Joyce—to emerge from the cloud of censorship into the glare of scandalous success. The public reception of Flaubert's first book, at all events, hardened those equivocal attitudes which had been poured into it. To avoid the accusation of immorality, he was pushed into the embarrassing position of a moralist. If the novel was not pornographic, it must be didactic—or had he stopped beating his wife? Taine spins an amusing anecdote of an English project to translate and circulate *Madame Bovary* as a Methodist tract, subtitled *The Consequences of Misbehaviour*. The respectable Lamartine, cited on Flaubert's behalf, declared that Emma's sins were too severely expiated. Why need Flaubert have been so much less merciful than Jesus was towards the woman taken in adultery? Partly because he was not exemplifying justice; partly because he may have been punishing himself; but mainly because her infractions of the seventh commandment were the incidental and ineffectual expression of an all-pervasive state of mind: Bovarism. Her nemesis, as Albert Thibaudet shrewdly perceived, is not a love affair but a business matter: her debt to the usurious merchant, Lheureux. When the bailiffs move in to attach the property, their inventory becomes a kind of autopsy. The household disintegrates before our eyes, as its component items are ticketed off, and we think of the auction in the *Sentimental Education*. This empty outcome—by the Flaubertian rule of opposites—is a sequel to the agricultural exhibition, where rural prosperity smugly dispenses its awards. And the lonely figure of Charles, left to brood among unpaid bills and faded love letters, has been foreshadowed by Père Rouault after Emma's wedding, "as sad as an unfurnished house."

The vacuum her absence creates for her father and husband echoes the hollowness of her own misapplied affections. Rodolphe's gallantry, after meeting her desires half way, proves to be no more than a cynical technique of seduction. Léon's sentimentalism is quite sincere, until she seduces him, and then it vanishes like growing pains. "Every notary bears within him the ruins of a poet." Consequently, amid the most prosaic circumstances, there will still be some spark of poetry, and in Yonville-l'Abbaye it is Emma Bovary. It is not, alas, the Princesse de Clèves,[9] nor could that model of all the compunctions have flourished there; for her delicacy presupposes reciprocal behavior on the part of others. Emma's dreams are destined, at the touch of reality, to wither into lies. Is that a critique of her or of reality? If she suffers for her mistakes, shall we infer that those who prosper are being rewarded for their merits? If we cannot, we can hardly assume—with the novel's apologists—that it preaches a self-evident moral. If it were a play our reactions would be clearer; we are more accustomed to facing her plight in the theatre; we disapprove of Hedda Gabler's[10] intrigues and pity the wistful Katerina in Ostrovsky's *Storm*. Though she possesses the qualities of both heroines, Emma is essentially a novelistic creation, set forth in all her internal complexities. Entrammeled by them, we cannot pretend to judge her, any more than we can judge ourselves. But, guided by Flaubert, perhaps we can understand her: *Madame Bovary c'est nous*. With her we look down from the town hall upon the exposition: a sordid rustic backdrop for Rodolphe's welcome advances. Again, at her rendezvous with Léon, the lovers occupy the foreground; but this time it is the massive cathedral of Rouen that looks down upon them; and its sculptured warriors and stained-glass saints, hastily passed by, are the mute upholders of higher standards than those which Emma and Léon are engaged in flouting. "Leave by the north portico, at any rate," the verger shouts after them, baffled by their indifference to Gothic antiquities, "and see the Resurrection, the Last Judgment, Paradise, King David, and the Condemned in Hellfire!"

The heavy judgment that Flaubert suspends, and which we too withhold, is implicit in this hurried exclamation. It affects the lovers as little as the extinct abbey affects Yonville, in whose name alone it survives. Yet oblique reference accomplishes what overt preaching would not, and those neglected works of art bear an ethical purport. The category of *moraliste,* which is more comprehensive with the French than with us, since *mœurs* comprehends both morals and manners, applies to Flaubert *malgré lui*. Whereas he seemed immoral to those who confused him with his characters, and seems amoral to those who take at face value an aloofness which

---

[9] The heroine of Madame de La Fayette's masterpiece, *La Princesse de Clèves* (1678).

[10] In Ibsen's play of that name (1890).

is his mask for strong emotions, he protested too much when he claimed to be impersonal. If he deserves Maupassant's adjective "impassive," it is because all passion has crystallized beneath the lucent surfaces of his prose. He is not above making sententious and aphoristic pronouncements upon the behavior of his characters: "A request for money is the most chilling and blighting of all the winds that blow against love." Nor does he shrink from stigmatizing Emma's acts as phases of "corruption" and even "prostitution." More positively he betrays his sympathy, when it seems most needed, by the adjective *pauvre*. The crippled groom is a "poor devil," and so is the blind man; the luckless Charles is "poor boy," and the gestures of Emma's agony are made by "her poor hands." The word regains its economic overtones, and Flaubert's tone is uniquely humanitarian, when he pauses before the "poor garments" of Catherine Leroux. The hands of this aged peasant woman, in definitive contrast to Emma, are deformed with toil. On the platform "before those expansive bourgeois," personifying "half a century of servitude," her mute and ascetic presence strikes the single note of genuine dignity amid the pomposities and hypocrisies of the agricultural exhibition. Flaubert deliberately classifies her with the attendant livestock, for whose impassivity he reserves his compassion. His irony intervenes to measure her reward—twenty-five francs for a lifetime of service—against two pigs which have just gained prizes of sixty francs apiece. An earlier and more cruel twist, which Flaubert finally left out, pictures her deaf apprehension that the judges are accusing her of stealing the twenty-five francs.

Here is Flaubert's response to those who criticize *Madame Bovary* for its apparent lack of positive values. The human qualities he really admired, the stoic virtues of patience, devotion, work, are not less admirable when they go unrewarded. His careful portrait of Catherine Leroux—together with many landscapes, small and subdued, of his fog-tinted Normandy—belongs with the canvases then being painted by Courbet at Ornans and Millet at Barbizon. Peasant faces, though never conspicuous, are always in the background; they watch Emma through the broken windowpanes of the Château. Animals, too, are sentient characters; her mysterious greyhound, Djali, is almost a demonic familiar. The people that Flaubert treats sympathetically are life's victims like the clubfooted Hippolyte: those whom Hugo would name *Les*

Misérables and Dostoevsky *The Insulted and the Injured*.
Surely the kindest person in the story is the druggist's errand
boy, Justin, whose dumb affection is the unwitting instrument
of Emma's death, and whose illicit reading matter is her
ironic epitaph: a book entitled *Conjugal Love*. The meek
do not inherit Flaubert's earth; the good, by definition, are
the ones that suffer; and the unhappy ending, for poor little
innocent Berthe, is grim child-labor in a textile factory. The
most downtrodden creature of all, the doglike Blind Man,
is linked by grotesque affinity with Emma herself. Conceiving him as a "monster," a *memento mori*, an incarnation
of fleshly frailty, Flaubert had originally planned to use an
armless and legless man; and accentuated Emma's disillusion
by the swish of the driver's whip that knocks the helpless
beggar off the coach. This, significantly, coincides with the
critical stroke that once laid Flaubert prostrate on a muddy
Norman road. His blind man dogs his heroine's footsteps
to her very deathbed, with a terrible mimicry which is not
unworthy of King Lear's fool; and there his unseasonable
song, a lyric from Restif de la Bretonne[11] about young
girls' dreams of love, finds its long awaited echo of rele-
vance. Emma's eyes open to a recognition scene "like a person waking from a dream," like Don Quixote when death
restores his aberrant sense of reality.

The counterpoint set up in the cathedral attains its fullest
resolution—far from the Hotel-de-Boulogne—in Emma's bed-
chamber. There priestly rites alleviate clinical symptoms; the
unction allays the poison; and, taking formal leave of her
five senses one by one, Flaubert breaks off his prolonged
sequence of associations between sacred and profane love.
In so far as orchestration is based on arrangement rather than
statement, Flaubert's can be best appreciated by comparing
this episode with a remotely analogous one from Dickens,
the famous sermon on the reiterated text: "Dear, gentle,
patient, noble Nell was dead." Flaubert, who evokes what
Dickens invokes and elaborates what the Englishman sim-
plifies, dismisses his heroine more abruptly and absolutely:
"She no longer existed." Thereafter Emma's deathwatch
unites "in the same human weakness" Father Bournisien,
with his holy water, and M. Homais, with his bottle of chlorine. Since religion is served by the priest as inadequately as

---

[11] An eighteenth-century follower of Rousseau.

science is by the pharmacist, it is not surprising that neither force has operated benignly on Emma's existence, or that the antagonists—as Bournisien predicts—"may end by understanding one another." Homais, the eternal quacksalver, is a would-be writer as well as a pseudo scientist, who practises the up-to-date art of journalism and is most adept at self-advertisement. Because his shop is the source of Emma's arsenic, he is an unconscious accomplice in her suicide; and he instigates the ill-advised surgery that poisons Hippolyte's leg and blackens Charles's reputation. When his own prescription, the antiphlogistic pomade, fails to cure the Blind Man's scrofula, it is typical of him to add insult to injury, persecuting his patient while continuing to pose as the benefactor of mankind. M. Homais is definitively shown up by the retarded arrival of Dr. Larivière, just as the introduction of Catherine Leroux is a standing rebuke to Emma's course of conduct. Hereupon Flaubert, inspired by memories of his father, dedicates a strongly affirmative paragraph to the understanding physician, who pursues the compassionate calling of medicine as religiously as a medieval saint. But the doctor is no god-in-the machine, and it is too late for an antidote. With a tear he immediately discerns the prognosis, and with a farewell pun he diagnoses the complaint of Homais. His difficulty is not *le sang* but *le sens*—neither anemia nor hypertension, nor indeed that lack of sense from which poor Emma suffered, but insensibility, the defect of her quality.

What is worse, the disease is contagious. With the rare exception of the stranger Larivière, and the dubious hope of agreement between the cleric and the anticlerical, nobody in Yonville seems to understand anybody else. And though collective misunderstanding is comic, failure to be understood is a personal tragedy. Though Emma, misunderstood by her husband and lovers and neighbors, misunderstands them and herself as well, at least she harbors a feeling of something missed; whereas the distinguishing mark of Homais is the bland assurance that he never misses anything. His Voltairean incantations, his hymns to progress, his faith in railroads and rubber, his fads and statistics, his optimism— a century afterwards—may seem as far-fetched as Emma's delusions of grandeur. His clichés, embedded like fossils in his newspaper articles, Flaubert was momentarily tempted to say, "would enable some future Cuvier of the moral sciences to reconstruct clearly all the ineptitude of the nineteenth-

century middle class, if that race were not indestructible."
Of that hardy breed M. Homais survives as our prime specimen. Neither a creation nor a discovery, he represents the
fine flower of the species that pervaded the *Comédie humaine,*
the ripe perfection of the philosophy whose accredited spokes-
man was M. Prudhomme.[12] This was enthusiastically at-
tested when Prudhomme's creator and actor, Henry Monnier,
sought permission to dramatize and enact Homais. The latter
is more successful in attaining their common ambition, the
decoration of the Legion of Honor; while his predecessor
must content himself, when the curtain falls, with "a decorated
son-in-law." The curtain-line of their spiritual relative, that
famous father-in-law, M. Poirier,[13] is his resolve to be "peer
of France in '48," a gesture which has meanwhile been
thwarted by the revolution. But the unabashed Homais goes
from strength to strength; the Empire will shower its ac-
colades on him and his brethren; and the dazzling glimpse
of him in his electric undervest is a veritable apotheosis.

When he equipped his bourgeois with a watchword, *"Il
faut marcher avec son siècle!"* Flaubert may have remembered his newly decorated friend, Maxime Du Camp, whose
Chants modernes were prefaced by a Whitmanesque declaration: *"Tout marche, tout grandit, tout s'augmente autour de
nous . . ."*[14] Any endeavor which aims to "keep pace with
one's century," as Flaubert realized better than his contemporaries, is bound to be outdistanced in the long run. He
took the province for his ground because it was an available
microcosm, because it exaggerated the ordinary, because its
dearth of color sharpened its outlines; but he did not assume
that provinciality was confined to the hinterland or, for that
matter, to any territory. M. Homais is historically, rather than
geographically, provincial. The habit of equating one's age
with the apogee of civilization, one's town with the hub or the
universe, one's horizons with the limits of human awareness,
is paradoxically widespread: it is just what Russian novelists
were attacking as *poshlost* or self-satisfied mediocrity. It is
what stands between Emma Bovary and the all-too-easily-sat-

---

[12] See note p. 342.
[13] A bourgeois whose daughter is married to an aristocrat in the
comedy *Le Gendre de Monsieur Poirier* (1884), by Augier and Sandeau.
[14] Everything is moving ahead, everything is growing, everything is
enlarging itself around us.

isfied citizens of Yonville. Her capacity for dissatisfaction, had she been a man and a genius, might have led to Rimbaldian adventures or Baudelairean visions: "Anywhere out of this world." As things stand, her retribution is a triumph for the community, a vindication of the bourgeoisie. Flaubert, who does not always conceal his tenderness towards those who suffer, now and then reveals his bitterness towards those whose kingdom is of this world. We cannot sympathize with the prosperous Homais as we could with Balzac's bankrupt César Birotteau; for, unlike his prototypes on the comic stage, Flaubert's druggist is not just a harmless busybody, a well-meaning figure of fun; he is the formidable embodiment of a deeply satirical perception which was adumbrated in *Le Garçon* and eventuates in *Bouvard and Pécuchet*. His Bovarism would be more illusive than Emma's, if the modern epoch did not conspire to support his bumptious ideology and to repay his flatteries with its honors. His *boutonnière*, like the one conferred on Tolstoy's Russian guardsman, symbolizes more than Napoleon intended—and less. For the symbol is an empty ornament, the badge of society's approval is meaningless, when it is unsupported by reality.

What, then, is real? Not the tawdry medal awarded to Catherine Leroux, but the lifelong service that earned it so many times over. And what is realism? Not the pathology of Emma's case, but the diagnostic insight of Larivière. Charles Bovary, for all his shortcomings, remains the great doctor's disciple, and retains the peasant virtues of his own patients; he is led astray by other motives than his own, by sentimentalism through Emma and pretentiouness through Homais. As the thrice-injured party, conjugally betrayed, professionally humiliated, financially ruined, Dr. Bovary is the neglected protagonist. If Emma is a victim of the situation, he is her victim, and her revenge against the situation is to undermine his way of life. The depths of his ignominy can be gauged by the idealized achievements of Dr. Benassis in Balzac's *Country Doctor*. Flaubert's ideal, though more honored in the breach than in the observance, fortifies him against those negative values which triumph in his book, and rises to an unwonted pitch of affirmation with the character sketch of Dr. Larivière: his disinterested skill, his paternal majesty, his kindness to the poor, his scorn for all decorations, his ability to see through falsehood. His most revealing epithet is *hospitalier,* since it connotes not only hospitality but Flaubert's birthplace, his father's hospital at Rouen, and also the stained-glass figure of Saint Julian the Hospitaler, whom the verger of the cathedral pointed out in an earlier draft, and who would later be Flaubert's knightly hero. The hospital and the cathedral: such, in retrospect, are the substance and the form of *Madame Bovary*. The attitude that embraces the distance between them, that comprehends both the painful actualities and the grandiose aspirations, and that can therefore make each paragraph comment dynamically upon itself, is Flaubertian irony. Irony dominates life, so Flaubert asserted by precept and example. So it does, particularly for those who are occupied with art as well as life, and unflinchingly face the problems of their interrelationship. Hence the irony of ironies: a novel which is at once cautionary and exemplary, a warning against other novels and a model for other novelists, a classical demonstration of what literature gives and what literature takes.

Realism in *Madame Bovary**
by Erich Auerbach

. . . In Flaubert realism becomes impartial, impersonal, and objective. In an earlier study, "Serious Imitation of Everyday Life," I analyzed a paragraph from *Madame Bovary* from this point of view, and will here, with slight changes and abridgements, reproduce the pages concerned, since they are in line with the present train of thought and since it is unlikely, in view of the time and place of their publication (Istanbul, 1937), that they have reached many readers. The paragraph concerned occurs in part 1, chapter 9, of *Madame Bovary*:

> Mais c'était surtout aux heures des repas qu'elle n'en pouvait plus, dans cette petite salle au rez-de-chaussée, avec le poêle qui fumait, la porte qui criait, les murs qui suintaient, les pavés humides; toute l'amertume de l'existence lui semblait servie sur son assiette, et, à la fumée du bouilli, il montait du fond de son âme comme d'autres bouffées d'affadissement. Charles était long à manger;

---

* From Erich Auerbach, *Mimesis: The Representation of Reality in Western Literature*, translated by W. R. Trask, Princeton: Princeton University Press, 1953. [Footnotes added by the Editor.]

*elle grignotait quelques noisettes, ou bien, appuyée du
coude, s'amusait, avec la pointe de son couteau, à faire
des raies sur la toile cirée.*

[But it was above all at mealtimes that she could bear
it no longer, in that little room on the ground floor, with
the smoking stove, the creaking door, the oozing walls,
the damp floor-tiles; all the bitterness of life seemed to be
served to her on her plate, and, with the steam from the
boiled beef, there rose from the depths of her soul other
exhalations as it were of disgust. Charles was a slow eater;
she would nibble a few hazelnuts, or else, leaning on her
elbow, would amuse herself making marks on the oilcloth with the point of her table-knife.]

The paragraph forms the climax of a presentation whose
subject is Emma Bovary's dissatisfaction with her life in
Tostes. She has long hoped for a sudden event which would
give a new turn to it—to her life without elegance, adventure,
and love, in the depths of the provinces, beside a mediocre
and boring husband; she has even made preparations for
such an event, has lavished care on herself and her house,
as if to earn that turn of fate, to be worthy of it; when it does
not come, she is seized with unrest and despair. All this
Flaubert describes in several pictures which portray Emma's
world as it now appears to her; its cheerlessness, unvarying-
ness, grayness, staleness, airlessness, and inescapability now
first become clearly apparent to her when she has no more
hope of fleeing from it. Our paragraph is the climax of the
portrayal of her despair. After it we are told how she lets everything in the house go, neglects herself, and begins to fall ill,
so that her husband decides to leave Tostes, thinking that the
climate does not agree with her.

The paragraph itself presents a picture—man and wife together at mealtime. But the picture is not presented in and for
itself; it is subordinated to the dominant subject, Emma's
despair. Hence it is not put before the reader directly: here
the two sit at table—there the reader stands watching them.
Instead, the reader first sees Emma, who has been much in
evidence in the preceding pages, and he sees the picture first
through her; directly, he sees only Emma's inner state; he sees
what goes on at the meal indirectly, from within her state, in
the light of her perception. The first words of the paragraph,
Mais c'était surtout aux heures des repas qu'elle n'en pouvait

plus . . . state the theme, and all that follows is but a development of it. Not only are the phrases dependent upon *dans* and *avec,* which define the physical scene, a commentary on *elle n'en pouvait plus* in their piling up of the individual elements of discomfort, but the following clause too, which tells of the distaste aroused in her by the food, accords with the principal purpose both in sense and rhythm. When we read further, *Charles était long à manger,* this, though grammatically a new sentence and rhythmically a new movement, is still only a resumption, a variation, of the principal theme; not until we come to the contrast between his leisurely eating and her disgust and to the nervous gestures of her despair, which are described immediately afterward, does the sentence acquire its true significance. The husband, unconcernedly eating, becomes ludicrous and almost ghastly; when Emma looks at him and sees him sitting there eating, he becomes the actual cause of the *elle n'en pouvait plus;* because everything else that arouses her desperation—the gloomy room, the commonplace food, the lack of a tablecloth, the hopelessness of it all—appears to her, and through her to the reader also, as something that is connected with him, that emanates from him, and that would be entirely different if he were different from what he is.

The situation, then, is not presented simply as a picture, but we are first given Emma and then the situation through her. It is not, however, a matter—as it is in many first-person novels and other later works of a similar type—of a simple representation of the content of Emma's consciousness, of *what* she feels *as* she feels it. Though the light which illuminates the picture proceeds from her, she is yet herself part of the picture, she is situated within it. In this she recalls the speaker in the scene from Petronius discussed in our second chapter; but the means Flaubert employs are different. Here it is not Emma who speaks, but the writer. *Le poêle qui fumait, la porte qui criait, les murs qui suintaient, les pavés humides*—all this, of course, Emma sees and feels, but she would not be able to sum it all up in this way. *Toute l'amertume de l'existence lui semblait servie sur son assiette*—she doubtless has such a feeling; but if she wanted to express it, it would not come out like that; she has neither the intelligence nor the cold candor of self-accounting necessary for such a formulation. To be sure, there is nothing of Flaubert's life in these words, but only Emma's; Flaubert does nothing but bestow the power of mature expression upon the material

which she affords, in its complete subjectivity. If Emma could
do this herself, she would no longer be what she is, she would
have outgrown herself and thereby saved herself. So she does
not simply see, but is herself seen as one seeing, and is thus
judged, simply through a plain description of her subjective
life, out of her own feelings. Reading in a later passage (part
2, chapter 12): *jamais Charles ne lui paraissait aussi dé-
sagréable, avoir le doigts aussi carrés, l'esprit aussi lourd, les
façons si communes . . . ,*[1] the reader perhaps thinks for a
moment that this strange series is an emotional piling up of the
causes that time and again bring Emma's aversion to her husband to the boiling point, and that she herself is, as it were,
inwardly speaking these words; that this, then, is an example
of *erlebte Rede*.[2] But this would be a mistake. We have here,
to be sure, a number of paradigmatic causes of Emma's aversion, but they are put together deliberately by the writer, not
emotionally by Emma. For Emma feels much more, and much
more confusedly; she sees other things than these—in his
body, his manners, his dress; memories mix in; meanwhile she
perhaps hears him speak, perhaps feels his hand, his breath,
sees him walk about, good-hearted, limited, unappetizing, and
unaware; she has countless confused impressions. The only
thing that is clearly defined is the result of all this, her aversion
to him, which she must hide. Flaubert transfers the clearness
of the impressions; he selects three, apparently quite at random, but which are paradigmatically taken from Bovary's
physique, his mentality, and his behavior; and he arranges
them as if they were three shocks which Emma felt one after
the other. This is not at all a naturalistic representation of
consciousness. Natural shocks occur quite differently. The
ordering hand of the writer is present here, deliberately sum-
ming up the confusion of the psychological situation in the
direction toward which it tends of itself—the direction of
"aversion to Charles Bovary." This ordering of the psychological situation does not, to be sure, derive its standards from
without, but from the material of the situation itself. It is
the type of ordering which must be employed if the situation
itself is to be translated into language without admixture.

In a comparison of this type of presentation with those of

---

[1] Never had Charles seemed to her so disagreeable, his fingers so
stubby, his mind so heavy, his manners so common.

[2] The language actually experienced and used by a speaker.

Stendhal and Balzac, it is to be observed by way of introduction that here too the two distinguishing characteristics of modern realism are to be found; here too real everyday occurrences in a low social stratum, the provincial petty bourgeoisie, are taken very seriously; here too everyday occurrences are accurately and profoundly set in a definite period of contemporary history (the period of the bourgeois monarchy)— less obviously than in Stendhal or Balzac, but unmistakably. In these two basic characteristics the three writers are as one, in contradiction to all earlier realism; but Flaubert's attitude toward his subject is entirely different. In Stendhal and Balzac we frequently and indeed almost constantly hear what the writer thinks of his characters and events; sometimes Balzac accompanies his narrative with a running commentary—emotional or ironic or ethical or historical or economic. We also very frequently hear what the characters themselves think and feel, and often in such a manner that, in the passage concerned, the writer identifies himself with the character. Both these things are almost wholly absent from Flaubert's work. His opinion of his characters and events remains unspoken; and when the characters express themselves it is never in such a manner that the writer identifies himself with their opinion, or seeks to make the reader identify himself with it. We hear the writer speak; but he expresses no opinion and makes no comment. His role is limited to selecting the events and translating them into language; and this is done in the conviction that every event, if one is able to express it purely and completely, interprets itself and the persons involved in it far better and more completely than any opinion or judgment appended to it could do. Upon this conviction—that is, upon a profound faith in the truth of language responsibly, candidly, and carefully employed—Flaubert's artistic practice rests.

This is a very old, classic French tradition. There is already something of it in Boileau's line concerning the power of the rightly used word (on Malherbe: *D'un mot mis en sa place enseigna le pouvoir*)[3]; there are similar statements in La Bruyère.[4] Vauvenargues[5] said: *Il n'y aurait point d'erreurs*

---

[3] See note page 14. In his *Art of Poetry*, Boileau praises the poet Malherbe for "putting the right word in the right place."

[4] La Bruyère (1645-96), a French classical writer, is the author of *Les Caractères.*

[5] Vauvenargues (1715-47), an eighteenth-century moralist, wrote *Maximes.*

qui ne périssent d'elles-mêmes, exprimées clairement.[6] Flaubert's faith in language goes further than Vauvenargues's; he believes that the truth of the phenomenal world is also revealed in linguistic expression. Flaubert is a man who works extremely consciously and possesses a critical comprehension of art to a degree uncommon even in France; hence there occur in his letters, particularly of the years 1852–1854 during which he was writing *Madame Bovary* (*Troisième Série* in the *Nouvelle édition augmentée* of the *Correspondance*, 1927), many highly informative statements on the subject of his aim in art. They lead to a theory—mystical in the last analysis, but in practice, like all true mysticism, based upon reason, experience, and discipline—of a self-forgetful absorption in the subjects of reality which transforms them ("by a marvelous chemical process") and permits them to develop to mature expression. In this fashion subjects completely fill the writer; he forgets himself, his heart no longer serves him save to feel the hearts of others, and when, by fanatical patience, this condition is achieved, the perfect expression, which at once entirely comprehends the momentary subject and impartially judges it, comes of itself; subjects are seen as God sees them, in their true essence. With all this there goes a view of the mixture of styles which proceeds from the same mystical-realistic insight: there are no high and low subjects; the universe is a work of art produced without any taking of sides, the realistic artist must imitate the procedures of Creation, and every subject in its essence contains, before God's eyes, both the serious and the comic, both dignity and vulgarity; if it is rightly and surely reproduced, the level of style which is proper to it will be rightly and surely found; there is no need either for a general theory of levels, in which subjects are arranged according to their dignity, or for any analyses by the writer commenting upon the subject, after its presentation, with a view to better comprehension and more accurate classification; all this must result from the presentation of the subject itself.

It is illuminating to note the contrast between such a view and the grandiloquent and ostentatious parading of the writer's own feelings, and of the standards derived from them, of the type inaugurated by Rousseau and continued after him; a com-

---

[6] There would be no errors that would not die of themselves, if they were clearly expressed.

parative interpretation of Flaubert's *Notre cœur ne doit être
bon qu'à sentir celui des autres*,[7] and Rousseau's statement at
the beginning of the *Confessions, Je sens mon cœur, et je
connais les hommes*,[8] could effectually represent the change in
attitude which had taken place. But it also becomes clear from
Flaubert's letters how laboriously and with what tensity of application he had attained to his convictions. Great subjects, and
the free, irresponsible rule of the creative imagination, still
have a great attraction for him; from this point of view he
sees Shakespeare, Cervantes, and even Hugo wholly through
the eyes of a romanticist, and he sometimes curses his own
narrow petty-bourgeois subject which constrains him to tiresome stylistic meticulousness (*dire à la fois simplement et
proprement des choses vulgaires*)[9]; this sometimes goes so far
that he says things which contradict his basic views: . . . *et
ce qu'il y a de désolant, c'est de penser que, même réussi dans
la perfection, cela [Madame Bovary] ne peut être que passable
et ne sera jamais beau, à cause du fond même.*[10] Withal, like
so many important nineteenth-century artists, he hates his
period; he sees its problems and the coming crises with great
clarity; he sees the inner anarchy, the *manque de base théolo-
gique*,[11] the beginning menace of the mob, the lazy eclectic
Historism, the domination of phrases, but he sees no solution
and no issue; his fanatical mysticism of art is almost like a
substitute religion, to which he clings convulsively, and his
candor very often becomes sullen, petty, choleric, and neurotic.
But this sometimes perturbs his impartiality and that love of
his subjects which is comparable to the Creator's love. The
paragraph which we have analyzed, however, is untouched by
such deficiencies and weaknesses in his nature; it permits us
to observe the working of his artistic purpose in its purity.

The scene shows a man and wife at table, the most everyday
situation imaginable. Before Flaubert, it would have been con-
ceivable as literature only as part of a comic tale, an idyl, or a
satire. Here it is a picture of discomfort, and not a momen-

---

[7] Our heart is best used in feeling that of others.

[8] I feel my own heart, and I understand all men.

[9] To say vulgar things at once simply and properly.

[10] It is saddening to think that even if *Madame Bovary* achieves perfection, it can be no more than passable, never beautiful, because of the
subject itself.

[11] The lack of theological foundation.

tary and passing one, but a chronic discomfort, which completely rules an entire life, Emma Bovary's. To be sure, various
things come later, among them love episodes; but no one could
see the scene at table as part of the exposition for a love episode, just as no one would call *Madame Bovary* a love story
in general. The novel is the representation of an entire human
existence which has no issue, and our passage is a part of it,
which, however, contains the whole. Nothing particular happens in the scene, nothing particular has happened just before
it. It is a random moment from the regular recurring hours at
which the husband and wife eat together. They are not quarrel-
ing, there is no sort of tangible conflict. Emma is in complete
despair, but her despair is not occasioned by any definite catastrophe; there is nothing purely concrete which she has lost or
for which she has wished. Certainly she has many wishes, but
they are entirely vague—elegance, love, a varied life; there
must always have been such unconcrete despair, but no one
ever thought of taking it seriously in literary works before;
such formless tragedy, if it may be called tragedy, which is set
in motion by the general situation itself, was first made con-
ceivable as literature by romanticism; probably Flaubert was
the first to have represented it in people of slight intellectual
culture and fairly low social station; certainly he is the first
who directly captures the chronic character of this psychological situation. Nothing happens, but that nothing has become
a heavy, oppressive, threatening something. How he accomplishes this we have already seen; he organizes into compact
and unequivocal discourse the confused impressions of discomfort which arise in Emma at sight of the room, the meal, her
husband. Elsewhere too he seldom narrates events which carry
the action quickly forward; in a series of pure pictures—pictures transforming the nothingness of listless and uniform days
into an oppressive condition of repugnance, boredom, false
hopes, paralyzing disappointments, and piteous fears—a gray
and random human destiny moves toward its end.

The interpretation of the situation is contained in its description. The two are sitting at table together; the husband
divines nothing of his wife's inner state; they have so little communion that things never even come to a quarrel, an argument,
an open conflict. Each of them is so immersed in his own world
—she in despair and vague wish-dreams, he in his stupid philis-
tine self-complacency—that they are both entirely alone; they
have nothing in common, and yet they have nothing of their

own, for the sake of which it would be worthwhile to be lonely. For, privately, each of them has a silly, false world, which can not be reconciled with the reality of his situation, and so they both miss the possibilities life offers them. What is true of these two, applies to almost all the other characters in the novel; each of the many mediocre people who act in it has his own world of mediocre and silly stupidity, a world of illusions, habits, instincts, and slogans; each is alone, none can understand another, or help another to insight; there is no common world of men, because it could only come into existence if many should find their way to their own proper reality, the reality which is given to the individual—which then would be also the true common reality. Though men come together for business and pleasure, their coming together has no note of united activity; it becomes one-sided, ridiculous, painful, and it is charged with misunderstanding, vanity, futility, falsehood, and stupid hatred. But what the world would really be, the world of the "intelligent," Flaubert never tells us; in his book the world consists of pure stupidity, which completely misses true reality, so that the latter should properly not be discoverable in it at all; yet it is there; it is in the writer's language, which unmasks the stupidity by pure statement; language, then, has criteria for stupidity and thus also has a part in that reality of the "intelligent" which otherwise never appears in the book.

Emma Bovary, too, the principal personage of the novel, is completely submerged in that false reality, in human stupidity as is the "hero" of Flaubert's other realistic novel, Frédéric Moreau in the *Sentimental Education*. How does Flaubert's manner of representing such personages fit into the traditional categories "tragic" and "comic"? Certainly Emma's existence is apprehended to its depths, certainly the earlier intermediate categories, such as the "sentimental" or the "satiric" or the "didactic," are inapplicable, and very often the reader is moved by her fate in a way that appears very like tragic pity. But a real tragic heroine she is not. The way in which language here lays bare the silliness, immaturity, and disorder of her life, the very wretchedness of that life, in which she remains immersed (*toute l'amertume de l'existence lui semblait servie sur son assiette*), excludes the idea of true tragedy, and the author and the reader can never feel as at one with her as must be the case with the tragic hero; she is always being tried, judged, and, together with the entire world in which she is caught, condemned. But neither is she comic; surely not; for that, she is understood far too deeply from within her fateful entanglement—though Flaubert never practices any "psychological understanding" but simply lets the state of the facts speak for itself. He has found an attitude toward the reality of contemporary life which is entirely different from earlier attitudes and stylistic levels, including—and especially—Balzac's and Stendhal's. It could be called, quite simply, "objective seriousness." This sounds strange as a designation of the style of a literary work. Objective seriousness, which seeks to penetrate to the depths of the passions and entanglements of a human life, but without itself becoming moved, or at least without betraying that it is moved—this is an attitude which one expects from a priest, a teacher, or a psychologist rather than from an artist. But priest, teacher, and psychologist wish to accomplish something direct and practical—which is far from Flaubert's mind. He wishes, by his attitude—*pas de cris, pas de convulsion, rien que la fixité d'un regard pensif*[12]—to force language to render the truth concerning the subjects of his observation: "style itself and in its own right being an absolute manner of viewing things" (*Correspondence* 2, 346). Yet this leads in the end to a didactic purpose: criticism of the contemporary world; and we must not hesitate to say so, much as Flaubert may insist that he is an artist and nothing but an artist. The more one studies Flaubert, the clearer it becomes how much insight into the problematic nature and the hollowness of nineteenth-century bourgeois culture is contained in his realistic works; and many important passages from his letters confirm this. The demonification of everyday social intercourse which is to be found in Balzac is certainly entirely lacking in Flaubert; life no longer surges and foams, it flows viscously and sluggishly. The essence of the happenings of ordinary contemporary life seemed to Flaubert to consist not in tempestuous actions and passions, not in demonic men and forces, but in the prolonged chronic state whose surface movement is mere empty bustle, while underneath it there is another movement, almost imperceptible but universal and unceasing, so that the political, economic, and social subsoil appears comparatively stable and at the same time intolerably charged with tension. Events seem to him hardly to change; but in the concretion of duration, which Flaubert is able to suggest both in the individ-

---

[12] No cries, no emotion, nothing but the steadiness of a thoughtful gaze.

ual occurrence (as in our example) and in his total picture of the times, there appears something like a concealed threat: the period is charged with its stupid issuelessness as with an explosive.

Patterns of Imagery: Her Dreams Too High, Her House Too Narrow* by Victor Brombert

Flaubert takes cruel satisfaction in ironic contrasts. Many of them are set up in a somewhat obvious fashion: the Bovary dogcart and the elegant carriages of the guests at the Vaubyessard ball; Charles's smugness and Emma's frustration; her exaltations and her moments of torpor; the alternations of ardor and frigidity; Emma's vibrating body still tingling from the caresses, while her lover, a cigar between his lips, is mending a broken bridle! At times, the antithesis tends to be more subtle: the knotty articulations of a peasant hand appear on the very page where the lovers' fingers intertwine.

These planned juxtapositions do, however, point to the heart of the subject. They emphasize the basic theme of incompatibility. Their implicit tensions stress a fundamental state of *divorce* at all levels of experience. But they also fulfill a dramatic function. If Charles's father happens to be a squanderer and an almost professional seducer, if Charles himself, while still married to his first wife, is drawn to Emma because she represents a forbidden and inaccessible love, these ironies are part of an effective technique of "preparation." And these very anticipatory devices—whether prophetic in a straightforward or an ironic fashion—are in turn related to the theme of "fate" which Flaubert propounds with characteristic ambiguity. *"C'est la faute de la fatalité!"* is Charles's pathetic, yet moving final comment. But the notion of "fatality" is of course one of the most belabored Romantic clichés; Charles's exclamation carries its own condemnation, at the same time that it implies a debunking of the tragic ending of the novel. Rodolphe, writing

* From Victor Brombert, *The Novels of Flaubert: A Study of Themes and Techniques,* Princeton: Princeton University Press, 1966.

his cowardly letter of rupture to Emma, hits upon the expression: ". . . accuse only fate"—and he congratulates himself on his skillful use of a word "which is always effective"! The expression coincides with the very devaluation of love. Similarly, Charles blames the pitiful outcome of the clubfoot operation on a malevolent destiny (*"La fatalité s'en était mêlée"*), when in reality only his hopeless incompetence is at fault. Yet who is to deny that, in addition to elements of pathos, the novel constantly suggests an all-pervasive determinism: Emma's temperament, the character of Charles, the effects of heredity, the erosive quality of small-town life, the noxious influence of books, the structure of the novel itself?

Flaubert significantly devotes an entire chapter to Emma's education in the convent. Her private symbolism of love, mysticism and death is determined by this experience. The "mystic languor" provoked by the incense, the whisperings of the priest, the very metaphors comparing Christ to a celestial lover, predispose her to confuse sensuous delights and spiritual longings. The convent is Emma's earliest claustration, and the solicitations from the outside world, whether in the form of books which are smuggled in, or through the distant sound of a belated carriage rolling down the boulevards, are powerful allurements. As for Emma's reactions to the books she reads, the image of a female Quixote comes to mind.[1] She too transmutes reality into fiction. Here, as in Cervantes' novel, literature itself becomes one of the strongest determinants.

Yet there is, in *Madame Bovary*, a necessity stronger even than the temperamental, social and intellectual pressures to which the protagonist is subjected. It is a necessity inherent in the inner logic and progression of Flaubert's own images. The very chapter on Emma's education (I.6) reveals a characteristic pattern. The primary images are those of confinement and immobility: the atmosphere of the convent is protective and soporific (. . . *elle s'assoupit doucement*); the reading is done on the sly; the girls are assembled in the study, the chapel or the dormitory. Very soon, however, images of escape begin to dominate. These images are at first strictly visual: ladies in castles (typically also claustrated, and dreamily ex-

---

[1] Harry Levin, in *The Gates of Horn* (p. 246), quotes a prophetic passage from Kierkegaard's *Either/Or:* "It is remarkable that the whole of European literature lacks a feminine counterpart to *Don Quixote*. May not the time for this be coming, may not the continent of sentimentality yet be discovered?"

pecting in front of a window the cavalier with a white plume);
madonnas, lagoons, gondoliers and angels with golden wings;
illustrations in books depicting English ladies kissing doves
through the bars of a Gothic cage (still the prison theme).
Soon, however, the images become less precise, giving way to
vaporous dreams ("pale landscapes of dithyrambic lands"),
and to an increasingly disheveled exoticism: sultans with long
pipes, Djiaours, Bayadères, Greek caps and Turkish sabers.
The suggested confusion of these images rapidly degenerates
into indifferentiation and ultimately even chaos, as palm trees
and pine trees, Tartar minarets and Roman ruins, crouching
camels and swimming swans are brought into senseless juxta-
position. Escape seems inevitably to lead to a manner of disintegration, even to images of death (perhaps even a suggested
death-wish), as the swans are transformed into dying swans,
singing to the accompaniment of funereal harps, and Emma,
infinitely bored by it all, but unwilling to admit it to herself,
continuing her dreams by habit or by vanity, finally withdraws
into herself, "appeased."

The chapter on Emma's education is revealing, not merely
because it proposes a parable of the entire novel, but because
the progression of images corresponds to a pattern repeated
throughout the book: from ennui to expectation, to escape, to
confusion, back to ennui and to a yearning for nothingness. But
whereas the symbolic detail is often, with Flaubert, part of a
deliberate technique, this logic of imagery associations, these
recurrent patterns depend on the spontaneous life of images,
on their mutual attractions and irremediable conflicts, on a
causality which operates at an unconscious, *poetic* level. The
novel as a whole is thus constructed around recurrent clusters
of images, all of which are part of definable, yet interrelated
cycles. These cycles, or cyclic themes, do parallel on a massive
canvas the inevitable movement, from boredom to self-destruc-
tion, which characterizes *Madame Bovary* in its overall conception as well as in its detailed execution.

First the patterns of ennui. This begins early in the novel.
The eternal sameness of experience is already suggested by the
weekly letters to his mother which the boy Charles writes
regularly every Thursday evening with the same red ink, and
which he seals with the same three wafers. Charles's working
habits are moreover compared to those of a mill-horse. The
primary means for suggesting an anesthetizing routine are temporal. Emma gets into the habit of taking strolls in order to

avoid the "eternal" garden. The days resemble each other
(". . . the same series of days began all over"); the future
seems like an endlessly dark corridor. And repeatedly, the
mournful church bell punctuates the return of the monotonous
hours and days with its characterless lament. The repeated use
of the imperfect tense, with its suggestions of habitual action,
further stresses the temporal reality of Flaubertian boredom.
Even comic effects contribute to an impression of sameness
(Flaubert's sense of comedy constantly exploits repetitions):
on the day of the agricultural show, the local national guards-
men and the corps of firemen are being drilled endlessly up
and down the Yonville square: *Cela ne finissait pas et toujours
recommençait*.

The underlying sense of hopelessness and monotony is also
conveyed by means of liquid images. There is a great deal of
oozing, dripping and melting in Flaubert's fictional world.
During Charles's early courtship of Emma, the snow is melting, the bark of the trees is oozing, one can hear drops of
water falling one by one. Later, when the bitterness of her
married existence seems to be served up to her nauseatingly
during their daily meals, Emma is aware that the walls are
"sweating." These liquid images, suggesting erosion and deterioration, are of course bound up with a sense of the emptiness of Time. A steady *écoulement*, or flow, corresponds to
feelings of hopeless waste and vacuity. These liquid images of
an annihilating temporality will be even more pervasive in
L'Éducation sentimentale. But *Madame Bovary* also brings out
this immense sadness of time's undoing. Old Rouault explains
that, after his wife died, grief itself dissolved (". . . *ça a coulé
brin à brin* . . ." I.3). The steady flow becomes the very
symbol of a chronic despair. After Léon's departure, Emma is
plunged again into a life of spiritual numbness: "The river
still flowed on, and slowly pushed its ripples along the slippery
banks" (II.7). Finally, the monotony of existence is conveyed
through a series of spatial images. The Norman landscape near
Yonville is "flat," the meadow "stretches," the plain broadens
out and extends to the very horizon—*à perte de vue*. This
colorless landscape is in harmony with the lazy borough
sprawling along the river banks. Emma, throughout the novel,
scans the horizon. But nothing appears which would relieve
the deathlike evenness.

This spatial imagery clearly constitutes the bridge between
the theme of ennui and the theme of escape. Once again, the

series of images can be traced back to the early pages of the novel which deal exclusively with Charles. Repeatedly, he opens his window, either to stare at the muddy little river which in his mind becomes a wretched "little Venice" and to dream of a yearned-for elsewhere, or to indulge in love reveries as he leans in the direction of the Bertaux farm. The window becomes indeed in *Madame Bovery* the symbol of all expectation: it is an opening onto space through which the confined heroine can dream of escape. But it is also—for windows can be closed and exist only where space is, as it were, restricted— a symbol of frustration, enclosure and asphyxia. Flaubert himself, aware that Emma is often leaning out the window, explains that "the window in the provinces replaces the theater and the promenade" (II.7). More, however, is involved than a simple taste for spectacle. Jean Rousset, in a brilliant essay, quite rightly suggests that the open window unleashes "mystical velleities."[2] In fact, the symbolic uses of the window reveal not only a permanent dialectic of constriction and spatiality, but an implicit range of emotions embracing the major themes of the novel.

Emma's characteristic pose is at, or near, a window. This is indeed one of the first impressions Charles has of her: . . . *il la trouva debout, le front contre la fenêtre.* Windows which are "ajar" are part of her literary reveries in the convent. The image, from the very outset, suggests some manner of imprisonment as well as a longing for a liberation. After her marriage, her daily routine brings her to the window every morning. When she goes through one of her nervous crises, she locks herself up in her room, but then, "stifling," throws open the windows. Exasperated by a sense of shame and contempt for her husband, she again resorts to the typical gesture: "She went to open the window . . . and breathed in the fresh air to calm herself" (I.9). The sense of oppression and immurement is further stressed after Rodolphe abandons her: the shutter of the window overlooking the garden remains permanently closed. But the imprisonment in her own boundless desire is intolerable. Emma's sexual frenzy, which reaches climactic proportions during her affair with Léon, is probably the most physical manifestation of her need to "liberate" her-

---

[2] Rousset, "*Madame Bovary* ou '*le livre sur rien*,'" in *Forme et signification*, pp. 109–133. Rousset sees the window in Flaubert as a symbol of the "limitless within the confined."

self. The window, as symbol, offers an image of this release. It is revealing that she first glimpses her future lover, Rodolphe, from her window. Similarly, she watches Léon cross the Yonville square. And it is characteristic also that, upon Léon's departure from Yonville, Emma's first gesture is to open her window and watch the clouds. The space-reverie at first corresponds to a sense of hope: either the surge toward emancipation, as after the Vaubyessard ball (Emma "opened the window and leant out"); or the process of convalescence (Emma, recovering from her nervous depression, is wheeled to the window in her armchair). But the space-hope is even more fundamentally a space-despair. From the garret where she reads Rodolphe's letter and almost commits suicide, all the surrounding plain is visible. The garret-window offers the broadest panorama. But it is a dreary view; the endless flat expanse provides a hopeless perspective.

Chronic expectation turns to chronic futility, as Emma's élans toward the elsewhere disintegrate in the grayness of undifferentiated space. Velleities of movement and flight only carry her back to a more intolerable confinement within her petty existence and her unfulfilled self. But expectation there is. Just as the chatelaines in her beloved Gothic romances wait for the dashing cavalier on his black horse, so Emma lives in perpetual anticipation. "At the bottom of her heart . . . she was waiting for something to happen" (I.9). Flaubert insists, somewhat heavily at times, on this compulsive expectance of the conclusive event. The frustrated local barber, dreaming of a shop in the theater district of some big town, thus walks up and down "like a sentinel on duty" waiting for customers. And Emma, casting despairing glances upon her life's solitude, interrogates the empty horizon. Each morning, as she wakes up, she hopes that this day will bring a three-decker, laden with passion to the portholes. Every evening, disappointed, she again longs for the morrow.

Images of movement reinforce the theme of escapism. Emma enjoys taking lonely walks with her greyhound and watching the leaps and dashes of the graceful animal. Restlessness and taste for aimless motion point to the allurement of a mythical *elsewhere*. Once again, the theme is ironically broached early in the novel, in pages concerned with Charles. "He had an aimless hope. . . ." Images of space and motion —the two are frequently combined—serve, throughout the novel, to bring out the vagrant quality of Emma's thoughts.

Departure, travel and access to privileged regions are recurring motifs. The "immense land of joys and passions" exists somewhere beyond her immediate surroundings: the more accessible things are, the more Emma's thoughts turn away from them. Happiness, by definition, can never be *here*. "Anywhere out of the World"—the title of Baudelaire's prose poem—could sum up Emma's chronic yearning for the exotic. "It seemed to her that certain places on earth must yield happiness, just as some plants are peculiar to certain places and grow poorly anywhere else" (I.7). By a skillful, and certainly far from gratuitous touch, Flaubert concludes Emma's initiatory stay at the Vaubyessard residence with a visit to the hothouses, where the strangest plants, rising in pyramids under hanging vases, evoke a climate of pure sensuality. The exotic setting becomes the very symbol of a yearned-for bliss. The "coming joys" are compared to tropical shores so distant that they cannot be seen, but from where soft winds carry back an intoxicating sweetness.

Travel and estrangement come to symbolize salvation from the immurement of ennui. Emma believes that change of abode alone is almost a guarantee of happiness. "She did not believe that things could be the same in different places . . ." (II.2). The unseen country is obviously also the richest in promises of felicity. Paris remains sublimely alluring precisely because—contrary to his original intentions—Flaubert does not grant Emma access to this promised land. Her first conversation with Léon typically exploits the Romantic cliché of the "limitless" expanse of the ocean, which "elevates the soul" through suggestions of the ideal and of infinity. And Léon's blue eyes seem beautiful to Emma because they appear more limpid than "those mountain-lakes where the sky is mirrored." The culmination of the travel imagery coincides with plans for Emma's elopement with Rodolphe (. . . *il fera bon voyager* . . . II.12) and with her visions of life in gondolas or under palm trees, to the accompaniment of guitars, in far-off countries with splendent domes and women dressed in red bodices. The very concept of emancipation is bound up with the notion of voyage. During her pregnancy Emma hopes to have a son, because a man is free: "he can travel over passions and over countries, cross obstacles, taste of the most far-away pleasures." And part of Rodolphe's prestige when she meets him is that he appears to her like a "traveler who has voyaged over strange lands." As early as her disappointing honeymoon (which, she feels, ought to have led to "those lands with sonorous names"), she knows that Charles did not, and could not, live up to her ideal of man as initiator to remote mysteries. She yearns for the inaccessible with a naive but pungent lyricism: ". . . she was filled with desires, with rage, with hate" (II.5). Her desperate escapism, which ultimately alarms and alienates both her lovers, is of an almost sacrilegious nature. It is significant that sex is repeatedly associated with mystico-religious images (the remarkable death scene pushes the association to its logical conclusion), and that the assignation with Léon takes place in the Rouen cathedral, which Emma's distorted sensibility views as a "gigantic boudoir." Emma's tragedy is that she cannot escape her own immanence. "Everything, including herself, was unbearable to her" (III.6). But just as her walks always lead back to the detested house, so Emma feels thrown back into herself, left stranded on her own shore. The lyrical thrust toward the inaccessible leads back to an anesthetizing confinement.[3]

The cycles of ennui and spatial monotony, the images of escape (window perspectives, motion, insatiable desire for the elsewhere), are thus brought into contrapuntal tension with an underlying metaphoric structure suggesting limits, restriction, contraction and immobility. The basic tragic paradox of *Madame Bovary* is unwittingly summed up during Emma's first conversation with Léon. They discuss the pleasures of reading: "One thinks of nothing . . . the hours slip by. One *moves motionless* through countries one imagines one sees. . . ."[4] As for the sense of limitation, the very site of Yonville (the diminutive conglomeration in the midst of a characterless, undifferentiated landscape) suggests a circumscribed and hopelessly hedged-in existence. As soon as one enters the small market town, "the courtyards grow narrower, the houses closer together, and the fences disappear . . ." The entire first chapter of Part II, which introduces the reader to Yonville, plays on this contrast between expanse and delimitation. The very life of Yonville suggests constriction. Viewed from a distance—for instance during Emma's prome-

---

[3] Georges Poulet, in *Les Métamorphoses du cercle,* points to the alternating rhythm of contracting and expanding movements in *Madame Bovary.*

[4] Italics mine. The French reads: "On so promène immobile . . ." (II.2).

nade on horseback with Rodolphe—the small community appears even more jammed in. "Emma half closed her eyes to recognize her house, and never had this poor village where she lived seemed so small to her." The same feeling of constriction is experienced inside her house, as Emma bewails "her too exalted dreams, her narrow home" (II.5). The entire tragic tension of the novel seems to be summed up in this experience of spiritual claustrophobia. The sitting room where Emma, in her armchair, spends hours near the window, is distinguished by its particularly "low ceiling." The predominant impression is one of entrapment or encirclement. In a somewhat labored but telling simile, Flaubert compares Emma's married life to a complex strap which "buckles her in" on all sides (II.5).

This imagery of restriction and contraction is intimately related to the disintegrating experiences of sameness, interfusion and confusion of feelings, indiscrimination, abdication of will and lethal torpor. Space is lacking even in the Yonville cemetery, which is so full of graves that the old stones, completely level with the ground, form a "continuous pavement." This absence of a hiatus has its stylistic counterparts in the tight verbal and dramatic juxtapositions. There is no solution of continuity between the platitudinous official speeches, the lowing of the cattle and Rodolphe's talk of elective affinities. The seduction scene at the *comices agricoles*—a chapter of which Flaubert was particularly proud—is almost a continuous exercise in telescoping of levels of reality. Everything tends to merge and become alike. Even the villagers and the peasants present a comical and distressing uniformity. *Tous ces gens-là se ressemblaient*.

Confusion, whether due to oppressive monotony, moral drowsiness or spiritual anesthesia, is one of the leitmotifs in *Madame Bovary*. Once more, the opening pages are revealing. When Charles reads the list of course offerings at the medical school, he experiences a spell of "dizziness." Riding toward the Bertaux farm, he falls into a characteristic doze wherein his most recent sensations "blend" with old memories: the warm odor of poultices "mingled" in his brain with the fresh smell of dew. *Confondre, se mêler* are among Flaubert's favorite words: *Et peu à peu, les physionomies se confondirent dans sa mémoire* (I.8). As the Vaubyessard ball recedes into the past, the sharp outlines dissolve and all the figures begin to merge. Emma's ability to distinguish between levels of values dwindles as the novel progresses. "She confused in her desire the sensualities of luxury with the delights of the heart" (I.9). Later, this commingling of sensations becomes increasingly habitual, until no clear notions at all can be distinguished.

Emma's lust, her longing for money and her sentimental aspirations all become "confused" in one single, vague and oppressive sense of suffering. While listening to Rodolphe's seductive speeches, she conjures up other images: the viscount with whom she waltzed at Vaubyessard, his delicately scented hair, Léon who is now far away. The characteristic faintness (*mollesse*) which comes over her induces an overlapping and a blurring of sensations which is not unlike a cinematographic fadeout. (. . . *Puis tout se confondit* . . . II.8). But this psychological strabismus is not here a technique whereby the author creates suspense or modestly veils the action. It corresponds to an abdication of choice and will, and points to the very principle of disintegration. As she is about to seek solace from the priest, Emma longingly recalls her sheltered life in the convent where she was "lost" (*confondue*) in the long line of white veils. The memory makes her feel faint (*molle*); and she yearns for anything which would submerge and absorb her existence (II.6). The latent yearning for annihilation or nothingness is probably the most fundamental tragic impulse of Flaubertian protagonists. Not only does Emma dream of dissolving herself in an all-absorbing whole, but approaching death is described as a *confusion de crépuscule*. Ultimately, not only all desire but all pain is absorbed in an all-embracing and all-negating woe. Thus Charles's retrospective jealousy, when he discovers Emma's infidelities, becomes "lost in the immensity of his grief." The frustration of all desire and of all hope is so great that nothing short of total sorrow and total surrender to nonbeing can bring relief.

A state of numbness or even dormancy is one of the chronic symptoms of *bovarysme*. *Mollesse, assoupissement* and *torpeur* are other favorite words of Flaubert. They refer most generally to a vague sensuous well-being, to a condition of nonresistance and even surrender. When Emma hears Rodolphe's flattering, if not original love declaration (he compares her to an angel), her pride "like one who relaxes in a bath, expanded softly" (*mollement*). The almost untranslatable *mollement* appears again, a few pages later, when Rodolphe puts his arm around Emma's waist and she tries "feebly" to disengage herself. Numbness and drowsiness occur almost regularly in a sexual context. During the nocturnal trysts in the garden, Emma, her eyes half closed, feels her emotion rise with the softness (*mollesse*) of the perfume of the syringas. Her physical submissiveness to Rodolphe is termed "a beatitude that benumbed her" (*une béatitude qui l'engourdissait* II.12). And when she meets Léon again at the opera in Rouen, she is assailed by the "torpor" of her memories.

The pathological nature of such torpid states is strongly suggested. Early in the novel, her torpor follows moments of "feverish" chatter, and corresponds to periods when Emma suffers from heart palpitations. But the real pathology is of the spirit, not of the body. Just as the somnolence of the listeners at the agricultural show reflects the dullness of the speeches and the intellectual indolence of the townspeople, so Charles's congenital yawning symbolizes his inadequacy. When the coach arrives in Yonville, Charles is still asleep. During the evenings at the Homais, he regularly falls asleep after playing dominoes. Such drowsiness seems contagious. Only Emma's takes on a more symbolic aspect. She suffers from an *assoupissement de sa conscience* (II.7): her very conscience is made numb. And in this numbness there is not only the principle of despair, but of death. All desire, like Baudelaire's *ennui,* leads to an omnivorous yawn. After Léon leaves Yonville, Emma's sensuous and sentimental frustration expresses itself through an infinite lassitude, a "numb despair." Her blinds are now kept closed (recurrence of the window motif), while she herself spends her days stretched out on her sofa, reading a book. The very atmosphere of Emma's burial will be one of monotony and sickening tedium. As Charles leads the funeral procession, he feels himself growing faint at this unending repetition of prayers and torches, surrounded by the insipid, almost nauseating smell of wax and of cassocks. A liturgical torpor invests him, and reduces all pain to a blurred feeling of weariness.

The very movement of the imagery in *Madame Bovary* thus leads from desire to frustration and failure, and ultimately to death and total undoing. Images of liquefaction and flow, which will be central to *L'Éducation sentimentale,* here also serve to convey the processes of dissolution. Emma almost perversely savors the slow disintegration of her being. The maraschino ice melting in her mouth corresponds to an entire past she wishes to negate. But the present, no matter how much one counts on it to beget change, never really disrupts the hopeless continuity of life. The tiny river near Yonville symbolizes a "time" which knows neither alteration nor respite (*La rivière coulait toujours* . . . , II.7). This temporal symbolism is bound up with the experience of loss and erosion: the great love with Rodolphe is like "the water of a river absorbed into its bed" until Emma begins to see the mud (II.10). During her convalescence, the falling rain is the background to the sick woman's daily anticipation of the "inevitable return" of the same petty events. But it is above all morbidity of spirit or body which is suggested through fluid or soluble metaphors. From the empty and bloody orbits of the Blind Man flow "liquids" which congeal into green scales. Similarly, a "black liquid" oozes from the blisters on Hippolyte's leg. And after Emma dies, a "rush of black liquid" issues from her mouth, as though she were still vomiting. Even the soil thrown up at the side of her grave seems to be "flowing" down at the corners. This fluent quality of life points not only to mortality, but to decomposition. "Whence came this insufficiency in life, this instantaneous rotting of everything on which she leant?" (III.6). Emma's question goes to the very heart of the book. For life, in the Flaubertian context, is a steady process of decay.

This relentless deterioration of everything is very different from the Balzacian wear and tear which is most often the price man pays for his tragic energy. Flaubert's heroes not only have a vocation for failure, but they fail independently of any investment of fervor. Charles's early fiasco at his examination foreshadows his entire career. Paradoxically, it could be said that unsuccess precedes the act of living. In Flaubert's world, life is not fought out and lost, but *spent*. It is only appropriate that Emma should be congenitally improvident. For she is a squanderer not only of money. In a strained but revealing simile, Flaubert compares her loss of illusions to a steady act of "spending." *Elle en avait dépensé à toutes les aventures de son âme* . . . (II.10). But it is, in reality, her own self that she is dissipating, as though urged on by the desire to fade or melt away. Flaubert elsewhere speaks of death as a "continuous swooning away" (an *évanouissement continu*).[5] The death-wish is a permanent reality in the fictional world of Flaubert; it most often reveals itself through an almost mystical desire to vanish or be absorbed by a larger whole. On her way to Father Bournisien, Emma dreams of the "disappearance" of her entire existence. The longing for nothingness is often linked to religious or pseudo-religious images. In Emma's mind, it is most often associated with memories of the convent, with a desire to return to it, as one might to a maternal womb. The desire to stop living ("She would have liked not to be alive, or to be always asleep," III.6) corresponds to a quasi-metaphysical fatigue, to the immedicable pain of having been betrayed by life itself. In the face of universal abandon, the Flaubertian heroine is driven to dissipation. She becomes the willing accomplice of all the forces of disbandment.

The Weaknesses of *Madame Bovary**
by Martin Turnell

Madame Bovary is a remarkable book because of the subtlety with which Flaubert explored his theme, but it is not the flawless masterpiece for which it is usually taken. Its weaknesses lie partly in its execution and partly in the novelist's attitude towards his principal character. When Stendhal used the story of Berthet as his starting point in *Le Rouge et le noir*, it became an *opportunity* for the display of his magnificent gifts and he created something which far transcended his original. Although the story of the Delamare family provided Flaubert with a discipline, it was also a *temptation*. We may suspect that he attempted a dispassionate analysis of the Romantic malady in the unconscious hope of curing himself of its

---

[5] Flaubert, *Bouvard et Pécuchet*, Chapter 8. On the subject of this expression, J. P. Richard writes: ". . . ever since his birth, the Flaubertian being has not ceased dying. He has lived through successive swoonings" (*"La Création de la forme chez Flaubert,"* in *Littérature et sensation*, p. 147).

* From Martin Turnell, *The Novel in France*, New York: New Directions, 1951.

ravages, but he was not really successful. It became an excuse, as we shall see, for exploiting all sorts of private manias.

Flaubert's relation to the Romantic Movement was a curious and an interesting one. Its impress is apparent on almost every page he wrote. But though it accounts for some of his most serious weaknesses, it also enabled him to make some of his most important discoveries. The French classic novel was the product of a small homogeneous society which possessed a common language. Its precision enabled the novelist to make a profound study of human nature, but he worked in a field which was necessarily restricted. He was confined in the main to the great primary emotions, to a settled round of feelings. The break-up of this society in the eighteenth century transformed the scene. Man became a problem to be explored and there were no longer any limits to the exploration, no longer any clear-cut outlines. The change did not come overnight. The process was a gradual one. Constant and Stendhal made discoveries about human nature, but they combined them with an eighteenth-century discipline. The "outsider" may be unpredictable, but we are aware of the rational being underneath. He never becomes a welter of conflicting impulses or a mere succession of moods. We do not have this feeling with their contemporaries. For the break-up of society led in the end to the break-up of man. The Romantic Movement did far more than release emotions which had been repressed by eighteenth-century decorum. It blurred the division between man and nature, dream and reality, creating a new kind of awareness which could not be expressed in classic French prose. Its writers had moments of insight, but their work reveals a progressive movement away from the psychological realism of the seventeenth and eighteenth centuries, and it tends to dissolve into a flood of unrelated words and images. Flaubert attempted, with varying success, to create a style which was capable of exact analysis and which would at the same time make use of the colour and suggestiveness discovered by the Romantics.

There is a striking passage in Part I, Chapter 7, which throws some light on Flaubert's originality:

> *Elle songeait quelquefois que c'étaient là pourtant les plus beaux jours de sa vie, la lune de miel, comme on disait. Pour en goûter la douceur, il eût fallu, sans doute, s'en aller vers ces pays à noms sonores où les lendemains de mariage ont de plus suaves paresses! Dans des chaises*

de poste, sous des stores de soie bleue, on monte au pas des routes escarpées, écoutant la chanson du postillon qui se répète dans la montagne avec les clochettes des chèvres et le bruit sourd de la cascade. Quand le soleil se couche, on respire au bord des golfes le parfum des citronniers; puis, le soir, sur la terrasse des villas, seuls et les doigts confondus, on regarde les étoiles en faisant des projets. Il lui semblait que certains lieux sur la terre devaient produire du bonheur, comme une plante particulière au sol et qui pousse mal toute autre part. Que ne pouvait-elle s'accouder sur le balcon des chalets suisses ou enfermer sa tristesse dans un cottage écossais, avec un mari vêtu d'un habit de velours noir à longues basques, et qui porte des bottes molles, un chapeau pointu et des manchettes!

[She thought, at times, that these days of what people called the honeymoon were the most beautiful that she had ever known. To savour their sweetness to the full, she should, of course, have travelled to those lands with sounding names where newly wedded bliss is spent in exquisite languor. Seated in a post-chaise behind curtains of blue silk, she should have climbed, at a foot's pace, precipitous mountain roads, listening to the postillion's song echoing from the rocks to the accompaniment of goats' bells and the muted sound of falling water. She should have breathed at sunset, on the shores of sea bays in the South, the scent of lemon trees, and at night, alone with her husband on a villa terrace, have stood hand in hand, watching the stars and planning for the future. It seemed to her that happiness must flourish better in some special places than elsewhere, as some plants grow best in certain kinds of soil. Why was it not her fate to lean upon the balcony of a Swiss chalet or hide her melancholy in some Highland cottage, with a husband dressed in a black, long-skirted velvet coat, soft leather boots, a pointed hat, and ruffles at his wrist?]

At a first reading one might pardonably suppose that this is no more than an unusually well-written description of a Romantic day-dream, but in reality it is far more than that. It is not only one of the central passages in *Madame Bovary*, it is also a landmark in the development of the European novel. The feelings are not in the nature of the undertaking very profound or very original, but in analysing the content of the Romantic *rêverie* Flaubert comes closer, perhaps, than any of his predecessors to the intimate workings of consciousness and his method clearly points the way to the inner monologue.

The passage, so far from being a straightforward description, is a deliberate piece of stylization which anticipates the method that was later used with conspicuous success by the Symbolists. For Flaubert translates feelings into *visual* images, enabling him to control expression by building each image into the final picture—in this case an imaginary voyage—and to register the transitions from one set of feelings to another with greater fidelity than had been possible before. The result seems to me to be a complete success and the passage an artistic whole. It is not, strictly speaking, a description at all, but the dramatic presentation of a "mental event." There is complete identity between image and feeling. Every image is a particle of Emma's sensibility and a strand in the final pattern. The *lune de miel* is the symbol of a vague feeling of happiness associated with Emma's childhood, but its function is complex. It is the first of a series of images—landscapes, sounds, perfumes—which lead naturally from one to the other, and it also marks the point at which Emma's contact with the actual world ends and the *rêverie* begins. Her feeling of happiness is the material out of which she constructs an adventure in an imaginary world which has the sharpness and heightened reality of an hallucination. The *noms sonores*, the *douceur* and the *suaves paresses* build up a general impression of softness and languor, a lazy voluptuous happiness. As they echo and answer one another, so too do the sounds—the song which reverberates in the mountains is answered by the tinkle of the goats' bells, mingles with the muffled sound of the cascade and finally dies away in the silence of a summer night. When we come to *Il lui semblait que certains lieux* . . . we notice a change in the tone of the passage. The note of exaltation symbolized by *lune de miel*, with which it opens, changes to a wistfulness as she contemplates a *bonheur* which already belongs to the past, and this is followed by a sudden sinking as the *bonheur* is transformed into *tristesse*. The image which dominates the first part of the passage and gives the whole its particular flavour is the image of the blue silk blinds with their smooth vivid tactile suggestions. Flaubert had a particular fondness for blue and we may suspect that here it was unconsciously suggested by statues of the Madonna which he had seen in churches. The blinds are drawn and are supposed to conceal strange depths of passion at play within the coach. So we have the impression of a blue mist radiating over the whole scene and enveloping it. The most striking thing about the passage, however, is the absence of the Romantic lover. The drawn blinds do not conceal an exotic passion, but an empty coach or a coach in which there is only a lonely woman. We catch a glimpse of *les doigts confondus,* but they are anonymous fingers—fingers without hands. There is, too, the *mari vêtu d'un habit de velours noir,* and we see the black velvet jacket with its long tails very clearly. We also see the *chapeau pointu,* but we never see the features of the man inside because there is no one there, only a tailor's dummy rigged out in extravagant garments.

The passage leaves us with a sense of absence and this is the crux of the book. The account of the *physical* absence of the lover here is completed by the account of his *psychological* absence in another place:

> *Elle se promettait continuellement, pour son prochain voyage, une félicité profonde, puis elle s'avouait ne rien sentir d'extraordinaire. Cette déception s'effaçait vite sous un espoir nouveau, et Emma revenait à lui plus enflammée, plus avide. Elle se déshabillait brutalement, arrachant le lacet mince de son corset, qui sifflait autour de ses hanches comme une couleuvre qui glisse. Elle allait sur la pointe de ses pieds nus regarder encore une fois si la porte était fermée, plus elle faisait d'un seul geste tomber ensemble tous ses vêtements;—et pâle, sans parler, sérieuse, ell s'abattait contre sa poitrine, avec un long frisson.*

> [On the eve of each of their meetings she told herself that *this* time their happiness would be unclouded, only to confess, after the event, that she felt no emotions out of the ordinary. Such recurrent disappointments were always swept away by a renewed surge of hope, and when she next saw him, she was more on fire, more exigent, than ever. She flung off her clothes with a sort of brutal violence, tearing at her thin stay-lace so that it hissed about her hips like a slithering snake. She tip-toed across the room on her bare feet to make sure that the door was really locked, and then, with a single gesture, let her things fall to the floor. Pale, speechless, solemn, she threw herself into his arms with a prolonged shudder.]

The first sentence describes with great insight the central experience of Flaubert's work. The sensation of "falling out of love" is not, perhaps, an unusual one, but Flaubert invests it with immense significance. He is the great master of negation. Some of the most impressive pages in his books describe the sudden collapse of all feeling, the void which suddenly opens at the supreme moments of life and the realization that not simply one's emotional life, but one's whole world has fallen into ruin. There is no crash, no disaster—it is this that makes it so horrifying—life simply comes to an end. When you look into it, you find that there is nothing there.

What I have called physical and psychological absence is combined in the *long frisson*. Emma's tragedy is twofold. It lies in her inability to adapt herself to the normal world and in her failure to construct a durable inner life which would compensate for its drabness. The *long frisson* reflects the tendency of the human mind to escape from the disenchantment of awakening and from the pressure of thought by deliberately submerging itself in primitive animal contacts, as Emma does here. It is a mental blackout, a voluptuous swoon in which the intelligence is completely suspended. The placing of the closing words and the punctuation—*et pâle, sans parler, sérieuse, elle s'abattait . . .* convey the sensation of someone losing consciousness, falling into nothingness. The words are interesting for another reason. They mark the limit of Flaubert's power of analysis. His preoccupation with negative states almost certainly reflects his own inability to penetrate deeply into the content of experience. This makes the contrast between *elle s'avouait ne rien sentir d'extraordinaire* and *elle se déshabillait brutalement* of particular interest. For here the novelist intervenes in the life of his creature. It is his own starved sensibility, his own incapacity for deep feeling that he portrays in Emma. The violent actions which follow are an attempt to whip up the feelings that he is convinced he ought to experience, to obtain a vicarious satisfaction of feelings which life had refused him.

"Je me suis toujours défendu de rien mettre de moi dans mes oeuvres" [I have always sought not to put anything of myself into my works], Flaubert had said in a letter to Louise Colet, *"et pourtant j'en ai mis beaucoup"* [and yet I did put in a great deal].[1] Although these words were written ten years before the publication of *Madame Bovary*, they suggest that he was already conscious of a divided purpose which later disturbed the unity of the book. *Madame Bovary* purports to be a study

---

[1] *Correspondance*, I, 254.

of the Romantic outlook, but it is only partly that and partly an expression of the novelist's personal attitude which could not always be conveyed through the symbols that he chose and was sometimes in flagrant conflict with them. *"Madame Bovary, c'est moi,"* he said on another occasion. She was, but she was also the narrator as well as the heroine of *Novembre*. The similarity of outlook between the autobiographical story written when he was twenty-one and *Madame Bovary* is striking, and it brings home forcibly how little Flaubert developed.

"In sum," wrote M. André Maurois, "Mme de La Fayette had studied love as a metaphysician, Rousseau as a moralist, Stendhal as a lover, Flaubert as a disbeliever and an iconoclast."[2] This comment draws attention to interesting possibilities. There was nothing new in Flaubert's preoccupation with sexual passion, but his approach differs sensibly from that of his predecessors. The great dramatists and novelists of the past had concentrated on it because it is one of the profoundest of human instincts and enabled them to make some of the most searching studies of human nature that we possess. In Flaubert it had the reverse effect, narrowing instead of widening the scope of his work. He was aware of its importance, but he was only interested in its destructive effect on personality, and he selected it because it was the most vulnerable point for his carefully planned attack on human nature. For when we look into the structure of *Madame Bovary,* we find that so far from being a detached study of sexual mania and in spite of its superficial moral orthodoxy, it is an onslaught on the whole basis of human feeling and all spiritual and moral values.

*

*   *

We cannot help noticing that Flaubert displayed a marked reluctance to give due weight to what was valid and genuine in Emma. She was not, as Henry James alleged, a woman who was "naturally depraved." She possessed a number of solid virtues which were deliberately played down by the novelist. It was after all to her credit that she possessed too much sensibility to fit comfortably into the appalling provincial society of Yonville-l'Abbaye and it was her misfortune that she was not big enough to find a way out of the dilemma. We cannot withhold our approval from her attempts to improve her

---

[2] *Sept visages de l'amour* (Paris, 1946), p. 219.

mind or from the pride that she took in her personal appearance and in the running of her house. The truth is that Flaubert sacrificed far too much to his *thèse*. These virtues express his instinctive appreciation of what was sane and well-balanced in the French middle classes. In sacrificing them to a doctrinaire pessimism, which was held intellectually instead of arising from his contemplation of his material, he destroyed the findings of his own sensibility and involved himself in a confusion of values. We may conclude, too, that it was this nihilism, this sense that nothing—neither religion, morals, nor love—has value rather than a few lurid scenes which really upset French *mères de famille* in the year 1857 and led to Flaubert's prosecution for indecency.

The critic is faced with another problem. While *Madame Bovary* is admittedly only partly successful on account of conflicting attitudes, it still has to be decided what value should be attached to Flaubert's pessimism, whether it was a mature conception of life or an immature cynicism which is masquerading as mature vision.

Thibaudet[3] was in no doubt about the answer:

> The world described in *Madame Bovary* [he said] is a world which is falling apart. . . . But in every society when something is destroyed, another thing takes its place. When the Bovarys' fortune collapses, Lheureux's rises. . . . The novel has two sides—the defeat of Emma and the triumph of Homais.[4]

The book does, indeed, end with a remarkable stroke of irony.

> *Homais inclina vers le pouvoir. Il rendit secrètement à M. le préfet de grands services dans les élections. Il se vendit, enfin, il se prostitua. . . .*
>
> *Depuis la mort de Bovary, trois médecins se sont succédé à Yonville sans pouvoir y réussir, tant M. Homais les a tout de suite battus en brèche. Il fait une clientèle d'enfer; l'autorité le ménage et l'opinion publique le protège.*
>
> *Il vient de recevoir la croix d'honneur.*

---

[3] See selected bibliography.
[4] *Gustave Flaubert* (Paris, 1922), pp. 120, 122.

[In pursuit of his ambition, he consented to bow the knee to Authority. Unknown to anybody, he rendered the Prefect great service at election time. In short, he sold, he prostituted himself. . . .

Since Bovary died, there have been three doctors in Yonville. None of them, however, has made a success of the practice, so violently hostile has Homais shown himself to all of them. He himself is doing extremely well. The authorities handle him with kid gloves, and he is protected by public opinion.

He recently received a decoration.]

There is no doubt that Thibaudet correctly described Flaubert's intentions. And if sheer technical power were sufficient, we should have to agree that *Madame Bovary* was one of the greatest of novels. Yet somehow we remain unconvinced by the irony as we are unconvinced by the pessimism. For Flaubert's figures will not bear the weight of the symbolism that he tried to attach to them. We cannot fail to notice that he was continually tipping the scales, trying to give these sordid provincials an importance which they were far from possessing. What he exhibits with superb accomplishment is in fact an immature cynicism masquerading as mature vision.

Class Consciousness in Flaubert*
by Jean-Paul Sartre

Flaubert was to spend his life painstakingly scrutinizing the commonplaces which we are always reciting to others or to ourselves. At the end of his life, he was to write in *Bouvard et Pécuchet*: "Insignificant things saddened them: the advertisements in the newspapers, the profile of a bourgeois, a stupid remark overheard by chance; when they thought about what people said in their village and that there were other Coulons and other Marescots[1] all over the world, they felt bowed down by the full weight of the earth."

Several questions come immediately to mind. Where does

---

* From *Les Temps modernes*, June, 1966. Translated by Helen Weaver. [Footnotes added by the Editor, except where indicated otherwise.]

[1] Two of the oppressively mediocre characters in *Bouvard et Pécuchet*.

he derive what M. Dumesnil[2] ingenuously calls "his amazing aptitude for noticing stupidities"? Why does he pursue them so relentlessly? And why was it that the stupidity of other people became such an intolerable burden to him?

We can begin to answer these questions if we renounce another commonplace: that one must be intelligent in order to spot stupidity. I am convinced that in these operations, intelligence is useless; often it gets in the way. Every writer knows it: when you are correcting proofs, printer's errors escape your attention if you consider the text from the point of view of meaning or style; if you want to notice whether a word has lost a letter or has one letter too many, you have to place yourself on the level of the type itself, make your mind a blank, and passively allow the printed characters to appear and disappear before your eyes. In other words, to discover a commonplace, one must experience it and not go beyond it, to its social application. If Flaubert is overwhelmed by preconceived ideas it is because he has been conditioned to perceive language at their level.

An example will give us a better understanding of his bias. If we open his *Dictionary* at the article on railroads we read, ". . . To go into ecstasies over the invention and to say, 'Why, just this morning, monsieur, I was at X; I took the train from X; I finished my business and by X o'clock I was back.'" They said them again, with slight alterations, when the automobile appeared; they are still saying them today, almost word for word, in reference to airplane travel. Thus the appearance of each new means of transportation elicits a certain speech, always the same, which refers to the speed of the vehicle and which is found on everybody's lips. Is this speech "stupid"? Is it a received idea? That depends on one's point of view. There is no doubt that we are in the presence of a truism: obviously, if we know in advance that an airplane travels at a speed of eight hundred kilometers an hour, we should not be surprised that in two hours it has transported us sixteen hundred kilometers from our point of departure. But to turn these remarks into a La Palisse-truth,[3]

---

[2] René Dumesnil: Flaubertian scholar and critic.

[3] A reference to the kind of redundant statement naively made in an old French song about Captain La Palisse, killed in battle in Italy in 1525:

> A quarter of an hour before his death,
> He was still alive.

one must have first decided to restrict oneself to concepts. If, on the contrary, one places oneself on the level of emotions, everything changes. Amazement at finding oneself in Moscow four hours after leaving Paris is certainly not a profound emotion; but there is no doubt that it is a genuine and spontaneous one. . . .

If, therefore, the same remarks keep springing to everybody's lips, it is not, in fact, because they have been introduced to each person by ear, but because they clumsily express a common reaction which is emotionally accurate, if not logical, to a situation which is identical for everyone. For everyone, that is, except Flaubert, for whom train rides were a terrible ordeal,[4] and who regarded the railroad as the symbol of an industrial civilization he loathed and a social progress in which he did not believe. Because he does not share the goals and values of other travelers, he does not recognize the statement that they all make as an expression of their sensibility. From the outset, their infatuation seems suspicious to him: they "are in ecstasies"; no wonder, then, that the phrases that they utter, divorced from the emotion they express, seem a mechanical product of conditioned reflexes. From childhood, Flaubert had an "amazing aptitude" for noticing commonplaces and stupidity because he was on the lookout for them and because he listened to the speech without considering the synthetic activity or the real intentions of the speaker. The question remains why he was like this: we already know the answer: he was what his family made of him. We know that from his very early childhood he was imprisoned in passivity. This is tantamount to saying that he was, at the beginning of his life, incapable of performing an act of affirmation. I showed earlier that at this time he had no experience of reciprocity—which is the sign of Truth—and that he had been condemned by the indifference of a gloomy mother to remain within the confines of simple belief. For this reason, he received language not as an organized body of tools that one assembles or disassembles in order to produce a meaning, but as an interminable commonplace which is based neither on the intention to describe nor on the object to be designated and which, though

---

[4] He suffered from what has been called "siderodromophobia."

retaining a kind of substance of its own, possesses him and is spoken through him, even designates him without the child so possessed being able to use it. . . . Thinking is a common and revelatory *praxis* which has no other tools but words but which, once it performs the work of reciprocity, dismisses the words in favor of the thing said. When this signifying activity —which moves closer to the world than the instrument it uses—disappears, the word reappears in its material density as a pure negation of the signified. In effect the word "ox" is a means of access to the real herd when it is part of a complex signal referring to a practical fact or an action (the ox is sick; we must bring in the oxen). But at the same time it ignored: nobody notices that it has been pronounced. When it remains in the passive flood of experience, it settles, a thing in itself, on the contrary, and presents itself as the negation of the ox, that is, as an auditory or visual determination which refers only to other determinations of the same kind. Flaubert never *thinks*: the supporter of "objectivism" has no objectivity; this means that he does not take his real distances from himself and the world; consequently language reappears both in himself and in others as an obsessing materiality. It does not therefore lose its essential quality, which is to signify, but the meanings remain in the words; ultimately, language refers only to itself. One might call it *alienated thought*— materiality imitating thought or, if you prefer, thought haunting matter without being able to emerge from it. Language, organizing itself in him according to its own system of relations, robs him of his thought (which is not explicit enough to govern words) and affects him with pseudo-thoughts which are "received ideas" and which belong to nobody since, according to Gustave, they are, in each of the Others, other than himself. On this level, Flaubert does not believe that *we speak: we are spoken*. Language, insofar as it is a pratico-inert and structured body, has its own organization of sealed materiality: thus, reverberating all by itself in us, according to its laws— that is, precisely according to the seal imposed on its inertia— it infects us with an inverted thought (a thought produced by the words instead of governing them) which is merely the consequence of the semantic work or, if you will, its counter-finality. Language, for Flaubert, is no different from stupidity, since left to itself, verbal materiality organizes itself into a semi-externality and produces a *thought-matter*.

In one sense he is quite right and we are all stupid insofar as every word we utter contains the counter-finality that consumes it. And, if you will, all of us, all the time, express ourselves by means of commonplaces. The word, in itself, is a preconceived idea because it is defined without reference to us by its differences from other words in the total vocabulary. But in another sense, we are all intelligent: the commonplaces are words in the sense that we move beyond them toward a thought that is always fresh to the extent that we use them. Does this mean that they do not rob us of our thoughts? On the contrary, they are constantly absorbing and distorting them. . . . But intelligence is a dialectical relationship between the verbal intention and the words. Always being distorted, always being recovered and controlled only to be distorted again—and so on *ad infinitum*—thought is caught in the trap of commonplaces when it believes it is making use of them, and inversely, when you believe it to be trapped, it goes beyond them and shapes them to its original intention. This uncertain struggle has varying results: but one thing is certain, it is a task that is never completed. To avoid waging this battle in all its rigor, Flaubert is constantly in a state of estrangement from language: it is the outside internalized, it is the interior grasped as the exterior. He writes and discovers with terror that a commonplace has flowed from his pen without his realizing it. This explains his rhetorical precautions. A hundred times he follows his sentence with this parenthetical remark: "as the concierge says," "to quote the grocer"; or again: "I sound like M. Prudhomme, who . . . ," "as M. Prudhomme would say," "I declare . . . (like M. Prudhomme)." This reference comes spontaneously to his mind; no sooner has he penned the word, than Flaubert sees it and no longer acknowledges it; some bourgeois must have stolen his pen. In fact, it is his own bourgeois nature which comes to him like a stranger and which he hastens to deny. He would have us believe that he is amusing himself, that he is imitating the clerks and shopkeepers. But why should he do it? And why *in this particular context*? Most of the time, in fact, the phrase hastily added, "as . . . would say; . . . to speak like . . ." sounds perfectly ridiculous; the letter is serious, passionate, eloquent, and the train of thought is suddenly interrupted by this unfortunate addition. In fact Flaubert is not imitating the bourgeois: he talks like a bourgeois *because he is bourgeois*. He did not write the offending sentence *in order to mock* his class: it came spontaneously to his pen, he noticed it all of a sudden and tried to save himself by lucidity. Oh yes, I know, I sound like a grocer—and at the same time to deprive his correspondent of the opportunity of telling him he sounds like Joseph Prudhomme: Come, now! Can't you see I was trying to?

But stupidity shines forth—stupidity in Flaubert's sense—above all when the double take fails him and he has let a sentence slip by without comment: his correspondence swarms with commonplaces and *prudhommeries*.

*   *

The fool he condemns irrevocably with the "ferocity" of despair. But folly itself, that impersonal anonymous substance, fascinates him. From adolescence to death he will collect *Received Ideas* with maniacal persistence. In doing this he is pursuing two contradictory goals. The first—the only one he clearly expressed—is, if you will, cathartic in nature. Nobody *sees* the commonplaces: people use them to communicate with others, to please; they are ways of establishing contact; but at the very moment you palm them off on your neighbor, their familiar appearance enables them to pass unnoticed. Since they are neither seen nor known, no matter how often they are repeated, they remain hidden in broad daylight. To make people horrified of them it would be enough to *show* them: nobody would dare open his mouth again. And this purifying presentation can be accomplished only by someone who has been excluded. But in order to present them, it is necessary to track them down, catch them on the wing and *write them down*. But by writing them down, one reinforces their consistency, one engraves them on matter; one participates—albeit the better to destroy it—in the ceremony. In the hatred Flaubert professes for the commonplace there lurks an indirect enjoyment. He is pervaded by it as he writes it down; if he is the only one not to benefit from the social unification, he takes his revenge by alone discovering and by noting—for himself at first—the instrument of this unification. . . . The ambiguity of his attitude can be clearly seen in the following lines: "I would attack everything (in the *Dictionary of Received Ideas*); it would be the glorification, down through history, of everything that is accepted. In it I would demonstrate that majorities have always been right, and minorities have always been wrong. I would sacrifice the great men to all the idiots and this in an extravagant, bombastic style. . . . This apology for human vileness in all its forms, ironic and shrill from beginning to end, full of examples, proofs (which would prove the opposite) and appalling quotations (that would be easy) is intended, I would say, to put an end once and for all to eccentricity of every kind. Thus I would fall in with the modern democratic idea of equality, and with Fourier's remark that great men will become useless, and it is to this end, I would say, that the book was written." Naturally, the intention is ironic. But the method is still surprising: the idea is to combat the stupidity of other people without ever attacking it, but quite the contrary, *by experiencing it,* by becoming its medium and its martyr—until he *manifests* it in his own person. In a word, Flaubert dreams of taking upon himself all the Stupidity in the world, of becoming its scapegoat, in order to save others from it and to lose himself in it for a moment, to denounce it and to carry it as far as the ignoble, that "inverted sublimity." As for the method itself—however obviously intentional its extravagance, so that not one reader would mistake it—it reveals much about Gustave's profound submissiveness to the family, to the social order. What's this? He starts his letter by announcing that he has "an uncontrollable urge to rail at the human race" and that he will do so some day, "ten years from now." Then he adds that *"in the meantime"* he is coming back to his old idea of the *Dictionary of Received Ideas.* This boy of thirty-one who is dying to rail at the bourgeoisie still hasn't the courage to do it? What is he waiting for? Fame? Fortune? Power? And why, immediately afterwards, does he take the trouble to explain, *"No law could touch me* although I would attack everything (in the Dictionary)." What precautions! And what an odd *attack* that wears the garb of submission! This is the essence of Flaubert, cunning and docile: he prefers to demonstrate the idiotic cruelty of the social commandments by means of the absurd, by a hypocritical eagerness, by an all-out demonstration of zeal. He prefers to yield seemingly, to exaggerate discreetly, to push to the limit and at the same time to *show himself*, pure passive result of the will of others, to become an object to give them a horror of themselves. To fight openly, directly: *never*. But in the case which concerns us, it is a question of robbing men of their materiality only to impale oneself upon it. On this level, the fundamental Stupidity *is his temptation*. And let us note that he seeks in it *both* the materiality and the social integration.

*

*   *

For a long time Homais was regarded as an idiot. This must have delighted Flaubert. But Thibaudet[5] smelled the trap: he pointed out that the pharmacist was undeniably *intelligent*. Better: in this lugubrious novel which ends in calamity, Homais alone triumphs, and all along the line. He knows how to pull strings; superior to the health officers, he reigns over the district; however fragmentary it may be, the scientific information he flaunts attests to a certain degree of education; the rise of the Homais family resembles that of the Flauberts: the son will be a doctor and the grandson will say, "We are *a family*." Flaubert meant, without any doubt, to describe a ridiculous free-thinker; but at the same time he meant to prove him right. How could it have gone unnoticed that Bournisien was deliberately conceived to justify the diatribes of Homais? What prevented the author from showing a less repulsive priest than this materialistic, illiterate cleric who eats and drinks for four, knows nothing about souls, and whose stupidity drives him to intolerance? What a strange mystification: in the same book, Flaubert shows us the odious stupidity of an anticlerical and the odious stupidity of a priest who fully justifies anticlericalism; in Homais he ridicules his own ideas. For after all it was he who wrote to Michelet, on June 6, 1861, that remark which the pharmacist would surely have approved: "The great Voltaire ended his least important notes with *E. L. I.*[6] Yours in the hatred of the Anti-Physis."[7] Inversely, what is so distasteful to Flaubert in the celebrated profession of faith that he puts in the mouth of the pharmacist? Let's look

---

[5] See selected bibliography.

[6] *Ecrasez l'Infâme*. (Sartre's note.)

[7] Anti-nature.

at it again: "I have my own religion," says Homais . . . "I
believe in a Supreme Being . . . who put us on this earth
to fulfill our duties as citizens and parents. But I don't have
to go into a church . . . Such things (the Christian beliefs)
are absurd in themselves and besides that they're completely
opposed to all the laws of physics. This proves, incidentally,
that priests have always wallowed in abject ignorance . . ."
The ignorance of priests? Flaubert is convinced of it. Dogmas?
He finds them utterly stupid in *all* religions. The superiority of
scientific thought over religious thought? He never ceased to
maintain it to the end of his life. Still better: Homais concedes
more than Gustave will ever concede: he has a religion, he
believes in a Supreme Being. As for Flaubert, we have seen
that he seeks in vain to believe in one. So where does the
ridicule lie? In the smug satisfaction of the pharmacist. Flaubert finds no fault with him for destroying the Christian
beliefs *by means of Science*; he does blame him for placing
an unqualified confidence *in Science*. His stupidity is revealed
in the words "opposed to all the laws of physics. This
proves . . ." Here a vast complacency betrays itself, a faith
every bit as stupid as the other. The Absolute has merely
shifted its position: Religion placed it in heaven, liberal Scien-
tism locates it in Human Reason. And this Supreme Being
in which the pharmacist claims to believe reminds Flaubert
of that revolutionary cult which the "hateful" Robespierre
had established. This abstraction has no other function than
to guarantee the rationality of the universe and the ethic of
the bourgeois: Homais' God in no way represents a challenge
to man; on the contrary, he deifies man and is there to serve
him. The whole difference is here: Flaubert, destined to be
a non-believer, observes with despair the absence of God, the
folly of myths, the abject ignorance and materialism of
priests; Homais, the heir of revolutionary deism, makes the
same observations with serenity; in fact, his peace of mind
depends on them. When the pharmacist sets physics over
against the Catholic dogmas, Flaubert has nothing to reply to
him, he who wrote so often, "I hate anti-physis." Nevertheless, the author loathes his creature: what he has against
Homais is the delight with which he crushes the great anxieties
of humanity under a pile of sharp and precise little truths.
This invincible and triumphant stupidity, whose well-managed
enterprises always succeed, and which ultimately accounts for

everything there is, for everything we are, reveals its hideousness, its abject complacency, its shortsighted materialism, only if we place ourselves at the standpoint of what should have been and has not been, the point of view of absence, of nothingness, of the void, of our vain desire and our abandonment. And after all, what is this caricature of a theory that Flaubert has lodged in Homais? None other than the experimental rationalism of Dr. Flaubert; it is simply Science, debased to the point of idiocy. When Gustave ridicules this pseudo-intellectual, this pretentious phony who dispenses antireligious propaganda by invoking the laws of physics, he knows perfectly well that the scientific movement taken as a whole is in conflict with Christian ideology. This is why he hates it. At the age of nineteen he wrote in his *Souvenirs*: "The day may come when all of modern science will collapse and people will laugh at us, and I wish it would." And later he often had occasion to condemn the Age of Enlightenment on behalf of an irrationalism which dared not say its name: "Fanaticism is religion: and the eighteenth-century *philosophes* who railed against the one overthrew the other. Fanaticism is faith, faith itself, burning faith, the faith that creates and acts. Religion is a changing notion, a matter of human invention, in short, an idea; the other is a feeling. What has changed on earth are dogmas . . . what has not changed are amulets, sacred fountains, votive offerings . . . priests, monks, hermits, in short, the belief in a force superior to life and the need to place oneself under the protection of this force."[8] It makes no difference: even as he condemns the analytic thought of the *philosophes*, the spirit of analysis haunts him. This dissolving principle remains in his mind just as it was placed there from infancy; as soon as an idea touches it, it immediately disintegrates. How could he renounce the surgeon's eye, the legacy of his father? That would mean surrendering the whole inheritance to Achille.[9] Unlike Achille, on the contrary, Gustave must claim the razor-sharp vision that dissects men's hearts. He does not restrain himself, in the

[8] Cf. also, much earlier, ca. 1838-1839, this idea, in the *Souvenirs*: "The eighteenth century understood nothing about poetry, nothing about the human heart; it understood everything that has to do with the intelligence." (Sartre's note.)

[9] Achille is Flaubert's brother; see the biographical sketch.

Correspondence, from asserting his merits as a psychologist: he is the prince of analysis. But this analysis is so repugnant to him that he never performs it: he always presents it as *already done*, that is, he pours forth in maxims the results of his experience, by which he means both the passive recording of his impressions and their surgical dismemberment. But Flaubert has no experience at all, who has? What he has disguised under this name is the pure principle of analysis which, as soon as it is established for itself and separated from scientific practice, ceases to be method and becomes theory and contains *a priori* utilitarianism, associationism, empiricism, etc. From this point on, we no longer have an observation to make, an experiment to conduct, an objective analysis to perform; we know in advance that the noblest action *must* break down into selfish impulses; we know that feminine idealism originates in the anus, etc. The point is that this so-called *a priori* knowledge is nothing but an abstract postulate which is concealed by rhetorical effects and which may be reduced simply to this: *analysis is always possible.* Thus everything has already been thought, is already known: Flaubert's experience is behind him, his principles are already established, the search for and discovery of Truth *has taken place.* But in what past? Flaubert's? That of his class or of the human race? Gustave does not tell us. And by his very passivity, he allows this *a priori* knowledge to present itself in him as an *alien knowledge.* The war between Science and Faith is waged in him without his taking part in it. Between the two forms of stupidity there is a reciprocity of envelopment: this is enough so that each is undone by the other. Flaubert will not lift a finger: he demands and denies each of the two in the same way. The ideal situation would be for the two adversaries to vanish together. The analytic stupidity, in short, is parasitic, it is precisely the negation of the fundamental stupidity which alone possesses the positive density of matter; nothing forbids us to hope that the first, by dissolving the second, will be deprived of all support and sink into non-being.

But it is a vain hope: no sooner destroyed, the Received Idea rises from its ashes and revives the Analytic that preys on it. Devastated by this doubtful and eternally renewed combat, Flaubert takes refuge in scepticism: "Stupidity is reaching a conclusion." He will be careful not to form ideas of his own: "There is no such thing as a true idea or a false idea. One accepts things very eagerly at first, then one thinks it over, then one doubts, and here one stops." All the same this scepticism works against analysis at the point when the latter, triumphant, tries to assert itself in blissful satisfaction as Wisdom and Truth. But this conflict remains passive. Read the *Correspondence* from beginning to end, and never will you catch Flaubert judging, arguing, making a critical study; never will you discover the birth of an idea, of a new insight, of an original view. Thought, with him, is never *an act*; it invents nothing, it never *establishes a relation*; it cannot be distinguished from the movement of life itself. A passive activity, swept along by the tide of experience, it is merely the verbal form of *pathos*; the sequence of the sentences sometimes resembles the shifting mists of dreams and sometimes the verbal associations of a patient on the analyst's couch. In this interminable monologue in which rhetorical connections constantly replace rational connections, the same resentments, the same rancors recur incessantly under the most varied disguises, the great surges of eloquence conceal the constant flight of the idea or more precisely, the flight *from* the idea. This bourgeois who demands his integration resents his exile, and can neither *see* his class nor forget it, since it is—as familial milieu—as much an object of desire as of contempt. He accepts himself insofar as he is rejected and rejects himself insofar as he demands acceptance. He arrogantly condemns the stupidity of others, that shortsighted conformism which hates his individuality, and he hates this individuality which prevents him from blending into the bourgeois community. In short, he is the martyr of Stupidity, he has installed it inside of him with all its conflicts, it rotates, consuming itself, and consuming him. He bleeds from its teeth but forces himself to remain immobile: since any idea of his can only reflect the materiality of the commonplace or the materialism of analysis, he outdoes himself in his painful passivity and rejects all forms of Thought. As early as 1841, in fact, he writes: "I am neither a materialist nor a spiritualist. If I were anything at all I would be more of a materialist-spettatore-spectator." Stiff, silent, stoical, he casts a disdainful glance at the conveyer belt of the world, and listens absentmindedly to the conventional chatter which is no different from his interior monologue. Flaubert is barely even a witness.

Flaubert's Silences*
by Gérard Genette

. . . Maxime du Camp tells how Louis Bouilhet (already responsible for the burial of the first version of *Saint Anthony* in 1849) persuaded Flaubert to sacrifice "many redundant sentences" and "extraneous passages which slowed down the action." . . . The docility with which Flaubert, though protesting, submitted to the censorship of Bouilhet makes one wonder, and the effects of this castrating influence are now impossible for us to evalute thoroughly. At least a comparison of the versions of *Madame Bovary* permits us to imagine what this novel would have been like if Flaubert had dared to follow his deepest inclinations. It would be tiresome to review all the moments of ecstasy (in the twofold sense of contemplative rapture and suspension of narrative movement) which were omitted in the final writing and which the publication of the rough drafts[1] has restored to us, but we must at least call attention to one page with which Flaubert himself—a rare enough occurrence—had at first manifested some satisfaction. His feeling was not unjustified. The passage occurs during the visit to the Vaubyessard chateau on the morning following the ball. Emma is walking in the garden and she enters a summer house that has a window of multicolored glass. She looks at the countryside through these pieces of colored glass: first the blue, then the yellow, then the green, then the red, then the white. These versicolor landscapes successively evoke different emotions, and finally plunge her into a deep reverie from which she will be pulled with a start by the passing of a flight of crows. During this time, Charles was looking at the crops and inquiring about revenue. This last touch integrates the episode into the body of the novel by bringing out the contrast between the two characters; but

---

* In *Figures*, Paris: Editions du Seuil, 1966. Translated by Helen Weaver. [Footnotes added by the Editor, except where indicated otherwise.]
  [1] See selected bibliography.

here again the development goes beyond its diegetic function and proliferates for its own sake, in an immobile fascination in which Flaubert perhaps participates more than his heroine. "Do you know how I spent the whole afternoon the day before yesterday? Looking at the countryside through colored glass; I had to do it for a page of my *Bovary* which, I believe, will not be one of the worst."

One of the distinguishing characteristics of these moments when the narrative seems to fall silent and congeal under what Sartre was to call *the great petrifying gaze of things,* is precisely the cessation of all conversation, the suspension of all human speech. . . . Even shallow or coarse persons like Léon, Rodolphe, Charles himself, experience these amazed silences. Here is a scene between Emma and Charles, before their marriage: "Since they had already said good-by to each other, *they would remain silent* . . . The sun shone through the iridescent silk [of Emma's parasol], illuminating the white skin of her face with shifting patches of light. She smiled beneath it at the soft warmth of the day, and drops of water could be heard falling one by one on the taut moiré." Another, with Rodolphe, during one of their nights of love, in the moonlight: "Lost in reverie, *they did not speak* . . . occasionally they heard the sound of a ripe peach dropping from one of the trees along the wall." A third, at Rouen, with Léon: "They heard eight o'clock struck by several clocks in the Beauvoisine quarter, which is full of boarding schools, churches and large deserted mansions. *They had stopped speaking,* but as they looked at each other they seemed to hear a kind of humming inside their heads, as though something audible were escaping from their motionless eyes. They had just joined their hands, and the past, the future, their reminiscences, their dreams—everything merged in the sweetness of their ecstasy." . . .

Such moments, as we can see, are doubly silent: because the characters have stopped speaking so that they can tune in to the world and their dream; and because this interruption of the dialogue and the action suspends the voice of the novel itself and absorbs it, for a time, in a kind of mute interrogation. What impressed Proust most in the *Education* was the "abrupt change of speed" that opens the next to the last chapter: not for the device, but for the way in which Flaubert, unlike Balzac, frees these narrative means of their *active or documentary quality,* "rids them of the parasitism of anecdote and the scoria of history. He is the first writer to set them to music." Thus it is possible to prefer above all else, in *Madame Bovary* as in the *Sentimental Education,* these musical moments when the narrative is lost and forgotten in the ecstasy of an infinite contemplation.

The extratemporal quality of interruptions of this kind is frequently heightened by a sudden shift to the present tense. . . . Let us cite that microscopic effect which, if one takes the trouble to examine it closely, is capable all by itself, like a well-placed grain of sand, of stopping a whole novelistic development. It is found in Chapter I of the third part of *Madame Bovary,* in the celebrated episode of the cab, one of the least defensible pieces of bravura in all realistic literature. The carriage, occupied as we know, drives through the town in all directions and at top speed. In the midst of this "mania for movement," Flaubert placed the following sentence: "The cab immediately started up again; it went through Saint-Sever, along the Quai des Curandiers and the Quai aux Meules, over the bridge again, and across the Place du Champ-de-Mars; it passed behind the gardens of the hospital, where old men in black jackets *stroll in the sunshine on a terrace green with ivy,* then went up the Boulevard Bouvreuil," etc. One doubts whether either Emma or Léon, at this speed and under these circumstances, have the leisure to contemplate a terrace green with ivy, and besides the blinds are drawn. Their unfortunate driver, exhausted and dying of thirst, has other things on his mind. Thus, from the point of view of the rules of realistic narration, this description, however brief, but here again prolonged indefinitely by its present tense verb, is as out of place, as dramatically and psychologically unjustified as possible. This motionless close-up in the middle of a frantic drive is the height of clumsiness. In fact, such an inadvertency forces us to conclude that this ambulatory love-making does not interest Flaubert very much, and suddenly, as the cab passes the gardens of the hospital, he thinks about something else. Memories from his childhood flash back into his mind. Once again he sees those "old men in black jackets, trembling on their crutches, warming themselves in the sun, on a cracked terrace resting on the old walls of the town," and he cannot restrain himself from devoting a line or two to them. Everything else can wait. From our point of view—need I say it?—

this second of inattention redeems the whole scene, because in it we see the author forget the direction of his narrative, and *go off at a tangent*.

Valéry found Flaubert (in *The Temptation of Saint Anthony*) to be "as if intoxicated by the secondary at the expense of the primary." If the "primary," in a novel, consists of plot, characters, psychology, manners, history, it is easy to see how this judgment applies to his novels, how his fondness for the detail, and not only for the useful, meaningful detail, as in Balzac, but for the gratuitous and insignificant detail, can undermine the effectiveness of his narrative. Roland Barthes remarks that a few unmotivated descriptions are enough to obscure the whole meaning of a novel like *Les Gommes*: "Every novel is an intelligible organism of infinite sensitivity: the smallest point of opacity, the slightest (mute) resistance to the desire which motivates and sustains all reading, creates an *amazement* which spreads over the work as a whole. The objects of Robbe-Grillet truly engage the situation itself and the characters brought together by this situation in a kind of silence of signification."[2] Although the descriptive style of Flaubert, so profoundly substantial, imbued with radiant materiality, is as far removed as possible from that of Robbe-Grillet, these remarks may apply to certain aspects of his work. . . .

Valéry could not accept the accessory and hence arbitrary element in that marquise who goes out at five,[3] and this is why the art of the novelist was to him "almost inconceivable." Flaubert, on the other hand, is preoccupied (and with him, his novel) with the accessory. He forgets the marquise, her appointment, her love affairs, and becomes fascinated by some material circumstance: a door which slams shut behind her and vibrates, *interminably*. And this vibration which imposes itself between a network of signs and a universe of meaning overthrows a language and establishes a silence.

This frustrated transcendence, the *flight* from meaning into the indefinite tremor of things, is the distinguishing feature of Flaubert's writing, and it may have been this which he

---

[2] In "Le Point sur Robbe-Grillet," *Essais critiques,* Paris: Editions du Seuil, 1964.

[3] "The marquise went out at five": attacked by Valéry and others as the kind of weak descriptive sentence typical of prose fiction.

achieved at such cost over the verbose facility of his early
work. The *Correspondence* and the youthful writings clearly
show that Flaubert was suffocating with things to say: enthusiasms, rancors, loves, hates, contempts, dreams, memories.
. . . But he formed one day, almost as an afterthought, this
plan to *say nothing*, that denial of expression which ushered
in the modern literary experience. Jean Prévost saw the style
of Flaubert as "the most remarkable petrifying fountain in
our literature"; Malraux speaks of his "beautiful paralyzed
novels"; these images clearly express what remains the most
striking effect of his writing and his vision. He never wrote
the "book about nothing," the "book without a subject" (and
nobody ever will), but he covered all the subjects with which
his genius teemed under that heavy layer of petrified language; that "moving staircase," as Proust puts it, of imper-
fects and adverbs which alone could *reduce them to silence*.
His plan—as he said more than once—was to die to the
world and be born to literature. But language itself becomes
literature only at the price of its own death, since it must lose
its meaning in order to achieve the silence of the work of art.
This reversal, this turning of speech onto its silent other side,
which, for us today, is the essence of literature, Flaubert was
clearly the first to attempt—but the undertaking was, on his
part, almost always unconscious or guilt-ridden. His literary
conscience was not, and could not be, on a level with his
achievement and his experience. The *Correspondence* is an ir-
replaceable document for the light it sheds on one of the most
acute cases of the *passion* of writing (in both senses of the
word passion), upon literature experienced both as a necessity
and as an impossibility, that is, as a kind of *forbidden vocation*: in this respect it can be compared only to Kafka's
Journal. But nowhere in it does Flaubert give a real theory of
his method, which remains a mystery even to him, at least
in its more audacious aspects. He himself found the *Sentimental Education* an aesthetic failure, lacking in action, perspective, structure. He did not see that this book was the first
to achieve that *de-dramatization*, one would almost like to say
de-novelization of the novel[4] which was to mark the beginning

---

[4] "He was, in the *Sentimental Education*, to anticipate something that
would come into existence much later, the novel that was not like a
novel—dull, indefinite, as mysterious as life itself, with denouements that
are all the more terrible because they are not materially dramatic."
(Théodore de Banville, May 17, 1880, reprinted in *Critiques*, Fasquelle,
1917.) (Genette's note.)

of all of modern literature, or rather he regarded as a fault what seems to us its chief virtue. From *Bovary* to *Pécuchet,* Flaubert steadily wrote novels, all the while *denying*—unconsciously,[5] but with every fiber in him—the requirements of novelistic discourse. It is this denial which matters to us, and the involuntary, almost imperceptible trace of boredom, indifference, inattention, forgetfulness that he leaves on a book that seems to strive for a useless perfection, a book which remains for us admirably imperfect, and as if absent from itself.

[5] Even so, he wrote to Louise Colet, speaking of the party scene in *Madame Bovary*: "I have to write a narrative; and that is something I find very tiresome." A vitally important aspect of modern literature appears in this distaste for storytelling. Flaubert was the first to challenge profoundly, although mutely, the *narrative function* which until then was essential to the novel. A tremor that was almost imperceptible, but decisive. (Genette's note.)

Selected Bibliography

I. Editions of Flaubert's work.

Oeuvres complètes. Paris: Louis Conard, 1910–1954.
Oeuvres complètes. Edition du Centenaire. Paris: Librairie de France, 1921–1925.
Oeuvres complètes. Paris: Société des Belles-Lettres, 1945–1948.

There is a two-volume edition of Flaubert's major fiction in the Bibliothèque de la Pléiade: *Oeuvres,* edited by René Dumesnil and Albert Thibaudet, Paris: Gallimard, 1951–1952.

Flaubert's outlines and early versions of *Madame Bovary* have been collected in Leleu, Gabrielle, *Madame Bovary. Ebauches et Fragments inédits,* Paris: L. Conard, 1936; and in Leleu, Gabrielle and Pommier, Jean, *Madame Bovary. Nouvelle version précédée de scénarios inédits,* Paris: José Corti, 1949.
A good inexpensive edition of *Madame Bovary* in French, edited by Edouard Maynial, has been published in the Edition des Classiques Garnier, Paris, 1961.

Excerpts from Flaubert's letters have been published in Gustave Flaubert, *Extraits de la Correspondance ou Préface à la vie d'écrivain,* edited by Geneviève Bollème, Paris: Editions du Seuil, 1963. For a choice in English, see *The Selected Letters of Gustave Flaubert,* translated and edited by Francis Steegmuller, New York: Farrar, Straus and Cudahy, 1953.

II. Criticism and Biography.

Auerbach, Erich. "In the Hôtel de la Mole," in *Mimesis: The Representation of Reality in Western Literature,* translated by Willard R. Trask. Princeton: Princeton University Press, 1953.

Bart, Benjamin F. *Flaubert*. Syracuse: Syracuse University Press, 1967.

Baudelaire, Charles. *"Madame Bovary* par Gustave Flaubert" (1857), in *L'Art romantique*. See *Oeuvres complètes*, edited by Y. G. Le Dantec and Claude Pichois, Bibliothèque de la Pléiade. Paris: Gallimard, 1951. (Also in *Baudelaire as a Literary Critic*, translated and edited by Lois Boe Hyslop and Francis E. Hyslop, Jr. University Park: Pennsylvania State University Press, 1964.)

Béguin, Albert. *"Madame Bovary," La Table ronde*, March, 1950.

Blackmur, R. P. *"Madame Bovary:* Beauty Out of Place," *Kenyon Review*, Summer, 1951.

Du Bos, Charles. "Sur le 'milieu intérieur' chez Flaubert," in *Approximations*, I. Paris: Plon, 1922.

Bourget, Paul. "Gustave Flaubert," in *Essais de psychologie contemporaine*, I (1883). Paris: Plon, 1920. (Also in *Studies in European Literature*, The Taylorian Lectures. Oxford: Clarendon Press, 1900.)

Brombert, Victor. *The Novels of Flaubert: A Study of Themes and Techniques*. Princeton: Princeton University Press, 1966.

Brunetière, Ferdinand. "Le Naturalisme français. Étude sur Gustave Flaubert," in *Le Roman naturaliste*. Paris: Calmann Lévy, 1892.

Demorest, Don L. *L'Expression figurée et symbolique dans l'oeuvre de Gustave Flaubert*. Paris: L. Conard, 1931.

Faguet, Emile. *Flaubert*. Paris: Hachette, 1899. (Translated by Mrs. R. L. Devonshire. Boston and New York: Houghton Mifflin, 1914.)

De Gaultier, Jules. *Le Bovarysme: La Psychologie dans l'oeuvre de Flaubert*. Paris: Cerf, 1892.

Genette, Gérard. "Les Silences de Flaubert," in *Figures*. Paris: Editions du Seuil, 1966.

James, Henry. "Charles de Bernard and Gustave Flaubert," in *French Poets and Novelists* (1878). New York: Grosset and Dunlap, 1964.

———. "Gustave Flaubert," in *Notes on Novelists. With Some Other Notes*. New York: Charles Scribner's Sons, 1914.

Lapp, John. "Art and Hallucination in Flaubert," *French Studies*, October, 1956.

Levin, Harry. "Flaubert," in *The Gates of Horn: A Study of Five French Realists*. New York: Oxford University Press, 1963.

Lubbock, Percy. Chapters 5 and 6 in *The Craft of Fiction* (1921). New York: Viking Press, 1963.

de Maupassant, Guy. "Une Étude sur Gustave Flaubert." Written for the 1885 Quantin edition of Flaubert's works, reprinted in the Conard *Oeuvres complètes*.

Poulet, Georges. "Flaubert," in *Études sur le temps humain*, I. Paris: Plon, 1950. (Also in *Studies in Human Time*, translated by Elliott Coleman. Baltimore: Johns Hopkins University Press, 1956.)

———. "Flaubert," in *Les Métamorphoses du cercle*. Paris: Plon, 1961. (Also in *The Metamorphoses of the Circle*, translated by Carley Dawson and Elliott Coleman. Baltimore: Johns Hopkins University Press, 1967.)

Proust, Marcel. "À propos du 'style' de Flaubert" (1920), in *Chroniques*. Paris: Gallimard, 1927. (See a summary in English of this essay in Strauss, Walter A. *Proust and Literature: The Novelist as Critic*. Cambridge, Massachusetts: Harvard University Press, 1957.)

Richard, Jean-Pierre. "La Création de la forme chez Flaubert," in *Littérature et sensation*. Paris: Editions du Seuil, 1954.

Rousset, Jean. "*Madame Bovary* ou le 'livre sur rien.' Un aspect de l'art du roman chez Flaubert: le point de vue," in *Forme et signification: Essai sur les structures littéraires de Corneille à Claudel*. Paris: José Corti, 1962.

Sainte-Beuve, Charles Augustin. "*Madame Bovary* par M. Gustave Flaubert," in *Causeries du lundi*, XIII. Paris: Garnier, edition published from 1853 to 1862. (Also in *Sainte-Beuve: Selected Essays*, translated and edited by Francis Steegmuller and Norbert Guterman. Garden City, New York: Doubleday, 1963.)

Sarraute, Nathalie. "Flaubert le précurseur," *Preuves*, February, 1965. (Translated by Maria Jolas, *Partisan Review*, Spring, 1966.)

Sartre, Jean-Paul. "La Conscience de classe chez Flaubert," *Les Temps modernes*, May and June, 1966.

———. "Flaubert: du poète à l'Artiste," *Les Temps modernes*, August, September and October, 1966.

Steegmuller, Francis. *Flaubert and Madame Bovary: A Double Portrait*. New York: Viking Press, 1939.

Tate, Allen. "Techniques of Fiction," in *Collected Essays*. Denver: Swallow, 1959.

Thibaudet, Albert. *Gustave Flaubert: Sa Vie, ses romans, son style* (1922). Paris: Gallimard, 1963 (revised edition).

———. "Une Querelle littéraire sur le style de Flaubert" (1919), and "Lettre à Marcel Proust sur le style de Flaubert" (1920), in *Réflexions sur la critique*. Paris: Gallimard, 1939.

Thorlby, Anthony. *Gustave Flaubert and the Art of Realism*. New Haven: Yale University Press, 1957.

Turnell, Martin. "Flaubert," in *The Novel in France*. London: Hamish Hamilton, 1950; New York: New Directions, 1951.

Ullmann, Stephen. "Reported Speech and Internal Monologue in Flaubert," in *Style in the French Novel.* Cambridge: At the University Press, 1957.

Wilson, Edmund. "Flaubert's Politics," in *The Triple Thinkers.* New York: Harcourt, Brace, 1938.

Zola, Emile. "Gustave Flaubert," in *Les Romanciers naturalistes* (1881). In *Oeuvres complètes,* edited by Maurice Le Blond, text of the Eugène Fasquelle edition, XLIV. Paris: F. Bernouard, 1928.